Sands of Lanikai

Much aloha !

Bob Hogue

May 2015

Sands of Lanikai

Bob Hogue

ISLAND HERITAGE™
PUBLISHING
A DIVISION OF THE MADDEN CORPORATION

Published and distributed by

ISLAND HERITAGE™
P U B L I S H I N G
A DIVISION OF THE MADDEN CORPORATION

94-411 Kō'aki Street, Waipahu, Hawai'i 96797-2806
Orders: (800) 468-2800 • Information: (808) 564-8800
Fax: (808) 564-8877
islandheritage.com

ISBN#: 1-59700-873-7
First Edition, First Printing—2009

*Dedicated to the memory of
my grandparents*

1 - DECEMBER 6, 1941

Only a natural catastrophe or an unnatural force could stop him from achieving his mission. He was sure of that. Very sure. But he must still be careful. Very careful. He spied the small island town that rose before him in the bay.

The half-moon cast serpentine shadows across the ridges of the island mountain range in the far distance. Its metallic light winked down at him sporadically when it broke from behind the clouds. The tops of small waves glistened in the moonlight, but made very little noise. The only sound he heard was the slapping of the waves against his tiny skiff.

He wanted total quiet, and he wanted the moon to go back into hiding. He didn't want to be noticed, but he knew it could happen. He would deal with that in his own way. His attention was focused on the tree-lined shore ahead of him, now no more than a few hundred yards away.

Through his fishing lines, he glared intently at the crescent-shaped beach; a wide and white sandy beachhead that arced for better than a mile. The only thing he could see, and the only possible impediment to his secretive landing, was a young couple walking along the sands. He slowed the approach of his fishing vessel and kept a watchful eye on them as the moon passed behind the clouds. Now, again, he was in total darkness.

He wiped the perspiration from his lips and tasted the salt water on his hands. He wondered if he would need to use his hands, as he had before, in a deadly manner. He knew he would if necessary. He dug his teeth into the semicircular scar that hooked across the back of his hand and remembered the bloody altercation that had created the disfiguring shape and had led to his opponent's death. He sucked at the ridges of the wound before spitting the salty taste from his lips. The memory quickly disappeared; his new mission dominated his thoughts. He clenched his fists tightly and waited. His tiny fishing vessel crept forward in the ocean waters, and he felt the iciness of his blood running through his veins. He was patient, yet vigilant.

But they never saw him. He was sure of that. He must be sure. He watched the couple intently as they strolled slowly, hand in hand, along the tropical beach just before midnight. They were too engrossed in each other to see the likes of him. He spied from a distance as they stopped to embrace and then continued their stroll.

His steely eyes pierced through the darkness, and when the moon once again showed its face, he could see their silhouettes lock together. They stayed that way for several moments before finally running off toward one end of the beachhead and eventually out of sight. He watched them leave, and for a few seconds, he wondered if his cover of darkness had been compromised. But he was confident that the couple never looked his way.

And then the moon disappeared behind the clouds again.

He told himself not to worry, that the plan he had was virtually foolproof. Who would be concerned about a late night fisherman in Hawaiian waters anyway, he thought? Before entering the bay, he had seen other night fishermen distantly along the shoreline, some of them with torches to light their way. But he had made sure that those torches were extinguished before he moved forward. His hope, his plan, was not to be noticed.

Now, as his boat bobbed and weaved on the shallow waters of Kailua Bay, he could feel his heart pumping with increasing intensity. He took his eyes off the spot where the couple had been and steered his small boat inside the reef. Over there, near the grove of ironwood trees—that's where he would come ashore.

A chilling gust crossed his face, in stark contrast to the dozens of miles across open ocean he'd already crossed. His journey leading up to this moment had been uncomfortably warm, despite the time of year. He still wasn't accustomed to the tropical humidity, and he felt the dampness of his dark shirt lathered in sweat.

He was now more than ready to go ashore and finish his December mission.

Small waves lapped along the shoreline. The stillness of the night magnified the sound of every wave brushing the sand in front of him. Other than the sounds of the waves and his fast-beating heart, it was incredibly quiet.

The town of Kailua, situated on the less-populated Windward Side of Oʻahu, was fast asleep. Only a few lights flickered in the distance, and none of them from the direction of the recently built naval air station to the west. The navy airmen and the other soldiers were probably fast asleep, too, or else out partying in Waikīkī on the other side of the island. No one was going to notice him, just as he had foreseen when he orchestrated his plan. He steered the boat over and through the breakwaters and leaped into the surf.

It took only seconds to pull his tiny craft onto the thick sand. He had a small duffel bag slung over his shoulder, and he made certain not to get it wet. Everything he needed was in that bag. His plan was to move silently and stealthily and disappear into the small town darkness. He was confident that in the morning, fully rested after a night's sleep in the former German naval officer's nearby carport, he would blend right in with the townspeople.

His organization skills were perfect. He had meticulously studied the makeup of the island's population, and he knew the locals came from many different ethnicities and cultures and from all over the world. Even the German fit in. Nobody in Kailua or anywhere else on O'ahu guessed that the German was secretly a sleeper spy. Knowing all of this, he was certain that he would fit in perfectly, also.

It was virtually impossible to tell by his facial appearance from where he'd come. He liked that ambiguity. He was often described as Asian, but was he Chinese or Japanese or even east Russian? He had been called all three in his lifetime, and he also had been mistaken as Burmese and Manchurian and Korean. His chameleon-like appearance simplified his life's work. He knew he had a face that no one could figure out. He belonged to no country, really; his allegiances were only to himself. Three or four days in Kailua at most; that was his plan. Then, during the chaos he knew would start the next morning, he would ready himself to forge on to the top of the nearby mountains. He had a most important mission—and the Japanese generals had agreed to pay him handsomely. Very handsomely. He had received some of the monies up front; his big payday would come after his job was accomplished. The signal he would send from the top of those mountains could help dictate the next course of the war in the Pacific.

The plan raced round and round in his head; he knew every step by heart. He dragged his boat thirty or so yards from the shorebreak to the ironwood trees. He would leave it there in the sand, not far from other fishing boats already along the shoreline. That was part of the beauty of his plan—who would notice yet another fishing vessel in this area? Kailua Bay was known for its great fishing avails—the waters were teeming with all manner of ocean fish, as well as lobsters and stingrays and more—and the local Japanese fishermen had their boats moored both in the waters of the bay and along the shoreline. His boat, tucked in among the others, should go unnoticed.

All he could hear now was his labored breath, until a sudden noise stopped his breathing completely.

When a small dog barked fearfully at him from a distance of no less than five yards away, he rose up and leaped into action. He dropped his duffel bag in the sand, pulled out a short knife from his waistband, and before the dog could let out another yap, he grabbed it coolly by the snout with one magnificently quick hand and scooped its hind legs with the other. Less than a moment later, his knife was deep in the dog's stomach, and after a small whimper the only sound was the lapping of the waves once again.

Nothing was going to stop him from his mission. He had taken the first important steps to make sure of that. He quickly buried the dog in the sand, picked up his duffel bag, and disappeared into the Kailua night.

2 – THANKSGIVING EVE MORNING, THREE WEEKS EARLIER

Young Paul Sands was restless with anticipation. His long arms dangled over the railing of the top deck of the SS *Lurline*, and he fidgeted with his hands. His eyes were focused on the shimmering slopes of Diamond Head in the distance, and he felt the coolness of the tropical trade winds in the morning air. The docking at Honolulu Harbor was only minutes away.

The sound of the *Lurline*'s purring engines was masked by the slapping of the waves in the deep blue waters off O'ahu's south coast. Sands looked down and could see such clarity in that water. He'd rarely seen an ocean so inviting. He wished the famous ship could hurry herself ashore so he could dive in and feel the warmth of this tropical ocean himself.

In the brief time since he had first laid eyes on these Pacific islands, he was quite certain that he loved Hawaii. He almost had to. It was his grandfather who had told him he would love it. The old man rarely talked about the islands during their lives together, but when he did, it was obvious that his feelings ran deep. How deep, young Paul always wanted to find out.

When his grandfather booked passage on the SS *Lurline* in

November 1941, he declared it a birthday present for his twenty-one-year-old grandson. As they sailed from California to Hawaii, Paul had high expectations and hoped the journey would lift his grandfather's spirits, as well as his own.

The old man had been very quiet during the ocean journey, and he smiled only briefly when he stood next to his grandson as they passed the picturesque slopes of Diamond Head. But Paul noticed that his grandfather's mood turned somber when young children excitedly brushed past them along the ship's railing. Paul's attention was diverted by the playful youngsters, and he watched them race around, zipping in and out among the throngs of well-dressed passengers on the top deck. When he finally looked back towards his grandfather, the old man was gone. Paul shook his head, figuring that he had gone back inside and down to his stateroom. No matter, he thought. He would relish in all the excitement of the mid-morning landing in Honolulu Harbor himself. The tall and lanky youngster breathed in the wonderful tropical air and basked in every minute of the arrival celebration that followed. He would tell his grandfather all the exciting details later.

Paul watched a tiny tugboat with *Mikioi* painted on its bough assist the giant passenger ship into the harbor. He heard the engines belch and roar as the huge ship slowed down on its approach. The landing area was lined with hundreds of people on virtually every dock. He had not expected such a large crowd and was amazed at the turnout. His hands and arms tingled with excitement, and he nervously rubbed his hands together in anticipation of landing.

Aloha Tower, with its giant clock at its apex, stood proudly as the tallest building along the Honolulu shoreline, as if it was standing guard over the entire proceedings. Paul could make out the giant letters A-L-O-H-A at the very pinnacle of the tower. He knew enough to know that the word meant both *hello* and *good-bye* and *love* and perhaps more. He was determined to experience as much of this *aloha* as possible. And with the sweet fragrance from hundreds of flower leis permeating the air, he felt almost intoxicated with the *aloha* spirit.

For several minutes, he reveled in the lively tunes of the Royal Hawaiian Band and marveled at the brown-skinned teenagers who dove deep into the dark blue harbor waters to collect shiny dimes that were tossed overboard by passengers. The boys carried the dimes in their teeth until they reemerged triumphantly, waving the coins from their fingertips. He watched the lovely hula dancers as they swayed their hips to the tunes of the band, and he waved back to the throngs of people who lined the docks amidst the fanfare and streamers. Honolulu, Hawaii, in November 1941 was an incredible sight to behold. Paul had rarely felt such excitement.

He went below to fetch his grandfather, to tell him about the sights he'd seen, about the thrill and pageantry of it all. With his long legs loping along the passageways, he was bursting with adrenaline. He couldn't wait to get ashore.

But by the time Paul returned to his stateroom, he would find a shocking discovery. The old man lay lifeless on the floor, his body twisted in an awkward heap in the middle of the room. Paul rushed to his grandfather's side and tried to turn him over, but felt the coldness of the old man's skin immediately.

Stunned, choked with emotion, and practically unable to breathe, Paul raced to fetch the ship's doctor. But nothing the grandson or the ship's doctor tried could revive the old man. No pulse, no breath, nothing. Together, they laid the old man's body face down on the small bed and covered him with a blanket from head to toe.

The doctor announced the time of death as 10 a.m.

Paul hunched over his grandfather's body for several minutes until the doctor told him to sit down. The young man hardly noticed when a couple of the ship's stewards scurried in and out of the stateroom. The doctor whispered quick orders to both of them before they left in a hurry. Paul was in a daze, too shaken to listen.

"How old was he?" asked the ship's doctor, a middle-aged man with a round face dominated by bifocals. He peered over the top of his glasses and held a clipboard in his hands; Paul would now have to suffer his unending list of questions. The youngster did not hear him, at first. The doctor repeated the question.

"Seventy, I think," Paul said, mournfully.

"What do you mean, you think?"

"I'm not exactly sure of his age. Um, I'm sorry. I mean he really was a very private man who kept most things to himself. That's my best guess."

"So, you're not sure."

"Yeah, I think I'm sure, but I'm also telling you that grandfather rarely talked about himself."

"Did he live with you?"

"Actually, I lived with him. My parents died when I was young, and I went to live with him in Hollywood, California. He's the only family I had left."

"Hollywood? Was he an actor?"

"No, he was in the shipping business." Paul's voice drifted off. The ship's captain popped his head in the stateroom and told them that the Honolulu police would be coming on board in a short time, along with the county coroner. He gave Paul his condolences. The tall young man, slumping noticeably in the stateroom chair, thanked him by nodding.

The ship's doctor wrote a few notes on the pages of his clipboard, then stepped back to the bedside, lifted the blanket, and gave another brief look at the old man's body. "He's not the only old fellow to die of a heart attack aboard ship."

"Is that what killed him—a heart attack?" Paul asked the question with anguish and concern.

"Appears so. The coroner will tell us for certain." The doctor stood up and went back to writing on his clipboard. "Name please?"

Paul looked at him quizzically, unnerved by the doctor's almost emotionless reaction to the death. He should already have the name from the stateroom roster, he thought.

"Just doing it for the record, son. Your name and your grandfather's name?"

"My name is Paul Sands. My grandfather's name was William—same last name."

"And you're both from Hollywood, you say?

"Well, he's from Hollywood. I'm not sure where I call home. I grew up in Los Angeles, then lived in New York City until recently—went to Columbia University—then only came back to Southern California a few months ago."

"You a student?"

"Not anymore."

"You're pretty tall—you a basketball player?"

"I was, but not anymore."

"Not anymore, huh. How tall are you anyway?"

"Six feet six inches." The ship's doctor whistled and wrote it all down.

"And your grandfather, you say he was in the shipping business?"

"He retired several years ago. Made a neat little fortune, enough to send me off to an Ivy League school. For the past few years, he's pretty much kept to himself, mostly at home."

"And you—what do you do now?

Paul coughed and cleared his throat. He stood up, and his six-foot-six-inch frame made the tiny stateroom that much smaller. He had dark, wavy hair, and his face had a certain gentleness about it. He was handsome in a boyish sort of way. He held a dark hat in his hands, and he fumbled with it, nervously. "I've tried a bunch of things, actually. After I dropped out of Columbia, I worked a bit waiting tables, at least long enough to get train money to go back to California."

"And what'd you do there?"

"Worked here and there, did some bookkeeping for a while, didn't like it. Tried my hand briefly in insurance—it didn't take long to realize I wasn't a salesman."

"That's a lot of jobs for a young man. How old are you anyway?"

"Twenty-one, sir. Yes, you're right; I haven't been too lucky in the job department."

"How come you didn't work for your grandfather?"

"He never asked me.'"

"Why didn't you ask him?"

"I don't know." Paul's voice drifted off again. He sat down and fumbled with his hat. After several seconds, he dropped it on the floor and reached down slowly to pick it up. The ship's doctor put his clipboard down at his side.

"You ever think about joining the military service? We can use boys like you."

"Tried to, but they won't have me."

"Why?"

"I'm 4-F on account of my knees. Injured them badly. That's why I gave up basketball."

"Oh." The doctor looked Paul up and down and shook his head. "You got a place to stay?"

"Um, not sure. My old college roommate is from here—from Hawaii, I mean. Grandfather and I, we figured we'd visit the islands and then his family. Not sure if I can bunk with them or not."

"Where's their place?"

"Kailua.

"That's a far piece from downtown Honolulu, son. Up and over the Pali. I hope you got another option." The ship's doctor went back to scratching at the papers on his clipboard. "Could you go over again how you found his body?"

Paul paused to try and get a handle on his emotions.

"I'm sorry, son. I just have to write it down for the record. "

Paul circled the room briefly and then started his story. "I, uh, was excited when we came into the harbor this morning, so I raced up to the top deck to see everything. You know, all the festivities out there." He nodded his head toward the top deck.

The ship's physician diligently jotted everything down on his clipboard. The young man fidgeted with his hands nervously and continued to talk, sometimes excitedly.

"I was up there for quite some time—seeing Diamond Head and Waikīkī Beach, listening to the bands, smelling the flower *lei*, enjoying the warm weather. There were these kids diving into the water for coins. It was really swell."

"And your grandfather didn't join you for this?"

"A little bit at the beginning, but he had been pretty quiet during the whole trip. All the talk of war had him pretty upset. He got sick of people talking about what was happening in Europe and Asia."

"That's pretty routine for these times, son. Was there a reason for that?"

"Not that I know of. He wasn't some kind of pacifist or anything. He just seemed consumed in his own thoughts. So I pretty much left him alone. I loved him, but he could get awfully sullen and sour. I felt it was better to leave him alone when he got like that."

"Had he been in ill health?"

"No, not that I was aware. He seemed to be in top shape—especially for a man of his age."

"How long would you say you were up on the deck?"

"Over an hour, I'm assuming. The last time I saw grandfather was when we rounded Diamond Head. He came up topside briefly, then went back to the room, and I stayed. The ship docked, and people started to disembark. It got very busy there for a while. I even saw several people coming on board; didn't really expect that."

"That's routine," the doctor said. "Porters and others come on board to help the disembarking passengers."

"It was chaotic, for sure. I'll admit I got caught up in it all. Finally, I went down to our staterooms—we had adjoining rooms because grandfather liked his privacy—and I knocked on his door. He didn't answer."

Paul stopped. The doctor looked up to see what stopped him. Paul wiped a tear from the corner of his eye and then took a deep breath.

"I wasn't sure if he was in there or not, but for some reason I thought it was kind of strange, and I noticed that the door was slightly ajar so I pushed it open. I can't tell you what I thought then because I was totally shocked. I saw him sprawled face-first on the floor. I ran to him immediately and checked his pulse, but there was none, so I raced out and called you."

The doctor wrote everything down. As he scribbled his notes, a man in a dark gray suit and hat arrived at the state room door. The man was thin, of medium height, and appeared to be in his midthirties, with jet-black hair cut short and neatly trimmed. He held a lit cigarette in one hand and took a couple of quick puffs before entering the room.

"Officer Jack Burns, Honolulu Police Department," he said. "I understand we have an unattended death here." He snuffed out his cigarette in an ashtray near the door and set his hat on the small dresser. He closed the door behind him.

"Yes," the ship's doctor replied, stepping away from the covered body. "A Mr. William Sands, age seventy, or thereabouts, of Hollywood, California. This is his grandson, Paul Sands."

Officer Burns nodded to young Sands, stepped forward, and kneeled down towards the body. He removed the blanket momentarily and then covered the old man again.

"Did anyone go through his belongings?"

The ship's doctor looked at Paul, who shook his head from side to side. Paul had a worried expression on his face. "Why do we have a policeman here?" he asked.

"Just routine, young man," the officer said. "Anytime there's a death in the harbor, or aboard a ship, we get called in to file a report.

Don't worry, from what I understand from the captain, there's no foul play."

The ship's doctor saw Paul's face cringe. He quickly followed up by stating emphatically, "Let me say for the record that there is no evidence of foul play."

"Okay," Burns said with a take-charge tone. "Please then note this for the record, too, Doctor. I'm removing the blanket, and I'll be checking his pants pockets."

The ship's doctor nodded.

Officer Burns removed some coins and a comb from one pocket. There was a silver money clip with a wad of dollar bills in the other pocket. The officer counted them all. "One hundred fifty-five dollars," he announced, looking up at Paul.

"He always carried a good deal of money with him," Paul stammered.

"The money clip is pretty old," Burns said, studying the clip as he tumbled it around on his fingertips. "I'm no jeweler, but this thing looks like it's been around for years. There's something inscribed on the inside, but it's been mostly rubbed away." He handed the clip to Paul for further study.

Paul looked at the inscription, or what was left of it, and shook his head. "I can't make out what it says either. The lettering is barely visible. I can see a few letters—maybe an *I* and an *N*, maybe a *W*—not sure." Paul tried to hand the money clip back to Burns, but the officer put up his hands and refused to take it.

"You keep it. It must have been important to your grandfather. Maybe someday you'll know what it says."

Just then there was an insistent knocking at the stateroom door. A small, rotund man in his sixties barged into the room. Sweat poured from his forehead—he looked like he'd been running a marathon. "Looks like you beat me here, Burns." The sweaty man pulled a handkerchief from his suit pocket and wiped his brow.

"Second time today," the officer responded.

"Frank Dillingham, county coroner," the sweaty, rotund man said to Paul and the ship's doctor. He made no eye contact. "Burns and I were on a homicide investigation earlier this morning regarding the death of a navy sailor on Hotel Street. It's been pretty intense around here lately, what with all the sailors and soldiers coming and going. You'd think we were going to war or something."

"Or something," the ship's doctor responded, almost disdainfully.

The coroner ignored the response and leaned down to study the old man's body. Officer Burns rose and stepped aside.

"This death has nothing to do with the war buildup," interrupted the ship's doctor. "Just a heart attack of an old man on holiday."

The coroner acted again as if he didn't hear him and continuously moved his hands up and around the body, inspecting the fully clothed corpse as thoroughly as possible. He stopped when he reached the old man's shirt pocket, where he found an old photograph. He pulled it out, studied it briefly, and shook his head a couple of times but said nothing. He then quickly wiped the inside of the old man's mouth and, just as quickly, gave close inspection to the old man's fingertips.

"I'm not so sure about that," the coroner said. "Take a look at this."

3 – FROM WASHINGTON DC TO KAILUA– FEARS OF WAR

John Gillespie was irritated. The frantic pace of life of working at the Navy Department in Washington DC was starting to wear on him. For nearly the entire month of November, as the brisk winds chilled the late autumn air along Pennsylvania Avenue, he had been hoping for a break from the endless phone calls and paperwork and the daily headaches that went along with them. It was the day before Thanksgiving, and he was definitely not in a holiday mood.

Still, despite the pressure of his job, he gave no inkling to others that he was troubled. It wasn't in his nature to complain. Argue his point, occasionally, but not complain. He marched down the long corridor of the old building that housed the various presidential cabinet departments, the sound of his shiny black shoes clipping along the marble floors echoing off the tall ceiling. He took a sharp right turn at the end of the hall and opened the first etched glass door. *Secretary of the Navy* was painted on the glass in block black letters. He found a seat quickly and sat quietly in the corner of the tiny foyer without uttering a word. He knew his time would come soon.

"The secretary will see you now," the petite and officious

woman behind the desk said. He nodded to her appreciatively and scooped up his papers before disappearing behind the big green door that separated the public lobby from the offices of the secretary.

"Thanks for coming back to the office so quickly, John" the bespectacled man in the office said.

"No problem, sir. You know that I'm always at your service." He sat down at the desk facing a nameplate that read *Secretary of the Navy* Frank Knox. The secretary, buried behind a large stack of paperwork, his tie undone and his shirt sleeves rolled up near the elbow, sat precariously alert. His suit coat hung over the edge of the desk, as if it expected to be grabbed up at any second for another spur-of-the-moment meeting at the White House.

"John, you've become indispensable to me," the secretary said. He looked up only briefly from his paperwork.

"Thank you, sir." Gillespie did not smile, despite the compliment.

"How long have you worked for me?"

"Nearly a year and a half, sir. I started shortly after graduation from Columbia in the spring of '39."

The secretary pondered the information for a moment and then signed his name on a document before continuing with his discourse. He kept his eyes focused on his papers, not on the young man who sat on the other side of his huge oak desk. "It's hard to believe that you've been in Washington such a short period; you grasp everything so quickly, with very good insight. We don't usually move interns into positions of responsibility so rapidly, but you are an exception."

"I appreciate that, sir." John fidgeted in his seat, but he kept his head held high. He was of average size, perhaps a shade over five feet eight inches, but he made up for his lack of height by maintaining an erect posture at all times and keeping his chin up and focused on whoever was speaking to him. He called it his right-and-ready position. He was wondering what the secretary was leading up to.

"I need you to stay on." The secretary said the six words quickly and emphatically, as if he was ordering a servant. John thought about stuttering a response but kept his cool. His eyes never lost their focus on the bespectacled middle-aged man before him, and he kept his chin strong and taught; he would appear right and ready, even if he had misgivings.

"That's a very interesting proposition," he said, slowly and deliberately. "But, sir, as you and I have discussed previously, I have already made plans."

"No buts, young man. You're smarter than most of the veterans I have around here. We don't get you Ivy League types very often, and few have your ability. I can't possibly let you go, as we—I mean, as you—previously planned."

"I understand, sir," John replied. For the first time, he dropped his gaze from the secretary and looked out the window at the Capitol building in the distance. "I'll admit that I was looking forward to seeing my family. I haven't been back to the islands since I went away to Columbia. That was more than five years ago."

"Yes, I know that. You've mentioned that to me before. But things have changed since we made our arrangement. The world has changed in five years—really changed. This isn't simply an internship you're doing. You've grown in your job. I've placed trust in you. Your research abilities, your innate intelligence, and your skills at navigating the bullshit around here make you, well, indispensable."

"Thank you, sir."

"I'm offering you a better job. I've talked with others in the Navy Department and in the White House, and we want to name you my special assistant. Can I count on you?" For the first time, Secretary Knox looked up and fixed his gaze square into John's eyes. The gaze said that there could be only one answer.

Gillespie knew what that answer was. "Yes," he replied, without hesitation. And when the secretary stood up and reached his hand across the desk, Gillespie stood, too, and grasped the secretary's hand.

"It's settled then. I'll need you back here at 2100 hours, sharp," the secretary said. "We have plans to go over Britain's response to the Japanese movements in the China and Pacific sectors."

"Very good, sir."

Gillespie exited the office as hastily as he had entered. He walked out into the hallway, down the long corridor, past the doorways of other special assistants to other cabinet secretaries, past the nearly wooden soldiers standing guard at the building on Pennsylvania Avenue, and out onto the street. The frigid winds of the November night in Washington DC smacked him across the face like a prizefighter. Dreams of going back to Kailua, Hawaii, his boyhood home, dreams of getting together in the tropical warmth with his family and friends and enjoying some time on the beach with his old college roommate, Paul Sands, invaded his thoughts. However, he knew all of this would have to wait.

He stopped for a moment to button up his jacket. He would phone home in a couple of days to break the news to his parents. They could relay the information to Paul. He looked down at his watch. He had a couple of hours to catch a bite to eat at a nearby diner. Before he knew it, 2100 hours, or 9 p.m., would come, and the secretary mustn't be kept waiting. John knew that it was going to be another long night of talk of impending war in Asia and the Pacific. His head ached again, already.

Five thousand miles to the west, on the Windward Side of O'ahu, Jorge Luis pulled on the reins of his quarter horse and stopped abruptly. "Goddamn soldiers," he said to no one.

A small convoy of army trucks passed in front of him near the junction of the Pali Road in Kailua and the blacktop leading to Waimānalo, the next town to the east. "Damn soldiers think they own the road now."

Jorge watched them pass, giving stink eye the entire time. A soldier in the final truck of the convoy shouted out, "Hey, Cowboy!

Hey, Joe!" but Jorge just stuck his chin into the air. He hated when people made fun of his name, even if they had no idea how it was spelled or how it was properly pronounced.

"It's George!" he yelled back. "George Goddamned Luis, and don't you ever forget it!" He yelled his name so loudly that all the soldiers at the end of the convoy laughed out loud and waved. He just sneered back. He had no use for these soldiers. In his mind, all they did was steal the land or trample over it. Ever since the new base opened up along Mōkapu Peninsula, he had seen fences busted open and locks broken, and he had spent days, even weeks, retrieving the Old Man's cattle. Jorge worked for the Old Man, a man he would do anything for. The Old Man was Harold Castle, who owned Kāne'ohe Ranch, and with it most of the property in Kailua and a little more in Kāne'ohe. He was definitely the largest landowner on the Windward Side of O'ahu, and Jorge had been working for him since he was a teenager.

Now, just over thirty years old, Jorge had become the ranch's number-one horseman in a town that fancied its horses. Jorge was looking forward to the next day, when he would race in the Turkey Day Cowboy Races at the Kailua Race Track. He confidently looked forward to thrilling the anticipated large crowd with his exploits.

He watched as the final truck passed and then continued on his afternoon ride. He had mended three fences, chased down more than a dozen stray cattle, and made sure the Old Man's Great Danes, his pride-and-joy championship dogs, had gotten a good run near the Kailua stables. He worked hard for his money, and he knew he earned every penny of it.

The last part of his day was spent making sure that all aspects of the huge property that covered Kailua and parts of Kāne'ohe were in order. He would phone in his report to Henry Wong, the ranch foreman, before sunset and then make his way home for dinner with the only family he had left in the world—his half sister, Healani.

He thought briefly about his younger sister, whom he adored

and was very protective of. She was the daughter of his father and his father's second wife, a local Hawaiian woman who had died a couple of years ago. His father—the man who gave him his Portuguese name but then pronounced it the English way—died soon after his second wife's death, and Jorge had vowed that he would keep his sister out of harm's way. Jorge was Portuguese, nearly full-blooded, and very proud of his heritage and its place in Hawaii's culture. His sister, the lovely Healani, was nearly ten years younger, and the mix of the Portuguese and Hawaiian backgrounds gave her brown skin a magnificent, if not exotic, tropical glow. Many times Jorge had fended off the unrequited advances of young soldiers who attempted to gain her attention.

He would have none of that. She must only enjoy the company of someone I can trust, Jorge thought. And with that, he gave his horse a kick and galloped off toward Kailua. A few hours later, his sister would have his dinner ready, and after his nightly phone call to Henry Wong, he would play on his ʻukulele, and she would dance her hula.

It would be another perfect evening in Kailua.

In nearby Kailua Town, Otto Kuehn darted up the darkened stairs and pulled the chain on a tiny lightbulb in the upstairs bedroom of his two-story Kalama tract home. When the light flickered on, Kuehn tiptoed to the black curtain and pulled it aside slowly, allowing just a little corner of light to pass through the window.

Then he pushed the curtain over the square window again. He let a few seconds pass and then repeated his effort—pulling and pushing the curtain to allow a brief flicker of light to the outside world. Each time he repeated his routine, the ray of light was shorter in duration.

He pulled back the curtain one last time and sat down in the corner of the tiny upstairs room. He looked up at the light bulb through his thick-rimmed glasses, as if to study the intensity of its wattage. He put his hands to his mouth and wondered if the light had been seen. And by whom?

He sat for a long time in the corner and then stood up and tugged on the chain to extinguish the light bulb. He stood quietly in the shadows and pulled a handkerchief from his back pocket to wipe his pudgy forehead. The handkerchief soaked up an ample amount of perspiration. God, it's hot, he thought.

It was also quiet. And he knew it must remain so. He only tested this routine when his wife, Friedel, and their daughter, Greta, were out of the house, working at the hair salon they owned in Kailua Town. They would be back soon, he thought, around sunset, and he must practice his routine incognito—usually in the late afternoon hours when no one would suspect what he would be doing later that night. Several hours later, after darkness fell on the Windward Oʻahu town and Friedel and Greta were fast asleep, he would quietly rise from his bed and repeat his efforts in the real darkness. He mustn't let them in on his secret.

No one must know. Not about this routine, nor about the signals he sent out from his other house on the beach at Lanikai. No one must know about his past as a captain in the Imperial German Navy during the Great War. It was vital that everyone must think of him only as an obscure furniture salesman in Kailua. No one could know what he was really doing. And, he thought, how could they? He wasn't all that sure what he was doing himself. And for whom?

Officer Jack Burns removed his suit coat and hat and tossed them on his chair. He was back at the Bethel Street headquarters of the Honolulu Police Department in downtown Honolulu, the place where his long workday had started hours before. He immediately lit up a cigarette.

The stuffy adobe concrete building served a dual purpose in these days of war talk. Amidst the daily clutter of regular police business, Burns' office on the second floor of the old building also housed a special FBI espionage unit. In his small, cluttered off. the back of the building, Burns was surrounded by three local Japanese men, all of whom had grown up in Hawaii, but who spoke fluent Japanese. They worked quietly and efficiently in one corner of the cramped room reviewing potential espionage files, while he sat in front of his rolltop desk in the opposite corner.

He smiled at one of the young Japanese assistants, a stocky young man in his late twenties, who shyly returned the smile. The other two, both small, round-shouldered men in their midthirties, barely looked up from the paperwork they were involved in. Burns said nothing; he was just glad they were doing their jobs so well.

He'd already had a busy morning and afternoon. Every day was busy for him now that he had to conduct his regular homicide work along with the added responsibility as HPD liaison to the FBI. He had been pulling double shifts for months, and there was no letup in sight. He pulled a small notebook from his pocket and flipped through a few of the pages. The day had started innocently enough, but then it quickly scrambled with an overnight homicide involving a navy sailor; he followed some leads on that case, and it appeared there would be a quick arrest. But another officer got credit for the actual collar, because Burns was called away suddenly due to the reported death of an elderly visitor aboard the SS *Lurline*. The department's personnel were spread so thin, he was forced to spread himself thinly, too.

He stood up and walked over to the glass door that separated his office from the rest of the department. He stuck his head outside the door. "Any word on the Sands paperwork?" he called out to the desk officer.

"Should have it quickly," the desk sergeant said. "Any cause of death, yet?"

"Nothing yet. We'll wait for the coroner's report." Burns looked down at his notebook and then tossed it back towards his desk. The notebook quickly disappeared in the array of papers that cluttered the desk top. Burns knew that a lot more paperwork cluttered the inside of the rolltop. He wondered if he would ever have time to get to it all. He stood in the doorway, empty-handed except for a lit cigarette in his right hand. He took a drag.

"What happened there?" asked the desk sergeant. "With the old guy on the *Lurline*, I mean."

Burns took another puff on his cigarette before answering. "Coroner said he found some white substance on the old man's hands. The old guy might have ingested it because they also found it on the inside of his mouth. Not sure if he died of a heart attack or by some other means."

"Strange," the desk officer said.

"I'll write it all down in the report once you get the other paperwork to me. I also have to go through his things from the state-room. I'll do that down at the harbor later." Burns took a few more drags from the burning cigarette that was now perched precariously on his lower lip. He exhaled a mouthful of smoke and then flicked the lit butt into a nearly full ashtray. Within moments, he lit up another cigarette. "I'm sure it's going to be routine."

The desk sergeant nodded at the last comment, then picked up a ringing phone. Burns, meanwhile, grabbed a cup of coffee, took a couple more drags on his cigarette, and then settled back into the chair of his corner office. His long legs found comfort in leaning against the wooden floor, and Burns took his first breather of the day by looking out the window at the palm trees and sunshine. For the first time, he finally realized what a beautiful day it was.

His forty-minute daily drive to Honolulu from his hometown of Kailua across Pali Road was nearly always made in the darkness before dawn, and he rarely had time to think about anything except his police work. Now, with the additional worries of the FBI assign-ment, his days became incredibly long. He took a deep breath and smiled at the sight of two young army privates ogling the leggy office girls walking past the building. So much for all the war talk, he thought.

"Here's the preliminary paperwork on Sands," the desk sergeant said, interrupting his peaceful moment. "Looks like it might not be as routine as you thought."

Burns thanked him and sat down at his desk. He looked over the forms and made a couple of notations where needed. The old man's death on the SS *Lurline* had been ruled an unattended death, but no cause of death was noted, pending an autopsy. That meant Burns would have some follow-up work to do. He would go back over to Honolulu Harbor before he headed home for the night.

Burns recalled the final moments in the *Lurline* stateroom as he and the coroner got ready to leave. He remembered how distraught the grandson had been. It was the part of the job that he detested; seeing how death affected the families left behind. He shook his head. He thought for a moment about this tall young man who had lost his only relative in the world—and on an otherwise peaceful voyage to the Hawaiian Islands. He felt deeply sorry for Paul Sands. He wondered what would become of him.

4 - KAILUA TOWN

The death of his grandfather stunned Paul, especially the mysterious circumstances surrounding it. He was too distraught to ask any questions of the coroner and Officer Burns when they left the stateroom. The coroner officiously reported his findings to the ship's doctor, had the body removed to the county morgue, and then was on his way to the next case. He said nothing to Paul as he left. At least Officer Burns tipped his hat on the way out the door.

All Paul was left with was a smudged money clip and an old, dog-eared photograph of a young Hawaiian woman. On the back of the tiny picture was a faded inscription that read "All my love, forever. Lani."

The coroner had taken one look at the photo, then checked the old man's mouth and fingers and found what appeared to be white powdery substance on both. He quietly conferred with Officer Burns, rechecked the body, and finished his work.

Within minutes of their departure, the ship's captain reentered the small stateroom and asked Paul his plans.

"I . . . I don't know for sure."

"The doctor said you had some friends here. Do you have a place to stay?"

Paul, breathing slowly and running his hands through his thick crop of hair, took his time to respond. "No. I, uh—I mean, we, my grandfather and I, were going to stay at the Royal. The Royal Hawaiian, I mean."

"You have that kind of money?"

Paul hesitated. "No, not now. That seems out of the question now."

"Would you like me to find you another place?"

Paul shook his head. He cupped his hand over his mouth and pondered his next move. "I can't believe this has happened."

"I'm sure it's a shock." The captain put a comforting hand on the tall young man's shoulders.

"We were going to visit a good friend over the holidays. My old college roommate is coming home to Hawaii in a couple of weeks. We were expecting to get together here."

"Where's he live?"

"The other side of the island, I believe. Lanikai, Kailua, something like that. We've talked about it a number of times."

"Does he still have family there?"

"Yes," Paul said, his voice starting to get a little stronger. He looked over at the bed where his grandfather had been laying just a short time ago. He glanced inquisitively at the old photograph and shook his head again. "Yes, I do know somebody there. John's parents, Mr. and Mrs. G."

"Mr. and Mrs. G?"

"Actually, Scotty and Nan Gillespie."

"They know you're here."

"Not sure if they know my exact timing. I'll give them a ring in a little bit. But not until I go down to the morgue to pay my last respects."

"I understand. I'll have a porter get your things."

The Hawaiian band was cleaning up from its performance by the time Paul exited the *Lurline*. He walked down the long gangplank into the warm afternoon air. Flowers, many of them terrifically fragrant, blessed the walkways surrounding the port. He moved slowly down the crowded Honolulu streets, jammed with parked cars lining the curbsides. The trade winds caressed his cheeks and tossed his hair carelessly from side to side. He hardly noticed; his head hung heavy, and he spent most of his time on the walk to the downtown morgue studying the photograph the coroner had given him. Who was this young woman, he wondered?

Despite the poor condition of the old photo, it was obvious to him that the woman was quite beautiful. She wore a white flowing gown, and her long hair spiraled down her back with little flowers seemingly dancing on her curls. He shook his head.

A half hour inside the morgue did nothing to brighten his mood. He hardly noticed the dozens of young navy sailors who brushed past him on the way back to the port. Servicemen were in abundance, but Paul was oblivious.

He kept repeating the same thing over and over in his head. "Why did this happen? Why did this happen?"

And who was Lani? He had never heard his grandfather mention her before. Who was she? And was she important in his life, or was it just some old photograph that he carried around for who knows what reason?

Hours passed, and after Paul paid his last respects in the dark and dingy Honolulu morgue, he wandered around the downtown streets for a while and then finally sat down on a small bench near the harbor. He didn't even notice the wondrous palm that he sat beneath. Shadows danced this way and that, and the sun seemed to shine from every angle. For late November, it was still delightfully warm, he thought. He wished his grandfather could be enjoying it with him. He sat silently in deep thought for several minutes.

"Paul Sands?" a voice interrupted.

Paul looked up to see a diminutive, balding man standing in front of him. The man, about sixty years old and well dressed in a light gray suit, held his coat jacket in one hand and his matching hat in the other. His face was feverishly dotted with light freckles, and he had a cherubic smile.

"Paul, is that you?" the man asked again, his voice tinted with a thick Scottish brogue.

Paul smiled weakly and nodded. "Mr. G.," he responded. He then unfolded his long legs from underneath the bench and stood up, towering over his roommate's father by nearly a foot. He extended his hand, but Mr. G. dropped his hat and gave the young man a warm hug.

"Good to see you again, Paul. What's it been, four, five years?"

"Something like that. I think I saw you last when you and your wife brought John to college at Columbia when we were freshmen. I think you visited New York City for a couple of weeks."

"You're right. A marvelous city," Mr. G. said. He rolled his r's like only Scots could. "Did you ever graduate?"

"No," Paul answered, bowing his head. He reached down to pick up Mr. G.'s hat and handed it back to him.

"I understand you've run into a spot of trouble. I'm very sorry to hear about your grandfather. You know you can stay with Nan and me for as long as you wish."

"I appreciate that."

Mr. G. ordered a porter to grab Paul's trunk and quickly had it loaded into his sparkling new 1941 Hudson, and the pair headed up the Pali Road towards the Windward Side of Oʻahu. Paul spent several minutes explaining what had happened during the earlier part of the day and showed Mr. G. both the photograph and the money clip. They were the only items seemingly available that could help him unlock the mystery of his grandfather's sudden death.

"Take a breath, young lad. I'm sure we can take a look into it. I don't know who the young *wahine* is, but perhaps we can find out."

Paul nodded and looked out the window at the lush scenery along the drive. Mr. G. perceived the young man's melancholy mood, and as the car rattled at the top of a windy mountain pass, he angled his car off to the side of the road. He pulled on the brake pedal and turned towards Paul seated in the passenger seat. "You've had a long run of bad luck, haven't you, lad?"

The tall young man mumbled yes.

"I know John mentioned your parents—they were killed in an automobile accident when you were a boy, if I recall. And now this. You have endured so much for a young man."

Paul nodded, his head hanging down.

"I'm not going to pry into your personal affairs, lad, but I am going try my best to help you. And the first step might be trying to take your mind off your troubles for a wee bit."

Paul looked up. Mr. G. pointed outside the car. He motioned for Paul to get out of the vehicle.

"Every time I'm feeling blue, I stop here," Mr. G. said. "I figure, no matter what ails you, a breath of this mountain air and this view can make you feel better. Every day, I try to enjoy what Hawaii has to offer. In fact, when the legendary Mark Twain was here at this very spot, he proclaimed it the best view in the world. Maybe he was onto something, don't you think?"

Paul smiled weakly.

"I'm not trying to make you forget your troubles, lad. I'm trying to get you to lift your head up. That's why we stopped. The scenic view at Nu'uanu Pali might help give you a clearer head. Why don't you try thinking that your next journey in life starts here?"

Paul slowly got out of the car, and the two men walked silently to a small wall that provided a good overlook. Mr. G. said nothing. He simply let his young friend bask in the view.

It was nearing dusk, but even in the dimming sunlight Paul was astounded at the view of the Windward Side of O'ahu. The strong winds from the pass practically slapped him across his face, but he hardly noticed; he was enraptured with what he saw before him. Mr. G. was right; it somehow made him feel better.

From left to right, as he stood on the edge of the road, leaning against the side of the car, he could see lush and sumptuous foliage. Small green hilltops seemed to pop up along the skyline. The white crests of waves could be seen along the Pacific Ocean shoreline. Beside the greenery of the tropical foliage and the ocean in the distance, wispy pink flares darted across the horizon of the light blue sky.

"Pretty amazing, don't you think?"

"In a word, gorgeous." Paul continued to look down at the expansive view below, where lush green hills and ridges were dissected by what appeared to be lakes or streams.

"See those two pockets of inland water? The one on the left is Kawai Nui, the one on the right is Ka'elepulu. Both are pretty much swamps now, but in ancient Hawaiian times, they were clear water fish ponds. In fact, the word *Kailua* means "two waters." You're looking at them."After about ten or fifteen minutes, the pair got back into Mr. G.'s Hudson and then slowly zigzagged down the mountainside, the car practically embracing the sheer cliffs for what seemed like an eternity. The color in Paul's face started to come back, and he felt much better. Mr. G. continued his positive demeanor, and he shared anecdotes about the island along the way.

"You know the story of the legendary Battle of the Pali?" the elderly man asked.

Paul shook his head no.

"This is where Kamehameha the Great conquered the islands. He won the decisive battle when his warriors chased their enemies up the Nu'uanu Valley from Honolulu, and then they forced the opposing soldiers over the jagged cliffs to their deaths."

Paul peered through the passenger window, and all he could see was the incredible drop-off, hundreds of feet into oblivion. The thought of such a battle seemed astounding to him. Mr. G. continued the drive. At one hairpin turn, he pointed out a huge hillside mansion and estate that was owned by the area's largest landowner, the Castle family.

"They call it Palikū," he said. "A beautiful place. When they built it in the late 1920s, they also brought in a bunch of Norfolk Island pines and Cook pines along here. Kind of gives it a Shangri-La-like feeling. I like that."

Further down the curvy road, Mr. G. announced their location. "If you're going to Kāne'ohe, you turn left. Straight ahead, where we're going, is Kailua," he pointed. "That small house there is the headquarters for Kāne'ohe Ranch, Castle's big ranch property." He pointed to a small green house at the junction. He told Paul that the area was called Maunawili, or twisted mountain.

Paul smiled again—he hadn't expected such a tour, but he appreciated the fact that the old Scot was going out of his way to brighten his spirits.

They drove ahead slowly, passing a small general store—Mr. G. called it the Kodama Store—then several fruit and vegetable stands that lined the highway. Farm fields, featuring everything from papaya to lettuce and tomatoes backed them up. Further down the road, they crossed a small bridge, and Paul began to see the town of Kailua emerge.

A movie theater stood perched on the left-hand side of the road as they entered the small village. The marquee announced that it was "Wednesday Night—Cowboy Night. Westerns starring Tom Mix and Hopalong Cassidy." Beyond the theater stood clusters and clusters of coconut trees, lined up in procession. For as far as you could see beyond the theater, tropical palms swayed in the tradewinds. "Used to be a coconut farm over there, but now it's a small housing tract," Mr. G. said. On the right side of the main road was a small gas station, the Flying A. They passed it slowly, plus the Bishop Bank building and Hughes Drug Store. Up ahead, across the street on the left, about a block past the theater, stood the Kailua Tavern, its bright lights already turned on. "Very popular," Mr. G. said. "Sometimes too popular with all the new servicemen in town, if you know what I mean."

The Hudson stopped at the T-intersection to allow a young couple, a navy sailor and his girl, to cross. There were several other pedestrians, all comfortably dressed for the seventy-five-degree temperature. When the trade winds kicked up momentarily, Paul couldn't help but notice the flaring skirts of two pretty teenagers walking along the roadside.

The town center was small and compact. Across from Kailua Tavern was a busy general store, Harada's. The store was much larger than the small Kodama Store they had passed near Maunawili. Next door to Harada's, there was a pool hall, but after the car turned right at the big banyan tree at the intersection, there was very little in front of them except pasture land.

"Blink and you'll miss the town," Mr. G. said, smiling.

It wasn't too long before they were driving past big ironwood trees that fronted a large dairy property. "Campos Dairy," Mr. G. reported. "Campos has been around here for years. They planted all these ironwood trees along Kailua Road. They make for a good windbreak for their dairy cows. The cows listen to music, if you've ever heard of such a thing. The workers turn the radio on full blast when they milk them. Apparently, the cows give more milk when the music's playing."

Paul laughed under his breath. He could tell that Mr. G. was trying to cheer him up. The events of the day were pretty over-whelming to a twenty-one-year-old, but the interesting mix of gorgeous scenery, musically inclined dairy cows, navy sailors, and pretty girls gave him at least a little comfort.

The small, two-lane paved road curved left and headed towards the ocean. In a small break in the ironwood trees, a grocery store, Lanikai Store, was visible on the left as they headed towards the beach. Kitty-corner from that was another small storefront property.

"That's Kalapawai Market," Mr. G. said. "Just a little place, but good chop suey at the cozy place next to it." They turned right in front of the tiny green building and continued towards Mr. G.'s home in Lanikai.

Eventually the road curved past an expansive beach that Paul would have to wait to explore during the daylight hours. A twenty-five-foot concrete pillar along the ocean side of the road greeted their arrival to the neighborhood. The pillar had one word engraved on its side—*Lanikai*.

"This is Alālā Point," Mr. G. said. "The developer marked the spot when he built the homes here about fifteen years ago. When they started development of Lanikai, they were planning to turn it into a mini-Venice, with canals and everything. But the developer had financial problems after a few years, his grand plans fell through, and he returned to the mainland. Now the fishermen use the pillar as a reference point for good fishing spots."

They bounced down the road, past several homes, and finally reached their final destination, just a block from the beach at Lanikai. The Gillespie cottage was small but delightful. Plantation-style in design but modestly built, it was nestled in the back of a large lot with plenty of parking in the front yard. Beautiful tropical flowers trimmed the house and the lot. Both Mr. G. and Paul stepped out into the warm temperatures of an early Windward O'ahu evening. Mr. G.'s wife, Nan, waited to greet them from the front lānai.

"You look terrific, my young lad," Nan said from the big porch that rimmed the front of the cottage. Paul smiled when he heard her friendly Scottish voice. You didn't have to convince him of the fact that the Gillespies were just about the nicest people he had ever met. Just like her husband, Nan was a petite woman, slight in stature, but big in heart. She wore a neat navy blue dress brimming with tiny polka dots. Not a button nor a pearl around her neck was out of place. She embraced Paul warmly. "I'm so sorry to hear about your loss," she whispered into the young man's ear. She hugged him tightly, then released him and stepped back. "Let's get some food in your stomach. You must be famished."

The threesome—two diminutive Scots and the tall *haole* boy from the big cities of Los Angeles and New York—marched arm in arm through the screen door and into the cottage. The hardwood floors creaked under their weight. The living room was cozy and warm, with a small sofa and rocking chair, a lamp, an end table, and, in the corner, a large radio console. Nan was a fastidious house-keeper, and everything in the living room had its proper place.

As modest as the living room was, the dining room, albeit small, was quite impressive. Nan had obviously laid out her best dinner dishes for her young visitor. The large teakwood table was complete with cloth placemats, fancy silverware, cloth napkins, and even napkin holders.

"Who are you expecting, the king of England?" Paul said, play-fully teasing his hostess.

"G'on," gushed Nan. "It's this way for us every night. And when the mister called and told me you were coming, I wanted to make it extra special."

"Sit down," Mr. G. intoned, respectfully. "I'll get your trunk out of the car after dinner. You can sleep in John's old room."

"Paul, we're so glad to have you. We can't wait for John to join us, too," Nan said, her voice almost twinkling with delight. She stood barely over five feet tall, and her silver hair almost glistened, with nary a hair out of place.

Paul and Mr. G. gathered themselves in their seats while Nan served up a feast of liver and onions, green beans with bacon, and a hearty helping of white rice. Paul recalled John telling him that his mother cooked up the best liver and onions in the world, and one taste of Nan's specialty had him clamoring for more. A second help-ing came with a smile, and the conversation flowed throughout.

"Show Nan the photograph," Mr. G. said after a second cup of hot tea.

Paul gingerly removed the withered old photo from his shirt

pocket and pushed it across the table.

"She's very attractive."

Paul nodded.

"Do you know anything about her?"

Paul shook his head.

"My grandfather was a very private man," the young man said. He got up from the table and walked around the room. It seemed easier for him to talk if he moved around.

"Even after my parents died, he rarely showed any emotions. I never met my grandmother—she died before I was born, so I don't know anything about their relationship, and he rarely spoke about his past."

"But you say you know he lived in Hawaii years ago?"

"That part I do know. A distant aunt on my grandmother's side of the family, a fairly wealthy woman who helped me get into Columbia, told me that grandfather lived in Hawaii in the 1890s, when he started up in the shipping business. She only knew that because she recalled his late wife, my grandmother, talking about it once, but she knew very little other than that."

"Is the aunt still alive?"

"No, she passed about the same time I left Columbia."

"Sorry to hear that. And your grandfather never spoke about Hawai'i all this time?"

"Not until recently, but that was only about this trip. I could tell he really cared about the islands, but I wasn't sure why. I'm actually embarrassed I don't know more about him. That's my fault, I guess. All I really knew was that he was fairly successful in the shipping business in southern California, but he never talked about his younger days."

"Why the trip then?"

"I think it was for my sake, more than anything else. I was having a difficult time holding onto a job, and when I left from my last position, he seemed to take pity on me and suggested a trip to the islands might help me. It was a very nice gesture."

"And you knew nothing of the photo?"

"Nothing."

"What about the money clip?" Mr. G. asked. Paul reached into his pocket and handed the aged and worn money clip to Nan.

"This also was with grandfather when he died."

Nan looked at it briefly, tried in vain to read the inscription, and then shook her head but said nothing.

"Why would the coroner say that the cause of death was unknown?"

"I think he thought grandfather ingested some kind of powder when he went back to the stateroom. He found remnants of some kind of white stuff on his fingertips and on the inside of his mouth. I don't know why the photo tipped him off to that thought, but he said it was clear cut to him."

"Do you believe that?"

Paul took a deep breath and continued to pace around the table.

"I don't know. I honestly don't know."

5 - KAILUA NIGHTS

Jack Burns was a notorious insomniac. At least that's what all of his friends thought. It wasn't uncommon for the Honolulu policeman to drop by a friend's home late at night or a local pub or tavern to discuss everything from politics to people to the latest news on one of his investigations. He was always on the move, hard-driving and resourceful, as if life was too short to accomplish all he wanted to do—he even managed to tend to a liquor store he owned in downtown Kailua.

On Thanksgiving eve, 1941, Burns finished his police shift, then dropped by his tiny liquor store on Oneawa Street to make sure that the day's receipts had been properly documented. He had expected it to be a busy day, what with Thanksgiving the next day, and he was happy that his assistant, a Japanese man named Kawekami who ran the counter and did the accounting work, reported brisk sales.

Burns tipped his hat to Kawekami on his way out the back entrance to the store and sauntered into the Kailua night. The Kailua Tavern was practically next door to Burns' place, and he figured on dropping by briefly before heading home to his tiny house in Coconut Grove.

The night was pleasantly warm with a light trade wind, and he could hear the rustling of the coconut palms in the distance. That crackling sound was so distinctly Kailua, he thought. He stopped to listen for a moment, took the last couple of drags on his cigarette, and proceeded to snuff out the butt on the ground. He was about to light another cigarette when he heard two women arguing in the not-too-far-off distance.

"Why must you be so headstrong!" he heard one of the women yell out. The other woman's voice, a voice that sounded much younger, screamed back something that Burns could not make out, but it was obvious she was very angry.

Burns hastily stuffed his unlit cigarette back into the pack and walked quickly in the direction of the voices. When he came around the side of the liquor store building, he saw two *haole* women—one middle-aged and one in her twenties—standing next to a car with an open driver's side door, struggling over some object. The older woman was clutching whatever it was they were fighting about, while the younger woman was trying to pull it away.

"Ladies, can I help you?" Burns asked as he approached them from about ten feet away. The two women immediately stopped struggling. The younger woman let go of the object and the older woman immediately put whatever she was holding behind her lower back.

Burns tried to see what the object was, but despite his detective's strong observation skills, he was unable to make a positive identification in the darkness.

"Is there a problem?"

"No, sir," the younger woman responded. She dropped her head and looked away.

"Are you sure you don't need my help? I'm a police officer, if you're wondering."

The younger woman gasped but said nothing. The older woman took a deep breath and then smiled. It was an uncomfortable smile.

"It's really nothing, officer. Just a mother and daughter having a tiff after work. I'm sure we can work it out between ourselves."

Burns moved closer to both of them. The younger woman turned completely away from him. The older woman held her chin up and tersely smiled again.

"You two ladies work in the hair salon, don't you? I think I may have met you before."

"Yes, Officer Burns, I recognize you now," the older woman said. Her voice had a thick German accent.

"It's Mrs. Kuehn, is that right?"

"Yes, Friedel Kuehn," she answered. "Yes, we probably have met before."

Burns took one step closer and removed his hat. He smiled back at her, reassuringly.

"I think you know my husband, Otto, the furniture salesman. And this is our daughter, Greta. I'm sorry—we're sorry—for troubling you like this."

Greta continued to look away, but Burns attempted to comfort her by placing his right hand on her shoulder. He felt her bristle and tighten up immediately. She's very nervous or still very upset, he thought. He tapped her gently and removed his hand.

"Glad to know things are okay. Have a wonderful Thanksgiving, ladies."

Friedel Kuehn smiled and nodded. Greta quickly walked around to the other side of the car and got into the passenger side. Burns glanced down at the object they were struggling with as the older woman got into the car. He could finally tell what it was.

It was a hairbrush.

Burns laughed to himself and then lit another cigarette as the Kuehn's car drove away into the night. He watched the path of their car lights until they disappeared around the corner.

He walked quickly from the parking lot and into Kailua Tavern. Before even setting a foot inside, he could tell it was a rowdy night.

The tavern was filled with local servicemen and the requisite number of young women, all drinking and smoking heartily. The large room that led to a big bar area was filled with smoke. It was just the kind of atmosphere that Burns liked.

"Burnsy!" the man from behind the bar called out to him.

Burns smiled at his barkeep friend, a big *hapa-haole* man with a quick smile and a loud voice, and sauntered up to the bar. "Hey, Kimo. Looks like a good night."

"You drinking tonight, Jack?" Kimo, the bartender, asked. He was a huge, dark-skinned man, nearly three hundred pounds, and an ethnic mixture of many races.

"You know I never touch the stuff," Burns smiled back at him. Despite owning a liquor store, he hadn't had a drop of booze in years.

"Just making sure," the bartender said.

"What's new in town?" Burns asked.

Kimo wiped his countertop. "A new detachment for the naval air station at Kāneʻohe Bay," he said. "Guess they're training these guys how to make amphibious air landings."

Burns looked around the room. Most of the men were in their early twenties—kids mostly. The number of servicemen had grown tremendously in the past few months.

"How long has it been? Six months or so, since they finished that new base there?"

"I think that's about right. Fort Hase was around for years, but this new naval air Station seems to be getting bigger every day."

"Any trouble?"

"Are you kidding me? You know these kids live to fight. They're just dying to get into a scrap, one way or another."

"They may get one."

The big bartender laughed. Burns grabbed the glass of water that was offered and walked towards a relatively quiet corner. He flirted briefly with a young and shapely waitress, who giggled back at

him. He accidentally bumped into an obviously inebriated serviceman who was on his way back to the bar from the restroom. The
drunken man momentarily looked like he was going to take offense
and start a beef, but Burns put up his hand and shook his head.
"Save the fight for the enemy, kid," he said, and sat down in the
corner and ordered his dinner.

Ironically, he thought, who knew exactly who the real enemies
were? If he believed his FBI and military friends, they were more
worried about sabotage from among the local Japanese population
than they were about an actual attack somewhere in the Pacific.
War talk was everywhere, and he was aware of ongoing negotiations
with the Japanese in Washington DC. He'd personally seen the
build-up of American troops all over the islands. Pearl Harbor was
busting at the seams, and so was Hickam and Schofield Barracks. On
the Windward Side of the island, the military had just increased its
presence on Mōkapu Peninsula between Kailua and Kāne'ohe with
the new naval air station, and at nearby Bellows Field, just beyond
Lanikai, near Waimānalo.

As the HPD liaison to the FBI, Burns routinely checked up on
local Japanese all the time. The FBI's favorite worries were the
Japanese churches and schools, and Burns had seen the long lists of
suspects. He personally didn't believe all of the names on the list
belonged, but he didn't argue. He knew this added job was an important one, and he appreciated it. Besides, if there was a way to protect
some of his friends, especially his many local Japanese friends, then
he was all for that.

He thought back to his early confrontation with the Kuehn
women. He knew that the FBI had done some background checking
on the husband, Otto Kuehn. Odd fellow, he thought. He was aware,
as virtually none of his Kailua neighbors were, that Kuehn had been
an officer in the German Navy in the last war. That fact the FBI had
discovered. He personally didn't think that it made Kuehn a Nazi,
but he found it interesting that the German could support two large

houses—a cottage on Lanikai on the beach and a bigger two-story house in the Kalama tract on the other side of Coconut Grove—on what he made as a furniture salesman and whatever the wife and daughter brought home from their work at the hair salon.

Burns decided that he would have an innocent chat with Kuehn in the coming weeks. Nothing formal, but he always followed up every lead and every thought. So far, Kuehn wasn't on anyone's list.

Halfway through his steak, he was interrupted by Kimo, the bartender. "Burnsy, got a phone call for you. Sounds pretty important."

Burns leaped up from his table and hustled over to the tavern phone. He listened briefly, then hung up. "Duty calls again," he said to the bartender. "Put it on my tab."

Kimo laughed, then sighed. He knew there was no tab.

Burns had no siren on his '38 Packard, but he drove quickly up the Pali Road towards Maunawili. His call had come not from police dispatch, but from Kailua's largest mansion estate—something about a woman behaving very strangely at the guesthouse at Palikū. Just chalk it up to another very long day, he thought.

It took less than ten minutes for Burns to get to the Spanish-style mansion in the foothills above Maunawili. He felt slightly humbled by the towering presence of the Koʻolau Mountains that rose steeply above the large mansion. He quickly got out of his car, where he was met by a Japanese servant boy.

"Come quickly," the boy said. Burns followed him down a pathway, past lush tropical flowers, to a small guesthouse behind the mansion. The room was dimly lit, but he could make out the figure of a large woman lying on the bed. Two men hovered over her. Burns recognized one of them immediately.

"Good evening, Mr. Castle," he said. "It's Officer Burns. How can I help?"

Harold Castle, the mansion's owner and the largest landowner in the Kailua-Kāne'ohe area, stepped away from the bed. His face was weathered by years of working on his beloved Kāne'ohe Ranch. The two men looked at each other, and Castle shook his head.

"I don't know why she's behaving like this," Castle stammered. "I think she's okay now, but I just don't know."

Burns looked over at the woman, a large, elderly Hawaiian woman, dressed neatly in a brightly colored *mu'umu'u*, who lay resting on her back with a local Chinese man gently patting her forehead with a wet towel.

"Who is she?"

"Rose Alston. Actually, she'll tell you Rose Kamakawiwo'ole Alston," Castle said. "She's a frequent houseguest here. She and her late husband are friends of ours."

Burns stepped towards Rose, but she didn't acknowledge his presence. The man helping her continued to stroke her forehead.

"This is Henry Wong, my ranch foreman. I think you two have met before."

"Yes, Henry, good to see you again. How's your golf game?"

Wong smiled. He and Burns had squared off a number of times on the golf course at nearby Mid-Pacific Country Club. Both were excellent players, even though Wong was not an official member. The unwritten rule at the time was that only *haoles* were allowed memberships.

"Fine, sir. Good to see you, too. I think she's better now."

"What exactly happened, and why did you call me?"

"Well, sir, I was just checking on the property, as I do every night before I go to bed, and I heard a distressed sound from one of the guest rooms. I was aware that Miss Rose was here alone, and when I heard a bloodcurdling moan, I went immediately to her door," Wong said.

Castle interrupted. "She often spends time with us since the death of her husband. We've been friends for many years. I think she likes the quiet and solitude up here. I let her stay in the guesthouse any time she wishes. She didn't even need to ask."

Burns nodded. "So what happened?"

"I'm not really sure. She only spoke briefly," Wong explained. "She continued to make the horrible moaning sounds. They were awful, almost unworldly. I called out to her, but she didn't answer. So I used my key and came into the room and found her wallowing on the bed here. I don't know what to make of it."

"Did you call a doctor?"

"No, just Mr. Castle and you."

"Why?"

"Didn't think I needed one, to tell you the truth. I deal with sick animals all the time. I calmed her down and had her vomit and then I placed her on the bed. When she was resting on her own, I got Mr. Castle, and he called you. I think she's fine now."

"Then I'm not sure I understand why you think this is police business." Burns stepped back from the bed and studied the faces of both Wong and Castle. Burns always looked into people's eyes, because he felt it could help him determine their motivations. But their eyes revealed nothing.

"It was something that she said. And she said it a few times, each time with a horrifying look."

"What exactly did she say?"

"At first, I couldn't quite understand, but then it became perfectly clear."

"What was it?"

"She said, 'He's coming. He's coming'."

Burns looked down at Rose again and saw the fear in her eyes. Wong reached down to comfort her and she calmed down relatively quickly. "I think she's going to be okay. I'll stay with her until the morning."

Castle looked over at Burns, his face still showing obvious distress. "Help us, Burns. What does it mean?"

6 - THE SUNRISE AND THE RACE TRACK

"The sunrise at Lanikai Beach is perhaps the single most spiritual event you'll ever experience," John Gillespie had told his friend Paul Sands when they were roommates at Columbia University in New York. Paul recalled that statement many times, and when he was unable to sleep any longer in the wee hours of Thanksgiving morning, he got up from his bed and dressed quietly in the darkness, hoping to witness the majestic sunrise.

Paul's mind obsessed on the events from the day before, and his thoughts raced. Nothing about the death of his grandfather made sense to him, but he refused to wallow in self-pity. If he had learned one thing in his short life—and the tragic death of his parents years before had painfully taught him this—it was that mourning was best handled by staying active in both body and spirit. He had reflected on that many times over the years. He would take John's advice and meander down to the beach only a couple of hundred yards away from the Gillespie cottage. Perhaps a walk and a sunrise could help him clear his head.

The last couple of years had not been good for him. His knees often ached, victims of the injuries he suffered during his junior season of playing basketball at Columbia. After those injuries, he got very sick, causing him to get behind in school and eventually lose his motivation. Despite John's insistence that he stay on and earn his college degree, Paul quit school and then wandered from one menial job to another. By the time he arrived back in Hollywood to live with his grandfather, he was a lost soul—aimless and without purpose.

Yes, he could use some spiritual guidance about now.

He took a deep breath as he stepped out in the darkness—he immediately thought he had never smelled air quite so fresh. The pleasant breeze liberated him from the normally cumbersome winter burden of coats, sweaters, and shoes. He would need none of that; the early morning temperature was quite pleasant, and he appreciated the light breeze that caressed his cheeks and comforted his soul.

But his newfound tranquility vanished at the thought of his grandfather lying cold in the Honolulu morgue. He looked skyward and saw the twinkling of the stars and silently asked for some form of guidance on how to deal with this terrible revelation. He must find out what really killed his grandfather. It was illogical to him that his grandfather might have taken his own life. He vowed to find the answers. He whispered a little prayer as he walked across the small road to the beachfront and felt the cool sand beneath his feet.

The homes along the beachfront were a little larger than the Gillespie cottage. This must be where some of the rich people of Honolulu live, he thought. Or at least, this is where they spend their weekends or vacations. He sat down in the sand and contemplated his life for a few moments.

Just who was he? A failed student, unable to hold on to a job, with no family now and no place he called home. What would he do? The only thing he was certain about at this moment was his vow to solve the riddle of his grandfather's death. His new journey, as Mr. G. called it, would start there.

His thoughts wandered, and he soon realized that just sitting in the darkness was spiritual enough. He could see the stars twinkling above the horizon. He lay back with his hand on the cool, dry, fine sand and tried to find the Big Dipper but couldn't locate it. It didn't matter anyway, he thought, as he could presently see hundreds of stars, more than he could ever count. He'd never seen so many stars in all his life.

He appreciated the serenity of the beach at that early hour. The tiny waves rippling the shoreline played like gentle percussion instruments. He listened to the rhythmic patter of the water nestling against the sand. It played out almost like the sweet jazz tunes he thoroughly enjoyed until closing time at the student bars of Harlem, near Columbia.

For the first time in the last twenty hours or so, he felt some peace. He closed his eyes and thanked the Lord for allowing him to be there. John was right. He could feel the spiritual wave overtaking him already.

The sky transformed from blackness to a soft gray as night turned into morning. He could make out the islands off the Lanikai coast. These were the Mokes, or Mokulua Islands, that John had told him about many times. He had seen their images only on postcards.

The two tiny islands blossomed out of the ocean about a half-mile offshore. The island to the left was slightly larger and had two small peaks, one no more than two hundred feet high, the other peak perhaps twice that. It also had a small sandy beach, which he could make out as the sky became lighter. The smaller island was a gentle pyramid-shaped mound with a crest also rising about two hundred feet above sea level.

Clouds hovered over the horizon beyond the Mokes, and for a moment he wondered if these clouds might block the sunrise. He didn't have to worry. In fact, the clouds would provide an even more spectacular sunrise.

Before the first rays of the sun even climbed to the horizon, he could see the edges of the clouds turning pink. He looked left and right and noticed that the colors were changing all across the sky.

From pink to lavender to crimson, the colors in the clouds grew brighter by the moment. The beauty was astounding. Finally, the tangential crown of the sun began to peek over the water's edge. The Mokes became almost a silhouette, as they were backlit by the emergence of a giant orange ball. Orange, at first, but then quickly yellow, with different shades of red, tangerine, and pink wrestling in the clouds.

Paul soaked in every solitary moment, eventually rising from the ground and standing reverently in genuine awe. He actually gasped audibly at what he figured had to be the crowning moment of the sunrise.

Within a matter of seconds, the sun climbed above the water, and the skies turned from a pale blue gray to a pastel blue. The Mokes became green emeralds, shining ever so brightly as they rose out of the water.

Paul took a few steps forward and felt the coolness of the waves as they broke over his feet. He walked forward, the water lapping first at his ankles, then his knees and thighs. He looked down and was amazed that he could see his toes so vividly. The water was that clear and transparent, and warm, too.

The ocean sparkled from left to right; like a field of diamonds, he thought. Each small wave of water glistened as the sun caught it just right.

If there is a heaven, he thought, it must definitely look like this.

He removed his shirt and tossed it back on the sand, then put his head down and dove in underneath the warm water. It was so clear he could almost keep his eyes open. He swam for several minutes toward the two tiny islands, then doubled back and headed for shore. The beach was empty except for a woman walking her small black dog along the pearly white shoreline. He smiled and waved to her, and she waved back.

He languished for a while, then grabbed his shirt and used it as a towel before heading back to the Gillespie cottage. The morning sun was already quite stinging. He didn't mind it a bit.

He felt at peace with himself.

"You missed breakfast, lad," Mr. G. said while pruning his prize hibiscus. "Nan wondered where you wandered off to."

"Just enjoying the sunrise. Wow, it was beautiful."

"One of the reasons I love living here."

Paul realized they weren't alone. In his peripheral vision, he saw a slight Japanese man, perhaps about forty years old or so, pop from the other side of the hibiscus bush. He was wearing a large hat to keep the sun off his face.

"Meet Kenji Fujimoto," Mr. G. said with a smile.

Kenji bowed, and Paul stuck out his hand. Kenji shook it gently, not bothering to take off his gardening glove.

"Kenji is a godsend," Mr. G. said. "He knows just about everything you need to know about keeping a yard looking fantastic."

The old Scotsman turned to Kenji and put his hand on the Japanese man's shoulder. "Tell Paul here your secret for keeping my hibiscus blooming all year round."

"Coffee grounds," Kenji said succinctly, his soft voice heavy with a pidgin accent. He pointed towards the plants as if to say, look for yourself.

Paul looked around the yard in amazement. The hibiscus blossomed in every direction. Yellow and red, pink and orange, the huge colorful petals opened wide in the morning Lanikai sun.

"You're kidding me," Paul said. "This is all because of coffee grounds."

"It like fertilizer," Kenji said. "I take what the missus throw away in morning trash. We use a little to help the plants."

"We fertilize a few times each year," Mr. G. said as he examined one of the larger yellow flowers. Five distinct yellow petals fanned out with a stiff, red pistil in the center. "The individual flowers bloom for longer periods during the summer, perhaps as much as several days. But our fair weather allows for blooms all year round. During this time of year, the blooms usually last only a day or two."

"You water them a bunch?"

"Hibiscus not like wet feet," Kenji replied as he went back to his pruning chores. "You can't overwater, or plants suffer. But don't let dry out either. Good moisture in soil and good drainage key to flower long life."

"The weather and drainage here is perfect for them," Mr. G. said. "They can thrive here for years. And the great thing is that each plant has its own personality. On this side of the yard, we prune them back to make a hedge. Over on the other side, you can see they're more spindly in nature."

The Japanese yardman went back to work. Paul pulled Mr. G. aside and told him he wasn't going to go through a long mourning period; he would instead focus his efforts on pursuing an investigation into his grandfather's death. The Scotsman listened intently and agreed that moving forward was the best thing to do. But he also told his young visitor that asking serious questions here might be a tremendous challenge, that working with Honolulu officials isn't quite the same as he might be used to.

"This isn't like Hollywood, you know, lad."

"I don't expect it to be easy, but I have to do this—I owe it to him. And to myself."

The little Scotsman took off his gloves and slapped them back and forth, removing some of the dirt that had gathered at each fingertip. "I've got an idea to keep us all active," he said. "Do you like horse racing?"

"I guess so," Paul stammered. "But what the hell has that got to do with anything?"

"Because today is Race Day in Kailua. Everybody who is anybody from all over the island will be there, including maybe someone who might be able to guide us. Notice, that's *guide us*, I say, not necessarily *help us*. As I said, this isn't going to be easy."

Paul put his hand to his mouth and pondered what he had just heard. "Okay."

"Go wash up, lad. I'll talk with Nan and phone my brother and his wife in Honolulu to join us. They're real racing fans and might have a few thoughts, too. We can catch Thanksgiving dinner at the Kailua Tavern afterwards."

A couple of hours later, Paul was introduced to Mr. G.'s brother, a man he and Nan affectionately called Uncle Rob. Like his older brother, Uncle Rob was a cherubic man with a bald head and lots of freckles. He also possessed an enormous set of teeth and grinned widely whenever he spoke. His wife, Constance, was just the opposite, petite and demure and quite taciturn.

In the Gillespie living room, Mr. G. and Uncle Rob spent their time going over the race ponies for the day. Uncle Rob had a copy of a betting sheet he brought from town. The two brothers carefully analyzed each of the races and meticulously scribbled down their picks on tiny pieces of paper. Then they stuffed the papers in their back pockets.

"Making certain nobody sees this but me," Uncle Rob said with a big grin.

"Gambling's not legal here," Mr. G. said quietly. "Only it is. You understand."

"That's the way it is here," Uncle Rob said, still grinning. "The territorial legislature tried to pass a pari-mutuel betting bill last year. They barely got it through, but then ol' Governor Poindexter vetoed it. Because it isn't legal, and so many people want to do it anyway, you've got to be a little sneaky."

Paul immediately understood. "Got ya."

Paul, Mr. G., Nan, Uncle Rob, and Constance piled into the Hudson and headed through Kailua Town to the race track. On each side of the main street of Oneawa, house lots were intermingled with dozens of coconut trees.

"We call it Coconut Grove," Mr. G. said. "The trees are clustered in checkerboard fashion throughout this area. There used to be a pretty good market for coconut oil, but not anymore. The property is owned by Kāne'ohe Ranch, like most everything else around here."

Near the end of the road, just past the Kailua Racquet Club, they ran into thousands of other racing fans. Mr. G. was correct in his assessment that it would be a popular place on this sunny afternoon, and the fans came in all ethnicities and all walks of life. Kailua Race Track wasn't at all large. The big oval track had bleachers on only one end, near the finish line. And they were uncovered bleachers, at that.

But that didn't stop several thousand horse-racing enthusiasts from joining in on the fun. "I'd estimate the crowd at upwards of five thousand," Mr. G. said. "Pretty typical since they started up last year. Before that, they'd gone some fourteen years without horse racing on O'ahu. Believe it or not, they plant watermelons here when racing is out of season."

The wooden grandstands were filled by the time they arrived, and Nan motioned them towards another area. "We're headed to the infield," Nan said. "We'll lay out a big blanket near the rail. And when it's race time, we can stand up at the rail and get a real close-up view." Nan and Constance peeled off towards the infield, while Scotty and Uncle Rob slithered off to an area underneath the grandstand. Paul followed them.

In this back area, a little man wearing a big hat walked around with his hands out, with dollar bills twisted around each finger. Mr. G. and Uncle Rob whispered something in the little man's ear and each handed him a small wad of bills and the pieces of papers they'd been working on that morning. The little man rolled the bills up quickly around his fingers and went on to his next customers. Mr. G. and Uncle Rob came away rubbing their hands together in glee.

"I guess you fellas are expecting to make some money today," Paul said.

"Indeed we are, boy. Let's get to the infield." But before they could get there, Uncle Rob was stopped by two men who looked like local business types. He motioned for Paul and Mr. G. to go ahead to the infield.

Paul looked back. The two men were dressed in slacks and dress shirts. The taller of the two men introduced a shorter man to Uncle Rob, and then the taller man left. Rob took the shorter man's card, said a few things to him, and then hustled over to the infield rail with the rest of the group.

"His name's Otto Kuehn," Uncle Rob said when he rejoined them back on the infield railing. "Says he wants me to take some photographs for him, but I told him I would have to get back to him."

Mr. G. interrupted. "Yes, Mr. Kuehn. Has a place on the beach near the end of Lanikai and another home not far from here. German fellow, I believe. Don't know a lot about him."

"His wife does our hair," Nan said, as if she were revealing a well-kept secret. "She and her daughter run the hair salon near Kailua Tavern. Kind of a busybody, if you ask me. The wife, that is."

The conversation abruptly ended. Paul watched Kuehn walk off toward the bettors. Everybody else's eyes focused on the race track. Paul watched the curious ritual of illegal gambling repeating itself again and again, then he turned his attention to the races.

The first race of the afternoon was at a distance of five furlongs. Five thoroughbreds answered the call and set a furious pace down the backstretch. Nan and Constance screamed the entire distance. The jockeys whipped their ponies in close quarters, driving them at breakneck speeds, knowing full well that any mistake, any trip or loss of balance, could possibly mean the end of their riding careers.

That first race ended in a driving two-horse finish, and Paul immediately observed Mr. G. and Uncle Rob's reaction when their horse didn't win. They both grimaced, and Uncle Rob let out a whine that made everyone laugh.

In between races, the fans were entertained by cowboy singers and trick ropers. One local cowboy even yodeled his songs while trick roping the entire time.

"That's Jorge Luis, one of the Portuguese cowboys who works for Kāne'ohe Ranch," Mr. G. said. "We call 'em *paniolo* here."

"*Paniolo?*" Paul repeated. "Kind of a strange word."

"I think it's a bastardization, if you'll excuse the term, of the Spanish word for *Spaniard*," Uncle Rob explained. "*Española* is the actual word, but like so many words in Hawai'i, it got changed a bit. Not sure why they're referred to as paniolo rather than *paniola*, but it seems that's the popular term."

"The Portuguese and the Spanish came here two or three generations ago and brought their horsemanship skills with them," Mr. G. picked up where his brother left off. "Many of the jockeys you see here today came from the famous Parker Ranch on the Big Island. I think Jorge is a local *paniolo*, but he's learned his skills from the best of the Parker Ranch boys."

Paul was interested but was feeling anxious again about his own quest. Mr. G. sensed it, put his arm on the tall young man's shoulder, and motioned that he wanted him to follow him towards the grandstands. "I think I see Officer Burns over there," he said.

Jack Burns looked much less formal than the first time Paul had laid eyes on him, the tragic morning before. He wore an aloha shirt and casual slacks plus a wide hat to block out the sun. "Jack," Mr. G. called towards the police officer, apparently off duty on this Thanksgiving Day. "You remember Paul Sands, of course."

Burns shook the tall young man's hand and once again told him how sorry he was about the previous day's events.

"I think that's what young Paul here would like to talk with you about," Mr. G. said.

"How so?"

"I think he wants to find out what killed his grandfather."

"I understand. I'm sure the autopsy will tell us more."

"Autopsy? How long will that take?"

"Could be a few days—could be shorter, could be longer."

"I don't quite understand what the coroner was trying to suggest when he found whatever it was that was on Grandfather's lips. You need to know that my grandfather would never do something wrong. It wasn't in his character," Paul protested.

"Just be patient, son."

Mr. G. interrupted by putting his hand on Paul's shoulders and nudging him away. He could tell that Paul was distressed. "How can we help the investigation?" Mr. G. asked.

"Were you aware that his grandfather was in Hawai'i many years ago?"

"I wasn't aware of that."

"Do you think Paul or I could scour some old records from when he might have been here?"

"Perhaps."

"Maybe we can find something that might give us a lead on the photograph or even the money clip," Mr. G. sounded almost confident.

"Perhaps so," Burns answered. "I understand your concern."

Mr. G. looked into Burns' eyes and noticed how tired the police officer looked, and so he backed off on what had practically turned into a civilian-versus-policeman interrogation. "You look tired, Jack."

"Spent much of the night up in Maunawili," Burns replied. "Some Hawaiian woman practically went out of her mind up at Old Man Castle's place."

"She okay?"

"Oh, she's fine now. I checked on her early this morning, and you would have thought that nothing at all had happened. She couldn't remember anything from the night before, and that was strange, because last night she looked absolutely scared to death."

"Strange story."

"It was strange—practically kept me up the whole night. Maybe I'll figure it out in the days ahead."

"Good luck."

"Thanks." Mr. G. and Paul shook Burns' hand. The officer disappeared back into the crowd. The old Scotsman and the young visitor returned to the railing just in time for the biggest races of the day.

The seventh race was called the Cowboy Relay. The horses switched from thoroughbreds to quarter horses, and the *paniolo* from all the different ranches all over the islands hooked up with their different relay teams. Paul kept his eye on Jorge Luis, who like other *paniolo* from Kāneʻohe Ranch wore red bandanas to set himself apart from the competition. The relays featured four riders, each taking a leg. Jorge had the fourth, or anchor leg, for his team.

The cowboys set off quickly, with the red-bandanaed rider in third place between the two leaders in the six-horse field after the first leg. In the second leg, the Kāneʻohe Ranch team had fallen to fourth. But the third rider was a big, strapping fellow on a fast horse, and he passed two opponents to move into second place.

That left it up to Jorge. He was a full-length behind when he started his run and still a half-length back with less than fifty meters to go. But he inched up in the saddle and grabbed his steed by the skinny hairs, whipping him hard on the backside. As they reached the final pole, he was neck and neck with the leader.

The driving finish brought the crowd to its feet. Jorge let out a primeval yell as he crossed the finish line first. He won by only a nose, but he and the entire crowd knew he'd captured it.

It was definitely the most exciting race of the day. And Jorge and his teammates milked the glory for all it was worth, galloping around the track in a victory lap, waving their red bandanas to the appreciative crowd.

"You know these guys?" Paul asked.

"Not all of them," said Mr. G. "But I've known Jorge for years. Good man. I used to do accounting work for his father. We'll see if we can run into him later at the Kailua Tavern. That's where quite a few of the riders and fans go after a day at the races."

Paul, Mr. G and Nan, and Uncle Rob and Constance bellied up to the rail for the final race, a one-mile free-for-all featuring four of the best thoroughbreds on the islands. The winner earned the coveted Kailua Cup, including a purse of five hundred dollars in prize money.

The favorite was a mare owned by a wealthy family from Maui. Uncle Rob and Mr. G. had their money on a local gelding by the appropriate name of Lani Kai.

"Lani Kai's jockey is Tommy Kaneshiro, one of the best jockeys in these parts," Uncle Rob said.

Lani Kai, with Kaneshiro aboard, battled the favorite down the backstretch throatlatch- to-throatlatch for nearly a quarter of a mile. Finally, when they turned for home, Kaneshiro gave his gelding just the right nudge, and Lani Kai galloped across the wire with a half-length to spare.

Mr. G. and Uncle Rob couldn't contain their excitement; they jumped for joy, with Nan, Constance, and Paul following suit. "I think we've made all our money back," Mr. G. said, laughing. "I'll buy the first round at Kailua Tavern."

After fighting the crowds back to their car and inching their way back towards Kailua Town, they eventually squeezed their way into the popular Kailua Tavern. The tavern was jam-packed on this early Thanksgiving evening with local racing fans, servicemen, and more than a fair share of cowboys. The air was thick with tobacco smoke and the sounds of reveling and laughter.

"Over here, Mr. G.!" a voice hollered out. Paul turned towards a group of *paniolo* in the back corner. The voice belonged to none other than Jorge Luis. He was standing at the end of a table, all cleaned up from the races. He wasn't very tall, but he had a commanding presence: strong-jawed, broad shoulders, thick and wavy jet-black hair, and to top off his handsome face, a smile as wide and bright as they come.

"Jorge, you were terrific today," Mr. G. said, reaching out his hand to grab his friend.

"Not bad for an ol' Portugee, huh," Jorge said, grabbing his old friend's hand and then giving him a strong hug. Jorge then gave up his seat for Nan; another cowboy gave his seat to Constance.

"Jorge, let me introduce you to my son John's best friend. This is Paul Sands. Hails from Columbia University, by way of Hollywood," Scotty said.

"Hollywood!" Jorge hollered out. "Hey everybody, we got us a movie star in the place."

Nearly everyone in the tavern turned and looked towards them. Jorge was obviously used to drawing attention. A few in the crowd yelled back. "Hollywood, Hollywood!" Paul, unused to the attention, turned redder than the bandana around Jorge's neck.

"Sit down, Hollywood. Let the ol' Portugee take care of you." Paul and Jorge hit it off right away. They sat, talking and laughing, all the while devouring hamburgers, washed down by the coldest beers Paul said he'd tasted since his days in New York City.

The joint grew louder while Jorge told wild stories of his days on the ranch. He had everyone laughing uncontrollably. Finally, it was time for Mr. G., Uncle Rob, and their wives to leave. They asked Paul if he wanted to stay or go, but the young man was feeling no pain, and he reassured them that he'd find a way back to Lanikai later.

After the Gillespies left, the vibrant tavern continued hopping. Jorge and a few of his local buddies strummed their ʻukulele and sang Hawaiian songs together. Things were going great, and everyone seemed to be having a good time, until a young navy sailor fell off his chair. Jorge made a wisecrack about it, and one of the sailor's drunken shipmates took offense.

Paul didn't see who threw the first punch, but it didn't matter. All hell broke loose in a matter of seconds. Jorge was right in the middle of it, his punches swinging wildly. He landed several but was also getting pummeled simultaneously by three or four navy guys when Paul finally pulled him from the fracas.

It took Paul several minutes to stop his new friend from continuing to flail away, but he finally got him settled down. With his long arms wrapped around the little punch-drunk cowboy, Paul pulled the *paniolo* into the parking lot outside.

"Dammit, Jorge, you got to know when to say when," Paul said, laughing.

"Goddamned servicemen," Jorge answered.

"Well, whatever they are, they were more than ready for a fight." The tall man and the feisty *paniolo* fell to the pavement, laughing hysterically. They sat there several minutes before an old truck pulled up alongside them.

A young woman got out of the vehicle, but Paul couldn't quite make out her face, as it was partially hidden by the darkness and by the large cowboy hat she was wearing. Jorge looked up at her, shook his head, and smiled. "Healani," he said. "Little sis to the rescue again."

The young woman said nothing and helped Jorge to his feet. Paul offered a hand, but she motioned him away. He was drunk himself and virtually spent from stopping the fight; he didn't have much energy left anyway. He fell back onto a grassy area to the side of the pavement and then pulled himself up into a sitting position with his face buried in his knees. He heard the sounds of the truck's doors slamming.

"Hey, Hollywood, you ride horses?" he heard Jorge holler out from the passenger side of the truck.

"Since I was a kid," Paul loudly slurred back.

"Then ride with us this weekend. I need some help moving a few ponies to Kāne'ohe. You can help my sis and me."

"I'll be there," Paul slurred back again. He felt his head hit the grass at the same time the screeching tires roared out of the parking lot.

7 - DC STORY

John Gillespie spent the morning after Thanksgiving wondering what might have been. He held a round-trip airplane ticket from DC to San Francisco in his hand, which he would never get to use. He already had booked passage on the *Lurline*'s sister ship to Honolulu, the SS *Malolo*, the first week of December. He wasn't scheduled to return until after Christmas.

But all those reservations would now be going to waste. He tore up the tickets and tossed them in the trash can in his tiny Georgetown apartment, just in case he might regret his decision later. There was no going back now. When he reported to work this morning, he was officially accepting his new post as special assistant to the secretary of the navy.

He put on his hat and straightened his tie. He looked sharp, as always. He thought about the meeting he had with Secretary Knox the night before last. Knox was convinced that the Japanese Navy was up to something but was unsure what it was. Intelligence reports gathered by British ships in the eastern Pacific were vague and somewhat sketchy. Knox demanded more information from his staff. He placed John Gillespie in charge of a special unit to help facilitate intelligence gathering in the western Pacific and the Pacific coast.

Other staffers would be in charge of other regions around the globe.

John was excited to accept his new challenge, and knew he must not fail his boss. He planned to place a phone call to his parents in Lanikai later that day. Transoceanic phone calls needed operator assistance and were only made during emergencies or equally important circumstances. John figured news of his promotion qualified as such.

A blast of frigid air sweeping across the Georgetown neighborhood slapped him hard when he stepped out of his walk-up apartment building. He tightened the woolly scarf around his neck and plunged into another busy day in DC. Winter was definitely coming, he thought. The warm breezes of Hawai'i were now a distant memory.

Jack Burns reported to work Friday morning, still mystified by the events from late Wednesday night. He still couldn't figure out why an elderly woman of a refined background would act so strangely. Furthermore, Rose Kamakawiwo'ole Alston's apparent lack of recollection of the turbulent events in question troubled him more. Why would she act so strangely one night and be perfectly normal the next morning?

He grabbed his hat and a pack of cigarettes and headed up Nu'uanu Avenue to Rose's home, located near Queen Emma's Palace in upper Nu'uanu. He heard from Henry Wong and Harold Castle that she had returned home safely on Thursday, where her Japanese houseboy was making sure she rested. Burns had talked with the houseboy briefly on the phone, enough to learn that the large Hawaiian woman went by the nickname Auntie Rose. According to her live-in servant, Auntie Rose was a polite, kindhearted woman, and her actions on the night in question made little sense to him.

Burns pulled up in front of her large Nu'uanu property and was impressed by the neatly trimmed yard and the tropical foliage that surrounded the big, two-story house. The house had been freshly painted white with a rich-looking forest green trim. One thing's for sure, either Auntie Rose or her late husband had money, he thought. He snuffed out his latest cigarette on the brick walkway that led up to the house and rang the doorbell. The Japanese houseboy quickly greeted him and motioned him inside.

"Auntie Rose in dayroom, sir." The servant bowed and made no eye contact. Burns, with hat in hand, walked slowly towards a small room on the sunny side of the house. A stream of light cast itself on Auntie Rose as she lay comfortably in a flower-covered *mu'umu'u* on a large futon bed in the corner.

"Come in, officer," she said, demurely. "Don't be shy."

Burns was impressed with the room's décor. Everything was brightly colored there was a tropical feel in every corner. A cool breeze blew down the Nu'uanu Pali through the open windows; the room felt comfortable. "How are you, ma'am?"

"I'm exquisitely fine, thank you. Sit down, if you please." Her perfect articulation impressed him. She is definitely well-bred, he thought to himself.

Burns set his hat down on a large *koa* table and sat down on the rattan chair opposite the futon bed. The Japanese houseboy delivered two glasses of iced lemonade, and Auntie Rose quickly motioned him away with a deliberate but thoughtful hand gesture.

"Ma'am, do you still not recall the events of Thanksgiving eve?"

Auntie Rose pulled herself up against her big, fluffy pillow and smiled. She was now sitting almost upright. "Only a little."

"Tell me what you remember."

She paused for a moment and rubbed her large, puffy hands across both of her cheeks. She was a large woman, but her eyes sparkled with the shimmer of her youth. Burns could easily discern remnants of a once-striking beauty beneath her aged countenance. She smiled warmly.

"I remember feeling peacefulness," she started. "I always feel at peace when I'm at Palikū."

"Why is that?"

"It's the place I met my husband many years ago when Mr. Castle, a dear friend, first built his dream home. My husband, he was such a kind man—he was the architect on the home, you must know. I had been through the area many times for years, in fact, even before the road was built."

"How so?"

"Why, you're a police officer and you didn't know that I was an attendant in the queen's court?"

"I'm sorry, ma'am. I didn't know that."

"I'm surprised at you officer. When I was a little girl, I traveled with the queen—lovely Liliʻuokalani—almost every year when she went over the Pali to her special place in Maunawili. It was such a lovely time." Her voice had a lilting quality, especially when she spoke Hawaiian words and pronounced the beloved queen's name.

"I'm sure it was."

Auntie Rose smiled and looked skyward, as if lost in her memories. Burns knew instinctively not to press her. In time, she would say what she wanted. After a brief pause, she continued her story.

"I met my husband in the 1920s, at a time when I started to wonder if I would ever marry. We met one springtime afternoon when I traveled back to Maunawili to revisit some of the places of my younger days. I was walking in the hills when I stumbled on the new Castle property. He was there, giving orders to the workmen in the early stages of the project. I think we fell in love on the spot."

Burns smiled but did not interrupt.

"Oh, the parties we had there over the years. Palikū became a special place for the pinnacle of Honolulu society. Anyone who was anyone was invited. We stayed in the guesthouses that Mr. Castle provided. He was always the perfect host."

Auntie Rose stopped suddenly. Burns leaned forward. "Are you okay?"

"I'm fine," she responded, but her distant eyes said otherwise.

"When my husband died suddenly of a heart attack, nearly five years ago, he left me with this huge estate. Every year on the anniversary of his death in November, I go back to Palikū. I saw his spirit there, walking in the mountains." She stopped abruptly again.

"Your husband's spirit?"

"What was that?" Auntie Rose looked confused. Her face turned ashen. She quickly lay back down.

"Auntie Rose, are you okay?" Burns stood up and walked over to her bedside.

"I need to rest," she said. "I'm exquisitely fine. Please go away now." She rolled over, showing only her ample backside.

Burns reached to touch her shoulder, but she bristled. "Please go away now. We'll talk later." The Japanese houseboy came running and motioned to Burns to leave the room.

Flustered, frustrated, and confused, Burns exited the dayroom and the beautiful Nuʻuanu home. He vowed to return and hopefully find an answer to the mystery of Auntie Rose.

In Lanikai, Paul Sands finished his tenth phone call of the morning and slammed down the phone in frustration. He had run into only dead-ends on every call he placed—from the coroner's office to the morgue to the offices of Matson Lines, who owned the SS *Lurline*, and even to the mayor's office at city hall in Honolulu. He received no help.

"You can't force this issue," Mr. G. cautioned him. But Paul just shook his head. He appreciated the old Scotsman's advice, but the blistering hangover clouded his head. And the steady malaise he felt all over his body prevented him from finding peace of mind. The frustrating phone calls didn't help, either.

Paul sat at the kitchen table with his grandfather's tattered photograph of the mysterious Lani near his left hand and the dilapidated money clip near his right hand. "I just can't figure it out," he said, shaking his head. He slammed his right fist on the table. The money clip flipped over.

"Hold on a second, lad."

Mr. G. slowly got up from the other side of the table and moved closer to the money clip. He readjusted his spectacles, moving his eyeglasses tighter to his face while Paul froze in his place.

"I think I just saw the glimmer of another letter in the sunlight when you flipped it over," the Scotsman said. He picked up the money clip and turned it towards the gleam of light that streamed into the kitchen. He moved the clip back and forth and watched it shimmer.

"Come and do the same thing, lad. Your eyesight is probably much better than mine, even with these glasses on."

Paul picked up the money clip and held it up in the bright light. "I think there are maybe two more letters. Do you agree?"

Mr. G. nodded excitedly. Paul placed the money clip on his pant leg and rubbed it back and forth several times in a buffing motion. He held it up to the light again. "I think I see another letter!"

"I think I know what the inscription is," Mr. G. announced. "Move it back and forth in the light."

Paul immediately complied. The money clip glistened in the sunlight.

Mr. G. inched closer to the clip, his eyes squinting hard under his eyeglasses. "I-W-A-L-A-N-I," he said, spelling out each letter deliberately. "That's Iwalani."

Paul studied the clip closer. "I believe it does, or I believe it could. Not every letter is there perfectly, but I think you may be right." He smiled broadly at Mr. G., and then he paused and wondered aloud. "Who is she? Who is Iwalani?"

"I have no idea," Mr. G. said, shaking his head and sitting back down. For the first time, Paul took a deep sigh and actually relaxed. The pair sat almost triumphantly for several moments. Their silence was broken only by the ringing of the phone.

"I'll get it," Nan called from the living room. She answered the phone on the third ring. "Yes, I'll accept charges," they heard her say.

A collect call meant important business. Mr. G. immediately popped up from the kitchen table and rushed into the living room. Paul followed him.

"It's John," Nan mouthed as she pressed the receiver hard against her ear. "Oh my," she repeated several times. Mr. G. nestled up against her and attempted to listen in. He nodded a couple of times, so he was able to hear at least part of the one-sided conversation. Paul saw Mr. G.'s eyes widen, and the old Scotsman mouthed the fact that John had received a huge promotion in Washington DC.

When John finished his explanation, Nan wished him the best of luck. "We're so proud of you, son. Here's your dad." Mr. G. grabbed the phone from her, but only briefly.

"Don't want to waste your hard-earned money, son. We know you'll do a great job. Your friend Paul here also wishes you Godspeed."

Paul could hear John's excited voice on the other end.

"Yes, he's right here," he said. "He's been staying with us here a couple of days, ever since his grandfather passed away suddenly on his arrival at Honolulu Harbor. Yes, that's right. Very sad, but Paul's doing okay." Mr. G. motioned to Paul to come to the phone. "He wants to talk to you," he said.

Paul looked surprised for a moment but followed the orders, taking the phone and pressing the receiver to his ear. "Yep, it's me. Yep, yep. Got here Wednesday, the day before Thanksgiving. Yep, yep, your parents have been great." He smiled in their direction, then paused to listen. "I appreciate your kind words. Yeah, it was very sudden, very shocking. I still can't believe it. Having some problems with the authorities here, but hopefully I'll get some answers soon."

He listened to John for a few moments and thanked him for his offer of help but also realized that his old college roommate had more immediate concerns in the nation's capital. "Congratulations, John. You're the right man for the job," he said. "Okay, good luck to you. We'll see you when the right time comes. Yes, I'll give them your love again. Bye now." He hung up the phone.

Paul looked at Nan and Mr. G., who both had looks of extreme pride on their faces.

"Wow, what a swell guy, that John," Paul said. "He seemed more worried about me than about the reason he called here. But his news is quite remarkable. Do you believe it—he's the special assistant to the secretary of the navy. Wow!"

Nan sniffed and wiped a tear from the corner of her eye. Mr. G. comforted her. "We couldn't be prouder, lad. I'm not sure we've ever felt prouder than this moment."

Paul felt the same way. He, too, was extremely proud of his old roommate, but he was also content with the fact that a small portion of his grandfather's mystery was beginning to unravel. For the rest of the day, he would make phone calls trying to find someone who years ago may have known a beautiful young woman named Iwalani. And what was her connection to his grandfather's death?

8 - SWEET HEALANI

On Sunday mornings, Jack Burns went to church. A devout Catholic, he never missed a service at Saint Anthony's, the little Catholic church located across the street from Kailua Bay on Kālaheo Avenue.

Kailua had three primary places of worship on Sundays—Saint Anthony's for the large Catholic population in town, the little white Methodist church in the center of Kailua Town, and the small Japanese Buddhist temple and Japanese language school that sat in front of the watermelon patches along Kuulei Road. All three churches enjoyed well-attended services.

Burns spent this late November Sunday officially greeting his neighbors, and when Scotty and Nan Gillespie arrived with tall Paul Sands in tow, the policeman gave them all a hearty handshake. Mr. G. then pulled Burns out of the greeting line to tell him of their latest information.

"Young Paul and I think we have a lead that can help us identity the woman in his grandfather's photograph," Mr. G. said in his typical Scottish brogue.

"What did you find out?"

"Paul was studying the photo and the money clip; he had

polished and cleaned the clip that morning and was making some phone calls, when we were able to get a closer look at the lettering on the clip in the sunlight. We agreed that we think it says *Iwalani*. It would then make perfect sense then that Iwalani is the Lani whose name is written on the back of the photograph."

"Now I understand why he left me all those messages," Burns said. "Sorry I didn't get back to him. It's been a busy weekend."

"So you agree that it's possible that it's the same person?"

"Possible."

"Will it help?"

Burns hesitated. He pulled out a cigarette from the pack he kept in his shirt pocket, lit it, and took a couple of puffs. "That's still pretty vague. I think you'll need a little more information than that. From what I've seen to this point, we don't have much to go on. The autopsy may tell us more."

"I see—so you can't help?"

"I didn't say that," Burns said, taking a few more drags and then snuffing out the butt before the cigarette was even half smoked. "I'll see if I can get some more information from county records. You say Sands' grandfather was here years ago."

"That's what the lad says. He said it was when his grandfather was much younger, perhaps in his twenties or so."

"Well, if old man Sands was seventy when he died, then I'll check back for his name in any of our records from about forty or fifty years ago. We'll see what comes up, if anything."

"Thanks."

"Just don't tell anyone that I'm doing this favor. I'm busy enough already." Burns lit up another cigarette.

Mr. G. smiled and walked inside the church. He nodded to many neighbors and acquaintances, including Henry Wong; the Campos family; and Otto Kuehn, his wife, and daughter.

Moments later, he found Nan and Paul in the pew directly behind Jorge Luis and Jorge's younger sister. He laughed quietly to himself when he saw the bruises on Jorge's face. But what caught his attention more was the staring eyes of young Sands. To say that he was enraptured was an understatement.

As he sat and stood at the middle seat of his pew, Paul couldn't look away from Jorge's sister. From the minute the services began, all the way through the Catholic priest's sermon, he was transfixed on the beautiful young woman who sat almost directly in front of him. As he stood for Holy Communion, he intently watched as she tossed her dark hair from side to side as she moved down the pew toward the aisle; he was almost embarrassed by how he felt, and he looked down momentarily, so as not to draw attention to his obvious staring. Inside, he could feel himself almost melting. But he couldn't avert his eyes for long.

He followed her every move: the gentle sway to her hips; the way she tossed her long, dark, wavy hair to the side to accept the priest's Eucharist; how she tilted her head back to drink the wine. Paul thought that she was more than beautiful; she was dazzling.

Paul looked away again and almost felt dizzy. He stood for a few seconds, his eyes closed, and tried to focus only on the singing of the church choir. He was practically frozen in place.

"Paul, meet my kid sister. This is Healani," he heard Jorge say. Paul opened his eyes, almost startled. Her beautiful four-syllable name seemed to flow off his tongue. It sounded almost magical.

He repeated it, slowly and phonetically. "Hey-ah-lonney," he smiled sheepishly. "Nice to meet you." He attempted to appear nonchalant. But he practically stammered his response. Inside, he was virtually turning somersaults.

She nodded and smiled pleasantly as she walked past him. She didn't need to say a word. As far as Paul was concerned, the smile said everything. It was the final piece to her perfection.

He would have melted away right then if he wasn't fighting hard to regain his composure. He tried not to stare as they stood to sing once again, but he couldn't help but glance repeatedly in her direction.

She wore a short-sleeved white blouse that exposed the richness of her caramel-colored skin. She was much darker than Jorge, her half brother. She had high cheekbones and rich, full lips, and her beautiful face glistened with an angelic glow. She wasn't wearing a touch of makeup. She simply didn't need to.

Nan caught Paul's darting eyes and muttered under her breath, "You seem a little distracted, Mr. Sands."

Paul turned about three shades of red and tried to reply but ended up saying something that only sounded like gibberish. Nan smiled and looked over at Mr. G., who also was smiling. They said nothing more, and soon the church services ended.

Nan and Scotty Gillespie waved good-bye to Jorge, Healani, and Paul as they stood under the partial shade of a group of coconut trees after the service. They knew that Paul would be joining the brother and sister for a day of moving horses, and they didn't want to get in the way of whatever was planned.

"Hollywood, hope you don't mind, but we've got to walk a few blocks to our house and change before we ride," Jorge said.

There was that nickname again. "No problem at all." Paul tried to act unruffled. Healani said nothing. They walked at a moderate clip along the coral-topped streets, leaving Saint Anthony's Church behind.

"My father never missed his Sunday church service," Jorge said. "We went with him to Saint Ann's in Kāneʻohe until they built Saint Anthony's in '33. Nice to have our own Catholic church here in Kailua. It's small, but we like it."

"How about you, Paul, are you Catholic?" Healani spoke for the first time. Her voice had a husky quality to it—gentle and yet strong at the same time. Paul, already enamored with her appearance, liked the sound of it.

"No, can't say I am. My parents were Protestant, but we didn't go to church much when I was growing up."

"Oh," was her only reply. And she said it in such a tone that it could have been taken as disappointment. Paul wanted to tell her that he was willing to convert right on the spot, but he was too tongue-tied to respond.

"Healani is a teacher. Finished tops in her class at the university," Jorge said, proudly. "She just started working over at Kailua School."

Paul looked at her placid face, but she said nothing as they turned the corner to their family property. The Luis house was tucked behind the heavy shade of ironwood trees, only a few hundred feet from the beach road.

"My father owned the property all the way from here to Kālaheo Avenue," Jorge said. "It's a pretty big lot, about twenty thousand square feet in all. Healani and I live in the small house out back here. We rent out the bigger house on Kālaheo to a couple of pilots from the naval base. We like the back house because we're closer to our horses."

Healani had already gone around back. Paul heard a door open and shut.

"Wait outside, and we'll be with you shortly," Jorge said.

Jorge went inside the tiny house. Paul waited outside in his blue jeans and polo shirt, looking decidedly unlike a cowboy. He was also wearing a sheepish grin from ear to ear.

When Jorge reappeared, he was wearing a bright orange shirt, dungarees, and a big brown hat with a wide brim. He tossed Paul a smaller, beat-up version of the same hat.

"You'll need this to keep the sun off your face, Hollywood. Wouldn't want your pale *haole* skin to turn into a lobster," he said, jokingly. He gave Paul a slap on the back. The tall young man reeled slightly from the power of the blow, and then he got that dizzy feeling again when Jorge's sister reappeared.

Healani, dressed in khaki pants and a red blouse, confidently walked two of their horses from the stalls behind the house. Her dark hair glistened in the sunlight. Paul realized that she probably could wear almost anything, even men's clothing, and appear drop-dead gorgeous.

"Here," she said, rather coolly, handing Paul a bridle and the reins to the chestnut-colored bay. Then she hopped onto a copper-colored mare. As pretty as she was, Healani she didn't say much. Jorge seemed to do all the talking in the family.

Jorge followed soon thereafter aboard a chocolate brown gelding with a brown and white filly in tow. Both brother and sister were accomplished riders, as though they'd spent half their lives on horses. They probably had.

"Here's the plan," Jorge said, very quickly and demonstratively. He waved his arms continuously, as if to give emphasis or direction with every phrase. "We'll be taking the four horses along the beach road, stop for a short break at the Central Corral, cross Kawai Nui Stream, and head past the naval base at Mōkapu and finally on toward Kāneʻohe Bay. It's about a five-mile trek, so we should be at our Kokokahi stables in a couple of hours. We'll drop off the filly, the mare, and the bay, and then I'll head back to Kailua on the gelding. We'll get you two to hitch a ride with one of the cowhands when he finishes the daily chores."

"Sounds good," Paul said. Paul looked at Healani, but she remained silent, looking straight ahead.

It took a while for Paul to feel comfortable in the saddle, but they say you never forget how to ride a horse once you learn. It had been several years since he last rode. Paul's father had taken him out riding on the back trails of the San Fernando Valley. He had taught his son well, so it didn't take too long until Paul was in near-perfect rhythm with his bay. All along the first part of their Sunday journey, Jorge kept up a steady stream of dialogue.

"Kailua's changing, Hollywood," he said. "I'm not sure if I like it or not. Used to be nothing but coconut trees inland and ironwoods along the beach, and grasslands and *kiawe* bushes from Mōkapu through the Oneawa Hills all the way to the Kawai Nui Swamp. We could graze our cattle in Maunawili or near the slopes of Mount Olomana and all over the swamplands of Kawai Nui in the summer and then bring them back to ʻAikahi and Mokapu in the winter."

Paul looked around. They were leaving the small neighborhood behind.

"Now, they've got more and more homes going up. We've nearly doubled our population since I was a boy. And Lanikai has totally changed. Used to be sandy fields filled with watermelon. Now, the people from Honolulu with their beach homes and their country club and all, not sure if I care for that."

Healani and Paul listened but said nothing. Pretty soon Jorge's voice rose in pitch. Eventually his monologue evolved into a bitter tirade.

"A few years back, they even started making plans to build a Royal Hawaiian–type hotel on Kailua Beach," he continued. "Thank goodness we stopped that nonsense while it was only in the talking stages. I can't even imagine Kailua with hotels."

Paul looked towards Kailua Bay and realized for the first time that unlike Honolulu's Waikīkī area, there were no hotels along this beautiful stretch of sand. He'd been in the area too short of a time to even consider the thought.

Jorge started cussing. Paul looked at Healani, but she continued to ride along with a passive stare, as if she'd heard all this before.

"What pisses me off the most is the military. Why, they took away our best winter grazing lands out on the Mōkapu Peninsula." He pointed forward and toward the ocean, where they could see a couple of navy planes flying over the large rocky mound that jutted out into the sea.

"That's Mōkapu," he said. "It was ours; I mean it belonged to Kāneʻohe Ranch. But it was our ranchland. We worked it." The angriness in his voice rose. "Best Bermuda grass you could find for the cattle. But they made the Old Man sell it to them. And then they reopened Fort Hase and moved their naval base there."

"You don't seem to mind renting your house to navy guys," Paul said.

"That's different—that's business. What I'm talking about is personal."

Paul tried to change the subject. "Who's the 'Old Man' you keep talking about?"

"Harold Castle," was Jorge's terse reply. "Kāne'ohe Ranch is his. You probably saw his big estate up on the Pali Road."

"Yeah, I remember Mr. G. talking about it."

"He and his family own most of the land over here; most of it. When the old Hawaiians divided the land, they called it the *ahupua'a*. This one extends from near the Pali Lookout to the ridges of Olomana and Keolu Hills past Ka'elepulu Pond and on towards Ka'iwa Ridge above Lanikai one way, then to the ridges surrounding Kawai Nui Swamp and Oneawa Hills, all the way to the Mōkapu Peninsula the other way. The *ahupua'a* is the entire watershed area, all the way to Kailua Bay."

Paul twisted on the top of his horse to get a scope of the large area Jorge was talking about. He could see how Kailua existed in a semibowl, surrounded by smaller hills, with the gigantic, green Ko'olau mountain range looming as a backdrop.

"The Old Man doesn't own it all. The Bishop Trust has some, and there are still a few Hawaiian landowners who have secured land from the days of the royalty, plus a few individual landowners, but he's got most of it," Jorge said. "I just want the country to stay that way. Country."

The trio of riders passed some of the Kailua homes that Jorge spoke of. Ironically, many lots were vacant, despite Jorge's claims of a population explosion.

"The only thing that slowed the growth around here was the

Depression," he said. "And now the war in Europe. And the trouble with Japan. It's got a few people scared. Definitely kept some people away. And a few people have moved back to the States."

Their ride hadn't gone too long before they reached the area that Jorge identified as the Central Corral. Located nearly adjacent to the Kailua Race Track, it was filled with a livery, stables, and a feedstore. Paul saw a blacksmith in the opening of the barn, pounding away at an iron horseshoe.

"We'll stop here for water," Jorge said. Healani hopped off her mare and headed into the store. She came out minutes later with a few morsels that she fed to all four of the horses.

"Keeps them happy," she said with a smile.

Paul smiled back. Wow, she can be friendly after all, he thought. He slowly walked in her direction and offered to help her, but when he tried to feed the horses himself, the mare reared back, causing Paul to stumble and fall. Healani laughed out loud.

"Takes a little getting used to, doesn't' it Mr. Sands?" She giggled, then finished the job herself. He sat on the ground, embarrassed and with a sheepish grin. "You'll be okay," she said.

The sound of dogs barking cut into the potential for conversation. Paul looked over, past the livery, to see two huge Great Danes inside a fenced area. He got up and dusted himself off.

"The Old Man has a dog kennel here," Jorge said. "He loves Great Danes and German shepherds. Every time you see him driving around the property, it seems he always has his dogs with him."

The trio was on their way again within a half hour. Jorge paused to open a cattle gate near a small bridge that crossed a local waterway. "Kawai Nui canal," he said. "The government built it to stop some of the flooding in these parts. Hundreds of years ago, all this area used to be underwater, so we still get flooded out periodically."

Paul, Healani, and Jorge crossed the bridge and their horses broke into an easy trot as they moved into the gap between the

Oneawa Hills on the left and the military station on the right.

"Kāneʻohe Naval Air Station and Fort Hase," Jorge said. A high fence surrounded the military fort. A small bank building stood just outside the front gate. They could see soldiers practicing drills in the fields behind it. Several small airplanes were also practicing takeoffs and landings, zooming over Kāneʻohe Bay and the Koʻolau and then circling back to the naval air station. From their markings, Jorge said they appeared to be P-36s.

"They've been more active in recent weeks," Jorge said. "Something's brewing. Don't know exactly what, but something's definitely brewing."

Before Paul had a chance to respond, Jorge clicked his horse and off he went. He galloped into the *kiawe* trees and up onto the hillside. It took only a few moments for Paul to discern what he was after. A couple head of cattle had meandered off from the rest of the herd, and Jorge sped ahead of the other two in an attempt to return the stragglers to the grasslands fronting Kāneʻohe Bay ahead of them.

"Black Angus," Healani said, describing the breed of cattle.

"Hmm. What other breeds?" Paul asked casually. Or, at least, he tried to act casual. He certainly didn't need to fall down again, he thought.

"I've heard my brother say that the best of the cattle is the Scottish Black Angus. That's the very best prime beef. The best you can find. We've got them here, plus the English Herefords. The Herefords are the ones with the horns. The Angus are hornless." Once again, Paul was struck by the confident sound of her voice—it had a country girl's huskiness to it—a voice that readily reassured her strength and independence.

Paul nodded. Without Jorge around, Healani grew more talkative.

"They also take care of a few dairy cattle—Guernseys, Holsteins, and Jerseys. In all, the ranch has well over a thousand head at any one time. Jorge and his coworkers work hard moving them around and keeping them together."

"I can tell by his actions that he cares deeply about what he does," Paul said. She nodded in agreement. She's very loyal to him, Paul thought.

He strived to keep the conversation going.

"I wonder how much all this has changed since my grandfather was here."

"You have family here?"

"Not anymore. My grandfather was here at some point; I think it was way back in the 1890s, or perhaps around the turn of the century. I'm not sure of the real story, but I think it was part of his growing interest in the shipping business. All I know is that he left suddenly and never returned. Nobody in the family really knows why."

"Sorry about his passing," she said. "Jorge told me that he died earlier this week. Said Mr. G. told him."

"Thanks. I appreciate your kind thoughts. It was very sudden."

"Is there a funeral planned?"

"We're told we have to bury him tomorrow, if that's what you call a funeral. And I'm waiting for the report on the official cause of death."

"Yes, Jorge told me a few of the details. Very, very sad. How's that going?"

"Not good. Not good at all. I'm interested in seeing the autopsy report. I should have it after the funeral services. That's all I know."

The two rode silently for a few hundred yards with Healani giving a concerned glance at Paul's face. He seemed deep in thought. She decided to break the silence.

"You asked about how much has changed around here. Well, a lot has quite obviously changed since then. You up for hearing about that?" she said.

"Sure," he replied. "Sorry, got caught up in my thoughts for a moment."

"That's very understandable. You mentioned your grandfather; well, my ancestors' story goes way back. My Portuguese ancestors came from the Azores near Portugal in the 1870s. My Hawaiian ancestors have been on Windward Oʻahu for hundreds of years, living in an area once called ʻĀlele here in Kailua. The two cultures blended easily, and that's why you see so many Portuguese-Hawaiian *paniolo*, like my brother."

"So both of you are Portuguese-Hawaiian?"

She laughed. "Actually, he's my half brother. His father is my father. His mother was Portuguese-Hawaiian-Chinese, a real mix of cultures and personalities. Jorge seemed to have inherited mostly the outspoken Portuguese side."

Paul smiled. "I can see that. And you?"

"My mother was 100 percent Hawaiian, and there aren't many of those left. So I guess I'm a *hapa* girl." She giggled.

Paul laughed with her. "Well, it's a lovely mixture," he said. She smiled back.

"Tell me more about your grandfather," she said.

"Well, I know my grandfather wasn't a cowboy; that's for sure. He spent most of his time at sea or around the docks. That was his business in California—shipping. And he was pretty good at it. Kept all of us comfortable financially. When my parents died, he took care of me."

"How did your parents die?"

"In a car crash in L.A. I was very young. It was a very long time ago."

"Oh my. Sorry to hear that. Were you okay?"

"As okay as you can be, I guess. My grandfather pretty much raised me as a teenager."

"And your grandmother?"

"She died many, many years ago. It was just me and grandfather until I went away to college. Then I moved back in with him in the last year, and recently we made the plans to come here for a while."

"I know this is hard, but did he seem close to death?"

Paul shook his head from side to side. "Not at all. I was totally shocked by everything—his sudden death, the way I found him, the mention of something on his lips. Everything."

"What do you know about his time here previously? Jorge said there was a picture of a girl, a Hawaiian girl."

"Yes, Lani is her name. How ironic that it's a part of your name, too." He looked at Healani as if he'd just realized that fact. "Here, I have the photograph in my pocket." They stopped and Paul hopped off his horse. Healani followed suit and quickly wrapped up the reins for all of the horses. Paul unwrapped the photograph, which he kept in a small envelope, and for a few moments, she studied the old photograph that he held in his palm. He flipped it over and they read the inscription—"All my love, forever, Lani."

"She's a very beautiful girl," Healani said. "If her name is Lani, it means 'heavenly.' And she truly is. How old would you say she is?"

"I've thought of that. Not quite sure, but maybe twenty or so. Very young and very pretty, obviously."

"And when was the photograph taken?"

"No idea. I don't know anything about her or who she is. It's possible that 'Lani' is short for Iwalani, but that's a guess."

"How do you know that?"

"My grandfather had an old money clip with him when he died. There was a small inscription on it with a few letters that we could make out. We—that is Mr. G. and I—we believe that it may say Iwalani."

"Heavenly seabird," Healani said softly.

"What's that?"

"The name Iwalani means heavenly seabird," she said.

Paul pondered the translation. "I don't know if that's a clue or not."

"Her dress should tell you something. I saw my mother wear

something like it when I was a little girl. It's called a *holokū*—it's worn only on the most special occasions."

The two studied the photograph for a few more seconds, then Paul neatly placed it back in the envelope and stashed it away in his pocket.

"Do you know anything more about him—about his story—anything?"

"Only something a distant aunt once said—something about him making an abrupt departure from the islands."

"Abrupt—that was her word?"

"Yes."

Healani seemed deeply interested in Paul's story. They got back on the horses and started moving forward again. "I'm sorry to suggest this, but maybe he did something wrong and he wasn't proud of it," she said.

"I've thought of that. I've asked myself dozens of questions. Was he a criminal? Was he dishonorable? I wonder sometimes what made him leave and never come back. And why didn't he ever like to talk about it? He took his secrets to the grave with him."

"Maybe it was simply about a girl," she said.

Paul pondered that comment and then smiled back at her. "Who knows, you may be right. A lot of things are always about a girl," he said. She looked at him with a twinkle in her eye. And for the first time, Paul felt a definite spark.

They continued riding towards Kāneʻohe Bay, Paul rocking back and forth on the saddle of his bay, Healani riding with ease, all the while towing the filly behind them. They smiled at each other more than once.

The clear skies and hot morning sun gave way to heavier cloud cover as the day wore into early afternoon. Soon they felt a couple of raindrops kissing their cheeks.

"Feels good, doesn't it? It's a cool blessing," she said. Her face broke out in a big smile and she turned it towards the sky. Paul followed her lead. Tiny raindrops danced on their faces. The drops then became heavier. Healani started to giggle. Paul laughed out loud.

The skies soon emptied.

The squall passed in less than a minute, but only after it had soaked Paul's hat as well as Healani's hair and shoulders. She tossed her hair from side to side and reached up to flip away some of the accumulated water.

"Grab me a towel from the saddle bag on the filly," she said. "I put a couple of small towels in the bag, just in case."

Paul complied immediately, moving his horse close to hers. He also took the reins of the filly and tied the reins to his bay, thus giving Healani a little more room to maneuver. Then he handed her a small blue towel. She dabbed at her hair and shoulders. Her dark hands were gentle in appearance, and she squeezed the towel as if she were checking the firmness of a tomato. Not too hard, not too soft. She patted away at her shoulders and neck and then fluffed up her hair. Then she handed the towel to him.

"Thank you, Healani. You're very sweet," he said, hoping not to sound too forward.

She smiled back.

"You're a nice man, Paul Sands. I can tell that about you. And you're very tall. Very tall! Do you play basketball?" But before he could respond, she started giggling again. And at the same time, she clicked her horse and broke into a gallop towards Jorge.

Stunned, and totally smitten, Paul tried to follow as quickly as he could, but now he had the filly in tow and had to watch his speed accordingly. He couldn't quite catch up to her before they reunited with Jorge. When they did so, Jorge took one glance at both of their blushing faces and gave a very harsh and disapproving look.

9 –THE FUNERAL

The Monday afternoon funeral of seventy-year-old William Sands was more a burial ritual than a heart-wringing ceremony. The only attendees in a steady downpour in Nuʻuanu Valley were grandson Paul, Scotty and Nan Gillespie, and a few umbrella-toting volunteers whose duty was to give comfort to the aggrieved friends and relatives. The only comfort Paul felt was Mr. G.'s statement that if legend says a good person is judged by the rain that falls at their funeral, then William Sands was a very good man.

The wet but traditional ceremony took only a few minutes, and Paul despised almost every moment. The cemetery's pastor, a sad-eyed *haole* gentleman in his late sixties, was respectful but impersonal. He went through the funeral rites nearly mechanically and said virtually nothing that made Paul feel any better about the situation. Paul was most grateful that it was over quickly. He thanked the volunteers for coming, thoughtfully paid his final respects to his grandfather, then slowly walked away from the gravesite arm in arm with the Gillespies. The rain lessened seconds later, and the sun began to emerge from behind the Koʻolau cloud cover within moments. Such was the beauty of Hawaiʻi.

Officer Burns, who had watched the short proceedings from a

distance, waited for the unhappy threesome with news that he hoped might brighten their day.

"I may have some information that could help you," he said, extinguishing a cigarette while leaning against his police car in the tiny parking lot that served a much larger Nu'uanu cemetery. Paul removed his hat and shook it dry, saying nothing.

"What have you got for us, Jack?" Mr. G. asked. He motioned Nan to continue walking toward their car.

Burns pulled a large manila envelope out from under his suit coat. He handed the envelope to Paul. The tall young man looked surprised at first but then quickly unsealed it. He carefully read through the first page of the document inside, then hurriedly shuffled through the high points of the next few pages. His demeanor changed noticeably. When he came to the end, he dropped the papers to his side. "This is not what I expected," he said.

"I thought you might find it interesting," Burns replied.

Mr. G. grabbed the papers out of Paul's hand and started reading as quickly as he could. "What does this mean?" Paul asked.

"It says your grandfather was in fairly good shape for a man of his age, and based on the preliminary autopsy, they don't know what killed him."

"That's kind of surprising, don't you think? Especially considering what the ship's doctor said that day. What I don't understand is that the report ends by stating that he died of unknown causes. In other words, the autopsy was . . . inconclusive? Why?"

"Well, because the pathologists didn't think his heart showed signs of the traditional heart attack. Usually, they say there will be some trauma to the heart, but there was apparently no evidence of that."

Paul stood silently for a moment. He wore a dazed expression.

"But . . . but, I thought the coroner was concerned about something else. Uh, what about some kind of white stuff or something? He noticed it around grandfather's mouth and fingertips? They mention it in their report—uh, I think they used the word *residue*—but then they dismiss it and say nothing else about it."

"I was surprised by that, too, and I talked with them about it this morning. They aren't sure what that is—all they know is whatever it was, it wasn't in his stomach or in his system. They also concluded it's not an illegal narcotic or medicine of some kind. They're sending it to the University of Hawai'i for further study."

Mr. G. finished skimming the documents. He repeated the same question that Paul asked earlier. "What does it all mean?"

Burns lit up another cigarette and took a quick drag. He pondered the question for another moment and blew out a big puff of smoke. "It means that the official investigation is not quite over. Sometimes, the official findings and the final wording on the death certificate takes time. The coroner's office took some tissue samples, and along with the residue, they've sent in on to the University for their review. The process could take a few weeks. We sent a wire to your grandfather's attorney, telling him everything. Not sure what this will mean with his estate. But we may still have questions."

"Questions! You got that right, plenty of questions," Paul interrupted, loudly. "I don't know about the estate, but more important, I don't even understand now how he died, or why." Paul was clearly distressed; his hands motioned up and down. "I don't understand the photograph or the money clip or why he even made this trip." He paused, letting out a deep, exasperated breath. "I'm sure I'll think of other questions, if you just give me time."

Mr. G. placed his hand on the young man's shoulder.

Burns took another two drags on his cigarette, then dropped the butt to the ground and crushed it under his shoe. "I think I might be of assistance in that department," he said.

"How so?" Mr. G. interjected.

"When we officially went through Mr. Sands' belongings—from his trunk to his stateroom drawers—we found this." Burns reached in through the window of his police car and grabbed a book from the front seat. "It's about Hawai'i."

Paul grabbed the book from the officer and thumbed quickly through the pages. "It's a textbook," he said, "and its marked property of the Los Angeles Public Library. Why is it significant?"

"Not really sure. None of the pages were marked or dog-eared. But we did find traces of the same residue that was on your grandfather's lips. Near as we can tell, the book is probably where he got the residue from. My hunch is that, whatever the white stuff was, he had it smashed in between a couple of the pages."

"Wouldn't you be holding on to the book for further examination?" Mr. G. asked.

"Oh, we've examined the book very closely," Burns answered quickly. "We removed the residue completely, and I've searched through every page looking for clues. I'm handing it over to young Paul here to see what he can find. Maybe he sees something in there that I don't."

Paul said nothing but nodded approvingly as he continued to rifle through the pages.

"By the way, I also followed up our conversation from the church and ran a check of some of our old records this morning. I came up with nothing on a William Sands."

"That's discouraging."

"But hold on," Burns said, lighting up yet another cigarette. He flicked away the match without so much as a care. "I found no William Sands, not anywhere, between 1890 and 1910. But another name caught my attention. I did find a William Sanderson. Have you ever heard this name?" He looked at Paul.

"No. Why should that mean anything? My grandfather's name is Sands, not Sanderson."

"I thought so, too. But this man, the man who called himself William Sanderson, was listed as a twenty-two-year-old employee of Honolulu Shipping Lines. His name caught my eye because I found it listed twice, once in 1893 and again in 1894. Once it was listed as

Sanderson, the next time as Sanderston."

"Why is that significant?"

"Because it's possible that this young man, however you spelled his name, went by an alias. Perhaps his name wasn't spelled either way. Perhaps it was Sands. Who knows? It's also possible that it was just a clerical error, but I think it's a lead worth exploring."

"So how do I go about finding more information? Are you going to help?"

"I think I've spent as much time as I can on this case, son. From now on, it's just a waiting game with the university, and I've got my hands full with a lot of other things. I'm just trying to help an old friend here," nodding in Mr. G.'s direction. "I'll gladly drop you off near city hall, and you can take it from there."

"Much obliged, Jack," Mr. G. said, shaking Burns' hand. Mr. G. told Paul he could catch a jitney ride back to Kailua after his investigatory work, then he walked away toward his own car. Paul curled into Officer Burns' vehicle and hitched a ride to city hall, located less than a mile away. When he was dropped off, he thanked the officer and headed into a building that he hoped might hold the key to unlock this ever-evolving mystery.

In Washington DC, the door to Secretary Knox's office was open. John Gillespie peered in to the see if the secretary had a minute for him. Knox, his back turned to the door, and leaning down to pick up some paperwork, didn't realize he had company.

"Mr. Secretary, can I bother you for a moment?"

Knox, startled, stood up quickly. "Sorry, John, didn't see you there. What can I do for you?"

John entered the semicavernous room and closed the door behind him. Knox's office was notoriously dark, and he lit the office only with a small desk lamp for reasons that John never understood.

"I'm concerned about Hawai'i," John said.

"That's not your territory, John. Your assignment is the Pacific

Coast region. Let others worry about the rest of the Pacific."

"But don't you see? That's the problem. I'm not sure who is sharing information with whom. Perhaps there is something that I have, or that you have, or that the British have, and we aren't sharing it properly."

"John, we have a chain of command—you know that. It must be followed."

"I understand that, sir."

"So why are you making these comments?"

"Well, for one thing, we've moved our carrier fleet to Pearl Harbor, and we may not have enough protection for it. It's not like it used to be when the navy fleet was located in San Diego. We had the whole Pacific to protect us."

"And you don't think Hawai'i is protected? Why, it's the most remote set of islands on Earth. It would take a miracle—and a damn good navy—to invade there. Nobody's got that kind of navy."

"I'm not so sure, sir."

"If you're talking about Japan's navy, that makes no sense. We've watched and the British have watched their buildup for years. It's obvious that Japan covets Asia. If the current negotiations with the Japanese break down, and I'm not sure they will or not, my guess is that Japan will continue to invade and perhaps try to occupy many places along the Asian Pacific rim, from China to Malaysia, as they have in the past."

"Why not the Pacific islands? And why not Hawai'i?"

"They'd have to be mad to consider that. Purely crazy."

Halfway around the world, on a small atoll more than a thousand miles south and west of the Hawaiian Islands, he meticulously combed his hair and shaved off his light beard. He had honed his razor sharp—very sharp—and he made certain to skim every hair follicle from his leathery face. He looked at himself in the tiny mirror and smiled mischievously. The shave had radically changed his appearance. He liked that change, and he smiled again, with his dark, steely eyes peering intently at the mirror.

It was a confident and knowing smile because he knew exactly what he was doing. He was a master planner, and he followed through precisely on all of his missions, even if it meant death to those who got in his way. But he also knew how to lay low. That was part of his craftiness. He had planned the next part of this important mission down to the most insignificant detail. He would be paid handsomely for his efforts, but that's not what drove him. He was driven by his own arrogance. He loved beating the odds and accomplishing something that seemed impossible. He had achieved that throughout his professional mercenary life—from Moscow to Shanghai to Tokyo and Manila. He had a face that blended in, and he took full advantage of it.

He knew his route, he knew his target, and he knew his ultimate goal. Everything about Windward O'ahu and Kailua, he felt he knew. From the beaches to the churches to marshes behind the town, he had studied it thoroughly. He knew the heights of the mountains and their distance from the town, and he knew if he gathered the right information, and if all went according to plan on the fateful day that lay in the immediate future, then it was his job to hike to near the top of 3,105-foot Mount Kōnāhuanui, the highest peak in O'ahu's Ko'olau mountain range. From there, he would be high enough to send a signal that could be seen by the Japanese submarines sitting patiently nearly a hundred miles off the coast, awaiting his sign.

Even if it meant death, he would reach the top of that peak. The idea of sending the signal that led to the next wave of attacks excited him. He could think of no bigger prize.

He had recently secured the name of a former German naval officer now living in Kailua from his contacts in Singapore. The German knew nothing of him. He was not supposed to know anything. The man's last name was Kuehn, and he was what those in the intelligence business called a sleeper spy.

The sleeper spy's responsibilities were never given in direct orders. And in many cases, his actions were somewhat inconsequential. Perhaps a specific task, perhaps a safe haven, perhaps a word or two of information, all of this was a possibility with a sleeper spy. But nothing was ever written. Oftentimes, they were good citizens in their hometowns, simply doing something for the fatherland. In many cases, they wouldn't know their helpful task until the circumstances arose.

He would utilize this man Kuehn, as needed, hopefully nothing more. He wanted to trust no one except himself. He was supremely confident. He must not fail. He knew that.

He gathered his small bag of belongings from his small hut, and he went to the shoreline to wait. He made certain that nothing was left behind. He had calculated that the Japanese submarine would be passing by the island sometime during the night. He must be ready to signal for pickup. He knew he was ready for the next step in his mission.

10 - KENJI

Paul Sands was frustrated. He had read his grandfather's book about Hawai'i from cover to cover and found no clues. The book, a college-level textbook narrative about the land and people of Hawai'i, was written in the 1920s, but there was no passage, no special wording that stuck out to him. And Burns was right; his grandfather had made no notations in the inside covers or in the margins or on any page. He wasn't sure why his grandfather had the book or what he had pressed inside it. He found it hard to believe that his grandfather would take something—whatever it was that was kept inside the book—that would kill him. That thought didn't make sense to him. When his grandfather's other remaining belongings were sent in a trunk to Lanikai, Paul went through everything but found nothing helpful.

Meanwhile, the days were passing along quickly, and he had made daily trips into Honolulu's city hall but with no results to speak of. His efforts to find a William Sands, a William Sanderson, or even a William Sanderston or some other close variation had come up empty. He was desperate to find out something. But it was Friday, and he could feel the workweek and the possibilities of answers to his many questions slowing down.

Nothing of consequence had shown up about the mysterious Iwalani, either. He was also running out of money fast, and his phone attempts to reach his grandfather's attorney had gone unanswered. In the meantime, he had bought an old beater of a car, a '31 Nash for fifty bucks, and he bounced back and forth across the Pali on a daily basis with little to show for it except feelings of frustration and exasperation. He realized he could only afford to stay on for a few more weeks, maybe until Christmas or so, before he headed back to California to clean up his grandfather's affairs. It was an ocean journey he didn't look forward to.

And now, with all the bad news in the newspapers, it didn't seem safe to consider taking such a trip.

Both the *Honolulu Star-Bulletin* and the *Honolulu Advertiser* were filled with stories about the bloody war in Europe and the ongoing U.S.-Japan negotiations. Japan had become increasingly antagonistic in its rhetoric. The headlines repeatedly reported that tensions between the two countries were mounting. Frankly, Paul didn't know whether to think that a war with Japan was inevitable or not.

In Hawai'i, Territorial Governor Poindexter was released from the hospital after a two-week stay at Queen's Hospital. The newspaper reported that he was exhausted from the recently completed legislative session. There were also reports about a potential vehicular tunnel from Honolulu to the Windward Side of O'ahu. Paul definitely saw the need for that. He sometimes was forced to drive his old Nash backwards up the steep incline of the Pali Road in order to get to the top of the Nu'uanu Pali and make the descent into Honolulu. An engineer made a public report in late November, stating that a tunnel through the Kalihi Valley to Kāne'ohe was his recommendation. He chose that route over the other two suggestions, Mānoa Valley to Waimānalo and Nu'uanu Valley to Kailua by way of the Pali Road. Paul disagreed with his first choice and hoped local officials in Hawai'i would, too. One two-lane tube should cost approximately 4.5 million dollars, the engineer's report concluded, and it was passed on to Mayor Petrie of Honolulu.

Paul devoured all the information that he read in the papers, hoping for a lead. He even read classifieds religiously. There were a couple of houses for sale in Coconut Grove, priced in the four- to six-thousand-dollar range. And a forty-thousand-square-foot business lot on Oneawa was going for six and a half cents per square foot. An especially large classified ad caught his eye. It announced that the owner was leaving the islands—only wanted $3,950 for a three-bedroom house in Coconut Grove. The threat of war was beginning to cause panic among some on the islands.

One morning, late in the week, the cable messenger dropped by the Gillespie cottage. He delivered a cable from John in Washington DC telling everyone that they were in his thoughts and prayers. He advised his mother to buy blackout curtains should they ever become necessary. He said he wasn't trying to be alarming, just precautionary.

"That's so much like John," she said, reading the cable aloud to Paul.

"He's the most thorough and prepared individual I've ever met," Paul replied with a smile. He tried to make small talk, because he knew John was Nan's soft spot. "Do you think he takes after you or Mr. G.?"

"Probably both of us. He's got my willful nature. That's what keeps him strong. But he also has Scotty's modesty and gentleness. And, most important of all, his loyalty."

She paused for a moment.

"Scotty probably never told you this, but it was his loyalty to his best friend that brought him here to Hawai'i," she said. "I think he secretly wanted to follow in his older brother's footsteps and join the military. But he had made a commitment to chaperone his best friend's bride-to-be out here, and nothing was going to stop that from happening."

"So how did you get here?"

"It was the custom to make sure that young ladies were always properly chaperoned. After he delivered his best friend's girlfriend to Hawai'i, he got a good job—working with Bishop Trust. Then, in a year, he bought a home in Mānoa, and he wrote for me to come. His brother, Uncle Rob, chaperoned me here to the islands. Scotty and I were married within a couple of days after I arrived at Honolulu Harbor."

"Romantic."

"Ironically, it almost didn't happen. I doubt if Scotty told you that he was going to leave Hawai'i after a year. Didn't like the back-room politics. Didn't like the threat of strikes at the docks. Didn't like the fact that he was required to wear a woolen suit to work in the tropical heat, at first."

Nan smiled and so did Paul.

"But he did love the people here. And when he wrote to me about the gentleness of the people, I said I had to come see for myself. So Uncle Rob brought me here, and Scotty and I were wed, and Scotty kept his job as an accountant with Bishop Trust ever since.

"Again, destiny set in a few years later. Scotty was ready to go back to Britain to fight in the Great War because of his loyalty to his older brothers. Several other islanders with British ties sailed to Europe, but fate got in the way for Scotty and me. I suffered a miscarriage, and Scotty stayed behind to tend after me. Later, when I was about to give birth to John in 1918, Scotty stayed at home with me for the last few weeks of the pregnancy. I was bedridden for many months afterward, so Scotty helped do just about everything for the baby. Yes, it hurt him terribly to know that both his older brothers fought and died for their country and he wasn't there to help them. He felt awfully guilty. But he also knew that his immediate responsibility was to be here for his wife and child. He was so dear. Still is."

Paul smiled again. Nan wiped her hands in her apron. "He's a very loyal man; I can see that," Paul said. "I've appreciated his willingness to get Officer Burns to help me."

Nan nodded and let out a big sigh. "That's another example of his loyalty," she said.

"How so?"

"Well, you're bound to find this out, so I might as well tell you. Jack Burns doesn't drink. Hasn't for five years or more. He was involved in a pretty bad car accident on the Pali several years back. Scotty came upon the scene and immediately recognized that his friend had been drinking. He didn't want to get him trouble, so he quickly got him to a doctor and took care of everything. After that, Burns swore he would never drink again. And he lived up to his promise."

"Sounds like a good friend to have."

"And a very good husband, too." She paused momentarily, her voice suddenly choked with emotion. "Well, go out and explore. You aren't finding out anything by sitting around here listening to me go on and on."

She shushed Paul off with her hands and quickly disappeared into the kitchen. Wonderful woman, Paul thought. Every day, she baked something different for dessert. Cakes, cookies, pies; there was always a smell of something special emanating from Nan's Lanikai kitchen. As he headed out the front door, Paul could hear her searching in the kitchen closet for the starting ingredients of her next concoction.

He decided to head down the long lane toward the beach. Perhaps a walk on the beach, or around the immediate area of Lanikai, might clear his head and give him some perspective, he thought.

Several beach cottages dotted the landscape. Few of the cottages were actually occupied during the workweek. Most of these beachfront homes, Mr. G. had informed him, were weekend cottages for the wealthy people of Honolulu. One exception in that area was a small white framed house with a large yard. The property intrigued him.

It was obvious that someone was living there at the time. A number of white sheets hung flapping in the Windward breeze along one of the clotheslines. Another clothesline, this one perpendicular to the other, sat empty. The sheets slapped hard against each other in the strong trade winds, and Paul was fascinated for a brief moment about their movement. He read the name on the mailbox as he passed by the house. "Kuehn," it read. He'd heard so much about Otto Kuehn lately that he made a mental note in passing.

Around the corner and across the street, Paul ran into Kenji. The little Japanese man was raking the yard at one of the beach cottages. The cottage had two large plumeria trees in the front yard, and they were dropping leaves by the dozens. Paul stooped down to give him a hand.

At first Kenji didn't acknowledge Paul's presence. The tall young *haole* squatted awkwardly for a couple of minutes, watching every meticulous move the Japanese yardman made.

"You do good work," Paul said, interrupting Kenji.

The little man looked up from his rake, but he didn't smile. He went back to his chores. Paul decided to forge on through the uncomfortable silence.

"I notice that some of the plumeria trees have both brilliant flowers and dark green leaves at this time of year, but others, like this one, don't. Why is that?"

"Plumeria mysterious plant," Kenji said. He chose his words carefully and spoke with patience. "Each one different. Some need gentle care, some need nothing. The rule of plumeria—no rules."

Paul laughed. "They sure are pretty and they sure smell great."

"Pretty flower to pick for your girl," he said. The comment actually made Paul blush for a moment—he thought immediately of Healani. "But make sure flower has staying power. Some flowers last for hours in pretty girl's hair. Some die quickly."

"Kind of like romance, huh?"

Kenji didn't respond. He continued raking for several seconds.

"You want to help me grow new trees?" he asked, standing up for a moment and stretching his back. He was a small man, no more than five feet three inches tall. His face was weathered from years spent in the punishing sun, but he kept it protected the best he could with a large straw hat.

"I can try to help you. But how do you do that?"

"Here." He stepped up to the plumeria tree and grabbed one of the smaller, lower branches. "This tree in dormant season. Best time to take cutting."

He sheared off a foot-long branch, cutting it at a forty-five-degree angle. Then he plucked off a couple of dead leaves from its tip. He did the same thing twice over.

"We'll take these three cuttings and put in warm, dry place," he said, walking over to the cottage's carport. Paul followed along as he placed the cuttings on a ledge. "It takes about two weeks to seal off area where I cut."

"Why don't you just put them in water?"

"No, no," he said. He wagged a finger in Paul's face. "I tell you plumeria mysterious plant. Some people say putting in waters works, but not for me."

Paul watched intently.

Kenji continued with his lesson. "We come back in two weeks and plant cuttings in small pots with good soil and good drainage. Then it takes about a month and half, maybe two months, to take root. You have three small new trees by spring."

"I wish I could be here to watch them grow," Paul said.

Kenji shook his head. Paul didn't know why. The Japanese yardman grabbed his rake and continued his work.

"How'd you get to know so much about plants?" Paul asked. He didn't get an answer for a long while, so he waited patiently.

"I learned from my father and mother. They both came from areas of Japan known for beautiful flowers. But my father's family very poor. He came to Hawai'i to make living."

Paul listened closely, trying to decipher every word because Kenji's broken English, what the locals called pidgin, was very strong.

"My father come to Hawai'i when Chinese and Portuguese workers threaten dock strike in Honolulu. That was around turn of century. Couple thousand other Japanese come here around same time."

"So he was a strikebreaker?"

"No, no, no. I think he believe he is a worker," Kenji said. "After couple of months living in terrible conditions in workers' camp, he want more for himself. So, he wrote to Japan, asking for bride. My mother is picture bride. She sent her photo, and they marry here without ever spent time together. I was born a year later, in 1901."

That made Kenji forty years old. Paul thought he appeared much older.

"Several years later, after his contract was up, we move to Kailua, and father and mother work in rice fields. Years ago, have many rice paddies near Kawai Nui. But water table drop. So my parents lease land by Coconut Grove and grow papayas. I work land there for many years but got lucky and found this job. Lots of rich *haole* people in Lanikai. They only here on weekends to go to beach. So I take care of their properties."

"Where do you live now?"

"My family and I live in small cottage behind big house near end of Lanikai." He pointed in the direction away from Kailua, towards the Bellows military base. "My wife take in sewing. My son, he eleven years old, goes to school in Kailua. We also have baby daughter."

"I'd love to meet them sometime," Paul said. He smiled briefly as he lifted a handful of leaves and tossed it into his pile.

"Going to make great mulch," Kenji said.

"Mind if I ask you a kind of sensitive question?" Paul asked. The two men continued piling up the leaves.

"Depends on what it is."

"I heard some of the people talking with some of the military people when I was downtown the other day," Paul said. "I know it's just idle chitchat, but everyone seemed worried about the local Japanese population. I guess the feeling is that if the United States and Japan go to war, lots of folks around here are wondering which side the local Japanese will be on. What do you think of that?"

"What do I think of what?" Kenji asked. His demeanor never changed. He could have been irritated at the question, but he never showed it. "Of fact they talk about us? Of fact they question our loyalty? Or fact that you may be asking because you're wondering, too? Which question you asking?"

"I'm not questioning anything about you," Paul said defensively. He stuttered and stammered his next couple of sentences. "I don't know what to think. I . . . uh . . . I'm sorry I brought it up."

"Don't ever be sorry, young man."

Paul stood up. Kenji never looked up at him. He just kept right on working while lecturing the tall young visitor at the same time. "Actions. Actions speak loudest. Remember that. Watch actions and then you won't have to ask."

Paul paused to think about what the little Japanese yardman said. "Thank you. I guess I better go." Paul thought about telling him about his grandfather's story but decided against it.

"I'm out for a hike this morning. Gonna clear my head," Paul said. "I think I'm going up on the ridge here and see what I can see."

"Plenty special things up there," Kenji replied. Then he stopped and looked up at the tall young man in the eye. "I won't tell you now, but you find out for yourself. Special place up there. All the mountains, special place, special feeling. You go find out for yourself."

Paul had no idea what he meant by that. And Kenji went back

to his yardwork before he might be asked another question. Paul waved to him, but Kenji had already turned to work in another part of the yard. Paul moseyed on down the road.

The neighborhood of Lanikai is just over a mile long and less than a half mile wide. The white strand of beach from Alāla Point to Wailea Point borders it on one side. Ka'iwa Ridge, the rocky ridge standing a few hundred feet high, makes a natural border on the other side.

Paul headed towards the ridge.

He found a small trailhead near the opening to Mid-Pacific Country Club, the golf course where Mr. G. did some of his accounting work. The trail meandered through heavy *kiawe* bushes. Paul had to push his way through in a few places. Residue from the *kiawe* stuck to his clothes, and he wished that he had been wearing long pants instead of shorts. But he forged on.

The trail got steeper but not so steep that he couldn't walk it fairly easily. The *kiawe* thinned out, replaced by thick grass. Only toward the top of the ridge did he have to scramble a little bit. In a couple of places, he reached down to brace himself. His injured knees handled the strain fairly easily, and it turned into an easy hike to the top. No more than a half hour.

The trail came in from the backside of the ridge. The top of the ridge cut off the airflow from the ocean, making it much warmer than the area below. Paul wiped sweat off his brow. And then he climbed up the final steps to the top where cooler air rushed across his face.

"Spectacular." Just another *wow* moment in Kailua, he thought.

From his vantage point atop Ka'iwa Ridge, he could see in all directions. Lanikai was directly below him. Different shades of blue water danced up against the coral white sands. Turquoise in the shallower water, a more royal blue in the deeper waters near the Mokes. The waters along the sand were almost clear.

Paul turned towards Kailua Town, where he could see the

layout of the nine-hole golf course below him, then the Campos Dairy beyond it, and then the small center of town. In the far-off distance, Kāneʻohe Bay was an awesome half oval of blue waters, rimmed by the steep, jagged cliffs of the Koʻolau mountains behind.

Paul turned again towards the Pali, and he could see what Jorge was taking about when he called it the *ahupuaʻa*. Mount Olomana, with its prominent peaks, stood out as the gem of the hills that surrounded Kailua. He could see the nearly black waters of Kaʻelepulu Pond and the swampy grasslands of Kawai Nui. All of it rimmed by the awesome spectacle of the Koʻolau, a range of mountains that defined the Windward Side of Oʻahu and cut it off from Honolulu.

The quiet of the moment was quickly quashed when he heard the engines of planes nearby. He looked skyward and saw a small squadron of U.S. Army planes overhead. He followed their direction by continuing his climb along the ridgeline.

They were headed eastward, coming from over the Pali, and he followed their flight path until they disappeared over the next hill near him. He continued his climb in that direction, where the ridge above Lanikai became less rocky and the trail eventually led to the rolling hills behind. He climbed the highest hill and looked down at Bellows Army Air Base, which was located just over the ridge from Lanikai and along the shoreline in Waimānalo.

From his vantage point, he could see where the planes landed, along an airstrip that appeared to be still under construction. The airstrip was cut out in a diagonal direction, amidst a virtual jungle of ironwood trees.

The base at Bellows was quite small in comparison with that of the Kāneʻohe Naval Air Station, which was located on the other side of Kailua. It sat alongside the shoreline, and he watched men and heavy machinery as they continued the construction work. As some planes taxied in, another small squadron of P-40s took off and headed over the nearby sugar plantation. His eyes followed them as they passed over hundreds of acres of agricultural land and then disappeared over the Ko'olau.

He could only guess at their mission. Perhaps they were headed towards Hickam or Pearl Harbor. He had no idea. In his short stay in Hawai'i, Paul had almost gotten used to the sound of plane engines and military exercises. His early mornings at Lanikai Beach were often interrupted by their sights or sounds. He wondered if they were truly planning to go to war.

After a short time observing the spectacles at Bellows, Paul made up his mind to venture into Kailua Town. School was getting out shortly, and he was hopeful that he would catch Healani down at the schoolyard. He hustled back down the trail in anticipation of seeing the most beautiful girl he had ever laid eyes on.

On his way back down the ridge, his eyes also caught a glimpse of what appeared to be sparkling stones. Brilliant actually. Perhaps the stones were the something special that Kenji spoke about. Or perhaps Kenji meant just being up above everything, seeing and feeling the incredible beauty. Paul wasn't sure.

He paused for a moment to try to see the sparkling stones up close, but while they glistened in the noonday sun, they were well off the footpath. He would have to go back through the *kiawe* bushes to see what was gleaming in the sunlight. He paused for a moment but decided he would leave that exploration for another time when he was better prepared for it.

By the time Paul got to the school grounds about a half hour later, he could hear the chatter and laughter of young students leaving the school. Boys and girls of several different shapes, sizes, and colors, from the first grade through the ninth grade, scattered in all directions. He peered into a couple of classrooms and finally spotted Healani, but she was deep in conference with one of her students. Based on her serious demeanor, it looked like the boy was getting a scolding.

Paul's attention was diverted by the sound of a bouncing ball.

He turned around to see a group of five or six boys shooting a basketball at one of the two hoops on the playground. Two taller boys—one *haole* and the other Hawaiian—stood under the basket waving their arms, hoping for a pass from the Japanese boy who always seemed to have his hands on the ball.

Paul was amused by what he saw. The Japanese boy with the ball was much smaller than the rest but also much more talented. He could dribble circles around his defenders and then fire off shots from any direction. If he missed, he also seemed to have a knack for getting the ball right back. His obvious talent frustrated the other boys, and soon a little scuffle broke out.

Paul hurried over to the playground to break it up.

"He's hogging the ball," whined one of the tall boys as Paul pulled him away from the pile.

"Hey, hey, break it up."

Paul turned to the little Japanese boy and said, "Why don't you give the other fellas a chance every once in a while?"

He said nothing. He just looked at Paul with a mischievous grin.

"Well, holding on to the ball may seem like fun, but basketball is actually about teamwork," Paul said, grabbing the ball out of the boy's hands. "The more hands that touch the ball on your team, the harder it is for opposing defenders to stop you. If only one player has the ball all the time, the other team will eventually find a way to stop him."

"How come you know so much?" the Hawaiian boy asked.

"Yeah," the *haole* boy blurted out. The Japanese boy said nothing as he kept his eyes fixed on the ground.

Paul started to answer, when another boy ran up and tugged at his shirt. "You're really tall, Mister. How tall are you?"

"Looks like you've got your hands full," a familiar voice interrupted. Paul turned to see Healani arrive. She was dressed in a white cotton blouse, buttoned high on the collar. But he noticed something was different about her. It was her hair pulled back and covered with a bright blue scarf. In any case, she still looks magnificent, he thought.

"Guess I got involved where I wasn't supposed to," Paul said, smiling.

"No problem. Boys will always be boys."

"Is that so?" Paul tossed the basketball back to the little Japanese boy.

"I'll give them some slack," she said, patting the Hawaiian boy on the head. "Besides, you could say that they're a little distressed these days. They lost their basketball coach—he went off to join the military, and so now many of the boys don't know what to do with themselves after school."

"Why don't you be our coach, Mister?" the tall *haole* boy said. "You're tall!"

"Well, I don't know. I'm only here for a short time. " Paul looked over at Healani, who gave a mocking frown. "Last time I was on the court, I hurt my knees pretty bad. I don't know." He kept his eyes on Healani, and her mock frown grew larger.

She walked away in feigned disgust.

"Let me at least talk it over with your teacher," Paul announced to the boys. "We'll see." They cheered and ran off. Paul watched as the little Japanese boy tossed the basketball to the tall Hawaiian boy, who made a nice layup.

"See, good passing helps," Paul called out.

He turned back towards Healani. She stood quietly with her hands folded together in front of her.

"So, what brings you here, tall man?" she said with a flirtatious smile. "I doubt if you were applying for the basketball coaching position. Or were you?"

Paul laughed as they started walking back towards her classroom.

"Well, if you must know, I was hoping you would go to the

movies with me tomorrow night," he said, trying to sound confident. Inside, he was an ocean of nerves. "It's Saturday night and all, and I thought we could make a night of it."

"Sounds intriguing. I'll see what my brother says."

"If it's a problem, ask him along."

She paused for a moment. "I think there's a way. Tell you what—I'll go to the movies with you tomorrow night if you come to the beach with me tomorrow afternoon."

"Sounds great."

"Oh, and one more thing," she said as she walked into her classroom. "You also have to agree to coach our basketball team for as long as you're here."

Paul stopped in his tracks. "I don't know. It's been a while, and I'm not sure that my knees could handle it."

She looked back over her shoulder and smiled. "You look fine to me." There was a twinkle in her eye. "Besides, it's the only way my brother would ever agree to let me go out with you."

"Why, that's extortion," Paul said.

"Yes, Mr. Sands, it is."

11 - THE SHARK OF KAILUA BAY

Paul felt very uncertain about his future. Yes, he had met a smart and beautiful girl, and he was looking forward to his beach date with her. But he was also very frustrated with his search for meaningful information about his grandfather's past and the elusive Iwalani.

His phone calls and visits to the big city of Honolulu had been fruitless, and no one in an official capacity, with the exception of Officer Burns, was sympathetic or even remotely interested in his quest to find answers. And now Burns was difficult to reach on this particular morning because he was tied up with other investigations. Paul hoped to see him in person again shortly. Meanwhile, Nan Gillespie had offered to help by dropping off the money clip at a jewelry shop she knew, but it was unlikely Paul would hear anything back about that until early the next week.

Worse yet, he had received a wire from his grandfather's attorney saying that the autopsy ruling may hold up the settling of the William Sands estate. Paul knew he only had a short time to find his answers.

Still, he remained hopeful. Healani may be able to help him, he thought. She had an easy style about her. And she made him feel better about himself than he could ever remember. He knew he could talk with her about all of this—he felt certain about that. He grabbed his towel and shorts and a change of clothes and headed to the beach at Kailua Bay.

Healani asked Paul to meet her at the Kalama Beach Club, a small private beach club located in Pine Grove along Kailua Beach. The clubhouse, a haven for well-to-do families getting away from Honolulu for the weekend, was located only a few blocks from Healani and Jorge's home.

As he waited under the shade of an ironwood tree, Paul watched children scamper in the clear, turquoise waters along the white, sandy beach. The waves were taller than in Lanikai, and the two- to three-footers knocked the youngsters off their feet time and time again. The crescent-shaped beach was also much larger than Lanikai Beach, perhaps three miles from Alāla Point all the way around to Mōkapu Peninsula. Except for the children playing in front of the beach club and a small group of teenagers walking in the direction of several fishermen and their boats on the Lanikai end, the entire length of the beach was virtually deserted.

Off the shoreline, a few of the fishing boats searched for their prey in the large bay. It was difficult to see where the boats met the water because each hull was painted a bright shade of ocean blue. Paul recalled Kenji telling him that the practice was considered a Japanese tradition—one that made the fishermen and their vessels "one with the sea." Paul watched the small fishing boats with great appreciation, a feeling he also had for the wise and thoughtful Kenji.

Two tiny islands dotted the horizon. To the left, toward Mōkapu Peninsula, was a small, rocky island that appeared to have no vegetation at all. The second island was to the right, toward Alāla Point, a totally flat island with some vegetation and birdlife. There were two fishing boats anchored just beyond the flat island.

Closer to Paul, a few of the children found a clever way to ride in the surf. They brought pillowcases with them, and they wet them down in the water and then ran along the shoreline scooping up air. When the pillow cases were properly inflated, they tied off the ends. Then they rode them like rafts in the surf. It helped them stay afloat for quite a long time.

How ingenious, Paul thought.

"Got any room under that tree?" Paul heard a familiar voice say. The voice made him smile, and he immediately sprang to his feet to greet her. Healani was breathtaking in a white one-piece bathing suit that revealed the gentleness of her shoulders and her generous curves. She wore her hair tucked into a bathing cap.

"Looks like you're already ready for a swim."

"I always say, 'swim first, relax later,'" she said. "Let's go."

Within moments, they were off, splashing past the young children and into the surf. Healani dove headfirst under a wave. Paul followed right behind her.

After a brief chill, the water seemed quite warm, even for late November. They swam together, side by side, for several hundred feet straight out into Kailua Bay. Then they turned back towards the shoreline. When they reached the small waves near the shore, Healani playfully slapped water into Paul's face.

But the serenity and flirtatiousness of the early afternoon swim ended abruptly. Waiting at the shoreline, wearing a cowboy hat, boots, and a menacing look, was Jorge. Healani pretended she didn't see him, but Paul wasn't aware of any problem, so he gave out a holler.

"Hey, Jorge!" Paul called out as he pulled himself to his feet and out of the water. Healani continued to swim in the surf. Jorge didn't respond; his eyes were riveted on his sister.

"Jorge, what's the problem?"

Jorge motioned his hand dismissively towards Paul. "This is not about you, Hollywood. Stay out of it."

"That makes no sense."

Jorge stepped back, but Paul could tell he was fuming. Paul tried to put his hand on Jorge's shoulder in a gesture of friendship, but Jorge knocked it away.

"Come on, Jorge, lighten up." But the stocky cowboy would have nothing of it—his eyes were dancing with anger.

But before the two could come to blows, Healani stepped between them.

"Jorge, go home!" she commanded. She got up in his face, nose to nose, but she kept her hands at her side.

"Me, go home? What the hell?"

Jorge continued to glare, but he stepped back. Healani motioned for Paul to move away from them. She stormed up the beach. Within moments, she had her towel in hand and angrily dried off. Jorge was right behind her. She turned and glared at him.

The stare-off continued for several moments, until Jorge finally relaxed. He looked skyward briefly, rolled his eyes, and shook his head. He reached out and tried to place his hands on his sister's upper arm, but she flinched backward.

"C'mon Healani." Jorge said, almost pleading.

"Leave now, Jorge. I can handle myself."

"But, Healani?"

She threw down her towel and walked with urgency towards Paul, only twenty or thirty feet away. She reached out her hand and Paul grabbed it. The two of them looked at Jorge, whose shoulders slumped. He shook his head again and sighed in exasperation. He mumbled something under his breath but said nothing aloud.

"Go home, Jorge. It's going to be all right. You don't have to watch over me forever."

Jorge pulled the brim of his hat deep over his face. Then he turned and walked slowly away, leaving the beach behind.

"What was that all about?" Paul asked.

"Oh, he was just giving me stink eye. It'll be okay," Healani replied.

She pulled him around and towards the water. Together they dove back into the shorebreak. Paul followed her as she swam with great strength and urgency deep into the bay. Several minutes into the swim, Healani veered east, and then she took the lead. Her long, determined strokes spurred Paul on. The swim was exhilarating for both, until she slowed down. Paul caught up with her and stopped.

"What's up?" Paul asked, kicking his feet furiously below him to keep his head above water.

"Shh," she whispered, putting her forefinger to her lips.

"Turn quietly and look over there," she whispered again, this time pointing towards the small flat island in the bay. "Turtles. Two of them. Right there in front of the island."

Sure enough, Paul could see the shadowy outline of two large turtles as they swam in front of them, perhaps no more than twenty feet away. Paul watched their tiny heads bob in and out of the water. They were shaped almost like what he'd imagined a Martian might look like—creepy, but almost human, too.

The turtles continued their dance in the waves, scavenging for food. They seemed oblivious to the presence of their peculiar guests. Soon, however, another shadow, larger than the others, joined them. Healani and Paul smiled at each other as they watched these incredible creatures enjoying the same beautiful bay. They continued to swim in place and marvel in the experience.

"Oh my God!" Healani blurted, her voice suddenly intense but dwindling to a mere whisper.

"What! What! What!"

"Be as still and quiet as you can be" she said, whispering very softly. "Don't say a word. Swim slowly, backwards with me."

Paul had no idea what was going on, but he swam with her, his eyes darting in every direction, trying to see what had changed her mood.

"The third shadow wasn't a turtle. It's a shark," she said, finally breaking the silence. Her voice was confident and resolute. "Try to stay calm. And don't splash."

Her words terrified Paul. But her calm demeanor in the face of danger inspired him to follow her every direction. Paul and Healani began to swim slowly but deliberately away from the shark, but they were more than a hundred yards offshore. With each stroke, Paul wondered if the shark was following right behind. But he was too terrified to look back.

They swam with great intensity side by side the entire way back to the shorebreak. When they reached an area where they could put their feet down in the sand, Paul instinctively put his arm around her shoulder, as if he were the protector now. He pulled her in close, and they helped each other, arm in arm and exhausted, to the water's edge.

"Thank you," Paul said, softly.

She nodded, catching her breath. "We'll have to warn others, but we must do it without a panic. I doubt seriously if the shark would come close to shore. It's not in their nature."

The duo beached themselves several yards away from where they started the swim, so they walked hurriedly back to the beach club. Healani started to run and grabbed Paul's hand to run with her. Only two youngsters, a young boy and a young girl, both around six years old, were still playing in the water when they returned. The rest of the children were well up on the sand. Healani nodded toward the two young swimmers and hurried ahead. Paul gathered one youngster under each arm, as if he were playing a game. They giggled all the way back to the towel area where their parents were sitting.

"That was fun. Let's do it again," the boy said.

"Wait just a minute," Paul said in a cautionary tone. When the two children tried to run back to the water, he stopped them. When he grabbed them, they squirmed and giggled again, but he held them tightly. "Hold on. No one's going anywhere until Mommy and Daddy say so."

Just then Healani reappeared on the shore. She had run up to the beach house at the same time he was bringing the two children out of the water. She came back with an elderly *haole* man. She pointed toward the flat island in the bay.

"First, let's make sure everyone knows what's going on," the elderly man said, as he removed his hat and wiped his white hair off his brow. A few of the people on the shore had gotten up off their towels and were standing around.

"No need to panic, folks," he said. "Healani and her friend have spotted a shark in the waters off the flat island."

A woman gasped. She pulled her small boy, a toddler, who had been playing in the sand, close up against her leg. The young girl and boy Paul had playfully gathered up from the surf were quickly hustled up by their father and mother.

"As I said, remain calm," the elderly man announced to the small crowd. "This is a very rare occurrence in Kailua Bay." The small group of beachgoers was hushed.

"There's a natural reef system out there that keeps sharks and most other large fish out. Judging from what Healani has told me, this shark might not be very large, and he must have gotten lost in the reef and now can't get out."

"Thanks, professor," Healani said. She motioned for the people to leave the area.

"I'll call one of my fisherman friends and have him take a look," the elderly *haole* man announced.

Just then the small group of teenagers Paul had seen earlier came running up.

"There's a shark out there," one of the boys hollered, excitedly. "We could see it from over there." He pointed down the shoreline towards Alāla Point, across from the flat island.

"We know, young man," the elderly professor said.

"My dad's in one of the fishing boats on the bay, and my uncle is down there at the point, ready to shove off," said another boy. "If we hurry, we can probably catch him before he goes."

"That's an excellent idea," the elderly man said. He put his hat back on his head and motioned for the boys to follow him. Healani and Paul followed right behind. The boys ran ahead.

"Let me give a proper introduction. This is Professor Granville. He teaches biology at Punahou School," Healani told Paul as they hastened their pace.

"Nice to meet you, sir," Paul said, extending his hand, but the professor barely acknowledged him. His attention was distracted by the task at hand.

"First, we've got to figure out exactly what type of shark we've got here," he said, looking out towards the bay. "We've probably got nearly forty different shark species in Hawaiian waters, but only a few are aggressive toward humans. Most are just curious and won't attack unless provoked."

"What species do we need to worry about?" Healani asked. The boys had reached their uncle at the fishing boat and were waving frantically for Paul, Healani, and Professor Granville to catch up with them.

"Most likely a tiger shark," the professor said. "Sometimes they follow the fishing boats around, looking for scraps. The fishermen should know almost immediately if it's a tiger shark. The markings on the shark are quite obvious. If it's another species, say a pygmy shark or a sandbar, or even most of the varieties of common reef sharks, we probably have nothing to worry about. If it's a tiger shark, then we're going to have to deal with it."

They hustled up to the fishing boat. Professor Granville and the fisherman exchanged handshakes. Healani gave the fisherman a hug and kissed him on both cheeks.

"This is Ichiro," Healani said. "He and his brother fish these waters all the time."

"We have no time for pleasantries," the professor interrupted. "We need to get someone out on the water to see exactly what species of shark we have out there."

"Hop in, Professor," Ichiro said. "You, too, Healani. And bring your friend, if he wants to tag along."

Paul didn't hesitate. The four of them jumped into the boat, a well-used twenty-footer.

"Push us off, boys," Ichiro commanded the teenagers. The small outboard engine purred. Within seconds they were on the bay, heading toward the flat island.

"We don't see sharks in here often, Professor," Ichiro said, speaking loudly so he could be heard above the sound of the boat's engine. "Maybe once or twice a year, usually in the winter. Don't know if this one followed one of the fishing boats or just got lost in the outer reef and can't get back out to sea."

"There it is!" Healani yelled out. She pointed to the left of the flat island. She could see the shark's shadowy figure just below the surface, perhaps fifty yards in front of the boat.

"Let's get closer," Ichiro said. He pushed his boat forward nearer to the flat island.

"It's definitely a tiger," the professor said as they moved to within ten yards of the shark. "You can see the distinct markings on its side. I'd say about ten to twelve feet, at least. That's a pretty big one."

Ichiro slowed his boat down and began maneuvering it, his hands whipping across the steering wheel. "Now, we just have to figure how to get it out of here," he said with urgency. He signaled towards two other boats with his waving arms and pulled his own boat around, facing the opposite direction. Within minutes, the other boats had pulled close enough that they were in shouting distance. Each was manned by two Japanese fishermen.

"A twelve-foot tiger shark," Ichiro yelled as he pointed. "Right in front of flat island. It's hugging close to the island, as if it knows it's in trouble."

The other fishermen looked in the direction of the shark. As each of them saw it, they became very excited.

"Let's try to spread ourselves out, so he can't escape," Ichiro commanded.

The two other boats moved almost immediately. One headed toward the left side of the island, the other to the right. Ichiro kept his boat in the center, right in front of the tiny island, no more than fifty yards away from the big fish. The tiger shark, obviously agitated, swam frantically back and forth. And now it was surrounded.

"Healani, help me with the bait," Ichiro yelled. "Professor, I think you know how to level the boat. Keep it steady while I bait the pole."

"No problem," the professor said as he stepped forward to take the wheel. Ichiro grabbed the strongest of his several fishing poles, and he and Healani went to the back of the boat. Ichiro reached into a large bucket and pulled some large sea remnants from the murky water.

"Octopus," he said, holding the large tentacles in his hand. "Caught it yesterday. Cut it up last night. Great for catching the bigger fish."

Healani held on to the fishing pole and Ichiro baited the hook. "This may take a few tries," he said. "Professor, move the boat closer to flat island. We'll try to bring the shark out by tossing some little bait overboard first."

The professor did exactly as he was told. Paul looked at the other two fishing boats, where similar scenarios were playing out. Paul then glanced back at the shoreline where a small crowd of people was gathering. Word had apparently already started to spread around Kailua that a shark was in the bay.

Healani tossed some smaller bait over the side, mostly fish remnants. The tiger shark attacked the bait, devouring it instantly. On each bite, he thrashed from side to side, showing his powerful presence.

"That could have been us," Healani said, turning towards Paul.

He just shook his head and held on tightly to the side of the boat.

The shark tried to make a break for the right side of the island, but the fishing boat on that side revved up its engine and the shark turned around. It was trapped.

The professor guided the boat perfectly and they inched closer in. Healani continued to toss small bait over the side. The shark, with its steely eyes, blunt snout, and dark markings, thrashed away at its lifeless prey and then searched for a way out of its predicament.

"Will it come at us? I mean ram the boat," Paul hollered out.

"Not likely," the professor said. "But never say never. It's probably more scared than we are."

"Time to go in for the kill," Ichiro said with confidence. He tossed his heavy line, baited with several long octopus tentacles, into the water. The tiger shark attacked the bait almost immediately. Paul watched as Ichiro kept a steady hand and then suddenly jerked backwards.

"Dammit, missed him," he yelled out.

After reeling in partway, the stocky Japanese fishermen tossed his heavy line into the sea again. The intensity in his face heightened. He was determined to catch the shark. He jerked back his line once again.

"Got him. Got him," he yelled. "Professor, let him run."

Ichiro dug his feet into the ribs of the boat for support. "Hey, kid," he motioned to Paul. "Give me a hand here. Come over and hold me around the waist." Paul didn't hesitate at all, wrapping up the fishermen with his two long arms. Paul braced himself as best he could and held on tightly. Ichiro kept both hands firmly on the pole as the line unwound rapidly.

The shark swam frantically, first towards the shoreline and then towards the open part of the bay. The professor kept his distance, allowing the shark to build up steam.

"We're going to tire it out, and then we're going to pull up alongside and give it a good whack," Ichiro said. The big shark frantically tried to get off the hook, but his thrashing efforts were fruitless. Each time he thrashed, he splashed up rooster tails of water. But it couldn't free itself.

The two other fishing boats followed. Finally, the shark slowed. The boat nearest to the shoreline came up alongside and one of the fishermen reached over the side with a large piece of wood and gave the shark a big whack on the top of its head. A few whacks later and blood began to flow on the surface of the water.

The professor slowed the boat down and circled back. Paul let go of his tight grip. Ichiro reeled in his line. The shark was all but dead. Ichiro dropped his pole and finished the big creature off with a couple of thrusts from a spear.

"That bugger was nasty," the professor said.

"Gave me a terrific fight. There were a couple of times I could hardly hold on," Ichiro said.

"Good job," Paul said. "I never realized how strong you have to be to pull one of those fish in."

"Now, everyone is safe," Healani sighed. The professor nodded in agreement.

By this time, the shoreline was packed with dozens of people. Two more small fishing vessels joined the cavalcade of boats, pulling alongside. Fishermen from each craft jumped into Ichiro's 20-footer and helped Ichiro tie up the shark for the ride in. The ride seemed almost like a parade, and the people on shore let out hoots and hollers of praise.

When the procession arrived on the beach, several people rushed up to see the shark at close range. Most were amazed by the size of the big fish and its monstrous, jagged teeth. Paul shuddered at the thought of what might have been.

"We were lucky," she said, as he put her arms around his waist. He pulled her close to him and gave her a kiss on the top of the head. She reached up on her tiptoes and gave him a kiss on his cheek. The two relished the moment for a short while until a low voice interrupted.

"Healani, Hollywood, hate to break it up, but you'd better come with me."

Paul and Healani turned quickly and saw Jorge standing by his truck. She was just about to say something when he cut her off.

"Not now, Healani, not now," he said in a somber tone. The change in his demeanor from earlier that day was quite noticeable; Healani didn't argue.

"Jump in my truck," Jorge said. "The military is going on full alert. I'll tell you all about it on the drive back to the house."

12 - FULL ALERT

Paul didn't see it until he and Healani squeezed into the passenger seat of Jorge's '37 Chevy. With Healani between the two men and saying nothing and looking straight ahead, Paul glanced over at Jorge and immediately noticed the deep cut between his right eye and right ear. His right cheekbone was also puffy.

"What the hell happened to you, Jorge?"

Healani immediately looked over and gasped. She quickly reached for the glove compartment and pulled out a small towel, but when she tried to touch his face with it, Jorge violently turned his head away from her.

"It's nothing."

"Let me take a look at it!" Healani scolded him.

Jorge still fumed, but he allowed his younger sister to tend to the wounds.

"You may need stitches," she said. "How did this happen?"

Jorge grimaced and shook his head. "Well, guess you could say this is how I found out about the alert."

Healani took the towel and pressed it against his cheek, but he pulled away from her again. He started the engine and drove away from the beach.

"Don't worry about me," he said. "Something bad is brewing. I got off work early today, and after I saw you and Paul at the beach, I was so ticked off, I headed to Kailua Tavern for a quick cold one. It took me a while to get over it, but I figured, what the hell—it's your life. I was standing at the bar, minding my business, when these two navy sailors came in."

"Uh-oh," Healani said. She'd seen her brother in this kind of situation before.

"Anyway, they were loud and obnoxious and I told them to shut up. That's when one of them took a swing at me."

"Must have landed a good one," Paul said.

"That's the only one he really landed. I punched out that guy real quick. Just a couple of rips to the face and one to the stomach and he was out. And when his buddy came over to help, I got him in a headlock and then held him down. Kimo, the bartender, called the MPs and they were there within minutes."

"Jesus, Jorge!" Healani interrupted. "What was everybody else doing during this time?"

"They know enough to let me handle my own battles. You should know that. It's not the first time I've fought with those sons of bitches."

Healani shook her head. Jorge grimaced as she pressed the towel on his cheekbone. This time he allowed her to wipe away some of the dirt and grime from the injured area.

"Let me tell the damn story," he said in an agitated voice. He spoke very fast, the words coming out like a torrent. "After one of the MPs handcuffed the guys and took them outside, his buddy was asking me for an incident report. I told 'em what happened, when, suddenly, the MP who went outside stormed back into the tavern—he told the other guy to drop what he was doing immediately. He said he just got word that they were going on full alert and they had better hightail it back to the base. Man, you should have seen those guys jump. Full alert, I tell ya. They took off like a flash."

Jorge paused for a moment to allow Paul and Healani absorb

the information. Then he continued, talking frantically.

"It was kind of weird because nobody else in the tavern was paying attention. I turned around to say something to Kimo, the bartender, but he was on the phone. I waited, and when he hung up I was going to say something about the full alert, but he interrupted me all excited. 'There's a shark loose in Kailua Bay,' he yelled out. Practically the whole tavern cleared out when we heard that. Anyway, I followed them down to the boathouse and watched you come in to the shore. That's all I know right now."

"What does it mean? Full alert? Going on alert doesn't mean war. It might be just a drill," Paul said.

"I doubt it. Those guys looked pretty rattled for a drill. I've seen how they react when it's some kind of war game or something. This wasn't that. I'm guessing they've got word of sabotage. I don't know. It could be anything. Let's get home quick so I can make a phone call."

"We can also see if the navy officers are there in the big house," Healani said. "Good bet that if they're gone, something's up."

Jorge's Chevy skidded into his dirt driveway. Jorge hurriedly cranked his hand with a twist to take the car out of gear and pulled up the parking brake. Then he hopped out and dashed for the small house. Paul and Healani quick-stepped it to the officer's house.

Healani knocked on the front door several times, but no one answered. She took a step or two and peered through their window. "No one's here. I don't see their car either," she said. "They usually have it parked out front."

They hustled around to the smaller house in the back. The door was wide open and they went in. The place was small and dark. Jorge was already on the phone, but Paul stopped quickly, suddenly overwhelmed by the strong smell of garlic and vinegar.

Healani glanced over at Paul and gave him a quizzical look. Paul pointed to his nose but said nothing.

She looked around and then burst out laughing, immediately

lightening the mounting tension. She picked up a metal lid from the kitchen sink and screwed it on a large glass jar that was filled with some sort of concoction. The smell was reduced tremendously.

"Jorge loves pickled pig's feet," she said with a smile. "It's a Portuguese delicacy, especially when left soaking in garlic and vinegar. He must have taken the lid off this morning and forgot to put it back on. You're right, it can get pretty strong if you're not used to it."

Paul smiled sheepishly. "Sorry," he said. "Just didn't expect it."

"You should see the look on your face," she said, giggling. She ran some water over a small washcloth at the sink and gently wiped Jorge's face while he talked on the phone. Jorge was so engrossed in his phone call that he hardly noticed.

"What a day, huh?" she said. Paul nodded. Jorge put down the receiver and turned to both of them.

"I called the Old Man," Jorge said. "He told me that the army and navy received direct orders from Washington DC to go on full alert. Apparently the negotiations with the Japanese took a turn for the worse, and they've received some strange intelligence information. He doesn't know what it is. He said the military authorities decided that it was best to place themselves on full-alert status for the immediate time being. He said he doesn't know of anything imminent, that this is a precautionary move."

"So who is involved?" Healani asked.

"All the bases. Kāneʻohe, Pearl, Bellows, Hickam, Wheeler, Schofield, Shafter, all of them. They're on full alert for the rest of the weekend, at least."

"How will this affect the civilian population? Or will it?" Paul asked.

"I asked the Old Man that same question. He said we're not affected at all, for now. He told me to just keep doing whatever I was doing. That all of us should just keep on going about our daily lives. He said most people won't even know anything is happening. He also said if the military wanted us to know more, they'd tell us more. Don't know about that, but I didn't argue with him. You don't argue with the Old Man."

Healani took a deep sigh. "That's a relief."

"Still, gives me the creeps, all this war talk," Paul said.

"Don't know if there's much more we can do," Jorge said, grimacing while massaging his injured cheekbone. "I don't know if I trust those military bastards anyway." Jorge grabbed a towel and compressed it against the side of his head and then walked out of the room.

"So I guess that means our date is still on," Healani said, looking at Paul. He laughed momentarily but then nodded in the direction where Jorge had exited, as if to say, what about him?

"He's going to be okay with it. I'll handle it. Don't even worry about it."

The mood was much more somber in the Washington DC offices of Secretary Knox. John and the remainder of Knox's staff had been working all through the night, and John knew they were headed for another long night. They had received and analyzed intelligence reports from the British and had heard from communications experts within U.S. Navy intelligence. The news was not encouraging even though much of it was vague. After a thorough review and analysis, but still with a great deal of incomplete information, it was Knox who finally recommended the alert to his U.S. naval fleet commanders, including the ones in Hawai'i.

But no one was happy.

"Where are the latest reports on the Japanese main fleet?" Knox asked.

"They're on the upper corner of your desk, sir," his receptionist answered from the doorway. She closed the door to his office and went into the foyer to answer phone calls. The phone had been ringing incessantly all evening long—and most of the calls were from the White House.

"Secretary of State Hull is furious with the alert status," Knox said to no one in particular. "He thinks we're overreacting."

"But he has the same basic information we have," John protested. "No one knows exactly where Japan's main fleet is right now. And talks with the Japanese have reached a low point. What exactly does he want us to do?"

"Not to overreact!" Knox pounded on his desk. John and the other special assistants said nothing as their boss shuffled through a massive buildup of papers.

"Secretary Hull says the negotiations are sensitive and we shouldn't be overplaying our hand." He paused for moment, his face reddening. "This is aggravating, dammit." Knox pounded the desk again. "We should have our focus on Southeast Asia. That's the most likely spot they'll hit."

He pulled out a map of the Pacific Rim and pointed out a number of strategic points, from Saigon to Singapore. John and the other special assistants had heard the tirade before. They knew exactly where their boss stood on the possibility of war with Japan and where he thought they would attack first if the situation continued to deteriorate.

Only John was confident enough to speak up. "But, sir, Hawai'i must be ready."

"Dammit, Gillespie, we've been through this before. The problem with Hawaii is from within, not from the outside. There are almost as many Japs in Honolulu as there are in Tokyo."

"Over 40 percent of a population of around four hundred thousand to be exact. But, sir—"

Knox cut him off.

"No more *buts*, Gillespie. Sabotage should be the main focus there. We need to make sure all our Hawai'i commanders know how to protect against sabotage."

Knox continued to shuffle through papers until he finally found the report he was looking for, gathered it in his hands, and stuffed it in his briefcase. "Gentlemen," he announced. "Make your reports, then go home and get some sleep. You'll need it. I'm going to meet with Secretary Hull and try to calm him down."

John watched as Knox put on his suit coat and hat, pulled the briefcase under his armpit, and marched out of the office. For good measure, he loudly slammed the office door on his way out.

Back in Kailua, Jorge and Healani were able to create a butterfly bandage, and Jorge was eventually all patched up. Paul ran back to the Kalama Beach Club to grab the change of clothes he had brought along with him much earlier in the day. As long as Jorge wasn't going to fight him about going out with Healani, he was ready, willing, and able to take her on a date that evening.

The few beachgoers who were still around that late in the afternoon thanked Paul for his assistance during the shark episode. When Professor Granville arrived back at the clubhouse, he told Paul that Ichiro was already talking about how to display the shark's teeth at Harada's, the general store in Kailua Town. "We pried open its giant jaws. Must have been a couple of feet in circumference," the professor said.

Paul shuddered at the thought. He thanked Granville for all his good work and said he hoped they'd meet again under different circumstances. The professor gave him a hearty handshake and wished him well. Paul quickly changed into his dry clothes.

By the time he got back to the Luis house, it was nearing dusk and his heart was racing with anticipation. Inside again, he saw that Healani was all dressed up, wearing a knee-length skirt and a light pink V-neck sweater. "You look lovely, Healani," he said.

"We walking or driving?" she asked flirtatiously. She wore a small, colorful flower just above her ear. Paul knew from his conversation earlier that week with Kenji that the flower was the sweet-smelling plumeria.

"Why don't we walk it," Paul answered. "It's only a little more than a half mile to the movie house. That will only take us only ten to fifteen minutes, and it's a beautiful evening." Paul extended his hand. She reached for it immediately. They walked out of the house and into the early evening air.

"How scared were you today?" she asked him.

"You mean about the shark or the military alert?" he answered playfully. "Both got me going. I don't want to minimize the alert. It's scary and all, but I think we're pretty safe out here in the middle of the Pacific. If we weren't, why would the military tell the Old Man for us to go on as usual? If it were unsafe, they'd be telling us to get off the roads right now."

"Agreed."

"On the other hand, that shark—oh my, that was unreal. I could hardly breathe when we were swimming back towards the shore. Having you swimming next to me was what kept me going. I don't know how you kept so calm."

"I wasn't," she said, looking up at him.

"Could've fooled me," Paul responded, tightening his grip on her incredibly soft hand. She squeezed back affectionately.

"I guess I've always been a little bit braver than the average girl. It might be my brother's influence. He's a pretty crazy guy, always has been. I think he treated me more like a little brother than a sister when I was growing up."

"I can't quite figure you two out. I can tell how much you care for each other. But it seems like he wants to lord over you."

"That's just the way he is. He wants to do the right thing; especially since our parents died. I can tell you he's chased many boys and many men away from me. You're actually pretty lucky—he must like you."

"I feel lucky."

"I've never met anyone quite like you," she said. "You're very caring, very sensitive; I can tell that about you."

Paul blushed slightly and smiled. "Not sure how to take that word—sensitive. Creative, maybe. I was always kind of interested in being writing, maybe even screenwriting—perhaps growing up near Hollywood made me think that way. But I'll admit I haven't followed through on it." He paused for a moment. "Truth is, I haven't followed through on a bunch of things."

"Why is that?"

"I really don't know."

"You finish college?"

"No, sad to say I didn't."

"You know what you're doing next with your career?"

"What career?" Paul shook his head.

"Well, screenwriting's not a bad ambition. I sure don't know any. Most of my brother's friends are ranch hands; tough, independent cusses. And the local boys I knew growing up here were all fun and games. They laughed and played and were fun to have around, but I never really dated any of them seriously."

"You mean, you didn't have many boyfriends? I find that hard to believe."

"Oh, sure, I went with a guy briefly when I was in high school. And I had a couple of steadies in college at the University of Hawai'i, but no one really serious. Besides, Jorge kept scaring them off. Plus, I guess I was too keen on making sure I got through school with good grades. I always wanted to be a teacher."

The Kālaheo beach road wasn't connected directly to a road to downtown Kailua, so Paul and Healani had to hop over a cattle gate and cut through a farm field. He was impressed by how easily she managed every obstacle; she was such a country girl, he thought.

"How do you like teaching at Kailua School?"

"It's a nice place. I just got my teaching degree last year from the university. Earlier, I went to Kamehameha School for Girls. I was lucky to get hired in my hometown. The principal remembered my father, and I think that helped me get the job."

"Just got to get your foot in the door sometimes."

"Kailua was the first public school run by the territorial government," she said. "We're an English Standard school. Most of the *haole* kids and some of the smart Japanese kids are in the English Standard section. More is expected of them academically, and most go on to high school. The rest of the kids, mostly Hawaiian, Chinese, Filipino, and the other Japanese, are all in the regular grades. Some of them also go on to high school, but many go to work on the farms or plantations like their parents did. Those are the kids I teach."

"Interesting system," Paul said. "I guess I'll meet them when I come to coach basketball on Monday."

"That's right!" she said, perking up. "I almost forgot about that. Coach Sands. Has a great ring to it."

"Hope my knees hold up."

"Your knees? You mentioned that before—what's the problem?"

"Hurt them badly at Columbia—first one, then the other. Got discouraged and ended up leaving school."

"You said that before; why didn't you go back?"

"Can't say for sure. Just couldn't figure out what do with myself. Didn't want school if I couldn't play basketball, didn't like work at the jobs I tried. Wrote a little bit, but nothing panned out. Got discouraged and quit most everything pretty quickly."

"You know what you need, don't you?"

"What's that?"

"You need to believe."

"How's that going to help?" he asked.

"Because if you believe in something, or in someone, or in yourself, good things happen." She smiled and winked at him. He smiled back.

"Maybe I'll start by believing that we're going to have a swell date."

He squeezed her hand and they laughed together as they walked past the Japanese school and community center and into Kailua Town. The pool hall across from the bus station was beginning to fill up.

"By the way, hope you don't mind me asking you so many questions, but how is your search going?" she asked. "Your search about your grandfather, I mean."

"It's okay to ask. Very frustrating, actually. I know very little except what Officer Burns told Mr. G. and me. They think maybe my grandfather went under an assumed name years ago."

"Why maybe?"

"Because I haven't been able to locate any records that help the search. The record-keeping from before Hawai'i became a U.S. territory is pretty sketchy."

"What about Iwalani?"

"All dead-ends so far. Worse yet, no one even seems to want to help. I get a lot of looks and cold reception on the phone that seem to tell me to leave them alone."

"They think you're a *haole*."

"Why should the color of my skin matter?"

"Not a *haole*, a *Haole*," she said, emphasizing the second word. "They think you're an outsider, not one of them. That's your problem."

He looked at her uncertainly. "How can I fix that?"

"By showing humility. And by learning about Hawai'i and its people—and showing your appreciation."

"Funny you should say that. My grandfather left something behind to that affect."

"What was that?"

"Oh, just a textbook about the land and people of Hawai'i. That's where they found whatever it was that was on his lips and fingertips."

"Inside the book?"

"Yes. They sent the residue to the University for analysis. In the meantime, Officer Burns gave me the book to read, and I've read it all, but I'm not sure what I've learned."

Healani stopped for a moment and gave him a look from toe to head. "Okay, schoolboy with a textbook. Let's start with something simple about where we are. You know much of what the names around here mean?" she asked.

"Why is that important?"

"Humor me."

He laughed and said okay. "About all I know is that *Kailua* means 'two waters,'" he said. "Mr. G. told me that. Other than that, not much."

"Well, you're going to learn and maybe it will help. Maybe that's why your grandfather had the book. Listen to your teacher," she said, smiling. "We'll start with this street we're going past now— the one lined with trees. It's Maluniu, a name that roughly means 'coconut,' although that's a very loose translation. If the developer spelled it correctly, it would have been 'Mala-niu' with an *a* instead of a *u* in the spelling. But you get the idea behind it when you look at all the coconut trees around here."

Paul glanced down Maluniu, a lane that was totally covered by tree branches from either direction. It was a picturesque country road, topped with coral but still unpaved.

"Another name from a land developer is where you are living now. *Lanikai* is loosely translated into "heavenly sea." Although Hawaiians might tell you that it should have been spelled *Kai Lani*, not the other way around. In any case, the area wasn't called that until the developer, a Mr. Frazier, changed it in the 1920s. He bought the area from Old Man Castle for a hundred thousand bucks and never finished his original grandiose plans. Castle once told my brother he wished he'd never sold it."

Paul listened intently. He was enjoying the lessons of his new teacher.

"At one point, the developer was going to build canals through the area and a pier for huge yachts that he envisioned sitting just offshore. He imagined grand estates with large pools and tennis courts to bring in the rich and famous people who could afford it. I once saw an old brochure my brother showed me—it said Lanikai would have 'the smartest homes this side of Santa Barbara and Hollywood' and was for 'neighbors of recognized standing.' I've never forgotten that."

They laughed as she pushed her nose towards the air in mocking fashion.

"It's still is quite beautiful, and some of the homes are rather nice, but nothing like they originally advertised. The developer was eventually forced to sell out, and he left the islands pretty much financially ruined."

"I'm listening and learning," Paul said, admiring her grasp of local history. "Tell me more, teacher."

"Well, the area we're walking in right now is called 'Ālele by the old Hawaiians," she continued. "It used be a big playfield, according to the legends. They held Hawaiian games, races, warrior war games, *hula*, and many other proud traditions."

They walked past the center of Kailua Town, past Kailua Tavern, and crossed Oneawa Street, the main street that goes in the perpendicular direction to Kailua Road. "That's *Oh-knee-ah-vuh*," she said. "Some visitors have trouble pronouncing it because it has four syllables—it means 'milkfish sand.' The waters around the street drain into Kawai Nui Swamp, which means appropriately 'big water.' The other big swamp in town, Ka'elepulu, means 'moist blackness.' If you've ever been by there, you know why. Lots of brackish water. But the local Hawaiians like it for fishing. Near Lanikai, the fishermen like to fish off Alāla Point. *Alāla* means 'awakening.'"

"Another fitting name, considering the gorgeous sunrises," Paul said.

"And Kālaheo Avenue, where Jorge and I live, means 'proud day,'" she added.

"Don't know if I'll remember all of this, but I'm soaking it up. I'll admit I didn't learn all this in grandfather's textbook. How about the towns nearby—Kāneʻohe and Waimānalo?"

"Those two names are not quite as attractive," she said, laughing. "Waimānalo means 'potable water,' and Kāneʻohe loosely translates to 'bamboo husband.' It's based on an old Hawaiian legend in which a woman is asked if she has a good husband, or a good man. She answers negatively, saying he is Kāneʻohe, or his cruelty cuts as sharp as a bamboo knife."

"Yikes."

"I don't think anyone will ever call you Kāneʻohe," she said, giggling. She brushed up against Paul, her shoulder touching his. He instinctively kissed her cheek and she blushed slightly.

Finally at their destination, they stopped in front of Kailua Theater to read the movie posters. The first fare on the double bill was *A Slight Case of Murder*, starring Edward G. Robinson. Paul had seen the movie a couple of years previously when he was a student in New York. He told Healani what a big movie fan he was, and she enjoyed his comments about the films they were about to see—the first film was actually a spoof of the popular gangster movies of the 1930s, about a guy who tries to go legit at the end of Prohibition but inadvertently finds himself with four corpses. Pretty funny, he said. The second film was the top-billed movie: *Dr. Jekyll and Mr. Hyde*, starring Ingrid Bergman and Lana Turner and one of Paul's favorite actors, Spencer Tracy, playing both the good *Dr. Jekyll and the evil Mr. Hyde*. Healani grimaced at the poster and held on to Paul tightly.

They bought their tickets and went inside. They bought a bag of popcorn and two cold bottles of Coca-Cola and sat down on the hard wooden seats for the double bill. They laughed out loud during the comedy scenes of the Edward G. Robinson movie. And practically right on cue, Healani grabbed Paul's arm during the scary parts of *Dr. Jekyll and Mr. Hyde*. He kissed her gently on the cheek again, and then she squeezed his arm affectionately.

Outside the theater, the night was still young, and Paul felt the electricity between them. He walked her into a shadowy area and pulled her closer to him.

"I'm going to kiss you here," he whispered. She practically melted in his arms and they exchanged their first kiss, a kiss that lingered for a couple of seconds. She giggled softly and hugged him tightly.

The door to Kailua Tavern was wide open and they could hear the band playing Hawaiian music from well across the street.

"Let's go," she said, and they sprinted across the street to join in the fun. They grabbed a small table in the back of the tavern, still fairly crowded despite the fact that no military personnel were present.

"I haven't seen it look like this since before they opened the base at Kāne'ohe," she said. "Still, it's a sign that not many people around here are scared."

"Should they be?"

"I don't know. I really don't know."

After a couple of Schlitz beers—she sipped hers and he gulped his—they made their way to the dance floor until the band decided to take a break. Back at the table, Kimo, the bartender, stopped by to see how they were doing. He was well acquainted with Healani.

"How you handling all this war talk?" he asked.

"I don't know what to make of it," she said. "I know the military is on full-alert status, but I don't know what that means. What've you heard?"

"I see the servicemen in here all the time," Kimo said. "None of them in here tonight due to the alert, but I know they're pretty worked up. I hear them always talking about the local Japanese population. I just play dumb and let them talk. I've heard them use the term *Fifth Guard*, meaning a so-called civilian backup that could help the Japanese if we ever went to war with them."

"You buy that?" Healani interrupted.

"I don't know what to believe. Hell, I'm part Oriental myself.

Let's face it: The Japanese have probably done more than any other nationality in Hawai'i to hold on to their ancient traditions, they rarely intermarry, they have their children go to Japanese language schools after school, and many have dual citizenship in both the United States and Japan. Knowing all that, I guess you might be able to see why some of the military brass is jumping to conclusions."

"I find that very hard to accept," Healani said. "I've known the Japanese families around Kailua, mostly farmers and merchants, since I was a small-kine kid. They've always been respectful and friendly. We have a Hawaiian phrase for how good they fit in— *kōkua mai*."

"I know. I know," he said, wiping the table. "I'm just telling you what the military guys are saying. You don't have to be a genius to know that the people who live here and the servicemen sent here to protect us come from separate worlds."

Healani nodded. The big bartender left the table, nodding himself.

After a couple more beers and another hour of listening and dancing to music, Paul walked Healani home in the moonlight. He went to kiss her good night on the cheek, but she surprised him by giving him her full lips instead. The passionate kiss lasted for a long while. She smiled again at Paul before letting herself in the house. It was a smile that let him know that they'd be seeing a lot more of each other.

Paul could probably have floated back to Lanikai at that moment, but he started walking, and then he was running. He was so caught up in the moment that he never saw the lights flicker off and on from the second-floor window of Otto Kuehn's large, two-story house in the Kalama tract near Coconut Grove.

Off, then on for a couple of seconds, then off, then on again. The flickering sequence went that way for nearly a minute and then repeated itself several minutes later.

13 - RUMORS OF WAR

JAPANESE MAY STRIKE OVER WEEKEND! was the banner headline in the *Honolulu Advertiser* on Sunday morning, November 30, 1941.

Mr. G. put the newspaper on the kitchen table, and he, Nan, and Paul crowded around to read the stories on page 1 after they arrived home from early morning church services. The report didn't mean an imminent attack upon Hawai'i but suggested that it could possibly occur in Southeast Asia. The smaller headlines read TALKS BETWEEN SECRETARY OF STATE HULL AND JAPANESE ENVOY NEAR COLLAPSE, CONCERN IN SINGAPORE, and ARMY FORCES IN HAWAI'I ON ALERT.

"Sounds like it's almost definite that we're going to war," Mr. G. said, breaking the silence. "I had been hoping that cooler heads would calm this thing, but everything is way too hot right now."

"And our John is right in the middle of it," Nan said. "I wish there was some way we could speak to him."

"I'll see if we can get a long-distance operator," Mr. G. said. "Usually, I wouldn't even consider making an expensive phone call like this, especially after we just talked to him, but maybe he can tell us what's going on in Washington."

Mr. G. went into the living room and got on the phone. Paul helped Nan clean up the breakfast dishes. Mr. G. came back into the kitchen within a few minutes.

"We can't make an overseas call right now," he reported. "The operator says she'll call us later this afternoon and let us know if they can arrange something."

"Guess I'd better be making those blackout curtains after all," Nan said. "We keep talking about these civil defense drills. Best get to being prepared."

"You think it's that serious?" Paul asked.

"We've been having blackout drills and air-raid drills for months. Why, Scotty here is the block warden if anything ever happens."

"'Fraid so, lad," Mr. G. said. He turned towards his wife. "Perhaps Paul and I can run into town and get you some curtains after our golf game."

"Oh, I totally forgot," Paul said. "That's right. I told you I'd caddy for you this weekend. They still playing with all this war talk going on?"

"Lad, they'd have to bomb us direct to get us off the course on a beautiful Sunday morning," he said, smiling. "Besides, this'll give my foursome something to talk about besides how much money I'm going to win from them."

The Mid-Pacific Country Club was practically a stone's throw from the Gillespies' house. Paul carried Scotty's bag for him just a couple of blocks and around the corner to the golf course.

"By the way, lad, we may run into Jack Burns here," Mr. G. said.

"He's here?"

"He's almost always here on Sunday. Right after church."

Three other members of Mr. G.'s regular foursome joined them for the Sunday round of golf: Stan and Bill, two local businessmen, and a guy named Chip from Honolulu. All of the members were *haole*, Mr. G. told Paul; the country club didn't allow nonwhite members, although they did allow nonwhites to play if they were with a member. Mr. G. said he and Burns had been trying to get the policy changed but were unsuccessful.

Paul found the playing partners very affable, and all of them shared their opinions on whether the United States was on the brink of war. Stan and Chip said it was inevitable; Bill said it was all blown out of proportion by the press. The players agreed that they would play only nine holes that day. "No need to go around twice," Bill said. He explained to Paul that Mid-Pacific was a nine-hole course with plans on the drawing board for another nine holes.

"How's the fundraising going on building the next nine?" Stan asked of Mr. G., who did the club's accounting on a volunteer basis after moving to Lanikai years earlier.

"What funds? You know as well as I do that we're floating in red ink here at Mid-Pac. We've got a long way to go before we get those other nine holes developed."

In the group ahead of them, just leaving the first tee, was Burns.

"Not a bad guy for a Democrat," Stan said in a voice just loud enough for Burns to hear them. All four laughed, and Burns gave the foursome a wave and a smile. It was a well-known fact that the territorial legislature, in fact almost all the politics in Hawai'i, was completely dominated by Republicans.

The round was interrupted on a couple of occasions by passing showers. Mr. G. and Stan had brought umbrellas, and they huddled under the partial cover when the showers got heavy.

"Never can tell the weather on the Windward Side once you get to this time of year," Stan said.

The showers moistened the greens, helping the golfers who had good short games. That favored Mr. G. the most. He didn't have much power off the tee, but he could control the little ball better than anyone Paul had ever seen.

On one occasion, on a short par-three, he knocked a high floating drive past the pin about twenty feet, and everyone watched from the tee box as the ball spun backwards to within inches of a hole in one.

"Scotty's still got it," Bill said.

Hole after hole, the other three golfers outdrove Mr. G., but when it came to around the greens, there was nobody better. He saved par from out of the sand; he one-putted from the fringe for a birdie; and on the final hole, he safely tapped in a two-putt for par to edge Chip by a stroke.

"Let's have a quick round of beers," Mr. G. said, as he accepted handshakes from his playing partners.

"Winner buys," Stan said, laughing.

"Always," Mr. G. said. "That's why I'm here, lads. Otherwise, you men would go home thirsty."

Inside the clubhouse, the discussion eventually got serious. War talk, mostly. The foursome joined Burns and his group, and Burns, sipping on a Coca-Cola, updated everyone on what he knew.

"Frankly, I'm worried," he said.

"I'll tell you one thing," Stan interrupted. "All this talk is bad for my real estate business. I've got places for sale all over Kailua and can't get a single offer. It's really sad."

"People are nervous," Mr. G. said. "We had a man from the bank up and leave for the States last month. He had a great job here, but said he was concerned about his family. I don't know if his wife pressured him, but they gathered up all their things, sold their house in Mānoa for a big loss, and sailed away."

"I've heard that story too many times lately," Bill said. Chip and Burns' friends left after one beer, but the rest remained for a couple more rounds. Eventually Paul changed the subject to his own search.

"Sorry I haven't returned your calls, son," Burns apologized. "I've been caught up in other business."

"That's okay. I'm not having a lot of luck."

"I understand. City hall can be a frightening place."

"I'm learning that."

"Tell you what, son. I'm going to send you someplace else. I'll scribble something on a piece of paper, giving you permission." Burns asked the waitress for a couple of sheets of paper. He grabbed a pen from his pocket. "Here, try this," he said.

Paul looked at the paper. It said that Paul Sands was authorized by the Honolulu Police Department to ask questions and get access to the Castle and Cooke archives and personnel records from the 1890s. It was signed by Jack Burns.

"You think that will work? Mr. G. asked.

"It better, or I'll kick some *'ōkole* down there," Burns responded, getting a laugh.

"I'm sorry if I'm stupid, but what is this Castle and Cooke?" Paul asked sheepishly.

"One of the biggest companies around here, son," Bill interjected. "You ever hear of the Big Five?"

"No."

"They pretty much run everything, businesswise," Stan said. "Shipping, banking, transportation, production, money factoring, you name it—they've got it locked up. Castle and Cooke has been around for years."

"If your grandfather was in the shipping business, as you say, then Castle and Cooke might have records of it," Burns said. "I should have thought of them before."

Mr. G. thanked Burns, who got up to leave. "Sorry, gentlemen, duty calls," the officer said. "A policeman's work is never done. Gotta go out and catch the bad guys. Who knows what evil lurks out there, as they say on the radio shows." He smiled. The four golfing friends exchanged handshakes around the table.

Stan and Bill left quickly, but before Paul and Mr. G. could depart, Burns pulled them aside. "You ever see Otto Kuehn much around Lanikai?" he asked.

"I've seen him occasionally, but mostly see him in town," Mr. G. answered. "Why do you ask?"

"Just following through on some recent information. All we know in our workings between the FBI and HPD—I tell you this confidentially—is that Kuehn is a former German naval captain who moved here several years back. He seems to have a healthy pension because what he does in the furniture business seems to bring him very little. And yet he owns a couple of houses. The one you saw on the beach at Lanikai and then another one, a big two-story place a couple of blocks off the beach in the Kalama tract. I can't tell you more than that because, frankly, I don't know more than that."

"I walked by his beach house the other day," Paul added.

"You see him?"

"No, but someone had to be there."

"Why?"

"'Cause there were lots of sheets flapping on the clotheslines."

"That's all you saw?"

"That was it."

Burns made a mental note and added nothing. "May mean something, may not. I'll have to drop by and ask him some questions."

Burns shook Paul's and Mr. G.'s hands. "I guess this meeting of the Committee of Mid-Pacific Golf is officially adjourned," Mr. G. said. Burns laughed and walked out the door. Paul and Mr. G. followed.

When they got home, the sun was shining again and the humidity was up, too. Nan noticed that both Paul and her husband were perspiring profusely.

"Looks like you two boys could use a tall lemonade," she said.

They sat down at the kitchen table with lemonade and freshly baked chocolate chip cookies and told her about the day at Mid-Pac and the brief conversations with Officer Burns.

"It's funny that you were talking about Otto Kuehn," she said.

"I told you his wife Friedel does my hair. She asks more question than any woman I've ever known. What a busybody! "

Mr. G. looked at Paul. "What does she ask about?

"Oh, everything. The weather, businesses, the naval base, the people coming and going. Why, she had one of the navy wives blabbering away for nearly an hour. I don't think I've ever heard so much about the new seaplanes they've been testing. The last time I was there, I finally had enough of it and asked if she could change the subject. I mean, who cares about all that base stuff when you're having your hair done!"

Mr. G. smiled and got up from the table. "I may have to call Burns back," he said. But his march toward the phone was quickly interrupted by an outburst from Nan.

"Oh, and good news," she said. "The long-distance operator called and we should be hearing from John at four o'clock sharp. And she said the government will be paying for the call."

"That's great news," Mr. G. said. He proceeded to the phone and returned within minutes.

"Burns said he would check it out. That's all."

At precisely four o'clock the phone rang. Nan leaped to her feet and ran to the phone. "Hello, hello," she said. "Put him through." Mr. G. and Paul followed quickly and the three of them huddled around the phone.

"Hi, John, how are you?" Nan asked, her voice bounding with excitement. They could all barely make out John's response as she held out the receiver. He was a fine, he said.

"How's your new job working out?" she asked. "It must be hard."

John said his job was going very well. Lots of long hours. Very tense at times.

"That's why we wanted to speak with you, son," she said. "We keep reading and hearing about all this talk of going to war. There's an alert here. We're very concerned."

John said he wished he could alleviate the fears, but negotiations were very delicate. He couldn't give any specifics over the phone except to say that the Washington diplomats were working hard to try to resolve the differences with Japan. He said he wished he could tell them more, but in his position, he couldn't.

"We understand, son," Nan said. "I know we can't stay on the line very long. We just wanted to know that you're safe and to let you know that we love you. Here, say hello to your father."

"I also wanted to say how proud I am of you, John. You're a credit to us all. Please give our regards from Hawai'i to Secretary Knox."

John said he appreciated the kind words and apologized for keeping the call short. He reminded them to get their black curtains ready.

"We'll do that, son. Any final words for Paul here before we let you go?"

"Tell him to leave at least one *wahine* for me," they heard John say. He said he had to hang up and get back to work. "Sorry, stay safe, I love you all," he said. "Stay safe." He repeated it again and then hung up. Nan wiped away a tear from the corner of her eye. Mr. G. put a loving hand on her shoulder.

14 - THE MONEY CLIP

Paul's jaw dropped when he received the Monday morning cablegram from Los Angeles. PAYMENT NEEDED ON WILLIAM SANDS MORTGAGE BY END OF MONTH. ESTATE IN LIMBO DUE TO QUESTIONS. FORECLOSURE PROCEEDINGS MAY BEGIN SOON. NEED CAUSE OF DEATH CLARIFIED. The cable was sent by Sands' attorney from Los Angeles. It was Paul's worst nightmare.

He shared the cablegram with Nan at the Gillespie cottage in Lanikai and called Mr. G. at his office downtown. Mr. G. told him he should go to Castle and Cooke headquarters immediately.

It was now December 1. He knew he had only thirty more days.

The anticipated forty-minute drive from Lanikai into downtown Honolulu took twice as long as usual. Paul's 1931 Nash stalled on the way up the Pali Road, and Paul spent several minutes on the side of the two-lane highway before finally turning his car around and driving up the steep road backwards. By the time he arrived on Fort Street in the heart of Honolulu, he was tired and frustrated and angry.

He was about to storm into Castle and Cooke's offices and demand they assist him, when he remembered Healani's comments.

"They think you're a *Haole*, an outsider" he remembered her saying. He took a deep breath and tried to shove his high-pitched emotions into his pockets. He would do as she said—he would make all his requests with humility.

The offices of Castle and Cooke were in an old brick building a few blocks from Honolulu Harbor. The Asian-looking receptionist smiled at him when he walked in through the double doors. His hat in hand, and with an almost apologetic tone, Paul showed the receptionist the note from Officer Burns. He smiled meekly. Within moments, she had called her office manager, and only minutes after that, Paul was walking down a long hallway toward the company's records department.

"We're only too happy to help the police department," said the office manager, a balding Caucasian man in his fifties. "But I don't have an extra staff person to help you. You'll have to do the search by yourself. I suggest starting over there." He pointed in the direction of a large file cabinet on the far side of the ten-by-ten-foot room.

Paul thanked him and watched as he left the tiny room filled with files from floor to ceiling. The claustrophobic cubicle had no windows or ventilation. The light from the ceiling was dim, at best. But Paul knew he would have to make do.

Beads of perspiration built up on his forehead as he painstakingly started going through the first set of files. Those first files he ran into were from the 1920s. He closed those drawers relatively quickly and moved to files from around the turn of the century. The search was slow and tedious—Castle and Cooke employed thousands of workers in a number of businesses, including Honolulu Shipping Lines, and the payroll sheets from that time period were all handwritten. Before too long, Paul was perspiring heavily. He decided to remove a number of files and find the coolest spot in the tiny room where he could sprawl out on the floor and search each one.

Nan usually enjoyed her shopping trips to town, but this time was different. She took the noon bus from Kailua to Honolulu and got off right in front of Liberty House, the city's number one department store. She had two items on her agenda. First, she must purchase black material for use as blackout curtains. Then, she would hustle down the street to Arakaki Jewelers, where she had dropped off Paul's money clip the week before.

It took all of her best gumption to pass by the sale racks in the ladies' department. Liberty House had a pre-Christmas sale going on and beautiful Christmas aprons were on sale for less than a dollar. Nan tried not to notice. She forged ahead, right to the sewing and fabric section.

The saleslady told her that she was lucky she still had some left over. Most of the black material had been purchased the day before when the alert notice appeared in the newspaper. "I think we're going to have to order more," she said.

Nan bought what little remained—at least enough to cover her living room and kitchen windows. If things were as bad as the newspapers were saying, then Scotty could always paint the bedroom and bathroom windows with black paint, she thought. She had a strong feeling all of this was needed, and she remembered John's warning—stay safe!

Nan thanked the saleslady and marched out the Liberty House doors feeling good that she resisted the temptation of seeing what else was on sale. She opened her purse and gave a couple of pennies to the Salvation Army lady who stood outside the store, and then she walked up the crowded street to the jewelry store.

"Oh, Mrs. Gillespie, good to see you," the middle-aged Japanese man behind the counter said to her when she opened the door. He was a very small man, not much taller than five feet, and he wore thick glasses that made him appear to be squinting.

"Hello, Mr. Arakaki. Were you able to help?" Nan put down her package of material and lay it against the jewelry counter.

"I don't know if I have or not. Let me get it for you." The Japanese jeweler went back behind the curtain that led to his tiny office and returned momentarily. In his tiny hands he carried a small cloth.

He carefully placed the cloth on the glass and slowly pulled the corners of the cloth to reveal the money clip that was wrapped inside.

"What did you find?"

"This is a very rare piece of silver, Mrs. Gillespie. I polished it the best I could," he said.

"And?"

"You were right about the name you said you thought was inscribed. You can probably see it better now." He rotated the cloth so that Nan could read the inscription.

"Iwalani," she said almost breathlessly.

"Yes, that's very clear now."

"I'm glad we've solved that mystery. I'll be able to tell the young man who is visiting us. He'll be able to know that we're on the right track." She smiled.

"I'm glad you're happy, Mrs. Gillespie."

She took out her purse and started to open it to pay him for his services but stopped. "Is there anything more that you can tell me?"

"Perhaps," he said, as he wrapped up the money clip in the cloth and placed it in a small paper bag. "I did a little bit of research because this grade of silver was so rare at that time—probably from the late nineteenth century. Clearly, only a handful of people could afford such a fine piece."

"And what did you find out?"

"Well, near as I can tell, and remember this was during the 1880s or 1890s more than likely, I think the piece is from the royal palace."

He had been traveling for days inside the Japanese submarine that was known only as I-72. The Japanese had a numbering system for their large battle-class submarines and a lettering system for their war plans. He knew what he was doing was all part of what was known only as Plan Z.

The long journey from the tiny coral islands in the southwest Pacific towards Hawai'i made him feel uneasy. He didn't like being cooped up, but he would have to live with discomfort for the time being. Because he was not a regular crew member, he was confined to just about the worst place on the ship. His bunk, which measured less than two feet high and five feet long, had him lying below the torpedoes, and he spent most of his day looking square into the impact cone of the projectile.

With so much time to think, and with the submarine running at periscope depth and with total radio silence, he mulled over how he had gotten to this point in his life. How long had he been paid for this kind of work? More than ten years he figured. He had helped the Japanese intelligence in their invasion of Manchuria. He worked briefly for the Russians, too—a fact he considered ironic since it was the native Russians who forced him and his mixed-ethnicity mother to leave his large home island of Sakhalin, located between northern Japan and mother Russia. They didn't know what to do with him— no one ever did. He was the product of a brief liaison between his Russian-Chinese-Korean mother and a Japanese soldier during the Russo-Japanese war. His father was killed in battle on the island, and his mother was forced to move him from town to town until they were banished to northern Manchuria, where his mother died. He quickly learned to live day to day, on the road and on the run, caring for no one.

Like the torpedo hanging above him, he developed a strong, steely exterior, always ready to explode underneath. He had managed to survive in a world that had gone mad with pride and power. He understood this feeling. He imagined how proud his soldier father might have been of him now. He felt the power of what he was about to do for the country he never had. This mission would solidify the respect he so desperately deserved. He began to go over the meticulous plan again in his mind.

His small fishing boat was tightly and safely tethered to the top outer hull of the submarine, as similar to the treatment of the mini-submarines that he knew were also involved in the impending attack on Hawaii. He and his boat would be unleashed from the larger submarine late on December 5, and then after "fishing" well off shore, he would come ashore on Windward Oʻahu late at night on Saturday, December 6, or the early morning of December 7. He would find immediate shelter on the property of the German Kuehn, who he was told would stash extra clothing for him in a closet area of the carport. If the German were somehow not available or had not followed through, he knew the layout of the town from maps and photos he had acquired. He was confident that he could easily blend in with the local Asian-looking citizenry, and, if necessary, he would sleep in one of the town's buildings, perhaps the local movie theater.

It would take at least two days, perhaps three, after Sunday's attack to assess the situation. He had no doubt that his appearance and manner would fool both the local soldiers and the citizens on the island. He had no idea how the planned Japanese attack would go, but he was hopeful that it would create chaos all over Oʻahu.

If so, and if he saw what he expected to see, he would cleverly sneak away from the town, away from where the military would be patrolling or stationed, and along the back trails through the Kawai Nui Swamp, past the twisted hills of Maunawili, and up the steep incline of the Koʻolau. He must not lose sight of his ultimate goal.

He focused again on the torpedo hanging precariously above his head. He had less than five more days of this living hell.

15 - AUNTIE ROSE

Paul spent nearly seven hours in the hot and tiny office cubicle meticulously pouring through old files. He found no William Sands, no William Sanderson, no William Sanderston, or anything remotely close to that. He had found the name Sandstrom in a couple of locations; however, the man's name was Joseph and the entries came from the early 1900s. Near the end of the day, he had few clues until he found something very intriguing next to an incomplete name in the 1893 and 1894 payroll records.

All of the payroll records for that time period were handwritten, and many names were listed simply by initials or by first or last names. Often, there was other information entered adjacent to those names. A listing for an A. Chun, for example, might be followed by five other Chuns and the entry next to the first name might say PAY UNCLE. Paul assumed that meant that the uncle received all the pay for his relatives and doled out the money from there. Other handwritten entries ranged from DISMISSED to TRANSFERRED to SENT HOME to MARRIED.

In the 1893 and 1894 records, Paul found a "William S." listed several times, meaning that he had worked for the company in some capacity for over a year. But the last entry for this mysterious "William S." was worth investigating. Next to his name on the last payroll in which he was listed was the word INCARCERATED.

Paul noted the date of the entry and was cleaning up what little mess he had created, when the office manager showed up at the door. "It's closing time, Mr. Sands. You'll have to leave now."

"I didn't realize I'd been here so long. Thank you very much for your assistance."

"I hope you found what you were looking for. Those old records are not always in the best of order."

"I may have found something," Paul said, putting on his hat as he left the room. He shook the office manager's hand. "We'll see what it leads to, if anything."

It was nearing dusk by the time he left Castle and Cooke, and he walked quickly to the Bethel Street police headquarters but was disappointed to find that Officer Burns was not in. He left a message with the desk sergeant, who said Burns would call him when he had a chance, but that Paul should be patient.

Later that evening in Lanikai, Nan told Paul and Mr. G. about the information she had acquired at the downtown jeweler. She gave the money clip back to Paul. Mr. G. explained the significance of the reference to the royal palace and the time period of the early 1890s. "Hawaii was a kingdom until 1893. That's when a group of local businessmen seized power from the queen and took over operations of the government. Hawaii became an independent republic for a few years before eventually earning the status of United States territory that it enjoys today."

Paul was intrigued by the brief history lesson, but wanted to know the significance as it related to his grandfather's money clip. Both Mr. G. and Nan agreed that Jack Burns was the logical next person to ask.

Burns had other issues. A murder investigation in Chinatown was going nowhere. He spent most of the night going from bar to bar along Honolulu's Hotel Street before finally giving up. As it was well after midnight, he decided not to drive home to Kailua that night. He found an old couch at police headquarters, curled up, and slept until dawn.

The next morning and afternoon were filled with meetings in his other capacity as the HPD liaison to the FBI. He wasn't always a fan of how the feds operated, but he knew his position was too important to criticize their heavy-handed methods. Besides, he'd seen such tactics himself at the Bethel Street police headquarters—it wasn't uncommon for a relatively clean-looking suspect to be booked for suspicion of a crime on one floor and then by the time he got out of the elevator with two policemen on the next floor to be totally disheveled. Yes, he knew the routine. That's how "information" was obtained. Burns didn't like the practice. He depended on hours of traditional legwork to get his information—whether it dealt with homicide or espionage.

"I know we've gone over this before. But let me reiterate— Washington wants a listing of every Japanese church; every Japanese language school; every person who is even remotely suspicious with ties to Japan, or Germany, or Italy—the three countries forming the Axis alliance," said Robert Shivers, the square-jawed, pipe-smoking director of the local FBI office. "Washington is very concerned about sabotage should any hostilities break out, and that looks like a good possibility."

"Where?" Burns asked.

"I have no idea. That information doesn't get to my desk. And I'm not sure anyone else knows either—that's the million-dollar question."

The meeting went on for hours with Shivers, his agents, and Burns exchanging lists and whatever little information they had. Burns had added the name of Otto Kuehn of Kailua to his own list and passed it over to FBI agents to follow through.

By the time the meeting ended, Burns went right into his homicide duties, once again combing the backstreets near Nuʻuanu and Hotel Streets. He was always amazed at how easily criminals could disappear in the dingy underworld of Honolulu. Once again, he came back empty-handed to the office late at night. Frustrated, he furiously smoked several cigarettes in succession while finishing his police reports for the day.

Once the reports were accomplished, he sifted through the growing paperwork on his desk and found the note from Paul Sands. The reference to a "William S—incarcerated" raised his curiosity. He left a note instructing the office clerk to go through the 1893 and 1894 police files and find anything about any name close to that and forward any information to him as soon as possible. This time the late-night drive over the Pali was just the tonic he needed to clear his head. He grabbed his hat, smoked another cigarette, and headed to his car for the midnight drive to Kailua.

Two days later, Mr. G. announced that the military's full alert had been called off. "Guess it was a false alarm," he said, heading out the door to a full day of work. Paul scoured the morning paper and was about to continue his search of Honolulu records, when he received an early morning phone call. Burns had left a message with the desk sergeant to call him. The desk sergeant told Paul to contact a Hawaiian woman in Nuʻuanu. Her name was Rose Kamakawiwoʻole Alston.

"Her name, at least her maiden name anyway, appeared in the bail records of a Mr. William Sanderston in 1893."

"Thanks," Paul said, excitedly. "Anything else?"

"Yeah, Burns said don't expect much. Said she can act pretty strangely."

"At least it's something." Paul hung up the phone and, gripping the Nuʻuanu address, drove as quickly as possible over the Pali. He was ecstatic that his old Nash didn't stall on the way over the Koʻolau. He thought it was a good omen.

A little more than a half hour later, he stood at the doorstep of a lush and lovely Nuʻuanu home.

The Japanese houseboy attempted to scuttle his visit, saying Auntie Rose was not accepting visitors. But she came to the door herself and quickly sent the houseboy scurrying off to his other duties.

"Come in, young man," she said with a lilting quality to her voice. She wore a bright yellow *muʻumuʻu* that fell all the way to the floor. Her smile was nearly as bright as her gown. Paul was quickly mesmerized.

"When I saw you standing in the door a few minutes ago, I was taken aback by your appearance," she said, speaking quickly. She immediately took Paul's hand and pulled him into her dayroom. She had him sit on a small love seat, while she took her place on the daybed. She talked away excitedly the entire time. "This may sound silly, but you look so much like my dear departed husband. I mean when he was younger. He was such a good-looking man. Many of us Hawaiian ladies fell for the handsome *haole* men, and I guess I was one of them."

She smiled and looked skyward for a moment. It was a rich, beautiful smile. Paul sat quietly and listened.

"Joseph passed on about five years ago. He was a very important businessman in Honolulu," she said. "I am Mrs. Rose Kamakawiwoʻole Alston. But people have called me Auntie Rose for years. I never had any children, or *keiki*, of my own. Unfortunately, I couldn't. But I've helped raise many, many *keiki*. And they all loved to come here over the years."

"Will you call me Auntie Rose?"

"Yes, I'm honored to do so. Thanks for seeing me, Auntie Rose," Paul said, smiling.

She got up from her daybed and walked towards the small fish-pond in the entryway. Dozens of colorful fish darted this way and that as she kneeled to put her fingers in the water.

"This pond has had so many tiny fingers splashing in it," she said. "Sometimes, I've wondered how the fish could survive. But they did. I guess it's the Hawaiian in them."

Paul gave her a quizzical glance. He wasn't sure at all what she meant. He agreed with Burns' assessment—she was indeed a strange woman, but in a very nice sort of way.

"I can tell you are puzzled by that," she said. "What I mean is that Hawaiians believe that life begins with the sea. All life. That's why the oceans are so special to us. And everything in them. The fish. The plantlife. The sand. The coral. Even the rain that pours from the heavens to refresh and replenish."

She paused again. "And what did you say your name was, young man?"

"I'm not sure I've told you," Paul laughed. "I'm Paul Sands and I'm living with friends in the Kailua area for the moment."

"Oh, I love Kailua," she interrupted. She was almost giddy with excitement. "I go there all the time—always have. I grew up the daughter of ali'i, the royal class. I'm seventy-one years old now, and I've seen so much change in Hawaii over the past seven decades. Some good. Some bad. When I was young, I was lucky enough to spend time with the queen."

"The queen?"

"Yes, Queen Lili'uokalani. She was a magnificent woman, very talented in so many ways. I told you I had memories of Kailua. I remember days when we used to go on horseback over the Pali. She had a summer residence there, in Maunawili. The Queen's Bath was there. It was a special place, so cool, so serene."

Paul leaned forward to the edge of the sofa. He found himself enchanted by her every word.

"On one very special day, our party was on a horseback ride. I was just a little girl, not even ten years old, but we were going to the Maunawili ranch of a man named Edwin Boyd. Another young Hawaiian girl met us at the gate to the ranch, and the queen was so touched when the girl gave us a *lei*. It touched her so deeply that she later wrote a song based on that memory. I know you've heard the song many times—'Aloha 'Oe.'"

"Why, yes. I heard the band playing it when I traveled here on the *Lurline*," Paul said. "It's quite beautiful."

"You think it's beautiful the way you hear it. But I hear it in my mind. I can see the words in my mind—and the images they represent." Auntie Rose closed her eyes; Paul sat spellbound.

Then she began:

Ha'aheo ka ua i na pali
Ke Nihi a 'ela i ka nahele
E uhai ana paha i ka liko
Pua 'ahihi lehua o uka

She spoke the first few lines in Hawaiian. Each word seemed charmed and enchanted as it flowed naturally off her tongue. And then she stood up and started to sing, most of it in Hawaiian, but some verses in English.

Aloha 'oe, aloha 'oe
E ke onaona noho i ka lipo
One fond embrace
A ho'i a'e au
Until we meet again

'O ka hali'a aloha i hiki mai
Ke hone a'e nei i
Ku'u manawa
'O 'oe no ka'u ipo aloha
A loko e hana nei

Maopopo ku'u 'iki i ka nani
Na pua rose o Maunawili
I laila hia'ia na manu
Miki'ala i ka nani o ka lipo

Paul applauded for her when she was finished. Chills ran down his spine. "What do the lyrics mean, Auntie Rose?"

She smiled when he spoke her name. "It's a lovely story, really. The queen wanted everyone to know that the people of Hawai'i meant so much to her. The people bring sweet memories. Loosely translated, it says 'For the true love shall never depart, I have seen and watched the loveliness, thou sweet rose of Maunawili. So, farewell to thee, until we meet again.'"

"I'm deeply honored that you've told me this."

"There's so much history in Kailua," she said. "I have been there many times since then, but I remember a night almost forty years later when my husband and I went to a weekend gathering to celebrate the opening of Palikū."

"Yes, the big Castle mansion; I've seen it from the Pali Road."

"My husband was a business associate of Mr. Castle's. They were good friends. It's ironic that Kāne'ohe Ranch became so profitable, because when Harold Castle's father, James B. Castle, first bought land on the Windward Side many years ago, many said it was not very smart. The land was hilly and almost inaccessible, but he had a dream, and Harold helped him realize that dream. Harold went to Harvard and then made smart business decisions. In the late 1920s he built his dream mansion high above Maunawili. My husband and I were honored to be there to see the fabulous property when he first moved in."

"What was it like?"

"Peaceful and serene. All Spanish-style architecture with a hacienda-like feel to it. I also remember the fireplace in a large living room with large, floor-to-ceiling windows. There was a panoramic view of the entire Windward Side from the *lānai*. It was quite a remarkable place. Oh, the parties they had there."

"I can only imagine."

"But it was also a place of unique happenings," she said. "Unexplainable, really."

"How so?"

"I think the mountains come alive at times and exhort their desires."

Paul wondered again if this was an example of her strangeness but said nothing. Her serious demeanor assured him that she meant what she was saying.

"One night when I was there, I was standing outside in the courtyard blissfully viewing the majesty of the Koʻolau all around me, when I felt someone come up from behind and tap me on the shoulder. But when I turned around, no one was there. I thought it was curious, but I mentioned it to the caretaker of the estate, and he said it happened all the time. He said he had not only been tapped on the back, but he'd actually been hit in the back of the head. By whom, or by what, he had no idea."

Paul's eyes widened. Auntie Rose continued her story.

"The strangest occurrence of them all, the caretaker told me, was a young boy who was fast asleep in one of the guest rooms. When his mother went in to check on him, she found him levitated above his bed, still in a sleeping position. She ran out of the room in hysterics, and the caretaker was summoned. Together, he and the boy's father brought the boy down to his bed. No one had an explanation for any of it. I'm told these kinds of things would happen there all the time."

Paul shuddered.

"Do you believe it's true?" she asked.

"I . . . don't know," Paul stuttered.

"Believe it, young man," she said, "Sometimes, you have to believe."

Auntie Rose ambled towards the dining area. "Would you like some tea?" she asked. Paul said yes, and she called to her houseboy to bring tea. He came out within minutes with two small cups and saucers. She took her time, slowly pouring the hot water into the cups, then gingerly dipping the tea bags.

She obviously had all the time in the world, Paul thought, but he still hadn't asked her about the news he had received from police headquarters earlier that morning. He started to tell her, but she was entranced in her own world. She kept her stories coming.

She told Paul of the ancient Hawaiians and how they arrived on the islands more than a thousand years before. She told him how the volcanoes were still active then, even on Oʻahu— at Diamond Head and Punchbowl Crater, and in Kailua at the Ulupaʻu Crater on the Mōkapu Peninsula.

"The Hawaiians had this great love of the sea, and their warriors protected themselves by watching the seas," she said. "On Mōkapu, on the shore cliffs below Ulupaʻu, warriors held watch there, looking out over Kailua Bay. They guarded the thousands of natives who worked the land that was watered by springs and streams. When the waters flowed, taro was cultivated in abundance."

Paul listened intently; her lilting voice was mesmerizing.

"Ironically, that is where the great Kamehameha came to unify all our islands," she said while taking a sip of her tea. "His ships landed along the Windward Side in preparation for his attack on Oʻahu. After landing between what is now Lanikai and Waimānalo, he gathered his troops in Kailua. He built his palace there, and that is where he and his chiefs organized the assault on their enemies. But it wasn't easy. First, there was a problem about feeding his many warriors. The land was suddenly scarce of taro, the plant needed to make *poi*."

Paul leaned forward, engrossed in every word.

"That was the sustenance of the warriors," she continued. "But they suddenly had none. But in their scavenging around the inland waters of Kailua, legend says they came upon a type of mud that was edible. The edible mud was nearly like *poi* itself. Kamehameha sent a few of his warriors to the secret place to gather what was called *lepo ʻae ʻae*. They used *pōhaku* stones to glean the edible mud from the waters. It was the sustenance provided by the *lepo ʻae ʻae* that lifted his warriors' spirits and gave them the energy to fight the great battle that lay ahead." `She paused for a moment. Paul could only imagine the sight of thousands of Hawaiian warriors gathering for war.

"Then Kamehameha sailed his fleet around the island at Makapu'u Point and attacked his enemies near Diamond Head. He was a very smart man and a great leader in battle. He used his cannon wisely and quickly turned the battle into a rout. His warriors chased the fleeing enemy up the Nu'uanu Valley where the Pali Road is now. Then, at the cliffs, his men drove hundreds of enemy warriors over the side and into the abyss. This battle proved to be his ultimate victory. Within a few weeks, he had unified almost the entire island chain under his leadership."

"Amazing," was all Paul could say.

"Ironically, it wasn't until a hundred years later that the actual numbers were known. That is, the number of warriors that were pushed over the Pali to their death," she said.

"How's that?"

"In 1898, work was begun on building a wider roadway down the Pali. Prior to that, it had been first a dangerous footpath, then a path with an iron railing, making it a more accessible route. Then, it was widened for horses and carts, and eventually a narrow roadway was carved out of the cliffs. It was in the 1898 construction that workmen found the skulls of eight hundred warriors from the battle a century earlier."

"Eight hundred!" Paul repeated slowly.

"The irony of that find is the fact that the same year, our former kingdom was declared a territory of the United States. The overthrow of the queen had happened five years previously."

"I'm glad you brought that up," Paul interrupted. He set down his cup and saucer. Auntie Rose finally allowed him to speak.

"It was around this time, the 1890s, that my grandfather was here. That's the reason I'm here to see you today."

Auntie Rose set down her cup of tea and folded her hands back to her lap.

"I'm all ears," she said.

Paul told her what he knew at that point, about his grandfather possibly working for Castle and Cooke during that time period, about how he was taken off the payroll sometime in 1894 with the word *incarcerated* penned next to his name. Paul told her about how his grandfather went back to California and rarely spoke about his time in Hawai'i. It was all very secretive, very mysterious, until his recent death.

"And what was your grandfather's name?" she asked.

"William Sands," Paul said.

She stood up quickly.

"William? Sands?"

"Yes, William Sands. But perhaps you've heard of him with another name. Sanderston, maybe?

She walked quickly out of the room and then she turned back.

"I think I know this name," she said. "You go now. You come back again tomorrow evening and we'll talk again."

She walked back towards Paul, opening her arms wide and gave him a hug. Then she leaned forward and kissed the air behind both of his ears. "You go now," she repeated.

Paul tried to ask her another question, but she had already motioned to her houseboy to open the door and let him out.

"You go now. Now!"

16 - FRIDAY, THE FIFTH

For the past few days that week, Paul had also lived up to his promise to Healani. After school and after following up any of his investigatory leads, he coached the youngsters in basketball at Kailua School. And despite his badly injured knees, which had led him to quit the team and then the school at Columbia, he was enjoying himself. His knees actually felt pretty good—he was much stronger than he expected. And with all the pressure he felt otherwise, he found that coaching kept him from going nuts. He needed a few hours each day to unwind from his pursuit of the mystery surrounding his grandfather's death.

His Kailua boys helped create the perfect diversion.

After school each day, he came by Healani's classroom and had his new team members gather outside. It was quite an ethnic mixture. There were two *haole* boys; Zach was tall and slender, William short and stocky. There were two Chinese brothers, Walter and Spencer, both of whom were very athletic. Keoki was a tall Hawaiian boy with strong shoulders. Paul immediately made him his center. Joseph was a tough Portuguese boy who also had a little size and feistiness to him. And they were all joined by four Japanese boys—Koy, Shigge, Yuya, and Hiro. The aptly named Hiro, whose name was pronounced "hero," was the little fellow who had so impressed Paul with his ball-handling skills the week before. He was the team's instant star and also happened to be the son of Kenji, the yardman.

The Kailua boys practiced next door, in the tiny gym of the Japanese Community Center. The little gym was poorly lit, and the basketball court was smaller than regulation size, but it was fine for what Paul had in mind. One by one, through the drills he ran, he began to learn about their work ethic and their personalities. Walter and Spencer, the two Chinese brothers, had stamina like none of the others. They developed it by running to school each morning all the way from the banana fields in Maunawili, a round-trip distance of more than five miles. Joseph, the Portuguese boy, lived practically across the street, but he was extremely competitive, easily the squad's best defensive player. He was also the team's energizer. He yelled and hollered and kept the other boys working hard. Zach, the tall *haole* boy, was still growing, and that made him slightly clumsy. But he made up for it by being very coachable. He was eager to please, and his eagerness quickly paid dividends. William, the stocky *haole*, was a tough little rebounder. Those five made up one of Paul's five-man units.

As for the Japanese boys, they worked together extremely well. He decided he would play them together as the other unit, with Hiro as the main ball handler and Keoki, the tall Hawaiian boy in their group, as the center. Shigge and Koy were outstanding passers, and Yuya could fling it into the basket from well outside the key. But the glue that held them all together was Hiro, the pint-sized point guard who could both lead a fastbreak and finish it. Shigge, Koy, and Yuya all came from the small farms near Kalāheo hillside. They were used to working hard and it showed. Hiro lived in Lanikai.

Paul didn't believe in long practices because he wanted his team to enjoy themselves while learning. He took advantage of their early enthusiasm, worked them hard, and then let them go. After each practice, he led them in a quick cheer and then sent them out of the gym until the next time.

Healani was impressed.

"You're a natural with them."

"I'm surprised how quickly they're coming along."

She smiled and came up to him and kissed him lightly. He grabbed her close to him and kissed her much harder. She giggled softly when their lips parted.

"Will you go with me to see Auntie Rose?" he asked. They had talked on the phone about the possibility the night before.

"I'm dying of curiosity just like you are. Let me get my things and we'll go."

By the time they reached Nuʻuanu, the sun was beginning to set on the Honolulu side of the island. Auntie Rose was waiting on her doorstep when Paul and Healani drove up to her home. Quick introductions were made, and Auntie Rose smiled and held Healani's hand as they all walked into her house.

Paul noticed immediately that there was a difference inside. The last time he had been there, the house was fastidiously tidy. Not a chair or a book or anything was out of place. This time, the living room was covered with papers and photographs. They were laid out all over the tables and the chairs, even the sofa. There wasn't a place to sit down anywhere.

"I've done a great deal of thinking about you and your grandfather," Auntie Rose said. "I knew that I knew this name. It took a while, but I have found it."

"That's terrific," Paul said, clasping his hands together in excitement. "I don't know how I can thank you." Healani smiled and put her arms on his shoulder.

"Oh, I don't know if you'll be thanking me when I'm done, but if you want me to tell you what I've found, then I will." She motioned Paul and Healani over to one of the corners of the room where she had a stack of old photographs.

"These are pictures of old Hawaiian nobility. You can see King Kalākaua there and his sister, Lili'uokalani. This was taken right before he died. Theirs was a tumultuous relationship. He appreciated her for her talents, especially her music. She didn't appreciate his political waverings, especially when he agreed to a new constitution. That constitution took away voting rights from most Hawaiians and all Orientals. It put all the power in the hands of a few *haole* property owners."

"I know the history," Healani said. "When she came to power, Queen Lili'uokalani attempted to put more power back in the hands of the Hawaiians and the monarchy."

"You're lucky to have her," Auntie Rose said of Healani. "Keep her close by your side, son." Paul gave Healani a quick kiss on the cheek, and she softly caressed his shoulders.

Auntie Rose, neatly attired in a long-sleeved, pale blue *mu'umu'u*, moved the photographs, giving Healani and Paul a chance to sit down at her dining room table to look at them closer. They both sat down in front of a table full of old papers, mostly yellowed and dog-eared.

"These papers tell the story of what happened next," she said. "The power struggle between the businessmen and the new queen escalated and escalated—eventually reaching new heights. The legislature got involved and so did her cabinet. On several occasions, her cabinet was dissolved, especially when she tried to have a new constitution written. It all came to a head in 1893. In January of that year, a group of well-connected businessmen calling themselves the Committee of Safety got help from an American warship, as well as the United States minister here, and they marched on to the grounds at 'Iolani Palace."

She paused to allow Paul and Healani to look over the papers.

"A large crowd of Hawaiians gathered around the palace to see what the queen would do. I know, I was there," she continued. "She was helpless against this show of force, even though she had a royal guard surrounding her. Luckily, no blood was spilled on that sad day, but power was taken from the queen after several tense hours. The queen surrendered to the Committee of Safety at sunset, saying she was doing so because of . . . Healani, you read what it says."

Healani carefully picked up the old news clipping so as not to tear it and read the words as printed: "Let me see; it says here that the queen capitulated to 'a superior force of the United States of America, whose minister plenipotentiary, His Excellency John L. Stevens, has caused United States troops to be landed at Honolulu and declared that he would support the said provisional government.'"

Auntie Rose looked at Paul. At first, he was tongue-tied, but he finally responded. "What does this all have to do with my grandfather?"

"I just wanted you to know a little about the tumultuous times when your grandfather was here," she said. "The businessmen took over the government and eventually declared a republic. Their immediate goal was to gain recognition from the United States and have Hawai'i declared a territory. But while the recognition came quickly, the territory status would have to wait five more years."

"And my grandfather, where does he come in?"

"Come over here, son, over by the couch," she directed Paul. Healani followed. "I have a couple of other photographs to show you." She took him by the hand and led him to the other side of the room. When they got to the couch, she gingerly picked up the corners of a small photograph.

"What do you see?" The photo was considerably scratched up and very old.

"It appears to be the picture of a young woman, a young Hawaiian woman," he said. "At least, I assume she's Hawaiian. The photograph isn't in very good condition."

"Here's another one of the same woman several years later,"

Auntie Rose said. "I think you can see her better in this one."

She held up another small photograph that revealed the same woman, several years older, with two children at her side, one dark-skinned and the other much lighter.

"She's definitely Hawaiian," Healani said. "This second photograph is much better, but who are these people?"

She set the second photograph on the edge of the couch, then pushed some papers aside to give all of them more room to sit down. She took a deep breath, and both Paul and Healani kept their eyes transfixed on her.

"I first met your grandfather more than a year after the queen's unfortunate overthrow," she said. Healani gasped out loud and grabbed Paul's hand tightly. "Yes, I knew him. Your grandfather worked down by the docks, right?"

"That's right, for the Honolulu Shipping Lines," Paul reminded her.

"In those days, everyone came to Hotel Street in downtown Honolulu after work. It was there that people of all walks of life gathered. And it was where your grandfather met a lovely part-Hawaiian girl named Iwalani."

"Oh my god," Paul said. He stood up quickly and reached for his pocket. He pulled out the old photograph that had been found with his grandfather and showed it to Auntie Rose. "Is this her?"

"Yes. She was my good friend, a very good friend. Where did you get this photograph?"

"It was my grandfather's," Paul said, his voice practically trembling. Auntie Rose took the photo from him and read the inscription on the back—*All my love forever, Lani.* She smiled and held it against her heart.

"That's so much like her to say that." She handed the photograph back to Paul.

"And these are photos are of her, too?" Paul asked.

"Yes, that's her. The first photograph was taken sometime

before she met your grandfather; the second was taken several years later."

"And where is she now? Can I meet her?"

"No, I'm sorry to say she passed on many years ago. She died nearly thirty years ago. Sad when people you love go before their time."

"Tell me, how did she die?"

"She was very sad, and her sadness overwhelmed her. She was not a strong woman, and she laid down one day and passed in her sleep."

Paul and Healani said nothing for a moment. They just studied the photographs. Paul was thankful that part of his mystery was solved, but he also knew that this information still couldn't help him solve the mystery surrounding his grandfather's sudden death. He needed more information. He showed Auntie Rose the money clip. She smiled and said she recognized it. It had disappeared under mysterious circumstances from Iwalani's bedroom. Now, she said, she understood where it went.

"So tell us more of my grandfather and Iwalani. What else do you know?"

"I know they saw each other frequently. It was difficult, at times very difficult. She was part of the extended royal family, and he was just a working man. I met him the first time when she came to me for help. She wanted to arrange a meeting but couldn't sneak away from her home anymore. I helped them get together near the China-town markets. Their meetings were brief but intensely passionate. Later I saw them together walking on a side street one evening near the palace grounds. They were always so passionate together, but that night they appeared to be arguing. That was right before it happened."

"What happened?" Paul asked.

"Well, as I told you before, the political situation in Honolulu was very unstable," she said. "Several people were still loyal to the queen. A small group stashed guns in the queen's flower gardens and in other buildings around town. I'm sure the queen didn't know what was going on because the efforts of these so-called royalists weren't very well planned. The new government in power heard about the gun hoarding, and they were able to capture the guns rather easily and quickly, along with a few of the men involved."

"You still haven't gotten my grandfather into all this. How was he involved?" Paul said.

"Bare with me," she said. "First off, this was several months after the overthrow. Once again, the government police got wind of guns being stockpiled and another potential conspiracy, this time near Waikīkī. And this time, the conspiracy was better planned, with royalists hiding on the slopes of Diamond Head and up in the valleys around Honolulu. It took several companies of regulars and volunteers to roust the royalists out of their hiding places, but eventually the potential uprising was quashed. Many men were arrested, including as it happens, your grandfather."

"He was part of the conspiracy?" Paul asked.

"I can't say for sure because I don't know," she said. "But the men who supported the new republic were out for blood. All of the men arrested in the uprising were convicted, and some were sentenced to death. None of those death sentences were carried out, but I do know that most of the *haole* men who were arrested and convicted were forced to leave the islands. Your grandfather was held in jail for a few months but was eventually released along with the other men."

"And what happened to Iwalani during this time?" Paul asked.

"All of us close to the royal family stayed in seclusion, as the queen was confined to her home, unable to leave," she said. "Few of us in our own homes said anything to anyone for fear that we might be implicated. Iwalani came to me one night, quite distressed, wanting to see your grandfather one more time. But he had just been released from jail, and I found that he sailed on the first ship out of the harbor that morning. They never saw each other again."

"That's it?" Paul stammered. "They never saw each other again?"

"Never."

"What a sad story," Healani said.

"And there's nothing more?"

"Nothing. That's all I can tell you. But perhaps it will help you." Auntie Rose got up from the couch and went over to the dining room table to tidy up the mess she had created. Paul and Healani spent a few brief moments staring at the scratchy old photo of the young *wahine* and the more recent photo of Iwalani and her two children.

"She was so pretty," Healani said, holding Paul's hand tightly. "How sad."

"You two should go now," Auntie Rose said as she came up from behind the young couple. Healani turned and gave her a big hug. The large Hawaiian woman returned the favor and gave Paul a kiss on the cheek as she ushered them out the door.

Healani sat very close to Paul on the ride home. They talked about young lovers and wondered out loud why Paul's grandfather would turn against his own employers. And they wondered why William Sands, if that was the name he actually went by at the time, would refuse to see his young love before he sailed away. And there was still the question of the circumstances of his untimely death. There were obviously many questions still unanswered. The puzzle had been unlocked, but the pieces still didn't all fit.

By the time they reached Kailua, it was nightfall, and neither Paul nor Healani were tired. They strolled along the beach until they happened upon Kenji and his son Hiro in the shallow waters where Ka'elepulu Stream spilled into Kailua Bay.

"I see you meet pretty girl," Kenji said. "Does she wear the plumeria for you?"

Healani squeezed tightly against Paul, who towered over the

Japanese yardman. Young Hiro acted as if he noticed no one. Paul had already noted that the young boy never said anything. Never.

"I hope she's wearing it for me." He smiled and squeezed her hand.

"Come, you two, join us for late-night fishing."

"Here? Now?"

"Yes. Here and now. Best time. I show you secrets."

Paul looked at Healani. Why not? she shrugged. The two carefully stepped into Kenji's small boat, just ahead of little Hiro, who continued not to utter a sound. Kenji followed.

"Aren't we going to bring some fishing poles?" Healani asked.

"I told you I show you secrets. Be still."

So without a fishing pole and just a bucket and a lamp, the four headed out into the blackness of Ka'elepulu Pond.

Kenji took them into the deep, dark alcoves of the pond, in places where "only the old Hawaiians knew," he said. When Paul dipped his hand into the black water, Kenji warned him, "Watch out for eels. If they bite at you, it feels like car door slamming on hand." Paul and Healani didn't know if he was kidding or not, but they kept their hands in the boat after that.

The small skiff navigated through the still waters with the help of the battery-powered lamp. That lamp was one of Kenji's secrets. "It's more than just to find our way," he said. Hiro's eyes got really big when his father said that. Paul and Healani smiled, and Hiro rubbed his hands together, as if anticipating impending excitement, but he said nothing.

In the blackness of the night, with just the small lamp creating a beacon of light near the boat, they found out why. Every few minutes, the mullet would jump at it. Paul and Healani couldn't believe their eyes as the fish would jump right out of the water, as if they were trying to reach out and touch the light.

Kenji would wait for them to jump and swing his hand out to bat them down into the boat. He missed more than he hit, but he still hit several. When he knocked one down inside the boat, Hiro would scoop it up and place it quickly in the large bucket that was their only other tool. Within an hour, both Paul and Healani were enthusiastically a part of the process. Soon, they had a bucket full of the fattest mullet they'd ever seen, all of them captured without the aid of one single fishing pole.

If they hadn't been there and seen it with their own eyes and caught the mullet with their own hands, they probably would have believed it was somebody's wild fish tale. Kenji made them true believers.

Kenji gave them a bag with half of the catch when they were done. Paul and Healani raced along the beach of Kailua Bay to her home to put the fish on ice. They stopped more than a few times to laugh and kiss.

Deep in the darkness and miles out to sea, another fishing expedition was about to get underway. A tiny fishing boat that had traveled tethered to a Japanese submarine for more than a thousand miles was launched into the night waters well north of Oʻahu. The fishing boat had only one man aboard. And that man, with his eyes piercing fiercely into the darkness, had his own fishing secrets. He, too, was a true believer—in his own cause.

17 - A PERFECT SATURDAY

On Saturday morning, December 6, at the behest of Mr. G. and Nan, Paul wrote a formal letter to the Honolulu city coroner asking for an appeal of the official ruling on the death certificate of William Sands. He knew he had no hard evidence, but he felt the information he had was compelling. In his letter, he cited the story of his grandfather's experiences in Honolulu in the 1890s, the information he had received from Castle and Cooke, Officer Jack Burns, and Rose Kamakawiwo'ole Alston. He also told what he knew of his grandfather's character and offered his opinion that William Sands had died of natural causes. He knew the letter was a long shot, but the Gillespies had suggested that with all the information that he had put together, he might at least get the coroner to give the case another look.

He appealed to the coroner to hurry the University of Hawai'i study of the so-called white powder. He said he was frustrated by the delay in their findings and concluded that the whole ordeal was causing tremendous hardship—both financial and emotional.

He planned to take the letter into Honolulu on Monday morning. Once again, the weekend would prevent him from getting more investigatory work accomplished.

He decided he would spend the rest of his time that weekend, or as much as possible, with Healani. They agreed to go horseback riding and hiking that afternoon, and Paul knocked at her front door sometime after one o'clock. He was stunned to see Jorge open the door. He was more stunned to see what shape he was in.

"Got in another scrape last night," Jorge said, grimacing and partially bent over. "It was nothing."

"Heck if it was," Healani interrupted. She gave Paul a kiss on his cheek and told her brother to sit down.

"How the hell do you know?" Jorge barked back at her.

"Calm down, Jorge!" Paul interceded. Jorge took a swing at him, but missed. The force of the missed blow knocked Jorge to the ground, and his injuries from the night before kept him there. Paul sat on the middle of his back, as he outweighed the stocky cowboy by several pounds, and Jorge decided not to fight. He was exhausted and had little strength left anyway.

"Do you know what happened to him?"

Healani nodded. She said she got a call from Kimo, the bartender at Kailua Tavern, only minutes after she and Paul returned from their fishing excursion the night before. "He told me that Jorge was hurt pretty badly. Apparently he got in a scuffle with two navy guys."

"Two navy guys and at least three army guys," Jorge announced loudly, facedown on the living room floor. Paul told him to be quiet and pressed his weight down harder. Jorge squirmed but gave up quickly.

"The bartender said the army guys stepped in to help break up the fight, but Jorge was flailing away at everyone, and this big navy guy came flying over the table and knocked Jorge clean out. Apparently it took several minutes to restore order. One of the army guys told the bartender that Jorge was the craziest person he'd ever seen. I told him I agreed with that assessment. "

She came over to where Jorge was still lying helplessly locked down to the floor, and she gave him a playful whack to his head. "But I love him anyway. Let him up," she ordered Paul. "He'll be okay."

Paul stood up and watched carefully as Jorge rose slowly.

"Dammit, Hollywood! You're almost as bad as they are." Jorge wiped a little blood from the corner of his mouth. Then he laughed and shook his head.

Healani grabbed a towel and tried unsuccessfully to wipe away some of the blood from his face, but he gently pushed her aside. "I'll be okay," he said. "You two get the hell out of here. And enjoy yourselves."

Healani threw the towel at him and it landed on the back of his shoulders as he went down the hallway to his bedroom. He waved at them as he went into his room. Within minutes, Paul and Healani could hear him snoring away.

They both laughed when they walked out of the house a little later.

"I'll take the quarter, you take the bay," she said, directing which horses they should mount.

"How about the other way around this time?"

"Are you ready for that?"

"I'm ready for anything," Paul said with a wink. She smiled back at him and nodded.

With Paul on the quarter horse and Healani on the gentler bay, they slowly sauntered off toward Kailua Town. Their eventual goal was Maunawili Falls, and both had packed bathing suits and towels in their saddlebags.

They rode into the town, past the Japanese Community Center and the school and Kailua Tavern and the theater and over the small bridge above the stream that marked the beginning of the town area. "Bet you think you're getting to know this place," she said. Paul nodded. "There's so much more you don't know."

"What, for instance?"

"Like this next area," she said, pointing towards the marshy area of Kawai Nui, just past the first of many Japanese vegetable stands that lined the beginning of the Pali Road. The first stand was located at nothing more than a wide spot in the road. A car was there when Paul and Healani rode up on their horses, and a man and a woman were buying bananas and papayas from the Japanese girls who manned the stand. Healani and Paul dismounted and walked their horses past the vegetable stand to get a closer look at the expansiveness of Kawai Nui.

"This all used to be water," she told Paul. "When the Hawaiians first came here, maybe as early as fifteen hundred years ago, they fished extensively in these waters. The full Hawaiian name was Kawai Nui Loko, or "big freshwater pond." The fresh water came from a number of streams that channeled down from the Ko'olau. For example, when it rains heavily around here, you can see the water running off the tops of the mountains. It almost looks as if the mountains are crying, but I find that it's actually quite beautiful. In fact, the deep crags in the cliffs on the Pali are caused by that runoff."

Paul followed her hands as she pointed out every detail. Kawai Nui was mostly grassy swampland by the time Kailua became a town, she said.

"You have to go deep inside the marsh to see where the streams still run. Most of the area has been overgrown with ferns and cattails and bulrush. But it can all become a lake again in a matter of hours. When the heavy rains come, it floods almost completely. That's why you don't see any homes down there. If you were to try and walk in there, you would find the footing unsteady. That's because the vegetation has created a kind of mat, if you will, maybe several inches thick. If you cut through the mat, there is water, and then a thick mud."

"I think Auntie Rose told me a story about Kamehameha's warriors and the edible mud," Paul said. "Was that here?"

"Oh, yes, there are plenty of Hawaiian legends. Like the legend of the Hauwahine."

They tied up their horses and sat down, and Healani told the story that she said she had heard from her Hawaiian grandmother years before. Paul was entranced with the easy manner in which she told her tales and enjoyed her passion for storytelling.

"A man saw two beautiful women sitting on the banks of a stream near Kawai Nui," she began. "But he felt his eyes were playing tricks on him. He didn't believe they were beautiful women at all, but actually lizards, or *moʻo*, pretending to be human. His wife said she would chant, and if at the end of her chant the two women were still there, that would prove they were indeed human. If they disappeared, they were lizards. At the end of the chant, the two beautiful women glanced at each other and then vanished into thin air. 'Now, I see,' said the man to his wife. 'The one lizard belongs here at Kawai Nui and is its guardian. The other belongs to the streams of Kaʻelepulu. When she returns there, the leaves of the *hala* trees and the *ʻuki* grass and the bulrushes in the water turn to yellow. This is the sign of the presence of the lizard.'"

"What's the moral of the story? Or do they have morals to stories in Hawaiʻi?"

She playfully whacked his shoulder. "It's a way for the Hawaiians to tell of the changes in the seasons. They have many legends like that, some to describe the elements, others to describe geological formations. For example, turn around. See that mountain over there?"

Paul turned around. Healani pointed across the Pali Road to the jagged, dark green peaks of a small mountain that dwarfed the area around it. It definitely was no hill because it stood well over a thousand feet with three distinct peaks. A mountain was the right description.

"That's Mount Olomana," she said. "Those distinctive peaks you see are also the stuff of legend, the legend of a great giant,

Olomana, who was so big, the legend says, that he stood more than six fathoms high."

Healani reached her right arm high into the sky. Paul tried to imagine the giant she was trying to portray.

"The legend says he came here from Kaua'i to fight another warrior on O'ahu," she continued. "The other warrior was very mean-spirited and cursed at Olomana. The giant asked him to stop, but the warrior refused. They battled and Olomana was killed. The warrior cut him in half, leaving only the jagged peaks behind. That's why the mountain is in that form today, or so the legend says."

Paul smiled. "You know so many stories. Do you believe these mountains are alive? Auntie Rose says she does."

"I do believe that," she said. "And I'll tell you why. Walk over here with me. Leave the horses here. They'll be okay."

They hiked into the deep grasses surrounding Kawai Nui, pushing away the branches of the monkey pod and guava trees. They climbed over the large roots of the big banyans.

"Down here," she said from a spot several feet below where they first started. Below them still was a large pile of rocks and big stones. They were layered in such a way that you could easily tell that this had been a large structure of some kind.

"This is the Ulupō Heiau," she said. "A *heiau* is a special religious place for the ancient Hawaiians. This one is very large, certainly the biggest one they've discovered around here. Legend has it that the *Menehune*, or little small men, built this *heiau* by passing the stones hand to hand from many miles away. Whether they did or not, it's obvious that the stones don't come from around here. So whether it was the *Menehune* or not, someone brought the stones in from a great distance."

"And you believe this same—I'll call it magic—could be still alive today, perhaps up in the mountains?"

"Absolutely." She smiled. "You need to believe." She kissed him gently. "Come!" she said, holding out her hand to grab Paul's and pull him up the trail. "I promised you a hike to the Maunawili Falls. Let's get back to the horses."

The day was warm, so after a brief ride further up the Pali, the two stopped at what locals referred to as the mama-san store to get something to drink. The elderly Japanese lady behind the counter, or mama-san, smiled at both of them as she opened two ice-cold bottles of Coca-Cola. They downed the Cokes on the spot and gave the bottles right back, getting a penny in return.

A couple of miles up the winding Pali Road, they pulled their horses onto a dirt pathway. "This is the old government road," Healani said. "Queen Liliʻuokalani used to have a home here in the summer. You can see why; it's a great place to stay cool. We can tie up our horses right over here."

With the horses safely tied up, Paul and Healani grabbed one of the saddlebags that included their swimsuits and towels and a couple of local delicacies—*manapua* and Portuguese sweetbread—which Healani had cooked up and brought along. But before they set off on foot, Healani grabbed a rock and went over to one of the nearby bushes and picked a large green leaf. She wrapped the leaf around the rock and placed it on the trail.

"It's a ti leaf," she said. "Now we know that we'll have good luck." Paul smiled.

He followed her at the beginning of the hike because the trail wasn't well marked. It was an easy trek through dense forests and then into several fields of ginger. Some of the ginger patches were so thick that they had to push their way through them. At one point, Healani stopped and allowed Paul to pick her a large flowering yellow ginger. She placed it neatly behind her ear and gave her tall *haole* boyfriend a passionate kiss.

They crossed a small stream several times and then climbed a series of hills before their final descent to the falls. The descent was the only arduous part of the hike, which in all took less than a half hour from the point where they tied up their horses. Paul helped

Healani climb down the final set of rocks as they reached their destination.

"Isn't it beautiful?" she asked.

It truly was, Paul nodded in agreement. The stream gathered in a large pool right in front of a cascading waterfall. From top to bottom, the water slid over the rocks and fell at least twenty feet into the deep pool. They stood in awe for several moments, not saying a word. The natural beauty of the area resonated loudly for both of them.

"Come on," Healani said as she grabbed Paul's hand, and they walked gingerly over the slippery rocks. Paul nearly fell a couple of times, but Healani kept him upright. By the time they reached the pool, they were giggling like schoolchildren.

"The water is very cold," Paul said, dipping his hand into the pool.

"That's the fun of it," she exclaimed excitedly. "That's where we're going to jump in from." She pointed to a rocky ledge several feet above the falls. "I'm up for it if you are."

"Okay. But if I die, promise me you'll bury me someplace where it's warm." They laughed and then quickly changed into their bathing suits, with Paul keeping his back turned the entire time. They set their towels and clothes on bushes at the side of the pool so they couldn't get wet. Then they scrambled up the big rocks above the pool.

Healani didn't even wait to jump. When they got to the top, she just went. She dropped over the side and disappeared into the dark pool of water with a big splash. She resurfaced within moments, yelling up at Paul, "Last one in is a rotten egg!" She laughed and then swam over to the side of the freshwater pool to give him plenty of room.

Paul stood there on the ledge, frozen for several seconds, his long legs practically knocking together at the knees.

"Are you afraid?"

Paul waved but didn't move.

"Come on, scaredy-cat!"

Paul sheepishly waved again but still was frozen in place.

"If you don't get down here this instant, Paul Sands, I may have to leave you right now!"

Paul knew he wasn't the bravest man in the bunch, but he damned sure wasn't going to lose this beautiful girl. This would definitely be a leap of faith. He gathered all the courage he could muster, closed his eyes, and flew out into the air. He kicked his legs furiously and held his breath at the same time. "Geronimo!" he whooped. When he hit the water, it was like crashing through into the frigid waters of the North Atlantic. "Oh my god, it's so cold," he yelled out when he came back up to the surface of the water.

Healani was laughing like crazy. She swam over to Paul in the middle of the pool and wrapped her arms around his shoulders. "Maybe this will warm you up," she said, softly. Then she pressed her body against his and kissed him very hard and very passionately. The spray from the waterfall danced across their faces and shoulders, but the two young lovebirds hardly noticed. They clung together, two lovers wrapped in amorous bliss for as long as they could stay afloat.

Several hours later, after they had cleaned themselves off and returned to town, they grabbed a bite to eat and then walked hand in hand in the moonlight from Kailua Bay toward Lanikai Beach. They didn't say a lot during that time; they didn't have to. They both knew how the other felt. For a long while, they strolled happily and quietly and then looked out above the waters and into the darkness. The twinkling of the stars and a cloud-covered moon didn't allow them to see very much, so the bobbing and weaving of a tiny fishing boat out in middle of Kailua Bay didn't even capture their attention. They were too wrapped up in each other to care about anything and anyone else anyway.

They kissed passionately and then quietly strolled on around Alāla Point to Lanikai, where they kissed each other gently this time. Then they laid a blanket down on the soft, cool sand, where Paul took Healani into his arms and held her as tightly as possible. They kissed and touched and caressed and then they kissed some more.

After lying side by side, they stopped for a brief moment and looked up at a star-filled sky. Paul then turned and looked deep into Healani's eyes and said the three words that he felt so strongly. "I love you," he said. She held him tightly and didn't hesitate. "I love you, too," she whispered.Sometime after midnight, when the sands of Lanikai were totally deserted except for the two young lovers, and the only sounds were the lapping of the tiny waves along the Lanikai shoreline, they made love. Sweet, passionate love. Then they wrapped themselves up in the blanket and fell fast asleep on the beach—knowing that their lives would never be the same again.

18 - THE RISING SUN

Healani and Paul watched the sunrise on the morning of the seventh of December. They huddled together with their blanket wrapped around their shoulders, hoping for time to stand still. But, of course, it did not.

After another long, impassioned kiss, they stood up on the white sandy beach and allowed the morning sunshine to dance on their contented faces. Paul held her tightly. They didn't speak for a long while.

He finally broke the lovers' silence. "You know, we're going to have to eat something."

She smiled, almost embarrassed. "I'm just drinking in the moment," she replied. And she kissed him on the cheek.

"Still, I should run over to Mr. G. and Nan's, at least to let them know I . . . I mean we . . . we're down at the beach and not to worry," Paul stammered. "I feel bad I never called them last night. You know, they feel responsible for me and they've been so considerate." He gently pushed some sand off her hair.

"That's fine. I'll stay here and wait for you. It's such a gorgeous day. I think I'll just sit back and enjoy it for as long as I can."

Paul kissed her on the forehead and ran up the beach and across the street to the Gillespies' Lanikai cottage. Nan was already outside, hanging laundry on the clothesline.

"Why, he lives and breathes," Nan somehow managed to say despite clenching clothespins between her teeth. She shook her head in mock disapproval. Paul blushed, then laughed.

"We're down at the beach," Paul said. "Healani and me. Where's Mr. G.?"

"He and the regulars are playing golf at Mid-Pac," she answered. "They had an early tee time this morning. I think Scotty wanted to get out there as soon as he could. I had him with me all yesterday, shopping for more of the black curtain material. I think he would have rather gone to the University of Hawai'i football game."

"No doubt about that. You don't mind if I grab a bunch of bananas from the kitchen, do you?"

"That's fine, lad. And give Healani my best. She'll make a fine wife."

The comment almost stopped Paul in his tracks, but he said nothing. He went inside the house, gathered a small bunch of bananas, and then decided he should also make a phone call. He suddenly realized that Jorge, too, would be worried about their whereabouts. So he dialed the prefix 2 for a Kailua number and called Jorge.

"Why, Hollywood, you son of a bitch," he said when Paul told him that his sister and he were in Lanikai together. He apologized by making up an excuse that the two had a few drinks and then fell asleep on the beach. Paul waited to see if he would get an angry response.

Instead, Jorge laughed. "It's all good. Say, why don't I drive over and pick you guys up. I'll meet you on the beach near Alāla Point."

Paul said fine and hung up. Then, with bananas in hand, he went running down to the beach again. Jorge, still a little bruised and battered from his fight the day before, joined Paul and Healani on the sand within a half hour. Healani gave her big brother a huge hug. He looked at her, shook his head, and hugged her back. He mockingly punched at Paul but then broke out laughing and reached out to shake the tall man's hand. Paul felt relieved.

"I just wanted to let you know that you two make a great couple," he said. "I can't believe I'm saying that, but it's true."

They sat down near the point and looked out toward Kailua Bay. From this vantage point, the crescent shape of the three-mile strand of beach was to their left. Mōkapu Peninsula, the site of the naval air station, with Ulupaʻu Crater standing guard on the peninsula's right-hand side, jutted out on the horizon, directly across from them. It was a spectacular view of one of the most beautiful bays in the world.

For several minutes, they sat and ate their bananas and laughed and talked about the beauty of the morning. Jorge heard the sounds first. "What's that?" he said, springing to his feet.

Paul and Healani heard it, too—the terrifying, but unmistakable buzz of gunfire. *Rat-a-tat-tat, rat-a-tat-tat*; Paul and Healani rose to their feet, and all three looked across the bay at Mōkapu Peninsula, where they saw gigantic plumes of smoke start to billow out above the Kaneohe Naval Air Station. A number of small planes buzzed above.

"They're starting their maneuvers a little early," Jorge said.

The planes increased in number. Several of them dove at rapid speed above the base and nearly touched the ground. The smoke above the base grew thicker.

"Why are they doing this at this hour?" Healani asked. She looked at her watch. She showed the time to Paul; it was several minutes before eight o'clock.

Jorge ran several feet down the beach to try and get a better look. Paul and Healani stood transfixed on the aerial circus playing out in front of them, not knowing what to think. Within seconds, two of the planes veered away from Mōkapu and headed toward

Lanikai. The planes couldn't have been more than two hundred feet in the air when they flew right above them. Healani gasped out loud when, all at the same time, they saw the giant reddish-orange ball on the plane's wings.

"My God, those are Japs!" yelled Jorge. "We're under attack!"

Healani grabbed Paul. He clutched her closer to his side, too numb to move. As they stood, transfixed in horror, they followed the flight of the first two planes and then saw them buzz past the beach at Lanikai, headed in the direction of the Bellows Army Air Base on the other side of the hill. They turned around to look back at Kailua Bay in time to see another plane headed in the same direction. This plane was even lower than the first two, perhaps only a hundred feet above them.

With the plane so close to the ground, Paul could see right into the cockpit. The pilot wore a white headband around his head and his goggles. Paul pulled Healani tighter to him and looked right into the pilot's eyes. As the pilot flew past them on the beach, he gave a quick wave. Then he disappeared over the Kaʻiwa Ridge towards Bellows Field.

"Jesus Christ, let's get out of here," Jorge yelled. Paul grabbed Healani's hand, and they ran up the beach toward the road where Jorge had parked his Chevy truck. Jorge turned on the radio as he gunned the engine. The radio station was playing church music.

"What the hell," he screamed out. "Does anyone have any idea what's going on?!"

Healani grabbed at his shoulder. "We have to get back to the house," she said sharply. "Usually, one of the officers is there on the weekends. He'll know what to do."

Jorge sped the Chevy past the boathouse and Kalapawai Market. He stopped the truck and jumped out in order to move a cattle gate that blocked their path, and then they raced down the road toward the Luis property on Kālaheo, passing Saint Anthony's Church along the way. Several parishioners stood outside the church, looking skyward above the naval base. From the expression on their faces, they were just as stupefied as the trio had been moments before. Jorge slammed on the brakes with a violent jerk as he pulled up in the front yard of his property, right in front of the officers' house.

"I've got to make a phone call," Jorge yelled out, as he headed out back towards his own house. "You two make sure Lieutenant Billings is up." Healani and Paul raced up to the officer's door and banged on it furiously. They were surprised when the still sleepy-eyed lieutenant came to the door in his pajamas.

"What are you people up to this early?" he asked rather nonchalantly.

"Better get out of those pj's, Lieutenant. It looks like we're under attack," Healani squawked. "The Kāne'ohe base is being hit by the Japanese." The Lieutenant looked at her face and knew right away she wasn't kidding.

"Oh my God! Wait right there. I'll be changed in an instant." He scrambled back into his bedroom, where he called out, "Can you give me a ride? Buddy has the car."

"Who's Buddy?" Paul turned to ask Healani.

"Lieutenant Masters," she answered quickly. "His roommate."

"We'll give you a ride. Is Buddy at the base already?" she yelled out.

"Yeah," said Lieutenant Billings, as he reappeared in his service khakis and a t-shirt. He anxiously held his navy regulation shirt in the palm of his hand. "He was supposed to take one of the PBYs on a maintenance run this morning. Let's get going." He hopped out the front door, trying to walk and wrestle with his socks and shoes on at the same time.

Just then, Jorge ran back towards them. "I can't get through to anybody official. I tried, but all the lines are tied up. Healani, will you stay here and keep trying?" He turned and looked at his sister.

"Sure, I understand," she said. "I'll keep calling." Then, she turned to Paul. "You going, too?"

Paul nodded. "Be safe," she said, and she gave him a very quick kiss. "Let's go!" Jorge yelled out as he and the lieutenant ran ahead of Paul to the Chevy. Paul followed right behind. "I'll also call Mr. G. and Nan," she yelled out, waving her arms. They slammed the truck doors shut, and Jorge laid heavy dust, screaming out of the driveway.

Within minutes, they heard the announcer on the radio interrupt the regular music broadcast with the warning that Pearl Harbor was under attack. "This is the Real McCoy!" he said.

"My God!" the lieutenant bellowed. "We've got most of our planes in the middle of the field. They're sitting ducks out there."

"We'll get you there as fast as we can, Lieutenant," Jorge said. The Kāneʻohe Naval Air Station was less than two miles way. They didn't speak much more after that, and Paul felt his heart beating at an enormous pace. He looked over at the lieutenant and saw the anxious appearance on his face. Jorge quickly got out of the truck a couple of times to open up the cattle gates, but he still made it to the base in a furious drive that took less than five minutes. An obviously dazed and confused sentry waved them through the gate when he saw the lieutenant stick his head out the window.

"They've damn right bombed us into oblivion," the lieutenant yelled out as they sped up the main road. "Pull over!" he commanded. The lieutenant jumped out and raced toward one of the burning buildings. The attack had momentarily stopped, and the wave of Japanese warplanes were nowhere in sight, but they had left little untouched. Fire, smoke, and blazing buildings were all around them. The overwhelming stench of charred buildings, mixed with gasoline and oil fumes, filled the air.

"Come on, over here!" Jorge yelled out. They rushed toward the hangar area where planes were still on fire. A charred body lay on the ground in the middle of the field. A mangled prop lay right beside him. Another man, this one bloodied from his face to his waist, staggered towards Paul and grabbed him before he fell to the ground. Gunshots were still going off in every direction, but there were no planes anywhere, and Paul couldn't see who was firing at whom. He was terrified.

The bloody man passed out in Paul's arms, so Paul carried him toward a shady area near one of the buildings that was still standing. The man was moaning, so Paul at least knew he was still alive.

"Jorge, water!" Paul yelled out. Jorge, who had stopped to help another wounded soldier, guided his less-bloodied man over to the same building and then set out for water. Paul ripped the blood-soaked shirt from the man he was tending and discovered a deep shrapnel wound to his shoulder. Paul and the less-injured serviceman then propped up the bloodied soldier's head. Paul cradled it gently.

"Jorge'll be back with the water soon," he said, trying to comfort the young man. The man said nothing. He looked at both of them, shell-shocked.

"Man, they came out of nowhere," the second serviceman said. "I thought it was some kind of sick joke when they first started shooting. I really did. But then I knew it was for real. They were everywhere." He was practically delirious and talked with his injury-free hand flying off in all directions. His eyes were wild. "They blew up the planes in the middle of the field in seconds. Just blew 'em up. *Boom!* Like that. Man, they knew exactly what they were doing." He looked wild-eyed at Paul. "You one of the construction workers?"

"No," Paul said, not really knowing what the serviceman was talking about.

The second soldier took a few deep breaths and started to calm down. He checked the other soldier's pulse while Paul tried to wipe blood away from the soldier's eyes.

"A bunch of construction workers were working on some of the new buildings, and they got shot up real bad. I thought maybe you were with them. You're obviously a civilian."

"No, just a guy from Kailua," Paul said, wiping more of the

blood off the face of the first wounded man. "I'm Paul Sands, officer."

"I'm Ensign Rothwell from Wichita, Kansas. God save us all."

Before Paul could respond, Jorge slid up next to them with a big pail of water and several towels. They spent the next few minutes cleaning up the wounds of both men. The sound of shooting had stopped.

"We're going to have to get this one guy immediate medical attention," Jorge said. "He needs a doctor real bad and he needs him now. We may have to do it ourselves, though. I don't see any medics in the immediate area."

"Everybody's just trying to regroup after the attack," Ensign Rothwell said. "If you gentlemen don't mind, I'll point you in the right direction, but I've got to find my unit and figure out how I can help fight this goddamned war!"

The young ensign pointed them toward an area that was being used as a makeshift base hospital, and then he ran off. There were no stretchers to be found, so Jorge and Paul carried the wounded man several hundred yards until they found help. They weren't mentally prepared for the scene they saw next. Paul gagged at the sight in front of them.

While the bloodied man they helped was still alive, many others weren't as fortunate. Several mangled or bullet-ridden bodies lay in the opening of the building that was being utilized as both the makeshift morgue and hospital. Blood was everywhere. The stench from a mixture of charred bodies, blood, and smoke choked the air. Paul gasped aloud as they placed the injured man on a mat. A doctor said nothing at first to them as he quickly approached and immediately began examining the injured serviceman.

"I think he'll be okay. Nurse!" he called out. One of two nurses that Paul and Jorge could see in the immediate vicinity hustled to the doctor's side. The doctor, the only one they saw, quietly gave her an order and then moved on to the next wounded man. Many of the men were moaning in terrible pain.

It was obvious that this one lone doctor and the two nurses were courageously trying to help those they could. Paul and Jorge were practically frozen in place, almost in a daze. Paul wasn't sure if he should offer help, but then saw Jorge slowly walking away from the horrific scene. He instinctively followed him.

They were walking silently back toward the car when they heard the distinct roar of plane engines again. The menacing sound grew louder and louder, and then shots rang out. Jorge and Paul dove to the ground.

"Here they come again!" they heard someone yell out. Jorge and Paul jumped up and ran for the cover of a nearby building. Bullets zinged above them and around them as the Japanese planes once again attacked the base on a strafing run. The crashing of steel against asphalt and concrete played out all around them. Paul felt a piece of concrete fall past his head and looked up and saw several new bullet holes directly above him. But there wasn't much he could do except crouch against the side of the wall, holding his arms protectively above his head. Jorge rolled himself into a little ball and squeezed down as tightly as he could.

The sound of war raged on in every direction. It was sound and fury like no other they'd ever heard. *Rat-a-tat-tat, rat-a-tat-tat.* The bullets zinged off buildings, pavement, cars, trucks, and everything else in sight. Then more planes came down on them with the sound of bombs being unleashed. The whistling of the bombs was a deadly shrill. Some bombs landed far away, others much closer.

Boom! Boom! The explosions were both large and small, sending smoke and debris in every direction. The two men covered their heads the best they could. The concussion from one bomb landed several dozen feet away from them. *Boom!* The shock knocked both Jorge and Paul off their feet, but they quickly scrambled back up. Smoke and fire sprung up everywhere.

"Let's get out of here," Jorge yelled at Paul. "There must be somewhere safer than this!"

But as they ran away from the building, a low-flying Japanese attack plane appeared practically out of nowhere, hugging the ground on another strafing run, no more than fifty feet off the ground. Paul and Jorge were immediately exposed, so they instinctively turned to run in the opposite direction, zigzagging across the open area. They could hear the thrashing of bullets smashing to the ground. Bullets zipped right past them, some kicking up dirt and pavement. Dozens of bullets scarred the ground only a few feet from them. Somehow they managed to elude the deadly shower as they dove headfirst into a cluster of small coconut trees.

"Over here!" someone yelled out. They popped up their heads and saw three helmeted men in a battery position perhaps fifty yards away. Two of the men were pumping antiaircraft shells out of the battery as fast as they could. The other man had a rifle and was motioning with it. "Get your butts over here!" Paul and Jorge quickly scrambled across the field and behind the small protective barrier to safety.

"Keep your heads down!" he screamed out, giving both Paul and Jorge a push to the ground. They practically tumbled on top of each other. "We're going to get one of these sons of bitches yet!"

The battery kept pumping away as the Japanese planes continued their horrible work. In front of them, a navy man was shot dead as he tried to run across the field to help one of his wounded comrades. The Japanese planes were shooting at anything that moved. Fires raged out of control all over the base.

More yelling and screaming ensued as bullets flew in every direction. "We got one of the bastards!" the man with the rifle yelled out. "Look at him, he's in trouble now."

Paul looked skyward to see a Japanese plane with smoke billowing from its tail section. The plane circled out over Kāne'ohe Bay and then turned around to face the base.

"Oh my God, he's not running. He's coming back," the navy man yelled as the battery continued to fire away.

Sure enough, the plane had turned completely around. Moreover, it was picking up speed in a desperate dive at the main hangar.

"He's going to crash it on purpose," Jorge yelled out. "It's a samurai thing!"

Paul looked back at the plane with its bright, bloody-red circle. Sure enough, the pilot was going out in a blaze of glory. But U.S. antiaircraft guns unloaded on him from every direction. He had no chance. The plane was hit several times and sputtered on its fatal dive, crashing short of its intended target. It bounced into a sand dune, where it came to a screeching halt.

A couple of navy men ran toward the fallen plane. They quickly waved to everyone to signal that the pilot was indeed dead—the first enemy casualty. Meanwhile, the other Japanese attack planes roared off; the second wave of attacks appeared to be over, as the Japanese disappeared over the horizon. However, sporadic shooting by nervous and itchy-fingered U.S. servicemen continued. Paul and Jorge kept their heads down, noting that for some unknown reason, the batteries were now turned in the direction of civilian cars that were observing the battle from the road outside the base. Several shots rang out in that general direction.

"Knock it off, you idiots!" a voice yelled out. The misguided shooting stopped.

"Somebody's a little jumpy," the navy man nearest to them said as he left the battery nest. Paul could see the look of exhaustion on the man's face.

Jorge and Paul said nothing to each other. They were exhausted, too, and just happy to be alive. With assurances from navy officers that the Japanese attackers had indeed left the area for the second time, they left their safe zone and went out onto the field to see whom they could help.

Paul wiped the sweat from his forehead. It was the most helpless feeling he'd ever experienced.

19 - AFTERMATH

Jack Burns was at Saint Anthony's Church when the first shots were fired at Kāne'ohe Naval Air Station. Within minutes, he was on the phone to authorities and then in his car driving over the Pali to Bethel Street police headquarters.

He stopped for a moment near the Nu'uanu Pali Lookout to watch the second wave of Japanese attacks. He saw the plumes of smoke that hovered over the Mōkapu Peninsula and the planes peel off from Kāne'ohe across Kailua Bay towards Bellows. Above him, a few stray planes flew across the Ko'olau, and he realized that no one out in the open was safe. Fearing for his own safety, he quickly got back into his car and hurriedly drove to police headquarters and then to the local FBI office.

Phones were ringing off the hook at both places. Every police officer, every FBI agent, and every worker he saw had grim faces. No one was sure when, or if, another attack was imminent.

He nodded to the FBI office secretary, who motioned him into the director's office despite holding a phone to one ear with her neck and shoulder while trying to shuffle papers with both of her busy hands. Director Shivers was on the phone. "Governor Poindexter," Shivers mouthed towards Burns, pointing at the receiver.

Burns nodded and sat down in the corner of the office. Out the window, he could see smoke billowing from Pearl Harbor several miles away.

"But Governor, it's absolutely necessary. We must declare martial law quickly," Shivers said, emphatically.

Burns couldn't specifically hear the other end of the conversation, but deduced from Shivers' facial expressions that the governor was arguing. Eventually, the arguing got loud enough that Burns could hear shouting emanating from the other end of the receiver. Shivers argued right back at him.

"I know that, sir, but you've got to issue the orders. And you have to do it quickly."

Shivers simmered down. Then he quietly listened for a long while. Burns waited patiently for the governor and the director of the Honolulu FBI office to finish their emotional conversation.

"We'll begin fingerprinting almost immediately, sir. Yes, that too. I believe the first sets of suspects will be arrested shortly. We have agents in the field already."

The conversation continued on with Shivers emphatic in his directions but then listening courteously when the governor went into one of his harangues or monologues. Eventually Shivers wrapped up, thanked him, and hung up. The highly charged call took several minutes.

"I can't believe that, Jack," he said. "The governor was actually crying to me over the phone. He was crying."

For most of the rest of that Sunday morning, Jorge and Paul helped out at the Kāneʻohe Naval Air Base wherever they could. They helped moving supplies; they helped carry both the wounded and the dead; the carnage surrounded and overwhelmed them.

They ran into a bloodied Lieutenant Billings at the makeshift base hospital. He was pretty badly shot up but still alive. The nurse said he tried to take off in one of the planes, but his engine was ripped away before he could get to the edge of the runway. She said he was going to be okay, but that they should keep their distance and let him rest. An ambulance roared up, and Paul and Jorge helped the stretcher-bearers get Lieutenant Billings and two wounded marines into the back area. The nurse explained that they were taking the more badly wounded to the Territorial Hospital located on the *mauka*, or mountain side, of Kāneʻohe Town.

Meanwhile, the makeshift base hospital was bulging at the seams, too small to handle the influx of wounded servicemen. A number of injured men were having their wounds dressed on the steps outside. Inside, a priest was soon giving a few men their last rites. Paul, who had come to grips with the entire scene, was impressed with the surviving men's courage. If they could still walk after getting their wounds patched up, they would grab their gear and run off to find their battle stations. Paul eventually heard that Jorge and Healani's other tenant, Lieutenant Masters, was unhurt, but the PBY he had been working on during the early morning was a total loss.

One of the problems in the latter part of that morning appeared to be lack of equipment. Paul heard one injured soldier complain that he hadn't been issued a rifle. But the man said he grabbed what he could and went off to report to his unit anyway.

Occasionally, there was misguided gunfire. Many of those who were issued guns were inexperienced, and they shot at anything that moved. Paul often ducked at the sound of gunfire. His nerves were shot. Jorge somehow managed to stay calm.

Outside the makeshift hospital building, they ran into a navy gunner who said the U.S. forces had shot down a second Japanese plane in the final moments of the second attack. The damaged plane had caught fire and crashed into Kailua Bay.

Hearing that story made Paul suddenly worry about Healani

and Mr. G. and Nan. "Did you hear about the town?" he asked. "Did the civilian population get attacked, too?"

The Navy gunner said he didn't know. Reports were kind of sketchy, he said, and rumors were rampant. He heard on the short-wave that the Japs had landed on the North Shore. But he didn't know for sure if that were true or not. Then he ran off.

"We need to get back to Kailua," Paul said to Jorge. "Looks like we've done all we can here. I'm worried about the others."

By now, it was early afternoon, and they thanked the nearest nurse and then ran off toward Jorge's Chevy. When they got to it, they found that its back windows had been shot through. Broken glass was scattered all over the truck bed. They opened the doors and found bullet holes in the back of the driver's seat.

"We're damned lucky to be alive," Jorge said. They got in the truck and were relieved to hear that the engine still ran. Jorge turned the car around, and they headed back to Kailua. Paul turned and took one last glance at the naval air station. The fires had been extinguished, but smoke continued to billow into the air. Huge chunks of metal and concrete lay all over the ground. But despite the devastation of the two attacks, Paul marveled at the fighting spirit of the U.S. Navy, Army, and Marine soldiers stationed there. Both he and Jorge were still alive because of the incredible bravery of the American servicemen.

Jorge tried to turn on the radio, but there was nothing but static. "Did they shoot out the radio stations, too?" he asked rhetorically.

They pulled up to the first cattle gate and saw a local Japanese farmer and his two small children walking along the side of the road. Jorge hopped out of the truck to speak with them. Paul could see them talking excitedly, but he couldn't hear their conversation. The farmer moved the cattle gate, and Jorge hopped back into the truck and they sped off.

"He said the town wasn't attacked at all," Jorge said. "He said the radio stations went off the air just before noon. He doesn't know why. He said he was taking his family to his friend's house but doesn't need a ride."

One concern that Jorge hadn't raised was left unsaid. The thought raced through Paul's mind about some of the comments he had heard in the previous weeks, comments about the loyalty of the local Japanese community. Knowing what he knew of the wonderful Japanese people he had met in Kailua, he had a difficult time believing that their loyalty was placed anywhere except to their families and friends and neighbors in Kailua, Hawai'i, United States territory.

"I'll tell you what, Jorge, this whole thing scares the hell out of me. If the Japs are going to follow this up with an invasion, we're in deep trouble."

Jorge didn't reply. Then he took his foot off the accelerator and let the Chevy slow down. "Look up ahead," he said.

As they slowed down, they could see Army soldiers already starting to dig in and make camp near Coconut Grove. Men and trucks were making haste with their activities, unloading ammunition and equipment. One of the helmeted men put out his arm and ordered the Chevy to halt. Jorge slammed on his brakes.

"Where you men coming from and where you going?" the soldier said as he came to the window. He was a fresh-faced kid, who looked more like an average teenager than a ferocious, fighting man.

Jorge answered his query. "We were at the naval air station, helping with the wounded."

"How bad was it?" the kid soldier wanted to know. He leaned his arms against Jorge's window, his rifle ready on his shoulder.

"Pretty bad. The Japs knocked out all the planes and lots of the buildings. But the good news is we got a couple of their planes, too."

"Yeah, we had a few dogfights above us, too," the soldier said. "We could see the planes going after each other above the Ko'olau. Then the Japs hightailed it out to sea. We haven't seen 'em in a couple of hours, at least."

"They coming back?"

"No idea, but we'll be ready. We've got orders to get an encampment started here and then wait. Another unit is digging in along the beach. Everyone's on the lookout. In the meantime, you be careful. I hear they're going to declare martial law, if they haven't already."

"Got it," Jorge said. "Be safe." The young soldier gave a salute. Jorge just half smiled back at him, and they drove off.

They drove past the Kailua Race Track, where another army unit was already unloading its gear. A number of service trucks passed them as they headed into Kailua Town. Jorge stopped the Chevy when they got to the T-intersection near Kailua Tavern. The streets were practically deserted, but Jorge jumped out of the truck and ran across the street to Harada's. He tried to open the doors, but they were locked. He ran around the corner, and then he came back to the main intersection with two old Filipino men. The two men excitedly made waving motions towards the sky, pointing this way and that, and then the conversation ended. Jorge thanked them and ran back to the car.

"They said the planes went back and forth between the Kāneʻohe base and Bellows and then over the hill to Pearl Harbor and the town bases. They said that Pearl got hit real bad. Real bad. The casualties there are horrible, they said. But neither of them had heard of any civilian casualties around here in Kailua. The shops that were opened early closed up real quick, and everybody got out of here. Mr. Hughes of Hughes Drug Store raced over here from his home and taxied all of his employees to their homes. Most other people were able to get home on their own."

"I don't know about you, but I'm exhausted," he added, "both physically and emotionally. It's been a helluva day."

"Let's go find Healani and make sure she's okay," Paul replied.

When they pulled up in front of the Luis property, they found a giant note tacked onto the front door. It read, "All okay. Meet me at

Gillespie house in Lanikai. Love, Healani." Jorge and Paul ran into the house and washed up. They grabbed a few essentials, including canned goods, juices, and a couple of blankets. Then they got back in the truck and drove off to Lanikai.

As they made the turn at Kailua Beach, they stopped for a moment to gaze back at the bay. What a change from the early morning. Smoke rose above the base at Mōkapu Peninsula, and a number of military vehicles were now parked along the beach. Groups of soldiers were digging into the sand. Barbed wire was being strung along the shoreline. Far out in the bay, several small navy crafts were patrolling the waters. One navy vessel was working near a downed Japanese plane that still floated on the surface. The navy boat was being assisted by two fishing boats.

Jorge and Paul said nothing as they continued on. Along the Kaʻiwa Ridge above Lanikai, several U.S. soldiers were already taking defensive positions. Several others had dug themselves into temporary foxholes along the beach. The entire beachfront was about to be covered with stakes and barbed wires—that work had already begun. Still, it didn't make either man feel any safer. They didn't have to say it to think it; they both knew that if the Japanese attacked again, or heaven forbid, they invaded, that everyone was in deep trouble.

Healani ran out of the cottage when they pulled up into the Gillespies' driveway. When Paul quickly got out of the truck, they embraced for a long time. "Oh, Paul, it's terrible," she said, tears streaming down her cheeks.

Mr. G. and Nan came out onto the front porch, and they helped Jorge with some of the provisions he'd grabbed. "Come in the house, lads. We want to hear all you know. The phone's been out for quite some time."

They all sat down in the living room, with Healani nestling up to Paul as close as she could. Mr. G. had his shortwave radio on, and they could hear the crackling of messages going back and forth.

"Lieutenant Billings was wounded," Jorge said. Healani gasped. "But they took him to the hospital. I think he'll be okay. Lieutenant Masters was unhurt, but his plane and all the other planes were wiped out. The naval air station is pretty much out of commission. I don't know how many dead, but maybe as many as a couple of dozen. The good news is that our guys fought back bravely; we saw our guys shoot down a couple of Jap planes. One of those planes is out in the drink on Kailua Bay right now."

"Oh my word!" Nan said suddenly. "Jorge, your leg is bleeding. There's blood on your right pant leg."

All of them looked down toward the ground, and sure enough, there was a noticeable bloodstain near Jorge's ankle. He reached down and pulled up on his trousers, revealing a small gash on the lower part of his calf.

"Shit, must have been hit sometime. Didn't even know it."

"Let me go get something for that," Nan said.

When she ran off to get her first aid kit, Paul told Mr. G. and Healani the vivid details about their brush with death that morning. "We're lucky to be here," he told them. Nan returned shortly and dressed Jorge's wound.

"We were on the third hole at Mid-Pac when we saw the commotion," Mr. G. said. "We thought it was some kind of military exercise at first, but then we saw the red circles of the Japanese planes fly over us. We watched for a few minutes. Frankly, I think we were all stunned, and then we ran back to the clubhouse. One of my playing partners today, Bill, works at Pearl, and he called over there and found out they were under heavy attack. Someone told him that the entire Battleship Row was lit up. I called home here and told Nan what was going on. She said she was safe and that she had already heard from Healani and a couple of the neighbors what was going on. Anyway, I had picked up Bill this morning, so I drove him to his home in Coconut Grove, and he made another phone call. When we were there, we saw the second wave of the attack hit the

Kāneʻohe Naval Air Station. Bill was told he and other workers at Pearl had to report immediately, and then he was off. I drove down to your house, Jorge, and I convinced Healani that she might be safer with us."

Healani nodded. "I tried to make a few phone calls, like you said," she interjected. She spoke excitedly. "I couldn't get through to anyone in town, but I did speak with Nan and a couple of my fellow teachers. Everybody was shocked by the news. One of my teacher friends had no idea that anything was going on. She said it seemed like a normal Sunday where she was in Maunawili. When I got off the phone, I ran down to Saint Anthony's Church. They had just received word of what was going on. One of the priests was called to go to the base. Sadly, I think it was his job to give the last rites to some of the soldiers. One of the parishioners gave him a ride. I went down to the beach and watched the activity at the naval air station from under the ironwood trees. I was there when the second wave of attackers hit. I felt so helpless. I finally left when I heard shells coming over my head, whistling through the treetops. I don't know where the shells were coming from, but I saw a few explosions out in Kailua Bay."

She paused for a moment, as if picturing the horrors in her mind. "And, Paul, remember where we went swimming the other day? Well, there was a small fishing boat in the area, and it was on fire on the beach. A total loss. Within minutes, there was a squad of soldiers who showed up, and they started to put out the fire. I ran back to the house. When I got there, Mr. G. showed up."

Paul clutched at Healani's hand. She laid her head on Paul's shoulder.

The chatter continued on the shortwave radio, and then they heard the sound of trucks outside. Mr. G. went out to determine what was going on. The others followed, but waited from the *lānai* as he spoke with an army soldier. After a couple of minutes, Mr. G. nodded, and the soldier moved down the street.

"The Governor has declared martial law," he reported. "The military general is in charge. The military has told everyone to stay in their homes unless it's absolutely necessary to move around. All of our phone calls, outgoing and incoming, will be monitored. They've also declared a 6:30 p.m. curfew and a mandatory blackout tonight until further notice. Then, those who can help are to report to Kailua School tomorrow morning."

"Better get moving on the curtains," Nan said. "I told you we had better be prepared."

"You were right," Mr. G. said. "I'll go explain to the neighbors." They all went back inside the house to prepare for the first blackout night. Healani fixed some sandwiches, the first food that Paul and Jorge had eaten since the early morning.

The sounds emanating from the shortwave radio didn't make any of them feel any better. "Reports of Japanese paratroopers landing in St. Louis Heights," a crackly voice said. "Check it out."

They didn't know if the report was true or not.

"Earlier, they were saying that the Japanese were invading the North Shore," Nan said. "But later someone confirmed that nothing was there."

"We just need to remain calm," Jorge said. "We should get the windows covered, bed down here for the night, and hope for the best."

Each of them took a different responsibility; it cut down on the anxiety to work on something. Mr. G. came back to the cottage in short order. He said all the neighbors had been apprised of the situation. He said he also checked in on Kenji and his family. They were scared but fine otherwise.

Frankly, they were all scared. Quietly terrified might be a better phrase. They ate a light supper after they hung the black curtains. Mr. G. checked carefully to make sure no light was showing. He even put a small piece of black fabric over the lights of the short-wave radio. As the late afternoon turned to dusk and then to darkness, others in the neighborhood weren't quite as careful. They saw a neighbor light up a cigarette from their doorway. That prompted one of the nearby soldiers to hurry by to angrily tell him to extinguish it.

Perhaps the hardest part about the curtains wasn't the darkness, but how it kept the heat in. The cottage became suffocatingly hot as the night progressed.

"You think they'll mind if I sleep outside on the *lānai?*" Paul asked, referring to the soldiers who were patrolling the neighborhood. Mr. G. said he thought it was fine. Within minutes, Healani, who was supposed to be sleeping in John's old room, joined Paul on the *lānai*. Jorge reclined on the couch in the living room and fell asleep, snoring away, before anyone else.

Paul and Healani huddled together under a blanket, not saying much at all. They couldn't sleep. Ironically, the blackness of the night that the military had demanded was not totally complete. The moon was bright and that allowed both of them to see shadows. And that only made things worse. Every movement, every gust of wind, was amplified. The only sounds they heard came from the shortwave, but most of that chatter had subsided. And it turned out that the paratrooper rumor was unfounded.

They continued to try to sleep but couldn't. Healani whispered to Paul that she had all sorts of thoughts racing through her head. She said she imagined waking up to invading Japanese armies come dawn. She imagined them coming ashore at Kailua Bay, at Lanikai Beach, up and down the Windward Side. Paul tried to reassure her, saying they would be okay. But he secretly wondered if it was so.

Sometime after midnight, after Healani had fallen asleep but Paul was still awake, he heard the distant sound of gunfire. He nudged Healani, but she had finally fallen into a deep sleep. He sat up for a moment and knew he could definitely hear something. The crackling and popping sounds continued for a couple of minutes. Then, silence again.

He didn't know what it meant—or where it came from. He

could only hope that it was just the sound of nervous and jittery soldiers. At least, if they were nervous and jittery, they were awake, Paul thought. Better that than being surprised for the second day in a row.

20 - THE DAY AFTER

He had been around wars and death and fighting for nearly his entire life, but he simply couldn't believe what he had seen the day before. How incredibly unprepared these sloppy Americans were! Perhaps because he had been planning his mission for so long, perhaps because he knew of the impending Sunday morning attack, he expected that those in the American military would have been much more ready than what he had witnessed. A successful surprise attack was always a goal, but he never expected that it would be carried forward so flawlessly. What buffoons, these people from Hawai'i were!

It had gone so easily for him, so incredibly easy. The only glitch had been the small dog that barked at him momentarily after landing late Saturday night, and he had taken care of that minor obstacle in quick and decisive order. He found shelter on Kuehn's large property, and there was a change of clothing for him, too, but he was careful not to make any physical contact with the German. He dressed quickly and quietly in the minutes before dawn on Sunday, stashed his belongings under thick kiawe bushes a few hundred yards away near the Kailua Race Track, and then sauntered into town like any other Sunday-morning churchgoer to see what was going on in the town.

He was quietly attending services at the Japanese church when he saw the reaction to the first news of the attack. He made certain that he acted like the other folks—surprised, concerned, and not drawing attention to himself. He made mental notes about how the citizens reacted and then how the military took over the town. No one tried to talk to him, and he only made very small talk with others, but he did a great deal of listening. He found out a lot, but not enough to decide when he should carry out his plan.

The next couple of days would tell him what he needed to know and determine his specific next move. He was certain to glean much more information by then. He would keep his eyes and ears open, and he would blend in with the citizens of Kailua and wait. He found a safe place to sleep—in a vacant building near the Kailua Theater. When the time was right, if the time was right, he would bolt for the Ko'olau. In his mind, the most important part of his mission had only just begun.

When President Franklin Delano Roosevelt delivered the line "a day that will live in infamy" on the floor of the joint session of Congress on December 8, John Gillespie was there in the gallery at the U.S. Capitol. Seated next to a glum Secretary of the Navy Henry Knox, John listened intently to every single word the president uttered. He found the speech both inspiring and daunting, and he proudly stood and joined in the standing ovation at the conclusion.

John had slept only intermittently since the day before, when he first heard the news. He and Secretary Knox and others in the navy department were stunned by the developments in Hawai'i and elsewhere around the globe. The casualties were staggering everywhere, especially at Pearl Harbor and the bases on O'ahu. There simply was no time to sleep; and when he thought about his parents and friends in Hawai'i, he couldn't sleep anyway.

Knox had ordered a full report of the losses up to that point. But the staggering numbers could only tell a portion of the real story. The president and the military and diplomatic minds in Washington needed firsthand knowledge of the terrible devastation.

Within hours after the December 8 speech, Knox was ordered to set up a secret mission to fly to Hawai'i to assess the damage. The mission had to be secret because no one knew exactly what information was compromised and what it meant and what exactly the Japanese were going to do next.

Knox needed someone he could trust implicitly and someone who knew Hawai'i, and thus he handpicked John as his chief aide. John's intimate knowledge of the island would be a tremendous asset. The two also briefly discussed the possibility that Japanese civilians might need to be rounded up. Secretary Knox said it was the right thing to do, considering the circumstances. John argued against it, saying loyal citizens should not be rousted from their homes. But the discussion got lost in an avalanche of more immediate concerns. What kind of shape was the U.S. Pacific Fleet in? Could our forces withstand another attack? What if the Japanese followed up with an invasion force? The questions were endless.

Together, Secretary Knox and John would fly by military transport along with other important military officials to the West Coast and then to the Hawaiian Islands by the end of the week. They would try to size up the losses and get some answers. Until then, they would have little time for sleep. The task ahead was more daunting than they could ever imagine in their wildest dreams—or in this case, their wildest nightmares.

"Get up," Jorge said, nudging Paul with his boot in the lower abdomen. Paul grunted and rolled over, tangling himself in his blanket.

"Get up," he whispered again, this time louder. "I need you to come with me." Paul sat up slowly and tried to shake the cobwebs out of his head. He rose into a sitting position, clutching the blanket around him. The darkness was just beginning to fade, and there was evidence that the sun would be coming up very soon.

"Where the hell you goin'?" Paul said, rubbing the top of his head. He glanced over at Healani, who was still fast asleep.

"I need to get to the corral. I have no idea what's going on, but we've still got cattle out there that must be fed. I just need somebody to ride along with me in case we get into trouble."

"Okay." Paul stood up and stretched. The two of them helped carry Healani into the living room. She stirred slightly, and Paul gave her a light kiss. She smiled and then went back to sleep.

They heard some movement in the back bedroom. Mr. G. appeared in the hallway. "What're you lads up to?"

"I've got some cattle business to tend to," Jorge said. "I need Paul here to come along with me and give me a hand."

"Not a problem, son," Mr. G. said, turning down the shortwave radio, then turning on the regular radio set. For a few minutes, all three men stood and listened to the news report. The information was devastating on all fronts. Jorge and Paul said nothing until Mr. G. broke the silence.

"At least grab something to eat before you go. I'll try to make a phone call in a little bit to see what's happening in town."

A local announcer came on the radio airwaves. First, he announced that regular programming had been cancelled, but that anyone listening should keep their radios on for important announcements throughout the day. He also said that all civilian authorities, plus all public employees, were to report to their preassigned areas at eight o'clock that morning.

"I've got to get over to Kailua School. I'm the neighborhood warden," Mr. G. said. "I'll wake up Healani in a little bit. I assume they mean teachers when they say 'public employees.'"

Paul hustled in to the bathroom and threw some water on his

face. Jorge quickly made some toast for all of them while Mr. G. made his phone call. After washing his face, Paul briefly went into the bedroom to grab a shirt. There, on the dresser, was the letter he was supposed to drop off at the county coroner's office that day.

He paused for a moment and picked up the letter and the envelope and realized that his own problems seemed inconsequential in light of what was going on. The letter would have to wait for now. He set it down and left the bedroom.

"Yes, I understand," Mr. G. said, as Paul reappeared in the kitchen. Then he hung up.

"The operator said they aren't allowing any personal calls at this time. The phone lines are all being monitored. Only emergency calls are being allowed through, until further notice. The good news is that there have been no further attacks in the islands. She couldn't give me any further information."

"Stay glued to the radio," Jorge said. "We'll meet up later today at the school. You need any help taking the curtains down?"

Mr. G. shook his head. "I'll get some help from the girls," he said. "Don't worry about us. We'll be fine."

"Tell Healani that I love her," Paul said, as we went out the front door. Mr. G. smiled.

Jorge and Paul got into the Chevy and drove off. It was now light outside, but it was a very dreary morning with heavy cloud cover. The sky was an ugly shade of gray, and it properly reflected the somber mood.

They didn't get more than a couple hundred yards down the road before they ran into two young soldiers. They were stopped briefly, but then the soldiers were interrupted by a call on their walkie-talkies. As they sat in the Chevy and waited, they could hear walkie-talkie chatter about something on the beach at Bellows. They couldn't make out exactly what the military chatter was about. The two soldiers waved them through and then jumped into their jeep and sped off.

Paul and Jorge had no idea what they were up to, and it was obvious that practically everyone seemed nervous and jumpy and probably fearful of another attack. In the meantime, at the top of the small incline in the road near Aāla Point, they paused for a moment to look out at how much had changed in Kailua Bay since the previous day.

Small groups of soldiers were positioned all along the shoreline. Machine-gun nests sat in many of the foxholes. A line of barbed wire crisscrossed the sand in every direction. Across the bay at Mōkapu Peninsula, the billowing smoke at Kāneohe Naval Air Station had ceased. The waters of the bay were almost devoid of activity, with the exception of a small navy patrol boat beyond the outer reef. A few local fishing boats were moored in the shallow waters, but they appeared dormant.

They resumed their drive along the beach road and drove past the two markets, Kalapawai and Lanikai Store. A Chinese man was tacking a sign on Lanikai Store that read CLOSED UNTIL FURTHER NOTICE. The streets were virtually empty. It was incredibly eerie; not even dogs were out.

Two army trucks passed in front of them, apparently headed for the new operations along the beach. In the center of the town, they could see tents and trucks near Kailua School but drove through the intersection before discovering more. Up the road, near the Kailua Race Track, the encampment they had seen getting started the afternoon before was now much larger. Men and trucks and rifles and military gear were strewn all over.

A soldier, much older than the kid who had stopped them on Sunday afternoon, took one look at Jorge's cowboy hat and stopped him. "Who goes there?" he yelled out.

Jorge responded with his name and pulled out his wallet while cursing under his breath. Paul cautioned him that asking to see driver's licenses or other identification was probably necessary under the circumstances.

The soldier gave Jorge back his identification with a warning. "They'll start fingerprinting in a couple of days. That's the word. Just so you know." Jorge started to say something, but Paul nudged his side, and Jorge stayed quiet. They drove on, slowly.

"I probably won't need your help once I get to the corral. Catch some shut-eye, if you want, Jorge said.

"I'll take you up on that. Stay cool, Jorge!"

"No promises, Hollywood." Jorge pulled up in front of the corral and quickly jumped out. Paul decided not to follow and, because he was exhausted, he leaned against the passenger-side window and fell back asleep like a rock.

It was nearly midmorning when Jorge got back into the Chevy. He shook Paul to wake him up.

"I'm going to have to get you back to Kailua."

"Why?"

"I'm headed to Waimānalo. Talked to the Old Man, and he wants my help with the army unit over there. They're taking over the old sugar mill, and everybody's pretty skittish. I guess they figure if the Japs are going to invade, they're most likely to come here on the Windward Side. They found a small, miniature submarine over there this morning."

"What?!"

"That's what the Old Man said. But who know what's true? He said that rumors were flying around that the Japs were landing in Waimānalo. Worse yet, the soldiers were chasing every rumor around. Everybody was getting pretty pissed off until they actually found the tiny sub and the sub's pilot washed up on the shore. Another guy on the sub was found dead."

"Is that true?"

"I'm telling you that's what the Old Man said. I'm headed over that way now."

"Why not take me?"

"You'll spoil my fun, friend," he flashed a grin. "Plus, you should see if Healani or Mr. G. need help in town."

Jorge drove the Chevy into Kailua Town and pulled up on the street adjacent to Kailua School. He dropped Paul off amidst a sudden hotbed of activity. Tents and cots were now up all over the school grounds, and civilians and soldiers worked side by side. A number of people were gathered near a table in front of a big Red Cross vehicle.

Healani was standing by one of the school buildings, saw Paul, and ran over to him immediately. She gave him a big hug. Tears welled up in her eyes.

"Oh, Paul. We have families here who were moved from Kāneʻohe Naval Air Station after the attack, and some of them have fathers or husbands who were killed. It's just terrible. We're trying to help them as much as we can."

Paul consoled her by holding her face to his shoulder. He petted her hair as she cried on his shoulder.

"I'll be okay," she said, finally. She pulled away from him and took a deep breath. "It's all so overwhelming. We've got refugee families from the base in one classroom and some wounded soldiers in the other classroom."

"Where's that?"

"Over there," she pointed. "I understand they took the worst of the wounded to the Territorial Hospital, but we've got some guys who are nursing smaller injuries. All the teachers and the principal are here to help. Everyone's been so wonderful. I just feel so badly for these people."

Paul looked up. The dreary skies above—very dark and very gray by Hawaiʻi standards-- added to the otherworldly scene. "It's as if God knows how horrible this day is."

Healani grabbed his hand and squeezed it.

"Let me know what I can do to help," he said.

"Check with Mr. G. He's over near the Red Cross people. I saw him unloading stuff over there a while back." Paul gave her a quick kiss and then hustled over to the location she noted.

"How can I help?" he said, touching the old Scotsman on the shoulder.

"Good to see you, laddie. We need some supplies, perhaps a little more food. I know the stores are closed, but you might be able to get someone to open up." He handed Paul a stack of blankets. Paul followed Mr. G.'s lead and dropped them off near the tents. Small children, oblivious to the horror of the day before, played in and around the tents while their mothers tended to their basic needs. Some women were being consoled by others.

"Where can I find food around here for them?"

"Try one of the food markets," Mr. G. said. He was all business that morning. "I think the store owner lives in Coconut Grove. Here."

He scribbled down a name and an address.

"Off with ya."

Paul knew there was no time for small talk. He watched Mr. G. go back to his work quickly. Paul ran off in a hurry.

It was nearing noon, but unlike the active school, everything else in the town was eerily quiet. A few people stood in doorways or their lānai. Paul asked an elderly *haole* lady where the store owner's street was, and she pointed that he still needed to go another street over. But before he could get there, he saw a big black sedan drive down the road and pull up in the driveway at the next house. Paul stopped in his tracks when he saw two men in dark suits get out of the vehicle and go up to the door. Moments later, they came out of the house with a middle-aged Japanese man in handcuffs, walked him to the black sedan, and pushed him into the backseat. The man's wife and children kneeled on the ground, sobbing in the doorway as the big black car drove away. Paul stood almost paralyzed on the side of the street while he watched.

He didn't know what to think. What had the man done? Should he go and help the family? He didn't have any answers. The man's wife gathered up her two small children, who were still crying, and she pulled them back into the house and closed the door behind her. Paul felt shame that he did nothing to help. But he was frozen with fear and decided to walk away and continue his mission to find the store owner's house.

When he finally got to the appointed address, he knocked, and a small, frail-looking elderly Japanese lady came to door. She opened the door slightly, not all the way, and peered around the edge. Paul asked if the store owner was in, but she didn't respond. She closed the door.

So Paul knocked again. This time, he heard voices inside, but he couldn't understand what they were saying. Paul stood at the door for a couple of minutes and knocked again. This time, a young girl, perhaps twelve or thirteen years old, came to the door.

"I'm sorry," she said. "Grandmother is very afraid."

"I understand, but why should she be afraid of me?"

The girl hesitated for a moment, as if gathering her thoughts, then spoke quietly and deliberately. "We heard this morning they arrested the teacher at the Japanese language school, and then we saw them take away one of our neighbors. We don't know what to think. You aren't coming to take us away, are you?"

"No, no, no," Paul said, stuttering. He felt just as shaken as she did. "I'm trying to find the store owner. We're hoping to help some of the wounded soldiers and refugee families from the base."

She nodded and opened the door wider. She turned to her grandmother, whom Paul could see huddling in the kitchen with another woman. The young girl spoke to them in Japanese. Paul didn't have any idea what she said, but she seemed to calm their fears. "I told them you were okay," she said.

She came outside and closed the door behind her. She said her father and mother were at the store, working quietly, and that Paul should go to the back door of the store instead of the front door. "They went down there this morning to make sure everything was safe," she said. "I think they said they were going to do an inventory."

Paul thanked her profusely. She smiled and bowed and went back inside.

Paul ran back to the main intersection and found the store boarded up. As instructed, he ran to the back and knocked. A petite and attractive Japanese woman came to the door and opened it slightly. Paul introduced himself, then told her what he needed, and she allowed him inside.

"We don't have a lot of stock," she said softly.

"Anything will do. Anything you can spare."

"We're trying to see what we have," she said, wiping her hands on her apron. "We were expecting another shipment from the mainland, but who knows when that will arrive now. We're just trying to figure out what we've got on hand."

Paul could see her husband working near the storeroom on the far end of the store. He kept right on with what he was doing, paying no mind to them.

"Perhaps I can give you some coffee," she said. "We seem to have plenty of that. And our bread won't stay, so you can have all of that."

She graciously helped Paul gather a number of foodstuffs in two large boxes. She topped them off with some bananas and papayas. "They won't keep anyway," she said, smiling.

Paul thanked her. Then she grabbed one box and Paul grabbed the other and they carried the big boxes of food a few hundred yards to Kailua School. When they arrived in the schoolyard, they were met with cheers from most of the townsfolk on hand. But Paul couldn't help but notice that one of the soldiers gave the Japanese woman a sour look. She saw the soldier's glare, and she dropped her head and turned around to walk away in silence.

"Thank you," Paul called out to her, but she never turned back. She walked quickly and quietly back to her family store.

At the school, a number of people huddled around a radio. Healani ran up to Paul and grabbed his hand. The look on her face was one of extreme concern. "Congress has officially declared war," she said.

They listened as the local announcer read excerpts of President Roosevelt's speech to Congress. The president said the United States would use all its might to avenge the horrible attacks of the previous day. The announcer's strong voice elicited a hopeful response from the local listeners—when the news report was finished, a few people cheered.

"We'll get those Japs, we will!" a man cried out, obviously oblivious to the fact that nearly a third of the people volunteering for duty at the school that morning were of Japanese ancestry. Amidst the hubbub, several people intently read the local newspaper. The photos from Pearl Harbor were devastating, and the accompanying stories were horribly tragic. The loss of life was enormous. Even a number of civilians had been killed in the Honolulu area. Rumors continued to spread about what may or may not be occurring next around the Hawaiian Islands. No one felt safe.

Beyond what was seen in the paper, the stories trickled in about what had happened on the other side of the island; at Pearl Harbor, Wheeler, Schofield, and Barbers Point and elsewhere. At one point, Mr. G. said he finally heard from Uncle Rob. He said his brother was scouting photographic sites for a wedding early Sunday morning and was along the Pearl shoreline when the bombings started. Rob spent the morning taking photographs of the attack. Some of those photos were expected to be published in the newspapers at some point. Mr. G. said he was just glad that his brother was safe. So many others were not as lucky.

People also sat around and talked of their experiences in Kailua during the attacks. It was different for virtually everyone. Some were aware of the Japanese planes almost immediately; others didn't find out until they heard it on the radio or from a neighbor. A few family members from the base talked about the horrible strafing and bombing that went on at Kāneʻohe Naval Air Station.

"No one was safe," a young blonde woman in her twenties said. "The planes were shooting at everything—everything!" She buried her face in her hands. Another woman consoled her.

Word eventually reached the school that all civilians would be fingerprinted and receive identification cards. But that wouldn't happen until later in the week at the earliest, they were told. Also, night driving would be disallowed except in emergency circumstances. Due to the blackout, car owners were instructed to cover their headlights and make a small slit in that covering to allow for minimal light.

The volunteers continued to assist the victims and the needy, and a few hours later, Mr. G. came over to the area where Healani and Paul were helping the base families. He pulled them aside. "I just spoke to a couple of FBI agents. They're arresting some of the local Japanese and also some Germans and Italians," he said.

"That can't be true. It has to be another rumor," Healani said.

"No, it's true," Paul interrupted. "I saw them arrest a Japanese man when I went to find the store owner. And I was told they arrested the teacher from the Japanese language school."

"Why is this happening?"

"They're very concerned about sabotage is what they said."

"Why were they here at the school?"

"They were just asking questions. I think they're very worried about sabotage or espionage—and what they're calling a Fifth Guard or Fifth Column."

"What's that?"

"They're worried that some of the people living here might secretly be sympathetic to the enemy."

"Do you think that's possible?"

"I doubt it, but it's not the first time I've heard it."

Mr. G. left them and went back to working near the Red Cross tent. Healani ran off to chase after a small youngster who broke away from his mother. It took several seconds for her to run down the giggling toddler.

Paul continued to be amazed at how some normalcies in life went on despite the horrific tragedies of the day before. He wondered if he would be able to get back to his own personal mission. But he also knew this was not the time to bother officials in Honolulu. He continued to help where he was needed—carrying blankets from here to there, assisting with putting up another tent, even shoveling dirt with soldiers who were digging a latrine.

"Let these men through," a sergeant hollered. "They've been up all night and all day. We're giving them a couple of hours to shower and rest before we get them back out on the beach."

A young officer motioned the tired soldiers towards the small shower facility. "There's only one shower," someone said.

"We'll make it work," the sergeant bellowed. Paul looked at the men as they passed in front of him. Most were red-eyed and dirty. One young soldier with corporal stripes on his arm came up to him and asked simply, "Do you have a place to lie down?" Paul showed him to a vacant cot. The corporal was sound asleep within seconds.

Paul took a visual survey of the area. It was both sad and inspiring—sad because of the death and devastation of the day before, but inspiring because of the hard work of both the soldiers and the civilian volunteers. Paul watched Healani move from family to family; she was a rock for all of them. Although she had broken down emotionally earlier in the day, she was a beacon of strength for everyone else. Paul's love for her had deepened with great respect.

As it was nearing dusk, and with curfew perhaps an hour or so away, Paul paused from what he was doing and saw Mr. G. walk over to the side of the road where a police vehicle had pulled up. He saw Officer Burns step out of the car momentarily and have a very brief conversation with Mr. G. Then he observed as Mr. G. shook Burns' hand, and the officer drove off.

Mr. G. turned back toward the school and saw Paul watching, so he walked toward him. When he got very close, he didn't wait for Paul to ask; he came right to the point.

"Burns said they just arrested Otto Kuehn."

21 - BLACKOUT

Burns was exhausted. He had slept only briefly the night before. But he didn't care about sleep. More important now was the safety of his beloved Hawai'i. He kept himself awake by downing one cup of coffee after another—that and his nonstop cigarettes. His duties were immediately amended to go full time in assisting the FBI. He would not have any regular police duties, at least for the foreseeable future.

From an FBI perspective, the concern was sabotage and espionage. No one could be trusted. With martial law in place, the rights of local citizens were tossed aside. Burns disagreed with this policy but did his duty.

In some cases, no official charges against those arrested were filed. "Just round 'em up," was the order. Burns argued that the locals he knew—especially the Japanese—were good citizens and loyal Americans. But his words were ignored. The arrests continued unabated throughout the end of the day on December 7 and all through the day on December 8, and Burns knew they wouldn't stop soon. Hundreds were arrested islandwide, more than 80 percent of them Japanese. The immediate question was where to house all the new prisoners—a place on Sand Island, near Honolulu, was selected, as one of the largest holding facilities.

The arrest of Kuehn came on the eighth of December. When the arrest was made, Kuehn's wife and daughter, Friedel and Greta, pleaded vociferously that Otto was innocent. Their protests were ignored. The wife and daughter were not arrested and did not appear on any lists. In Otto Kuehn's case, charges of espionage against the United States were filed by the end of the day.

Due to information Burns obtained—including the story told to him by Paul—and anecdotal comments from a couple of Kuehn's neighbors, the former German naval officer was suspected of attempting to send signals to someone or something off the coast. Specifically mentioned in the charges were flashing light signals sent from the upstairs front window of his house in the Kalama tract, plus the waving sheets on his clothesline from his beach home in Lanikai. His alleged ties to the German military were the greatest evidence against him.

Burns was told privately that Kuehn was suspected of being a sleeper spy and that sleeper spies are not always actively involved in spying duties but that their actions in a specific situation are nonetheless vital to their own cause and potentially extremely dangerous to their enemies. Thus, a sleeper spy was charged with espionage just like a regular spy. Burns didn't have to be told that if the espionage charges were proven true, then Kuehn could receive the death penalty.

As the time for nightly curfew came close, Jorge drove back to the Gillespie cottage after his long day in Waimānalo. He gave his friends the update on the capture of the Japanese midget submarine and the activity at Bellows. The story was indeed true. The submarine washed up in the waters off Waimānalo Beach after it malfunctioned and went off course during the raid on Pearl Harbor. One Japanese midget-submariner was captured alive, while another drowned in the surf.

Jorge also reported that while American forces lost several

aircraft during the bombing, some American B-17s were able to land at Bellows after being detoured from Hickam on Sunday morning. The encouraging news was that although some of the B-17s were damaged, they should be able to fly again soon.

He said U.S. Marines and Army personnel had already stationed themselves all along the beachheads at Waimānalo and around Makapu'u and on the ridges above Lanikai and Kāne'ohe Bay. No one had sighted further Japanese activity, despite a wild rumor that the Japanese were already landing along Waimānalo Beach. That rumor had apparently sent several soldiers scurrying earlier in the morning. He said he spoke with an army captain about that particular incident, and the officer was very upset.

"He said they were spinning their wheels a lot because of all the rumors."

"We've heard plenty ourselves," Mr. G. said.

"Well, keep your lips buttoned up. The officer I spoke with said they were sick of it all. He said he might just arrest the next person who came up to him with some wild story. I could tell he wasn't kidding."

The four of them decided that they would all continue to stay in Lanikai for at least the next few days. There was safety in numbers.

That evening, after driving home before curfew, they sat in the Gillespie kitchen eating their supper in the darkness. Nan prepared a stew with some of her leftover meat and vegetables. Nothing would go to waste. With the blackout curtains drawn and no lights allowed on, it was hard at times to see their food. But they managed. They had no other choice.

They made small talk for a while, talking about the day and about how everything had changed so suddenly. Nan commented that Paul might have to wait to deliver his letter to the county coroner's office.

"That almost seems trivial now," Paul replied.

"But it's not trivial at all," Healani cut him off. "You can't give up."

"I don't know."

"Where do you have the letter?"

"It's on top of the dresser in the bedroom, but I might as well throw it away."

"What?"

"What am I supposed to do? I can't make all of this go away." Paul waved his arm in the darkness and knocked over a small glass. It crashed on floor and smashed into pieces. Nan quickly began picking up the pieces. Healani stood up and hovered over Paul.

"Don't you realize what's still at stake here? There's a cloud over your grandfather's death! You owe it to him to find out what happened. You can't just let it go and quit."

"I . . . I don't know," Paul stammered.

"Paul Sands! You told me before that you've quit too many things already. Don't quit again!" She turned in the darkness and stormed out of the room. Nan reached over and put a hand on Paul's shoulders.

"She's just tired. We're all tired."

Paul put his head down.

"Get some sleep, everybody," Mr. G. commanded in a fatherly voice.

Paul fell asleep in the middle of the living room floor, but this time without the comfort of Healani by his side. Once she left the table, she stayed in the bedroom and didn't come out. Paul weighed his next options. He could continue on aimlessly, or he could follow Healani's lead. He could try to make contact with officials in Honolulu, or he could also take the first boat back to California once all the craziness ceased, if that ever happened. He didn't know what he was going to do next.

He looked up in the darkness and felt terribly alone. He longed for the peaceful serenity that he and Healani had experienced just days before. He shook his head. With Jorge snoring away on the couch, he lay awake listening to the taped-up radio for a while. He had heard so many announcements and so much bad news during the day that he had finally become numb to it all. Finally, the announcer's melancholy voice put him into a deep sleep.

In the middle of the night, he was awakened by the sound of gentle rapping, but he couldn't quite decipher where it was coming from. He opened his eyes for a moment and looked towards the couch. It was nearly impossible to see anything, but Jorge was still snoring away. The rapping came again, but it was still very light. He sat up quickly, not knowing if he was dreaming. In the blackness of the night, he could see nothing. But the gentle rapping sound continued. It sounded as if it were coming from the front door.

Without waking Jorge, Paul crawled on his knees toward the sound. He opened it cautiously, and he heard a man whisper, "Let me in, Mr. Paul, hurry."

Paul knew that pidgin voice. And as he looked up, he could make out the silhouette of Kenji. He opened the door wider and let the little Japanese yardman into the house. Then he closed the door behind him as quietly as possible.

"I need your help very bad," he said, still whispering. "Can you wake Mr. G.?"

"What's happening?"

"Do as I say, Mr. Paul."

Paul shook his head momentarily, but then decided to honor his request. Although he still couldn't see him very well in the darkness, he could hear the quivering desperation in his voice. Paul rousted Mr. G. out of bed without waking Nan. He and Kenji and Paul walked into the kitchen, hoping not to wake the others.

"What's going on, Kenji?" Mr. G. asked as they sat down at the table as quietly as possible. He, too, spoke in hushed tones.

"I fear men will take me tomorrow."

"What?"

"Shh!" Kenji put his forefinger to Mr. G.'s lips. Paul sat stunned.

"They arrest many of our people," the little yardman continued. "We hear many bad things." His pidgin was very thick. Paul leaned forward so he could understand better.

"What things?" he asked.

"That if you with Buddhist temple or Japanese language school or if you make trips to mother country in Japan, you are suspect. My wife sister of Buddhist priest. And I travel to Japan only last year to bury my grandfather."

"That doesn't make you a criminal," Mr. G. said, his voice suddenly louder.

"Shh," Kenji cautioned him again by pressing his whole hand against Scotty's lips. "Everyone scared. Nothing make sense now. I know this inevitable."

"It doesn't have to be." Mr. G. protested, but kept his voice down.

"I know it is. I need your help."

"How can we help you? How can we make sure you're not arrested?"

"I told you. This inevitable. That not help I need."

"Then tell us how we can help you? We will always do our best for our friends."

"I need to hide many personal belongings. If I don't hide them, I don't know if they be safe."

Mr. G. didn't hesitate. "Consider it done," he said. "But how will you get them here? You've risked your life coming here in the night. You could have been shot."

"I understand. But I have plan."

Quietly but with determined intensity, Kenji told them his plan. He would stay at the Gillespie cottage the remainder of the night. Then, right at daybreak, he would go outside and begin working in the yard, just as he always does. In the meantime, Paul would be sent to his small house at the end of Lanikai and would retrieve a large bag of mulch. Mixed in with the mulch would be the personal property, including prized family heirlooms that Kenji wanted them to protect. Nothing in the bag would mean anything to anyone except his family, he promised them that.

"But it must be saved. If not saved, then when they arrest me, they will take it all away. We will lose our ancestral heritage—everything!"

"We understand. Go on with the plan."

He said he didn't expect the soldiers would bother a man carrying a bag of mulch—especially a *haole* man. The bag, with all his prized personal belongings, would then be left in the Gillespie's safekeeping. After he helped unload them, Kenji would return home in the daylight and wait for his expected arrest.

Mr. G. was visibly angry.

"We have to stop this," he said, his voice low and gruff. "We'll proceed with your plan, but we can't allow our good neighbors to be treated like this."

Kenji got up and bowed to Mr. G. to show his respect. "This inevitable," he repeated. "Just give me corner to lie down." Mr. G. rustled him up a blanket and then went back to his bedroom to try to finish his sleep. Amazingly, during this entire time, Jorge just kept snoring and missed everything. As he curled up in the corner of the kitchen, Kenji asked Paul to sit down with him for a few minutes.

"One more thing I need tell you," he said. "Not everyone here is good neighbor like Mr. G. say."

Paul listened as the little Japanese man spoke in a soft whisper.

"I fear there may be someone in our midst who should not be. My wife told me of strange man coming and sitting in back of our church Sunday morning. She say she couldn't see his face well, but she said there something in way he carry himself that make him different from others. It make her feel uneasy. She say she also see Mr. Kuehn come into the church and look at the man. She say it strange because the man not notice Mr. Kuehn."

"Are you aware that Otto Kuehn has been arrested?"

"Yes, I have heard this."

"Why did your wife notice that Kuehn was there?"

"Because he not belong to our church. She think it very odd that he suddenly show up there on Sunday morning and then leave. Then, bombing happen and people get plenty shook up."

"Did she see the man again?"

"Only for a moment, but she remembers."

"What does she remember?"

"That the man have scar on the back of his hand shape like crescent."

"What does it mean?"

"I do not know exactly. But my wife felt terrible feeling in her stomach. She said something very wrong and this man up to no good."

"Then why don't you and her tell the authorities?"

"We cannot tell them; I tell you now. They not trust someone like me—not now."

"Then why are you telling me this?"

"Because maybe they trust you," he said.

"Why didn't you tell Mr. G. or wake up Jorge and tell them this?"

Kenji paused and spoke slowly and deliberately. "They, the men who come to arrest me, they not trust local people, not any kine local people."

"What?"

"Local people fill their head with rumors. Men not like rumors."

"So, why me? Why are you telling me this?"

Kenji reached over and poked Paul directly in the chest. "Because you are like them."

22 – A SPY AMONGST THEM

Kenji was arrested late the next day. None of them actually witnessed the arrest, but they heard about it from Nan when they came back from Kailua School just before dinner. Nan said she heard the story from neighbors. She said two government men drove their big black car into Lanikai and took Kenji in for what they called "questioning." Kenji's wife and two children were home at the time but were not taken into custody. They apparently told her they didn't know when or if he'd be back home. The neighbors said she was petrified by the ordeal.

The arrest had the entire neighborhood upset, especially coming on the heels of Kuehn's arrest, since he also had a house in Lanikai. Nan said some neighbors wondered if the two arrests were somehow related, since Kenji often did yardwork at Kuehn's home. But no one knew for sure. Nan said she heard rumors that all Japanese, Germans, and Italians would soon be placed in internment camps.

"If that's true," Mr. G. said, with a heavy touch of sarcasm in his voice, "then they're going to have to get a bigger island. There's more than 150,000 Japanese in Honolulu alone."

In the meantime, Paul and Mr. G. had secretly hidden Kenji's personal belongings in the carport closet, under some tools. Most of what they saw before hiding it seemed innocuous—some religious articles, certificates, family heirlooms, and a box of coins—but they were important enough to Kenji, and that was all that mattered to them.

Paul mentioned Kenji's story about the strange man at his church only to Jorge, who quickly told him that it sounded, in his words, "like BS." Jorge told him emphatically to shut up about it. With all the talk of rumors, and with the warning that Jorge had received the day previously, he decided to heed Jorge's advice.

Besides, Paul had another, more immediate concern. Healani was keeping her distance from him. Paul was confused and hurt and unsure of how to handle it. Jorge had no advice in that department.

By Wednesday, December 10, some of the life in Kailua was beginning to return to a certain degree of normalcy. The stores reopened for business that morning, and there were long lines out the doors. Patrons were asked not to hoard food. One market sign read WE SELL TO OUR REGULAR CUSTOMERS ONLY— ONLY IN LIMITED QUANTITIES.

The stores had spent the previous days performing mandatory inventories. Military authorities wanted to know the amount of foodstuffs on hand, including rice, canned milk, wheat flour, potatoes, onions, fats and oils, canned meats, canned vegetables, soups, plus canned and dry fruits.

Tips on food conservation were prominently placed in the morning newspaper. The newspaper stories read DO NOT WASTE. COOK PORTIONS A LITTLE LESS THAN USUAL. EAT SMALLER PORTIONS. CONSERVE MILK AND EGGS FOR CHILDREN AND PREGNANT WOMEN. CONSERVE FATS AND BOIL INSTEAD OF FRY. SAVE AND RESAVE FATS. PROTEIN FOODS SHOULD BE USED SPARINGLY. SHARE WITH NEIGHBORS. "

With the edict of martial law came the word that all civilians would need identification cards by the end of the week. A small table was set up in one of the Kailua School classrooms, and lines of people went through the fingerprinting and photo process. It was slow, but people didn't grumble. Locals were a little bit less tolerant of the next edict, that rationing also would begin immediately. Gasoline and alcohol were among the commodities rationed. All radio and camera sales were stopped. Japanese families had even stricter rules. They were ordered to turn in any cameras, radios, binoculars, and weapons of all kinds. The last part of that order was especially difficult for some families, because it meant turning over ceremonial swords. Paul now understood why Kenji was so protective of his own personal stash.

Many of the families who came to Kailua School were helped by the Red Cross, whose volunteers had worked tirelessly since the time immediately after the attack. Meanwhile, after going through the identification lines, Mr. G. returned to his work at the bank in Honolulu. Jorge went back to his work at the ranch. Healani, still not speaking to Paul, helped families at the school put together what one volunteer lady called evacuation knapsacks. The knapsacks included blankets and clothes, water and canned goods, a flashlight and a first aid kit. Families were told to keep these items close at hand in case of an emergency. In Kailua people were told to evacuate to the Kawailoa Girls School near Mount Olomana, should another attack occur.

The digging of bomb shelters also began. At Kailua School, volunteers helped dig large trenches. The shelters and the trenches were crude, at best. Paul worked with soldiers to shore up one end of the shelter, but they consistently ran into problems with cave-ins because of the sandy soil.

At three o'clock that afternoon, the entire island went through a mandatory fifteen-minute air-raid drill. In Kailua, civilians and soldiers cleared the streets and took advantage of the closest cover.

The experience sent shivers down Paul's spine, as he relived the unpleasant memories of the airstrike.

A few minutes after the drill, they all huddled around the radio to hear an address from General Short, the new military governor. In his brief speech he said, "You must obey military personnel instantly and without question. Avoid the slightest appearance of hostility. Certain enemy agents have been apprehended and detained. Civilians who go about their regular duties have nothing to fear. Keep your heads up and do your duty as Americans."

Later, there was another radio message, this one from Lieutenant Colonel Fielder. He praised the people of Hawai'i but also cautioned everyone.

"Promiscuous spreading of wild rumors will only contribute to confusion. Check carefully the authenticity and accuracy of rumors you may hear. There have been very few acts of sabotage. Reports of parachutists and glider troops have been proven false. It was rumored that the *Lurline* was sunk. I can assure you that it arrived safely in San Francisco."

He spoke for a while about United States military efforts, reassuring the listeners that everyone was being well protected. Then he spoke of local efforts. "A number of enemy agents have been detained. Many others have been apprehended on suspicion but were found to be innocent and released. There is no desire on the part of authorities to organize mass concentration camps. Continue to pull together," he concluded. "Your armed forces can only operate effectively and successfully when we are not hampered by a citizenry that is divided and discordant."

The short speeches were both uplifting and troubling. Paul looked over at Healani, and she at him, momentarily. But then she looked away. Paul knew that the immediate future was uncertain, both his and theirs. He did not have any answers, and slowly, and with a heavy heart, he went back to digging with the soldiers.

An hour later, the local news announcer came back on the

radio with another important announcement. He said that all evacu-
ated military families would be allowed to return to their homes the
next morning. A huge cheer went up from everyone around the
school. "Finally, a bit of good news," Paul said aloud.

He looked for Healani but could not find her in the mass of
people. As curfew approached, he was dismayed when she walked
away from the school grounds toward her own home. He couldn't
muster up enough guts to chase after her. Disconsolately, Paul made
his way back to Lanikai, knowing that a lonely night in the blackout
was ahead. He quickly fell asleep without eating, feeling empty and
very alone.

He was awakened from his early morning stupor by the furious
tone of a ringing phone.

"Come quickly to my house," Jorge told him when Paul picked
up the phone.

"What's happening?"

"Just come. I need help with the horses," Jorge said on the
other end of the line. Then he hung up.

The phone message was vague indeed. What could he mean?
Paul wondered. He understood why he did it, though. Phone
conversations were being monitored. Whatever was bothering him,
he couldn't say, and he wouldn't say. Without eating breakfast, Paul
drove through the town and met Jorge as he quickly as he could get
there. He looked for Healani briefly, and when Jorge saw him, he
said that she was already off to the school grounds.

He told Paul to saddle up with him. Paul started to ask questions, but Jorge waved him off.

"I'll tell you as we go." They saddled the horses. Jorge took the
quarter and Paul the bay. They sauntered at a steady pace through
Kailua Town with Paul saying nothing. The soldiers stationed along
the way paid them no mind—they were already used to the Kailua
cowboys doing their daily chores.

Finally, Jorge broke the silence as they passed the tavern and then the theater.

"Somebody, I don't know who, but somebody has been staying in a building near the theater. I saw him slip in and out of there just before curfew last night and thought it was odd, but I was tired, and I headed home. It didn't mean anything until I thought of what you told me yesterday."

"About Kenji's story?"

"Yeah."

"You're saying you think the man at his church could be this same man. How could you know that?"

"I couldn't, but this morning I was up very early, and I drove the Chevy over near the theater where we have a small feeding area. A few other people were up and about, and I saw the same man as he nonchantlantly walked past me, no more than five to ten feet from where I was working. He looked just like anyone else around here, but for some reason, I looked at his hands because he was carrying a small duffel bag and what looked like a fishing pole on his back, and I saw the crescent-shaped scar that Kenji's wife talked about."

"Why didn't you stop him?"

"I'll admit I was kind of startled, and it took a while to sink in. I continued on with my work while I watched him out of the corner of my eye as he began walking toward the Kawai Nui Swamp as if he belonged there. I followed him for a while but not too closely. I thought maybe he was a fisherman: I wasn't sure. But then I figured he had to be up to something because he didn't follow the regular roads."

"Why didn't you keep following him?"

"I thought then I should tell someone. I ran over to the area where some of the army guys were camped, but the sentry there told me that they'd been told to stop chasing after wild rumors. When he called over his superior, it turned out to be one of the guys that I got into a fight with at Kailua Tavern the other day. He took one look at me and told me to get the hell out of there. Called me crazy, among other things. In fact, that was probably the nicest word he used. In any case, I knew they weren't going to believe me, so I went back home and tried to call the Old Man or Henry Wong, but they weren't in. So, I called you. Figured we'd track him together."

"You are crazy!"

So with limited information and essentially a hunch, they moved their horses toward the trails leading to Kawai Nui. They had no weapons with the exception of the machete Jorge used to clear away bushes and deep brush. They had no plan, not even any ideas for a plan. They were doing this strictly on instinct.

Paul wondered if Jorge's hunch was right. He wasn't sure, but he remembered the way Kenji looked when he told them his story. He would trust both of his friends at this stage.

They crossed the small bridge that was the entry to Kailua Town and walked their horses slowly up the Pali Road. Jorge pointed in the general direction of where he had last seen the person that they soon started calling simply "the man."

Where was the man headed? What was the man's mission?—that is, if he had one.

And, most important, where was the man at the moment? They speculated endlessly.

It was Jorge's opinion that the man was headed toward the Pali itself. "You can imagine how destructive it would be to cut off the flow of traffic, including military vehicles, to the Windward Side. Maybe it's his mission to blow up the Pali." Jorge's imagination was running on overdrive.

Paul's own mind was also going crazy with the possibilities. Everything sounded both bizarre and plausible. He didn't know if they were going on a wild goose hunt or not. "Let's just see if we can find this person and let the authorities deal with him. They can take all the glory."

Jorge answered with a bunch of cuss words and Paul immediately shut up. Paul had already learned that his cowboy friend didn't like anyone to disagree with him. But he also figured that if he was ever in a fight, Jorge was the guy he wanted on his side. So he let him know that he didn't need to worry. They were in this thing together, wherever it led them.

At first they slowly scouted the shoreline of Kawai Nui. Jorge got off his horse near the side of the road where the Japanese vegetable stands had been doing a furious business just a few days before. The stands were empty now. Most of the Japanese farmers and their families were too afraid to come out of their homes.

Jorge and Paul stayed close, walking their horses behind them. Paul was scared as hell but said nothing to his friend. He let Jorge take the lead.

"We're going to have to leave the horses behind and forge ahead on foot," Jorge said. "Tie them up over there." He pointed at one of the sturdier vegetable stands. They quickly tied the horses down and gave them access to food and water.

They pushed their way through the deep brush that bordered the swamp. "Look over here," Jorge pointed. "You can see some recent footprints in the mud. I think we're on the right trail."

Jorge used his machete and hacked his way through the straw-berry guava and the Christmasberry bushes. Paul cautioned him about the noise, but Jorge said he wanted to make his presence known. "I'd rather know that he knows somebody else is out here. It might make him move faster, and then he'll get careless. Remember, I know the land here. If this man is really new to these parts, there's no way he's going to elude us."

Within moments it began to rain. First it seemed like a passing shower. But then it got heavier. Paul and Jorge paused under a banyan tree to take cover. They talked about how long they should wait. And they even talked about abandoning the chase altogether. But they finally agreed that they had to press on.

Out of the cover of the big banyan, their clothes were soaked within seconds. But the rain actually helped their tracking. Every few hundred yards, they would discover a fresh footprint or two in the mud. The man's trail still led toward the Pali, but it had shifted away from Kawai Nui and up into Maunawili.

Jorge knew this area intimately. He had chased cattle through every thicket and every stream of this land. When the man's trail eventually started moving along Maunawili Stream, Jorge said, "We've got him where we want him now. If he stays with the stream, he's going to run out of room. The only way out will be to climb up the cliffs."

But they couldn't move as fast as they wished. The footing along the banks of the stream became more treacherous as the rain grew harder. Soon it was a torrent. The waters of the stream rose extremely quickly, and within minutes, it was ankle-deep and then knee-deep. They were not only wringing wet but also extremely cold. They knew they had to get away from the stream, and they eventually found shelter in an abandoned shack near the Old Government Road.

Wet and weary, they tried to regroup. Their respite lasted about a half hour, and the heavy rains dissipated some. Jorge found some old rags in the shack, and both men tried to dry themselves. Jorge even took off his jeans and hung them over a broken chair.

Then Jorge let out a yell. Paul didn't know what he was hollering about at first. But then he looked down at Jorge's lower leg. While he was drying off, Jorge tore away the bandages from the wound he had suffered during the December 7 attack. The wound was badly inflamed.

"God damn it!" Jorge shouted, holding his lower leg. "I knew it hurt. I didn't realize how bad it was until I tore off the wet bandages." He sat on the ground and applied pressure to the area.

"It's infected," Paul said. He looked in Jorge's red eyes, and he could see he was in deep pain.

"How long have you been hurting like this?"

"It's been bad the whole time. I just didn't want to say

anything. I'm stupid, I know it."

"We should head back and get you to a doctor."

"Nope," he answered quickly. "We have to go on."

Paul decided against arguing with him again. There was no point. They did the best they could to clean the wound and covered it with torn pieces of rags they had found in the abandoned shack.

"I don't know how long that's gonna last," Paul said.

"Long enough," was Jorge's quick retort. But Paul knew his cowboy friend was in terrible pain.

By the time they left the shelter of the small shack, the rain had ceased. But the old dirt road was extremely muddy. Then they got lucky. As they reached the top of one of the ridges, they had a good view of the immediate lowlands. Up ahead, perhaps a half mile or so, Paul got his first glimpse of the man, who appeared to be fighting his way through the deep Maunawili forest. He couldn't see his face, but he could definitely make out the shape of a small, stocky man scrambling toward the foot of the Koʻolau.

"There he is," he said to Jorge, who was now lagging behind by several yards. He caught up with Paul, albeit slowly.

"I'm sorry, I'm not any help," he said. "My leg is getting worse. Dammit. I'm really having trouble walking."

"What are you going to do?"

"I don't know what I can do, dammit. But if we're going to catch him, I think you've got to go without me." He sat down in the mud and propped his leg up on a rock.

"I can't do this alone," Paul argued.

"Yes, you can, Hollywood," he said, looking him squarely in the eyes. "Don't quit now, you hear me. Don't quit."

Paul started to protest. Jorge grabbed the tall man's chin and shook it. "Don't give up. This is too important. This man is obviously up to something, and only you can stop him. Take the machete, in case you need it." He handed the machete to Paul, who hesitated to grab it at first but then reluctantly took hold.

"And what will you do?"

"I can stay here and give you signals from this vantage point," he said. "It's a pretty good view of the landscape. He may not stay in this area for long, so you have to move quickly. No more talking. Just do it."

Paul looked at him incredulously. He started to say something, to argue back again, but Jorge reached up and pressed his forefinger against his lips. Then he commanded, "Go!"

Paul stumbled forward down the hill, losing his footing. He looked back a couple of times to make sure he could still see Jorge, and for a while, he could see his friend giving him hand motions. He followed the motions the best he could. He clutched the machete against his side and felt the sharpness of its steel. He hoped to God he wouldn't have to use it.

Pretty soon he was out of Jorge's sight range. He was alone now.

He tried hard to imagine how a hunter might move, slowly, quietly, and with courageous determination. But he knew he wasn't quiet. His long legs and bad knees made his climb through the area difficult. He was unsteady and he knew it. He fell down on two occasions; the second time was facefirst and he let out a yelp. He knew he scared up a few birds in the area, and he wondered what else he scared up.

The forested area grew thicker and thicker. And it began to rain heavily again. The forest became like a dark jungle around him. With water fiercely pouring onto his head and into his face, he could hardly see anything. But it didn't rain as long this time, and when the rains slowly began to dissipate, the cloud cover dropped so low that it created a thick, deep fog. Soon, Paul couldn't see more than twenty feet in front of him.

Eventually, the plants and bushes around him were so thick that he could hardly move. He pulled his machete from his side and hacked away. He quickly realized that he had not only lost total sight of Jorge, but also the man he was tracking. He was hopelessly lost.

And then his feelings of fear and trepidation got worse. A sudden fear crept into his soul. Behind him, somewhere in the fog, in the depths of the thick forest, he could hear something—or some-one—moving.

23 - TERRIFIED IN THE KO'OLAU

He was now less than a few hours away from completing his long-planned mission. The rains couldn't stop him, nor could those two worthless locals who had been following him. He adjusted on his back the small signal beam that he had patiently assembled from the pieces in his knapsack. Assembled, it was a clumsier piece of equipment than he'd expected, but if he had to drag it up the goddamn mountain, he would do exactly that.

The Japanese submarines, waiting clandestinely nearly a hundred miles offshore to avoid American patrol boats and scout planes, couldn't wait much longer for his signal. He understood that from the original plan—his signal had to come within the first four days after the attack; after that, the subs would have to leave their position, and his mission would be a failure. He couldn't allow that to happen. From what he had seen and observed, O'ahu was immediately vulnerable to a follow-up invasion. He was prepared to send the signal.

In his meticulous planning, he had hoped to be at this place and time at least a day earlier, but he observed soldiers frantically repositioning themselves in the days immediately after December 7. Thus he had to confine his location to the town. He found that as poorly prepared as the Americans were, they had patrolled reasonably well in the first few days after the attack. Only when military officials made the decision to allow local citizens to go back to work—thus opening up the floodgates of people and commerce and relaxing military tensions—did he find the opportunity to finish his mission. He would hike through the swamp and foothills and heavy forested areas during daylight, then make the final assault on the mountainside after darkness. His signal needed the height of the high mountains so it could be sent a distance of up to one hundred miles, where it would be best seen in the darkness before tomorrow's dawn.

Now, partway up the Koʻolau, he looked ahead of him, through the deep thicket, and toward the ridgeline. The taller of the two men who had been following him now pressed forward on his own. The other man had disappeared. He spied through the deep forest to see if he could catch a glimpse of his would-be tracker. For brief moments, in the misty light between the branches, he saw his adversary. From this vantage point, all he could discern was that he was a very tall man, and he moved awkwardly and hesitatingly in the irregular terrain. From all observations, he didn't appear to be a threat.

But he decided to keep his distance for the time being and to spy occasionally, because he was unsure what had happened to the second man who had been following him earlier. Perhaps the other tracker was circling him; maybe there was a trap. He wasn't going to fall for any trap; he was much too clever for that.

He had one goal—complete the mission.

Paul's heart pounded violently inside his chest. He had never felt such fear.

"Damn," he thought to himself. He could hear the definitive sounds of human movement below him; the consistent rhythm of crackling leaves and branches. He knew those sounds weren't coming from the rain. There was no denying it. He was overcome with the realization he was no longer the hunter; he was the hunted.

The man they had been tracking since morning was now behind him. The thought mortified him—it meant there was no escape, except to get to higher ground.

Paul was cold and wet and terrified. He couldn't see who or what was out there. He just knew that he was now being followed. He paused briefly to catch his breath and regroup his thoughts. He wondered what the hell he was going to do next. If he could somehow stay above his new adversary, he thought, he felt he might have a chance to regain the advantage. If he couldn't achieve that . . . well, he didn't want to think about the alternative.

Still new to the terrain, Paul had a general idea of where he was because of his hike with Healani the week before. He retraced the day's journey in his mind. He knew that he and Jorge had chased their intended prey up the Maunawili Stream and then headed into the hills above Maunawili Falls. The trees and foliage had thickened to the point where he knew he had to be almost up against the base of the Ko'olau, perhaps somewhere on the same horizontal plane as the Palikū mansion.

He tightened his grip on the machete and then scrambled up nearby rocks, trying to see as far as he could. The rain had let up to no more than a heavy mist, but the cloud cover still hugged every tree and morsel of ground. Paul hunched atop a giant, moss-covered boulder and surveyed the area.

Suddenly he heard a branch snap loudly. The cracking sound sent chills down his spine and intensified his fears that he was in a precarious position. The man couldn't be far away.

So he kept moving, scrambling up more large rocks, then turning to see if there was anything he could see below him. The cloud cover began to lessen. At first he thought that was a good sign because he could get his bearings. But then he quickly realized that the more he could see, the more he could be seen. That fact terrified him more. He scrambled higher up the ridge.

At one point, he became so frustrated at the intermittent sounds following behind him that he grabbed some loose stones in the area and threw them down the hill. The sound below him stopped—at least momentarily.

That gave Paul an idea. Perhaps he could cause a rockslide of some sort. He looked around at the ground before him and quickly realized that he didn't have the proper tools. He would need something greater than the strength of his own power and that of his machete to move some of the giant boulders around him. He knew quickly that the idea wouldn't work.

So he kept climbing onward. And as he moved, the clouds began to disappear. The air became still. He looked around, knowing that the storm had finally passed.

Cascading waterfalls came crashing down the cliffs of the Koʻolau. Every crevice was dominated by the falling water. It was as if the mountains were crying.

But there was no time to gaze at the amazing sight. He nervously scanned the area behind him but saw no glimpse of his adversary. He looked back at the cliffs and realized he could no longer go straight forward. The rock face in front of him was nearly vertical and perhaps a thousand feet high. To escape this position, he needed to move and find a ridgeline.

Because the skies were beginning to clear, it meant that Paul's ability to see his surroundings was restored. He began to run, at least where he could run. Where he couldn't run, he scrambled. The footing was slippery, but he knew he had to keep moving. He slipped a number of times along the muddy path, but recovered each time without falling to the ground. He glanced desperately behind him to the area where he had just been and saw nothing. But he knew he was still being followed.

Eventually, he came upon an opening in the deep forest. He scrambled to the highest ground he could find and surveyed the entire area. No signs of anything or anyone in the dense thicket immediately behind him. In the opposite direction, he could see what appeared to be another ridge. He instinctively ran toward that ridge, falling but once.

By the time he reached the base of the ridge, he could tell it was midafternoon. Strangely, it was brighter than it had been all day long. The black clouds of the morning, followed by the heavy rains, followed by the thick dense cloud cover—all had conspired to block out most of the early daylight. Now, although it was not fully sunny, the skies were brighter, and Paul could see a great distance.

As he continued to scramble up the ridgeline, he could now see all the way from Waimānalo to Kāneʻohe. Below him was the dense forested area of Maunawili, and in the distance, perhaps a half mile away, he could make out the roofline of the Castle mansion just off the Pali Road. He wondered if he could yell and bring help.

He decided against it. He wasn't sure why he was making this decision, but was concerned that if he started yelling and screaming, the man would come out of nowhere and attack him. Fear consumed him.

He wondered why his adversary didn't shoot at him. His only guess was that the man didn't have a gun or he didn't want to make a loud sound that tipped off his whereabouts. If he truly was a spy, as Jorge and Kenji suspected, then he would want to go out of his way to be undetected.

Paul continued to move on. He was exhausted and running totally on adrenaline. As the ridgeline narrowed and became steeper, he slipped and fell and hit his head against the rocks. The machete bounced out of his grip and careened down the side of the ridge. He cursed aloud, realizing that there would be no way to get it back. More than a hundred feet below him in an inaccessible ravine, he saw the machete resting atop thick bushes.

Now he was without a weapon of any kind. He had no time to think about the consequences; he kept on moving higher and higher. Soon he figured he had climbed several hundred feet at least, maybe even more than a thousand feet.

He was perspiring heavily, but when he went to wipe his brow, he felt a stinging cut on his forehead. Now he felt the blood trickle down his temple. He gathered up the lower part of his shirt in his hands and then pulled it up toward his face. He wiped the blood away the best he could. He wondered if he could go on much longer. He paused for a moment and tried to gather his strength.

Suddenly, he felt a stinging pain go through the back of his right leg. "Oh my God," he cried out in agony. He hit the ground hard, and he felt the pain shooting through him. For a moment, he thought he was shot. Maybe he was wrong about the man having a gun—but he realized quickly he had heard no gunfire blast. Then he thought the pain had come from his knee giving out on him. He wondered if he would be able to go on. Lying flat on the ground, he slowly straightened out the leg; the pain finally subsided.

Of all things, he realized, he had simply suffered a muscle cramp. But regardless, he knew he couldn't stay in this vulnerable position for long. He looked at the steep incline of the ridgeline above him and decided he was either going to have to continue his difficult climb or take a detour.

Up ahead, the drop-off was not as great and there appeared to be some covering near one of the many waterfalls. He decided to slide down the opposite side of the ridgeline, or away from the Maunawili side. He scrambled ahead and then looked down. He could see thick shrubbery below and believed he might be able to hide there for a while, perhaps until dark, and then escape. On the other side of the shrubbery, the water cascaded down the cliffs and splashed into the rocks. His goal was to get to that waterfall.

The slide down the ridge was much harder than he expected. The ground was wet and grassy, but underneath the rocks were razor sharp in places. Paul felt the piercing pain of the sharp rocks as he dropped into the thicket below. He caught his breath and rolled into the bushes. He kept right on rolling, breaking several branches, until he came to a stop in a muddy pool at the base of the tiny waterfall.

He plopped his head into the muddy water, and he lay there in the shallow pool for several seconds. He felt the coolness of the water and let it soak into his cheeks. Then he pulled himself up and let the streaming water pound against his entire body. He opened his mouth to taste its sweetness; never had water tasted so good or been so appreciated.

However, he still knew he was in grave danger. In fact, he realized he may have locked himself into a less defensible position. He quickly looked around and felt the paranoia of a hunted animal sweep over him. He sat with his head back to the side of the cliff, soaking in the falling water, but also keeping a watchful eye on the ridgeline above him.

He waited for a sign that he was either out of harm's way or right in the middle of it.

He realized that it was a wonder his body could function like this. His knees were somehow holding up, but his legs ached. He had fulfilled his thirst under the waterfall, but he felt the deep pangs of hunger in his gut. He suddenly realized that he had not eaten in nearly a day and a half. He was amazed that adrenaline was what was keeping him going and what had brought him to this point. But he wondered if he had enough strength to keep going. He felt weak and knew he needed something to fill his stomach.

He looked around for something, anything. But there were no berries or fruit at that elevation. The hunger pangs consumed his thoughts. He felt more weak and scared; ne needed strength if he was going to go on.

As he searched around on his hands and his knees, his mind raced. The predicament made him recall the story Auntie Rose had told him of Kamehameha's warriors eating the edible mud after they landed in Kailua. According to the legend, that edible mud was the sustenance that empowered the soldiers before their decisive and victorious battle at the Pali.

As absurd as it sounded, he thought if he had to, he would eat anything, even mud. He was desperate. He didn't hesitate.

He leaned down and splashed his hands in the muddy pool of water around him. He dipped his fingers into the shallow mud and scooped some of the slimy black muck off the surface. He put the mud to his lips and grimaced at the first taste. But he swallowed it anyway. Quickly, and without thinking further about it, he dipped his fingers twice more and ate every muddy morsel. Then he washed his mouth with the streams of water that continued to cascade from above, and then he drank more of the water. At last the hunger pangs subsided.

He felt a slight renewal of strength as he considered his next move. He couldn't believe the mess he was in. Over three weeks had passed since he sailed across the Pacific on one of the great ships of the era. But then his grandfather died suddenly, and in his frustrating search to get the answers for his death, he found and then lost a new love. And then there was war.

War. It made people crazy and irrational, and it directly led to the desperate situation he was now in, clinging to life in a deep crevice below the Pali. When faced with adversity in his life to this point, he had always taken the easy way out; he quit. Now quitting was not an option.

Both Jorge and Healani were right. He couldn't quit anymore.

Reenergized by water and "food," he looked up and decided to climb back up to the ridgeline from where he had come. Emboldened by his renewed belief in himself, he crawled away from the waterfall and began his challenging ascent back up the side of the hill. It was a slow climb, and he slipped several times as he inched his way up. His arms bled due to the cuts from sliding against the rocks. Each time he tried to go up, he failed.

He had slipped partway back down into the crevice again,

when he suddenly heard the sounds of movement above him. It was an unmistakable sound. Someone was moving along the ridgeline. He pressed his body as hard as he could against the side of the hill, attempting to stay out of sight. The deliberate sounds of someone climbing the ridge continued. He listened intently as the sounds passed directly over head.

He lay still for several moments, frozen by fear. Only moments before, he had felt almost irrationally confident in his ability to meet his challenge. Now he was overcome with the reality that death could be a mere few feet away.

He closed his eyes and his thoughts raced. Should he continue to hide and then scurry down the hill? Should he scream as loud as he possibly could? Should he run? Should he engage? Should he quit after all? He was overwhelmed with the sense of helplessness.

Slowly and deliberately, he made up his mind. He began to crawl back up towards the ridgeline. He had no plan, nothing. It took him several minutes to reach the top, but he finally made it, and he continued to hug the ground as he reached the precipice. He had no idea what he was about to do next.

He looked up toward the top of the mountain. He could see its peak reaching towards the sky. As he turned his head to determine if he could see his adversary, the bright rays of the sun flashed through the cloud cover for the first time during the day. It was a glorious sight.

But there was no time to marvel in amazement because seconds later, he spied the silhouette of a man inching upwards about a hundred yards above him. The man was scrambling hurriedly forward on all fours and dragging something behind him. The sounds of whatever it was he was towing rattled against the ground.

Paul was overcome by fear. And he simply couldn't breathe. His mind raced and his heart pounded, and then he suddenly leaped into an almost suicidal rage and began charging up the ridgeline.

As he ran, he threw caution to the wind, moving faster than he could ever imagine. Every step was fraught with peril, but in the stir-craziness that had overtaken his mind, he knew he mustn't fail. Failure meant death.

He screamed as loud as he could, and he heard the sounds of his booming voice echo off the walls of the cliffs around him. The man heard the sounds, too, and halted his steep ascent momentarily. From the startled look on the man's muddied face, Paul knew that his wild attack had caught him off guard. The man hesitated for just a moment and then quickened his pace. Paul couldn't tell if he was trying to escape or if he was just going to blindly go on to finish his mission, whatever that was.

Paul didn't care. He was filled with delirious rage. He yelled and screamed as he scrambled and climbed faster and faster. He was less than fifty feet away when the man finally turned, ready to fight. Paul saw the flash of his knife as he pulled it from his belt. The man held the knife over his head, and Paul could see the wildness of his adversary's steely eyes.

Paul didn't stop. He just kept coming hard, expecting it might be the final moment of his life. Thirty feet. Twenty feet. Ten feet. Five feet. And then he lunged.

He screamed the most vicious sound a man could ever make. And he grabbed for him. But he came up with nothing; nothing at all. He landed hard, facefirst on the rocky ridgeline. He felt the sudden impact of the hard ground and tried to let out another yell. But he had nothing left in his lungs. He tried to rise up again to fight, but felt an enormous pressure on his back. He couldn't move.

He was out. Out cold.

24 - A QUESTION OF LOYALTY

Paul awoke from his stupor. It was nearly dark and in the throes of the last moments of dusk. He slowly pulled himself to his knees and then reached up to touch his face. He could feel blood on his forehead, but not a lot. Mostly scrapes. His head hurt a great deal, and he massaged an area near his left ear that was severely bruised.

It took him several moments to realize that he was alone. And then he wondered why he was still alive. He knew he missed his target when he crashed to the ground. But where was the mysterious man he had been chasing all day?

In the dwindling light, he looked above him and saw nothing but the peak of the dark green mountain. He rose to his feet slowly and deliberately. It hurt to move, but he knew he had to get off the ridge or he would be stranded there for the night. He looked around full circle and saw no movement at all. He wondered what had happened.

Without warning, some kind of force field pushed against him. Try as Paul might to get himself away from the powerful feeling, he was unable to move except in the direction that the force led him.

Slowly, he was being nudged from the top of the ridge toward the edge of the drop-off several feet away. There was no rational way to explain what he was feeling, but he was positive something was forcefully moving him. He wriggled this way and that, and he tried to twist his torso to get away from it, but he couldn't escape the feeling. He dropped to his knees and wondered if he was experiencing some sort of vertigo. His balance must be off because of the hard fall, he thought.

He tried again to get to his feet, but once again he felt the strange force push him. The sensation made his head spin, and he felt suddenly sick to his stomach. His body was reeling and he could take it no more. He vomited. He stood hunched over, his head hanging down toward the ledge of the cliff, and he gagged repeatedly.

Finally, he began to breathe normally again. And his senses began to recover. He shook himself, stood up straight, and tried to study his surroundings. With his eyes finally beginning to focus, he became aware of a large object in the dense overgrowth below him. He dropped to the ground and strained to see.

In the bush and tall grass more than a few hundred feet below, he could see a large shape. He strained to look closer and realized it was the shape of a man. The man laid motionless, his arms draped awkwardly around a twisted tree. A small bag and a mangled piece of metal lay beside him.

Oh my God, Paul thought. It's him. He stared for several moments. No one could have survived that fall, he realized. His adversary was dead. There was no doubt about that. He moved slightly to the downhill side to get a better look, but the dead body lay deeply under the heavy growth, twisted amongst the branches and bushes at the bottom of the ravine. Paul moved back to his original position, realizing that it was the only place from which the body could be seen clearly.

Paul sat down momentarily and pondered his fate. How in the

hell had this happened? What force had allowed him to live and the man to perish? He couldn't answer.

He rose slowly and once again felt the large bruise on his head. Damn, it hurt. But he shook off the pain. He stood transfixed for several moments, wondering what he should do next. Get off the damn ridge, he quickly realized. The man who could have been a spy, and who at the very least was definitely up to no good, was dead. It was nearing darkness, and Paul knew he had to come down off the mountain for his own well-being.

Quickly, he started walking down the ridgeline toward Maunawili. He had survived a most dangerous situation, certainly the most harrowing event of his life, but he wondered how he did it. How could he tell anyone about it? Who would believe it?

It was pitch-black by the time he reached the Old Government Road. Wounded and weak, he dragged himself to the nearest sign of civilization. A hundred yards in front of him, where the Old Government Road met the Pali Road, he could see two tiny slits of light. Even in the darkness, he could make out the shape of a vehicle. A man stood outside a truck.

"Hollywood, is that you?" the familiar voice of Jorge Luis rang out. It was the first human words he had heard in hours. He strode forward in the darkness to greet his friend, but he said nothing.

"I thought we were going to have to organize a search party," Jorge said when Paul reached the car. He grabbed his tall friend around the back of the shoulders and gave him a big bear hug. Paul then felt the strength of Jorge's arms as the stocky cowboy gave him two firm slaps in the middle of his back.

Paul's body started to shake uncontrollably until he convulsed in wracking sobs.

"Hollywood, you okay?" Jorge asked, as he extended his arms outward and looked the tall man in the face. But Paul couldn't see him through his tears; his body heaved desperately. Jorge said nothing more. He just let Paul stand in the darkness until he had cried himself out. Then he reached into the car and pulled a blanket from the front seat. He wrapped it about his friend's shoulders and led him into the passenger seat.

"I'm sorry," Paul whispered quietly when Jorge started up the car.

"I'm the one who should be sorry. I'm the one who couldn't go on. I really let you down. What the hell happened up there, anyway?"

"I wish I could tell you. I don't know really know, to tell you the truth. Something happened up there, I'm not sure what." Paul stammered and stuttered, making very little sense. "Uh, I trailed him. Um, I lost sight of him. I thought I was done for. Then I saw him again trying to climb the peak. I'm not sure really want came over me, but I went after him. I don't know what happened then. All I know is that he's dead."

"The man, dead? You sure?" his voice rose excitedly.

"Very sure. And I doubt anyone's going to discover the body for a helluva long time."

He looked over at Paul, expecting him to tell him more. But Paul said nothing, offering no more details. Jorge tried to pry, but gave up when his tall friend sat in a trancelike state.

Under the blanket, Paul was trembling silently. He honestly didn't know if he had somehow murdered a man. Or if the man had accidentally fallen to his death. Or if something else he couldn't explain at all had happened. What was that powerful force he felt after he was knocked out? He didn't know. And he didn't know how to feel. He was consumed by both relief and regret.

Along the drive back to Lanikai, Jorge tried to cheer Paul up by pulling up his pant leg and revealing a huge layer of bandages. "Good as new," he said. Paul smiled weakly at the news that his friend's wound was now okay.

The Chevy motored forward slowly in the darkness. The small slits in the headlights revealed only the immediate road ahead. Near the Kodama Store, a lone sentry came on to the road and stopped them.

"You gentleman have business here?" the young soldier asked sternly. "You know you're not supposed to be out past curfew unless you're on official business." He was wearing a doughboy helmet strapped tightly to his chin. He held a rifle in his right hand. The heavy bags under his eyes revealed he'd had very little sleep the last few days.

"We work for Kāneʻohe Ranch," Jorge said. He showed the young soldier his identification papers. "Just chasing some cattle that got caught up near the pass. We had to redirect them down towards Kawai Nui. Took longer than we thought. We'll be home within minutes."

The soldier looked over at Paul. He appeared to be studying the scratches and bruises on Paul's face.

"What happened to him?" he asked Jorge.

"That's why it took so long. One of the steers got the better of him," Jorge lied. "Knocked him over something fierce. Hurt both his body and his pride."

Jorge and the soldier laughed. Paul just tightened his grip on the blanket. The soldier let them pass with the warning not to let it happen again. Jorge thanked him and they moved on.

"What do you want me to tell the others?" Jorge said a minute or so later. "We've got to have some story."

"Sounds like you already made up a good one," he said in a hushed tone. "That's good enough for me."

Paul and Jorge both knew they couldn't blab the truth. Nobody had believed Jorge in the first place, and Paul couldn't come to grips with what actually happened on the ridge. Both of them decided that they would have to lie for the time being.

Slowly they drove into Kailua Town. With the exception of a car passing in the other direction with its two slit-covered head-lights, the streets were empty. The theater, the tavern, Harada's general store—all were locked down due to the curfew. They drove silently through the town. At the turn going into Lanikai, Paul looked down at the edge of Kailua Bay. In the moonlit sky, he could see soldiers manning their foxholes and machine-gun nests behind the barbed wire. His heart ached for the men. For once, he knew of the fear that must overwhelm them all.

Nan and Mr. G. met them at the door. Nan didn't ask any questions; she simply wrapped a blanket around both of Paul's shoulders and helped him towards the couch. They stepped into the dark house. Once inside, Mr. G. closed the front door and then adjusted the black curtains to make sure that no light escaped. Only when they were all inside were they able to turn on a small light that the curtains hid from the outside.

Paul leaned awkwardly against the back of the couch. "You want to eat something?" Nan asked him. Paul mumbled something, but it made no sense. Nan reached down to touch his forehead.

"He's burning up. Get him into the bedroom now; I'll get a cold compress."

Jorge and Mr. G. helped the gangly and reluctant hero into the bedroom, where he flopped face-first onto the pillow. Very rapidly, he was consumed by fever. Flashes of heat were followed by dizzying cold spells. Paul curled into a ball atop the bed and felt Nan's warm hands trying to comfort him. But Paul was desperately ill, and he finally fell into a deep sleep.

When he finally woke up, it was three days later, and he was lying in a hospital bed in Honolulu.

"Welcome to the world, young man," a pleasant-sounding voice said.

Paul glanced toward the foot of the bed, where he saw a nurse peering over a clipboard. She was a large *haole* woman in a white dress, her dark hair pulled up underneath a small, white hat.

"Glad to see you're among the living," she said. She came around the edge of the bed and grabbed Paul's wrist. He instinctively pulled away. "It's okay. Just taking your pulse."

Paul started to come to his senses. His eyes darted around the sterile white room. He looked down at his other arm and realized that he had a needle inserted, with long tubing draped over an L-shaped contraption.

"Where am I? Um . . . uh . . . how long have I been here?"

"You're in Queen's Hospital in Honolulu. I guess it's been two and a half days."

"What?"

"What is right! I recall they carried you in on a gurney a couple of days back. You had a fever of 105."

"Gee, uh, I don't remember anything."

"We were all quite worried about you for a while there," she said, as she removed her fingers from his wrist. "Pulse is normal. Let me take your temperature." Paul opened his mouth and she inserted a thermometer.

"The doctors were mystified by your symptoms. It wasn't until we pumped your stomach that we found what might have been the culprit. What have you been eating?"

Paul said nothing.

She pulled the sticklike object from his mouth. "Down to 99-point-9," she said. "Guess you really are getting back to normal. By the way, we've got a very lovely young lady outside in the waiting area. She's been here almost the whole time you've been here. We told her to go outside on the couches and take a nap. But she wanted to make sure we woke her if you came around."

"Healani?" Paul asked, suddenly excited. He pulled his body up and propped himself up on his elbows. But he fell quickly back down, showing just how weak he was.

"Calm down, young man," she scolded him. "I'll get her and the doctor, too."

Five minutes later, Healani was in the hospital room. She embraced Paul tightly, her hands clutching the back of his head. Big tears welled up in her beautiful eyes.

"Oh, Paul, you were so sick!" she said, her voice cracking with emotion.

"Very sick indeed," a man's voice said. Healani released her embrace, and Paul could see a doctor in a white, knee-length coat enter the room. He was a young Chinese man, perhaps in his early thirties.

"I'm Dr. Lum," he said as he stepped up to the edge of Paul's bedside. "You're a lucky man, Mr. Sands."

"That's what I've been hearing. I don't remember much."

"You ingested something you shouldn't have and severely irritated your stomach lining. The lab reports confirmed it. Your body simply reacted violently until we were able to purge your system. Do you recall eating anything out of the ordinary?"

Paul looked at the doctor and then at Healani and the nurse. He thought about telling them his story, but quickly changed his mind.

"I . . . uh . . . recall falling in a muddy pool of water when her brother and I were chasing after some cattle," Paul said. "If I remember right—and I can't remember much right now—I stumbled and fell in face-first. I think I must have swallowed some of the muck at the bottom by accident."

"Well, whatever you consumed, it seemed to have had a powerful effect," the doctor said.

Paul said nothing more. He listened to the doctor give the technical name for his malady but glossed over that information when he heard the good news that if his vital signs stayed normal and his fever disappeared in the next twenty-four hours or so, there was a good chance for discharge in a couple of days. Paul thanked him. Both the doctor and the nurse left, allowing Healani and Paul some privacy.

He looked into her eyes and she kissed him softly.

"I'm sorry," he whispered.

"So am I."

"I wish I could explain what happened."

She put her forefinger to his mouth and shook her head from side to side. She hugged him again and kissed him several times on his cheeks and his forehead, and then she leaned back and smiled.

"Oh, good news," she said, perking up. "That is, if there can be any positive news with the war and everything. Your friend John Gillespie is on the island."

"What?" Paul sat up straight.

"Yes, because of the terrible attacks at Pearl Harbor and Kāneʻohe, the navy department sent him, along with several other officials, to see everything close up."

"No kidding!"

"He arrived last night with Secretary of the Navy Knox. It's pretty hush-hush, but Nan told me and said it was okay to tell you."

"Thank her for that."

"I guess they're surveying the damage at Pearl and the other bases, but Nan said John might have a few hours of free time before they head back to Washington. He wasn't certain about that, but hopeful."

"With John, it's always duty first. As much as I'd like to see him, I know he's got a very big job."

"One other thing. I took the liberty to give your letter to Officer Burns when he was in Kailua yesterday. He made no promises, given the current situation, but he said he'd try and see what he could do."

Paul leaned over and kissed her gently on the lips. She squeezed his hand. "You better get some rest," she said. He lay back down and closed his eyes. She sat at his bedside for the next couple of hours while he dozed on and off. It was hard for them to finally say good-bye for the evening, but the shadows began to dim on the hospital room walls, and because of the curfew, Paul knew he had to let her go. The nurse came in to say it was time. She left around dusk, driving Paul's old Nash back to Kailua.

As night fell over Honolulu, all the lights went out in the hospital and blackened curtains were drawn in every room. Paul sat alone in the darkness and felt extremely uncomfortable. It had been one thing to sit around with a family in a small house in Lanikai during the blackout. That had been scary enough. But to sit in a lonely hospital room in virtual blackness made him feel incredibly uneasy. Luckily, the nurse came into his room to check on him, and after she walked out, she left the door to his room partially ajar. Then he could hear the doctors and nurses and other personnel moving around in the hallway. Because they obviously needed some light, they did their jobs in only semidarkness, and the dim lights from the hallway caused shadows on the wall of the hospital room. As he lay there alone in his room, Paul couldn't help but notice every sound, and when he opened his eyes, the shadows played evil tricks on his mind. For all he knew, each shadow could indicate the start of another attack. Paul tried hard not to think about it. Eventually he fell asleep.

He woke-up startled at around midnight. He heard voices in the hallway and the *clickety-clack* of dress shoes walking towards the room. By now, he recognized the familiar sound of the doctor's and nurse's shoes; this was something else.

The door opened slowly. With his eyes adjusting to the darkness, Paul could see two shadowy figures. A man in uniform. And another man in a suit. At first, he failed to recognize either man.

Then an extremely familiar deep voice whispered in the darkness. Paul knew the soothing sound of that voice in an instant. It was his good friend, John Gillespie.

"Paul, you awake?" the soothing voice said.

"Hey, John," Paul said, his own voice suddenly animated. He immediately propped himself up on his elbows.

"Let me get your pillow." John stepped in next to the bed and fluffed up the hospital pillow behind Paul. The tall young man pulled himself up as straight as he could and sat against the hospital headboard. Then John motioned for the soldier who was with him to leave the room. The soldier nodded, and went out in the hallway.

"You're looking a little peaked around the gills," he said.

"It's been a rough couple of days."

"I'm sure it has, but I want to tell you that you're a sight for sore eyes. In fact, you look a helluva lot better than what I expected from listening to Dad and Mom. They told me you were really sick for a while."

"I'm okay. I'll be out of here in no time. Man, it's good to see you. You're looking a little skinny yourself. Washington must be causing you a lot of stress."

"You sound like Mom," he said. He let out a huge sigh and pulled up a chair next to the bed. "You have no idea what it's been like. We were up day and night before the attack, hoping that we could fend off the inevitability of the damn war. But it appears the Japanese were playing with our minds all the time. They had no intention of working with us during the negotiations."

"The surprise attack must have caught you guys off guard."

"There had been rumors for days. And we had a meeting scheduled with the Japanese ambassador early that Sunday afternoon. Apparently, they were supposed to deliver their war intentions before the attack, but they couldn't get their documents in order quickly enough. The ambassador was in our State Department waiting room when we got the call about the bombing. Secretary Hull was infuriated."

"He should be. I witnessed some of it firsthand at Kāne'ohe Naval Air Station," Paul said, recounting the December 7 attack. "Death and destruction were everywhere; you can't even imagine. It was awful."

John responded sympathetically.

"I saw it up close the last twenty-four hours. We flew in last night and toured the devastation at Pearl all morning and afternoon.

Seeing it up close like that was mind-boggling. The destruction is staggering. More than two thousand dead, and dozens of ships destroyed or in need of major repairs. We've got an unbelievable amount of work to do. If there's one bit of good news, it's the camaraderie and fighting spirit of the men and women who survived it. They lived through hell, and they're all willing to do whatever it takes to get us back on our feet quickly."

He paused. Paul could tell that the experience had affected him greatly.

"Eventually, I broke off from the group to tour the base and facilities at Kāneʻohe. I headed over the hill to Kailua and Kāneʻohe, just before sunset," he said. "From what I saw at the naval air base there, they were practically wiped out. All the planes there were destroyed. There's no getting around it, we got our butts kicked. It's going to take a while before we can get everything operational, but I know we can do it."

"How long you here for?"

"Just a few more hours. The president and Secretary of State Hull want a full report. Secretary Knox and I and the rest of our small group are flying back before dawn. I stopped off briefly in Lanikai to see Mom and Dad and they told me about you. I figured I'd catch a quick visit here at the hospital on my way back over the Pali and into town."

He paused for a moment. "It's still pretty scary, what we're up against. Up at the pass, near the Pali Lookout, I saw some army guys setting landmines up there in the darkness. Don't tell anybody, but the brass has plans in place to blow up the highway if the Japanese ever invade."

"What do you think the chances of that are?"

"No idea, really. We caught a lucky break when the Japs didn't follow-up on the two attacks they did make. Our carriers were all out to sea, and they stayed away from the oil tanks and refineries for some reason. So, it's possible we could be up and running again within a few months. Or it could take much longer. It's going to take a great deal of people a good deal of time to get us in war shape. Our concern right now is watching the shores and patrolling the nearby waters. And the biggest concern, according to everyone at headquarters, is the potential for sabotage."

"That must be why they're rounding up so many people—so many of the Japanese, Germans, and Italians," Paul said.

"They're still not sure what to do about it. I know they're pulling all the local Japanese out of the Territorial Guard. Some of the brass in Washington are really worked up about a so-called Fifth Column. My boss, Secretary Knox, wants to put these people in internment camps. I don't think that's a good idea at all. I lived with these people here in Hawai'i for years. I don't buy the argument the brass are making."

"You should know they picked up Kenji Fujimoto the other morning," Paul said with a long face.

"Our yardman? That's ridiculous! Kenji wouldn't hurt a flea, unless it was bothering Dad's hibiscus."

Paul smiled, but they both knew that Kenji's predicament was no laughing matter.

"Somehow Kenji thought it might happen," Paul told him. "He came to your dad and me the night before they arrested him. I guess he has some ties to Japan or something, but he maintains his innocence. A lot of the local Japanese have dual citizenship, I've heard. But I can't believe his loyalty would come into question. Isn't there something you can do about it?"

"There has to be," he said. "These people are as American as you and me. I'll see what I can do. You have my word on that."

That was all Paul needed to hear. He knew John well and had a great deal of respect for both his accomplishments and his character. He held out his hand as John stood up and got ready to leave. John shook Paul's hand firmly.

"There's one more thing, John, that I should probably tell you,"

Paul said.

But before he could say another word, the soldier came into the room and told John it was time to leave. "Just a minute. I'll be right there." The soldier nodded and stepped back outside the room.

John turned back toward his friend, and Paul started to speak again, but the young man from Washington DC put his finger to his lips.

"Shh," John whispered. "You don't have to say anything. Nothing at all. It's all been taken care of."

Paul looked at his friend in the darkness and wasn't quite sure exactly what he had just heard and what exactly was meant by it. But he didn't argue. He was almost too stunned.

As he stood silhouetted in the doorway, John had one more thing to tell his friend. "By the way, I heard about your problem with your grandfather and I was so sorry to hear it. Just know that you've got good people who really care about you and are there to support you. Very good people. Get well, soon, Paul." He gave a quick wave, and then he was off into the darkness.

25 - A TWIST OF FATE

Paul felt virtually back to normal within the next two days. The nurse reported that his fever was totally gone. A quick visit from the doctor on Monday morning confirmed the fact that Paul would probably be discharged the next day as long as he was strong enough.

It had now been a full week and a day since the surprise attack. Paul still couldn't believe the events that had unfolded in that time period. He reflected back on seeing the Japanese planes above Kailua Bay, surviving the strafing attacks at the Kāne'ohe Naval Air Station, then the terrifying night of the first blackout, and the constant fears of an impending invasion. He thought about the bizarre episode that he and Jorge had gone through—of how they had chased a man they truly believed to be a spy into the Ko'olau and how the chase miraculously ended with the intruder lying dead in the deep overgrowth and Paul in the hospital. There was no other way to describe it except as miraculous. Jorge had proven what a good friend he was during the ordeal.

Paul thought about how Mr. G. and Nan had handled all the horrible events with a plucky resolve. Nan had predicted an attack was possible and was prepared for the blackouts before anyone else. And Mr. G., he was a rock. You could see where John got it from. He thought a lot about John's visit the night before last. He couldn't even imagine what it must be like at the nerve center of all the decision-making. He wondered if he would have the time to help Kenji, and he further wondered about John's final comments.

And he didn't just think about Healani, he also dreamed about her. Her beauty. Her touch. Her presence. He didn't know what his future held, and he knew he would have to go back to California soon, but he hoped with all his heart that she would be in his future--somehow. That future, which became very cloudy after he arrived in the islands right before Thanksgiving, was now more uncertain than ever.

He was still in a dream state during a late-morning nap when he heard her sweet voice whisper in his ear. "Time to wake up, darling," she said. "I've brought someone to see you."

She kissed Paul on the cheek and he smiled. He opened his eyes and Healani pointed toward the doorway. There, at the end of the bed, stood the proud figure of Auntie Rose. Next to her was a tall *hapa* man in his mid to late forties and a younger Hawaiian woman, probably in her early thirties. Auntie Rose introduced them as Keoni and Pomai.

Keoni and Pomai said they could only stay for a few minutes. Keoni, a man with friendly face and a huge smile, said he worked as a volunteer with the hospital and often provided greetings to people in the hospital rooms. They asked how Paul was doing, and he said a few nice things about the hospital and the staff and Keoni smiled.

"I'll be sure to pass on your good comments," he said. Pomai nodded in agreement, and then the two were on their way.

"You've got a wonderful young lady here," Auntie said, motioning toward Healani. "She's come to visit me a couple of times in last couple of days."

Paul looked at Healani, who just smiled. Auntie Rose came

around the bedside and gave Paul a big hug. She placed a flower *lei* around his neck and kissed both his cheeks. "I don't know if the nurses will let you keep this on for too long, so enjoy it while you can. It's *pīkake*."

The room was immediately filled with the small flowers' sweet scent. Paul thanked her. The nurse came into the room and smiled. Auntie Rose seemed pleased that the nurse didn't ask Paul to take the *lei* off. Healani and Auntie Rose talked about some of the events of the last few days as the nurse brought his lunch. Paul didn't speak for quite a while; he just listened. He was enjoying the light meal of jello and chicken noodle soup. It was the first full meal he had eaten in days.

After the nurse left and cleared away the lunch tray, the two ladies pulled their chairs close against the bed. Healani held his hand tightly.

"Auntie has a wonderful surprise for you," she said. She looked at Paul as if she could see right through him.

"I'm not sure anything could surprise me anymore," he said.

"Oh, I think this might qualify." She brought Paul's hand to her lips and kissed it gently several times. Paul looked at her with a quizzical expression. Then, he turned his gaze towards Auntie Rose.

"Remember when you came to me that first day," Auntie said. Paul nodded. "Your story, or actually the story of your search for your grandfather, startled me. It brought me back to times that I had not thought about for a long, long time. I actually knew your grandfather much more than I let on. He was a wonderful young man, just as his grandson is."

Paul smiled, but still had a puzzled expression. Healani clutched his hand tighter.

"The young Hawaiian *wahine* that your grandfather met and fell in love with—Iwalani—she was actually my younger sister," she said. Paul sat there with his mouth agape. Healani looked over at Paul and nodded.

"Wait, there's more," Healani whispered.

"I'm sorry I couldn't tell you earlier, but I didn't know I was strong enough to tell you until I heard about you and Healani and your search and your courage and your love for each other. I thought about it for a long while. I knew I had to tell you the truth."

She looked at the two young lovers with a great deal of love in her eyes. Then she began to update her story of Paul's grandfather and Iwalani.

"Those were turbulent times in our tiny island kingdom," Auntie Rose began. "I say *kingdom* because that's what we truly believed it was. The overthrow had turned us into a republic, but we knew how it really should be."

Paul pulled himself up closer to this grand Hawaiian woman and listened intently.

"Despite the overthrow and the tensions it created, your grandfather and my sister fell deeply in love during that time period. My family wanted no part of it, so my sister came to me for help. Being the oldest sister in the family gave me certain privileges, and although I cautioned her about falling in love with a *haole*—how ironic, huh?—I knew I could help her." She gently squeezed Healani's arm.

Then she continued. "I set up places where they could meet in a clandestine manner, often in the dank buildings of Chinatown or around Honolulu Harbor. And I made certain that no others would talk about it. At the same time, political pressures were rising. Unbeknownst to me at the time, your grandfather and my sister had befriended some of the people who were hoping to restore the monarchy. These people had guns and ammunition and needed a place to store them. Eventually, my sister, despite the strong objections of your grandfather, felt sorry for the men and allowed these monarchists to hide their guns in one of those secret meeting places. That decision almost broke up their relationship, but the passion between them was too great. Despite arguments about whether they should get involved, they continued to meet secretly and make love passionately."

Paul looked over at Healani. She was wiping away tears from her eyes.

"Then, one day around noon, my sister came to me with big news," Auntie Rose continued on. "She announced she was with child. She had visited a discreet doctor who had confirmed the news that morning. She was excited to tell your grandfather about their child later that night. But she would never get that chance."

"Why?" Paul blurted out.

Auntie Rose put up her hand. "Just listen," she said. "Before their meeting took place, the republic police found out about the potential uprising. All over the town, they began arresting those they believed to be in on the plot."

"But my grandfather wasn't involved directly, at least according to what you've said," Paul interrupted. "Why was he arrested?"

"That, my boy, is a noble story. And a sad one, too. My sister came to me in a panic later that afternoon. She confessed to me about allowing the guns and ammunition to be stored in their love nest. She asked me to warn your grandfather. I agreed and took a carriage down to his office near the harbor. He told me that he had to remove the guns and ammunition out of the building so it could never be traced back to my sister. He told me that he loved her so much that he could never allow her to be arrested."

"Are you telling me that my grandfather ended up taking the fall for her?"

"I guess that's what I'm telling you, yes," she said. A small tear welled up in the corner of her eye. "I don't know what exactly happened immediately after that, but I do know that your grandfather was found and arrested with several others in Pālolo Valley the next day. The people in power were incensed and cried out for vengeance. They demanded death to all the revolutionaries."

"But, of course, he didn't die," Paul said. "He left."

"No, he didn't just leave," she said. "He and the others were locked up in jail for several months. My sister was beside herself because she couldn't visit. Neither could I. The best we could do in the next few months was to secretly slip your grandfather a letter in his cell. My sister professed her love to him in that letter, but she never told him of his child. When he was released from his jail cell, six months later, he was taken immediately to a waiting ship in the harbor and sent off. He was allowed no communication with anyone."

"Are you saying he was deported without knowing that he had a child here in Hawaii?" Paul asked.

"Yes."

"Then, what happened to the child?"

"Actually, I already showed you some photographs. Remember?"

Paul thought back to the second day he spent in Auntie Rose's home in Nuʻuanu. He recalled the photograph she had of the beautiful young Hawaiian woman—Iwalani—that she now revealed was her sister. And Paul pictured the second photograph of the same woman, years later, accompanied by one dark-skinned child and one light-skinned child.

"I do remember," Paul said. "What happened to them all?"

"My sister died many years later. They said it was the flu, but I truly believe it was a broken heart," she said. Her youngest child, a girl bestowed on her from a brief and loveless marriage, had died from a mysterious illness the previous year. But her eldest, the son born out of wedlock, the son of your grandfather, he is still alive."

"And you say my grandfather never knew about him."

"Never."

"That sounds very difficult to believe."

"But it's true. I also wondered what would happen if he found out. I always thought about the love between your grandfather and Iwalani and how they had it so good for such a short time. And then never again."

"Do you think they ever wrote to each other?"

"Not that I am aware. And I am a deeply aware person. I would have known if that happened. For whatever reason, and they took their reasons to their graves, they never were in contact again."

"That is very sad."

"But that doesn't mean they didn't think of each other. That strong feeling I can sense, too. And I could strongly sense that something was going to happen days before I met you. When I'm in that state—that state where I can best feel these things over the years— I've gone to Palikū, the Castle mansion in Maunawili."

"Why there?"

"Because something spiritual, something almost supernatural, happens to me when I'm there. I can't explain it, but I know it happens. There's something almost magical, almost mystical, about being there in the midst of the Ko'olau."

Paul sat up straighter in his bed.

Auntie Rose looked into his eyes. "You know what I'm talking about it, don't you?"

Paul pondered for a moment. He thought about what she'd said, and then he considered his own recent experience near the top of the mountains. A smile slowly came over his face. "Yes, I think I might have an inkling."

"It's a very special feeling, isn't it?"

"Yes, it is," Paul nodded. He leaned over and gave Healani a kiss on the cheek. She smiled and squeezed his hand.

"I could feel your grandfather's presence there the other night; I really could, and I think it scared me."

"Why?" Healani asked.

"That part I cannot be sure of. But I think I was just scared of the secret. Hearing from Healani and then seeing the two of you together, I'm not scared anymore. I don't care who knows."

Healani gripped Paul's hand tightly, but his immediate attention was riveted on Auntie Rose.

"So what else did you think about my grandfather?" Paul asked. "Did you sense his death?"

The large Hawaiian woman thought about the question for a moment. She looked up briefly and walked slowly around the room. "I almost feel like I can sense your grandfather's presence with us here today."

Paul and Healani looked around the room and then at each other. Paul wondered if Auntie Rose was beginning to act "strange," as Officer Burns once said.

"I'm okay," she said. "You don't have to worry about me. I simply have this awareness. I know you are worried, but you don't have to be. Your grandfather died peacefully and of natural causes. In a blissful moment of peace, his heart simply stopped. I know that."

"How can you tell?" Paul asked.

"Because I know these things. And because I believe them."

"Would you be willing to share this story with the county coroner?" Healani asked excitedly, squeezing Paul's hand again.

"I told you I'm not afraid of secrets anymore. Seeing you, feeling your love together, makes me know that. I will share that with anybody."

"Thank you for that," Paul said. "I appreciate that." He gave Healani a light kiss on the cheek after she nuzzled up against him.

Paul then had a follow-up question. "But you never said what became of the love child of my grandfather and Iwalani. You say the child is still alive. Does he know who his father is?"

"He does."

"How does he know?"

"Because that particular secret I have shared with him. And until now, I have asked him to not reveal it. He will be glad now that he doesn't have to keep it any longer. I know he must be very glad."

"Who is he and where is he now? And can I meet him?"

"You already have," she said. Paul looked at Healani, who shook her head and shrugged.

Auntie Rose smiled; she had a sweet gleam in her eye. "You just met him here in the room a little bit ago with Pomai."

"You mean the volunteer that came with you?" Paul stammered. "What was his name—Keoni?"

"Yes, Keoni is the one. In fact, Keoni is now mine, because after Iwalani and his sister died, I took him as my own. I am his *hānai*, or adoptive, mother."

"Keoni," Paul repeated.

"In Hawaiian it means 'the righteous one,'" Healani said. She was smiling and wiping away tears from her face.

"Yes, Keoni is your grandfather's son, or your uncle," said Auntie Rose. "And because he is my *hānai* son, my dear Paul, I guess that makes me your new grandmother. I hope you can know that this is the whole truth and can believe this. We are your new family."

26 - A GAME OF HOPE

On Christmas morning, 1941, Jack Burns arose before dawn and drove his car from his home in Coconut Grove up the Pali Road to a place where an old shack called the halfway house once stood. The place had a special meaning to Burns because it was in this spot where an old man helped motorists who struggled to get back and forth over the steep and zigzagging highway. That old man had once helped Burns when his own car broke down. He had also shown the police officer a hidden path that led to a beautiful grove of trees that were as perfectly shaped as Christmas trees.

On that morning, Burns got to the place early and watched the sunrise from the vantage point that was halfway up the Koʻolau. The beauty of the sunrise was just what he needed. He watched silently and then marched in along the hidden path and cut down a six-foot tree with a small axe. He loaded up the tree in the back of his car and drove home with the present that he knew would please his own family.

The previous two and a half weeks had been extremely difficult for Burns and everyone else, as a period of nervous tension took over the island. More and more troops arrived on Oʻahu, and the signs of war were everywhere. Military and civilian officials finished the fingerprinting and identification process and then followed up with the issuance of gas masks. Every man, woman, and child received their own personal gas mask. Bomb shelters were also built, and children, who had gone back to attend school, practiced daily air-raid drills.

Meanwhile, the arrests of local Japanese, German, and Italian citizens continued. Burns had been sickened by one incident that directly affected the town of Kailua. It was the sad story of a teenage girl who lived with her Italian family in Coconut Grove. Her father was an Italian immigrant who had been arrested during the round-up of suspects the day after the bombings. Burns and others told authorities that the Italian man was a prominent citizen in Kailua and active in several community projects. His pleadings were in vain.

While the man sat in a jail cell awaiting disposition, the entire island was in blackout. During the middle of a December night, his daughter arose in the blackness of their two-story home and apparently became disoriented. In the pitch black, she accidentally walked off the second-floor balcony and fell to her death. Her father had to be notified of the tragedy in his jail cell. He was allowed to leave briefly to attend the funeral, but then was locked up again.

The tragic story of the Italian family strengthened Burns's resolve and underscored his strong belief that the arrests must stop and that loyal, local citizens should return to their homes. With many federal officials recommending internment camps, Burns fought hard against the idea. He reminded them that they were violating the civil rights of American citizens, the same rights they were fighting for in the wars in Europe and the Pacific. Luckily, he had help from others in the Hawai'i community, and he hoped that common sense would soon prevail. In the meantime, he would continue to do his part to secure the release of local citizens who had been jailed or detained as soon as possible.

On this day, he hoped to set aside the sadness of recent weeks and spend time with his family and friends. He returned home to decorate his new Christmas tree and doled out presents. Then he drove around the town and delivered other presents to selected friends in the community.

In Lanikai, he stopped by the Gillespie cottage and gave Mr. G. and Nan a bottle of scotch. The Gillespies appreciated his kindness and exchanged a box of shortbread cookies that Nan had baked up for friends and neighbors who dropped by.

Burns also had a special gift for Paul. It came in the form of a letter. He watched as the tall visitor from California opened the envelope and emptied its contents. He smiled when Paul gave him a huge bear hug after reading everything. The letter was from the Honolulu coroner's office. It said the lab at the university had examined the white residue that was found in the Hawaii textbook and on the lips and fingertips of William Sands after his sudden death. The examination had determined that the residue came from crushed flowers. The cause of death of William Sands was now officially listed as "death by natural causes."

The official letter gave Paul hope because he could now go on with his life. But he still wasn't sure exactly what that meant. He knew only three things, really—that he had a new family to learn about in Hawai'i, that he was deeply in love with Healani, but that he must also go back to California to settle his grandfather's estate. He was able to book passage on the first passenger liner that was allowed to sail from Honolulu since the time of the attacks, leaving the night of December 31—New Year's Eve. He was unsure of what would happen after that.

With each passing day, the threat of an imminent invasion began to seem less and less likely, and a kind of nervous calm descended on the island. Daily commerce picked up tremendously, and people became less fearful about going outside. After a week of closure due to war construction just before Christmas, the Pali Road also reopened and traffic flowed between the Windward Side of the island and Honolulu.

The biggest difference between the Kailua of New Year's Eve and the Kailua of December 6 was the strong presence of the military. Encampments were clustered from Coconut Grove to Mōkapu, and the beaches were still guarded day and night. Other than that presence, the center of the small town had become busy again, and people tried to go about their daily business. It was an uneasy peace but a near-return to normalcy nevertheless.

When the lead local officer, an army colonel, called a town meeting at Kailua School to come up with ideas that could boost the morale of both the troops and the general population during this time, Healani suggested a basketball game. She said that the school had a basketball team and that their boys would like to play another team, and it might be a community event that everyone could enjoy. The colonel announced it was an excellent suggestion, and so it was agreed that a basketball game between the Kailua boys, coached by Paul, would take on a team bused in from Honolulu. The game would take place at midmorning December 31 on the outdoor black-top at the school. Everyone was invited.

An overnight rain had threatened to wash out the game, but when the New Year's Eve dawn arrived, the clouds were whisked away as if by magic. The skies cleared to a perfect azure blue, and the sun looked down on the town with a warming smile. It could not have been a more perfect morning.

By the time Healani and Paul arrived at the court an hour before game time, the ten boys on the Kailua team were already present. They could not have been more excited. For a period in the days leading up to the game, both Paul and Healani wondered if all ten boys would be allowed to play. The mothers of two of the Japanese boys were reluctant to send their children outside, but with the help of Mr. G. and Healani, they convinced the mothers that it was safe.

The backlash against local Japanese, which some had feared,

never materialized. And many of the locally based military officials, who came from other parts of the mainland United States, were beginning to realize that they had nothing to fear from the local population. In fact, some of the Japanese, Italians, and Germans arrested and interrogated in the days after December 7 had already been released, but there was still no word on Kenji Fujimoto.

But Kenji's son, Hiro, was ready to play in the game. Although he never said a word, his actions on the court spoke loudly. He took control of the other boys and ran them through a number of pregame dribbling and shooting drills. He didn't even look intimidated when the Honolulu town team arrived on the court, sporting seven boys, four of them at least two inches taller than every boy on the Kailua team.

A half hour before the game, Paul and Healani were surprised by the approach of something they both thought they'd never see. Jorge Luis walked right towards them, decked from head to toe in a suit and tie and holding a suit case.

Paul's eyes practically bulged out. Healani rushed up to her brother and he whispered something in her ear. She immediately kissed him on the cheek.

She turned toward Paul. "Jorge just joined the service!" she exclaimed excitedly.

"What the hell? Have you forgotten all the things you ever said?" Paul asked while quickly walking in their direction and then shaking his friend's hand.

"A man's gotta do what he's got to do. I joined the Marines because it was the fastest way I could get into the action," Jorge said. "Sorry I won't be able to stay for the game. My unit is pulling out right away. I just wanted to stop by and say good-bye."

"Well, if you can't beat 'em, join 'em," Paul said, laughing. He draped his long arm around Jorge. "You look great all dressed up. You'll look great in a uniform, too. The Marines are definitely getting the right man. Give 'em hell, buddy!"

The three exchanged hugs and Healani gave her brother an extra kiss of approval. She whispered in his ear that their father would be very proud of him; she said she was, too.

A few minutes before game time another surprise came. Walking up to the court was the stately Auntie Rose. She was escorted by two small children, a boy and a girl about four or five years old, and a lanky *hapa-haole* man. It took Paul only a moment to recognize his new uncle Keoni.

"How're you doing, nephew?" Keoni asked, a warm smile erupting on his face. He emphasized the word *nephew*. Paul gave him a big, strong bear hug.

"Welcome to the game, Uncle." Paul smiled and gave another hug to Auntie Rose. She introduced Paul and Healani to Keoni's two young children, Ke'a and Ki'i.

"Your new family is growing," she said.

"Thank you for coming. It means so much to me." Paul smiled proudly.

When the game began, the crowd on hand was nearly one hundred people. The crowd rimmed the court all the way around, and the colonel gave a brief welcoming speech, thanking everyone for their support of the boys in uniform, as well as the Red Cross during this challenging time.

When the game began, those in attendance didn't seem to mind the fact that the boys struggled a little bit to get going. So many players were rusty that their skills were not at their strongest. But all the boys tried hard, and "Coach" Paul substituted liberally with his five-man rotations. The boys from Honolulu led the game by five points at halftime.

Paul gathered his team around him during the short intermission and tried to give them encouragement. The boys' hopeful faces lifted his spirits.

"We're going to pick up our defense all over the court," Coach Paul said. "We've worked on it, so you know what to do. Cut off their dribblers and jump into the passing lanes. You'll have to hustle like crazy. And that means you're going to get tired. Just signal to me and I'll get a fresh substitute in for you. We've got them outnumbered, so our quickness might wear them out."

Coach Paul pulled the boys together for one last cheer before they hit the court again. At the same time, he was startled to hear Healani let out a scream. Not a scream of horror, but one of out-and-out joy.

He wheeled around to see what she was jumping up and down about, and he saw the figure of a small Japanese man limping toward them. There was no doubt; it was Kenji.

Hiro let out a scream, too. It was the first sound any of them ever heard the small boy utter. He raced up to his father and hugged him around the leg. Kenji stopped and patted his son on the shoulder. Soon, they were joined by his wife and baby. The four of them clustered together, but only briefly. Showing no emotion, Kenji motioned Hiro to get back to his team. As Hiro ran back towards his teammates, Paul bowed in Kenji's direction. That was all the emotion that was needed, Paul thought; Kenji was home where he belonged.

His appearance also gave the entire Kailua team a lift at exactly the right moment. Coach Paul's strategy worked, and the Honolulu boys were completely baffled by the attacking defense. Hiro was the most effective. He swiped the ball from the opposing guards on the back-to-back occasions and drove in for layups. By the fourth quarter, the game was tied. The crowd, including a growing number of army soldiers from the encampment along Maluniu, was in a frenzy.

The game seesawed back and forth, with the crowd cheering every effort, and then with about a minute to go in the contest, the Kailua boys trailed by a single point. The crowd got so loud at that moment that if another attack had come, it's doubtful that anyone there could have heard it. The soldiers were probably cheering the loudest. They grew even louder when Hiro stole the ball near mid-court. Coach Paul called time-out with only thirty seconds to play.

The young coach's heart was beating furiously, and he tried to calm himself down. The boys all looked directly into his eyes, and he knew immediately it was up to him to help decide their fate. It was also at that moment that he knew that he wanted to do this for the rest of his life. It was a feeling that he had never experienced before—working with young people, guiding them, mentoring them, and helping them achieve all that they could. That's what he would do; he could hardly wait to tell Healani.

He stepped back to gather himself and looked across the court, where he saw Kenji and his family stoically looking on. Flanked on both sides of this tiny Japanese man and wife were two big American soldiers. But they were all rooting for the same result. All they wanted was a chance to succeed. Paul looked in the other direction and saw Keoni and his children with Auntie Rose, Healani, Mr. G. and Nan. They were his family, and he knew it, and they were supporting him, no matter how this game turned out.

All of this took only seconds. Finally, Coach Paul was able to maintain his composure and lean in toward the boys. "They're going to put all their pressure on Hiro. So, we'll have to run him off a couple of screens to get him free. Once we accomplish that, and we will, I want us to spread the court with two of you at half court and two in the baseline corners. With just over five seconds left, I'll give the signal for Hiro to drive. When he does that, they'll probably double- or triple-team him. But this time, instead of shooting, Hiro, I want you to give it up to one of the boys sliding in along the baseline. You got it."

The boys nodded and Hiro uttered the first sentence Paul had ever heard from him. His voice was much stronger than Paul anticipated. "We'll do it, Coach, for the team," he said with tremendous confidence.

The next thirty seconds played out as if in slow motion. Coach Paul inserted the following five boys into the final lineup—Keoki, the tall Hawaiian; Zach, the tall *haole*, Joseph, the tough Portuguese boy; Spencer, the quick Chinese guard; and of course, Hiro, the lightning-quick Japanese guard and the team's best player. The five players on the bench—William, Koy, Walter, Shigge, and Yuya, all cheered on their teammates. Ten strong—they were a team in every way.

Paul had learned from his many years of playing the game that you can tell a lot about the character of players by the way they handle pressure situations. He felt his Kailua boys reacted with the greatest courage that he could possibly imagine. With the stresses of the past few weeks, and with the buildup to this moment, in front of a crowd that was in a total frenzy and with their team down by one point to a much taller squad, they could easily have crumbled.

Instead, they set up for the final play with the greatest of confidence. Keoki took the ball out and inbounded to Zach. Zach's job was to wait for Spencer and Joseph to set screens to free up Hiro, who was double-teamed. For a moment, it looked like Hiro would get bottled up, but Joseph set a mean second screen, and Zach was able to dump the ball off to the team's dynamic little playmaker.

As the seconds ticked down, Keoki and Zach retreated to the baseline corners and Hiro continued to use screens from both Spencer and Joseph as he dribbled down the clock. When the clock operator yelled "ten seconds," Hiro looked over at Coach Paul. The young coach held his hand up for a brief moment and then yelled "Go!"

With the crowd screaming at the highest decibel, Hiro dribbled between his legs and then spun, thus breaking away from the double team. With less than five seconds left, he dribbled into the middle of the free throw lane, looking as if he were going to take the shot himself. But it was a ruse. Both opposing defenders took the bait and collapsed on him. Meanwhile, Keoki and Zach dropped in from behind along the baseline. Hiro bounce-passed to Zach, who then laid the ball off to a wide-open Keoki for a layup. The clock operator's horn went off as the ball nestled through the twine. Final score: Kailua boys, 31; Honolulu town team, 30.

The boys started jumping up and down and Paul jumped right along with them. For several seconds, he ran around the court looking for someone to hug. Finally, he spotted Kenji. The tiny man looked pretty startled when the tall young *haole* grabbed him and gave him probably the biggest bear hug he had ever received. Coach Paul whirled him around a couple of times and they ended up on the ground, with Paul laughing deliriously and Kenji looking as if he wondered what hit him. Within seconds, the boys from the team started piling on them, one after the other. Paul eventually felt the air knocked completely out of him, but at that point, he couldn't care less.

Eventually, order was restored and the entire team thanked the visitors from Honolulu for coming to play. Townspeople and soldiers alike came up to both Coach Paul and the opposing coach and thanked them for a great game.

"Thanks for reminding us what we're fighting for," an army soldier with corporal stripes told Paul as he shook his hand.

Paul had never thought about it that way, but he was right. These soldiers were fighting for freedom and the American way of life. Only in Hawai'i could a Japanese boy, a Chinese boy, a Portuguese boy, a Hawaiian boy, and a *haole* boy come together like this and make everyone proud. Prejudice was dead that day.

The two teams and their supporters lingered for a while afterwards. Joseph's parents had brought freshly baked Portuguese sweet bread, while Spencer's grandmother had cooked up some pan-fried noodles and Chinese vegetables. Everyone enjoyed the nourishment. But mostly they enjoyed the camaraderie. After a very short while, you couldn't tell the winners from the losers. That scene, even more than the victory itself, made Paul certain that this was what he wanted to do with the rest of his life.

Mr. G. and Nan and Officer Burns offered their congratulations. Burns told Paul that he thought it was one of the best coaching jobs he'd ever seen, especially considering the circumstances. Paul told the police officer that he obviously had the skills of a politician—he knew exactly how to say the right things. Burns smiled and shook his hand.

As the afternoon wore on, the town team, along with Auntie Rose and Keoni and his two children, headed back over the Pali. "We're now a big *'ohana*," Auntie Rose said with a hug and a smile before she departed.

Later, the Kailua boys also slowly headed back home to their families, one by one. Coach Paul gave each of them a hearty handshake when they left.

When it was time to say good-bye to Kenji and his son, Hiro, Paul took a little extra time.

"Thanks, Coach Paul," Hiro said.

Just hearing the boy speak was worth more than all the winning baskets in the world. "Great pass," Paul told him. "See, teamwork pays off."

Hiro smiled and nodded.

"You take care of your dad now."

"I will."

Kenji stood stoically. He reached out and shook Paul's hand with a firm grip. "I know what you did. You are great friend. Thank you for all you have done for my family."

"Thank you, Kenji. Welcome home. You're a great American."

The Japanese man nodded. "I am," he said.

Paul watched as the Japanese American man turned and walked away. Within moments, Paul saw Kenji's son reach out his tiny hand and clasp it together with his father's. The scene of a boy and his father walking home after the big game was one of many scenes of that day that Paul would always treasure.

With virtually everyone else gone, Healani and Paul took a slow walk together toward the open field behind the school. Under the shade of a tree, they sat down.

"I'm so proud of you," she said. She clutched his two hands and held them in front of her.

"I love you so much," Paul said. "I don't want to leave you."

Tears welled up in the corners of her eyes. Paul looked down at the ground, hoping he wouldn't start crying, too.

"There's something I need to tell you," he said, his voice choked back by emotion. Healani patiently waited for him while pushing back the wavy dark hair that had fallen into his eyes. Then, she placed her hands in his again, gently.

"We haven't talked about it yet," he began to speak, haltingly at first. "But it has to do with why I ended up in the hospital. I need to explain."

Healani leaned forward and tightened the grip on both of his hands.

"Stop," she whispered. "You don't have to torture yourself. I already know."

"What? How could you?" Paul stammered.

"You were a very sick man at the time. For a while, we actually thought we were going to lose you. You don't know how tragically close you came. Mr. G. and I kept questioning Jorge until he finally broke down and told us the story of your chase into Maunawili and the mountains. Mr. G. convinced Jorge that the two of them had to retrace your steps to find out what must have happened to you."

Paul looked at her and his shoulders slumped.

"The day before you woke up in the hospital, Jorge and Mr. G. went back into that area on horseback. It was Jorge who finally found the telltale signs of your climb up the ridge. Together, they came upon the dead body of a man in a deep ravine. It took some doing, but they got the body and the stuff around it out of there. Jorge had wanted to bury it immediately, but Mr. G. convinced him to take it back to Lanikai, wrapped in a huge sack, until they determined what to do with it."

"They did all that?"

"They did. That night, John came home after his tour of the bases and Mr. G. told him the whole story."

"Okay, that might explain something to me. What happened then?"

"We were all there that night in Lanikai, and John inspected the small bag and twisted metal. He told us to get rid of immediately and how to properly dispose of the body. And when all that was accomplished, we were to be sworn to secrecy, as you and I are about this subject from this day forward. John told us that we must never speak of this again."

"Why would he do that? Why would he decide not to report this to the authorities?"

"His father asked him the same question, but John was very clear and decisive on that. He said that if the story ever got out that the Japanese were successfully able to land here and then infiltrate someone into our island community, that it might incite panic and mistrust. He had seen too much of that already. It could not go on. The body must be disposed of and the secret must be kept. As far as he was concerned, the matter was closed."

"They agreed on that, all of them together?"

"They did. We all did."

Paul reached over and pulled Healani towards him. He held her in his arms for what seemed like eternity. He told her over and over again how much he loved her. She kissed him sweetly and told him that she loved him, too.

They sat there for the longest time, saying nothing. Finally, Paul looked skyward and broke the silence.

"What kind of tree is this?" he said, looking up at the large-leafed tree that was providing them great shade on that sunny afternoon. "I've seen them in several places around Kailua and I need to know."

"A *hau* tree," Healani said. "Why?"

"I remember when I was a small boy sitting in my grandfather's backyard in Southern California. I remember looking up and seeing the same kind of twisted limbs and rounded leaves. It was a tree much like this. My grandfather told me once that he had planted it there. But he didn't tell me why. I never knew anyone where I lived there who had one like it."

Healani hesitated and then sat up. "Oh," she said. "That explains a lot."

"What do you mean?"

"About your grandfather and Auntie Rose's sister, Iwalani," she said. "After hearing the story, I always believed that they truly loved each other very much despite the fact that he never ever returned for her. The fact that your grandfather planted a *hau* tree in his backyard way across the sea undoubtedly confirms that love."

"How?"

"You and I have spoken before of the legends of Hawaii. Listen closely to the legend of the *hau* tree and think of how it relates," she said. "It goes like this: Many years ago, a boy and a girl met and fell in love here in the islands. It was an intense love, much like the love your grandfather had for Iwalani. But that intensity led to a lovers' quarrel. Whatever was said and why it was said doesn't matter; the two lovers parted and he left this island, going across the sea to another. Just like your grandfather."

She looked deeply into Paul's dark brown eyes. He was entranced with her story. She continued. "The years went by, and the two lovers still pined for each other. He longed for her beautiful face and smile and the light in her eyes. She tried hard to forget him, but it was difficult. One day, as he slept on the beach in the faraway island, he felt the leaf of a *hau* tree come down and land on his head. He looked up at the twisted tree and knew exactly what he should do. He ran to the cluster of *hau* trees and quickly picked all the blossoms. He threw those *hau* blossoms one by one into the sea and watched them float off." Healani mimicked the scene of throwing blossoms into the ocean. Paul smiled.

"Meanwhile, back here on Oʻahu," she continued, "the beautiful *wahine* was visiting the shoreline and playing in the surf. She came upon the trail of *hau* blossoms, and when she touched one of these love-laden flowers, she began to tingle all over. Immediately, love reblossomed in her heart. She followed the path of the *hau*, one by one all the way across the sea, and back to the arms of her lover. Or so, the legend says." She leaned over and kissed Paul on the lips.

"Seems your grandfather might have heard the same legend," she whispered.

Paul put his forefingers to his upper lip. The corners of his mouth curled upwards in a slight smile. "It makes sense." He nodded. "You think the ground-up flowers the university lab said were found on his lips and on his fingertips were *hau* tree blossoms? The report didn't disclose the actual flower."

"Of course, it makes total sense. And my guess is that he kept the crushed blossoms in the book about Hawaiʻi because that's where his heart was," she said. "My guess is that when he arrived in Hawaiʻi, he was so overcome with emotion that he wanted to touch and feel and taste the blossoms that were dear to him. The memories were so strong and powerful, that his heart just stopped—like Auntie Rose said. He died of a broken heart."

Paul nodded and smiled again and pondered the theory. "Auntie Rose also told us you have to believe. And I believe you're right."

They paused and looked around at the beauty of the area that surrounded them. Healani broke the silence this time.

"Maybe your grandfather also brought you to Hawaiʻi for another reason," she said.

"What would that be?"

"I think he wanted you to find something."

Paul thought about the comment, then smiled to himself.

"That also makes sense. I guess I had to find out about him," he said with a gleam in his eye. "Plus, I had to find you."

"I think you had to find yourself!" She smiled and kissed him. He returned the favor by kissing her ever so passionately back.

They sat together in each other's arms, enjoying the last moments of the late afternoon until his scheduled departure that night.

"You know, I won't need a pathway of *hau* blossoms," Paul said. He looked deeply into Healani's eyes. "I've found exactly what I've always been searching for my entire life. Great friends, a loving family, and a place worth fighting for. I've found it here in the most beautiful place on earth, and I've found with you, the girl I want to spend the rest of my life with—in Kailua."

EPILOGUE
SIXTY YEARS LATER

"The war started right over there," the old man said, pointing across Kailua Bay toward a peninsula that jutted out into the Pacific.

The young reporter looked across the vast expanse of turquoise-colored waters, past the miles of palm and tropical ironwood trees in the direction of the modern military base—Marine Corps Base Hawaii—that sits on the Mōkapu Peninsula. The base is located on a rocky volcanic piece of land that separates the towns of Kailua and Kāne'ohe in Windward O'ahu.

"A lot of people think the first Japanese bullets and bombs were at Pearl Harbor, but they weren't," the old man said. The reporter nodded.

The old man, his voice strong and commanding, waved his pointing finger toward the horizon. "That's where their planes hit first, several minutes before their main fighter group struck Pearl."

The young newspaper reporter looked down at his small notebook and dutifully scribbled down the quotes. He was here with the old man to report on a story for a major Honolulu newspaper. The two men walked barefoot along the white sandy beach at Lanikai, some three miles east of the place of that first attack wave in 1941.

"I can see it like it was yesterday," the old man said. "The plumes of smoke. The explosions. The utter chaos. I'll never forget that day. The Japanese planes flew right over my head, right here, on their way for a strafing attack on Bellows."

The old man stopped and fell suddenly quiet. "It could have been so much worse."

"That's what I wanted to talk to you about," the young reporter said. "When we first heard about you at the paper, someone said you might have an interesting twist on the story."

The young reporter, a short and stocky young man of Asian descent, looked up at the old man, as if expecting him to reminisce more. But the old man, his forehead deeply wrinkled and his Caucasian complexion tanned from years spent in the sun, appeared deep in thought. The two were silent for several moments

"We're doing a follow-up story on John Gillespie. Someone said you knew him." The old man was still silent. "Was he here then? I mean, was he here when the war broke out?" the young reporter asked.

"No. He came a few days later."

"How well did you know him?"

"We met in college," the old man said. He began walking again, slowly, but with good strength for a man in his eighties. He was a tall man, and he towered over the younger Asian reporter, who had to be nearly sixty years his junior. The old man wore a large straw hat to shade his face, and the hat made him appear even taller.

"We were all so naïve, everybody but him."

The young reporter looked up at the old man and then furiously scribbled all the words down in his notebook and flipped to the next page.

"How so?"

"He just knew the right thing to do. I don't know if it was his upbringing here in Kailua and Lanikai, or if it was his parents, or if it was some innate sense he had, but whatever it was, he had it."

The old man stopped again. Once again, he fell silent. The young reporter waited. He liked the old man. He could tell he was going to eventually open up, to spill the story, but it would take patience. He was sharp enough to recognize that some interviews can't be rushed. He would get his story, hopefully the full story, without being pushy.

The old man walked over to a soda can that someone had left in the sand, picked it up, and then sauntered over to a nearby tree, where another someone had tied a plastic trash bag to the trunk. He tossed the can in the trash bag. The old man loved the beach. But he's stalling, the reporter thought.

"Sounds like John Gillespie made quite an impact on your life," the young reporter said.

"More than you know. All of them made an impact."

They walked back to the water's edge. The water was so clear that both men could see small gray fish swimming a foot or two below the surface no more than five or ten yards away. Small waves lapped up near the old man's toes. The young reporter waited patiently for more information.

"What do you mean, 'all of them'?"

"Everyone here in Kailua at the time. It wasn't like it is today. Hawai'i is different. The whole world was different. I don't think anyone knows the whole story."

"The whole story?"

"It may surprise a few people, that's all," the old man said. He paused to look out toward the small islands off Lanikai. He waved back at a middle-aged couple passing the shoreline on bright yellow kayaks. A woman raised her paddle towards him and then paddled on. "Nice people around here."

The young reporter smiled. The old man obviously cared deeply. The reporter had tracked him down in the weeks after Gillespie died. Gillespie had received international notoriety, meaning that his obituary, including national and local reaction, was in all the local papers.

The reporter had found out about the old man from friends in Kailua. It took some convincing, but he eventually coaxed the old man into this meeting at Lanikai Beach.

"Why would your story surprise people?" He tried to get his elderly subject to focus on the interview. The reporter was patient, but he also realized that he could move the interview along if he nudged a little harder. He stepped into the shallow water and moved directly in front of the old man.

"Can you tell me what was surprising? Does it have to do with anything involved with December 7? Is there something we don't know?"

"There's lots you don't know, young man." The old man smiled. "There was a lot I didn't know then, either." He chuckled under his breath, finding his own comment mysteriously amusing.

The young reporter loved a good mystery. He thought about pushing again, but kept his poise. He wasn't sure if the old man was playing with him or not. He waited for more information, but the old man seemed more interested in picking up litter and disposing of it than anything else. After several minutes, the old man had deposited seven more cans in the rubbish bag. The reporter watched him from the shallow waters along the shoreline. Still stalling, he thought.

"Tell me what you know," the old man hollered out, pausing at a small concrete wall under a *hau* tree, some twenty-five feet from the shoreline. The big-leafed tree made for some nice shade on this hot day on the white sandy beach. The wall cordoned off the small strip of a shoreline from a luxurious beachfront home. The old man sat down on the edge of the wall. The young reporter splashed out of the shallow water and hustled to get by the old man's side, his pen practically married to the top line in his small notebook.

"I thought I was interviewing you," the young reporter said, laughing. He liked the old man. He was willing to play the game.

"I'm not playing around with you, young man. I'm just kind of ruminating in my mind, that's all. It was sixty years ago. None of this was here," he said, waving his hands toward the expensive homes that lined the sands of Lanikai. "The beach was much wider then, not narrow like it is today. There was space to live and grow and the people gave you your space. There was lots of space—wide-open space, in fact."

"I understand. I wish I could have been here. Maybe you can help me see it through your eyes?"

The old man smiled. He had a mischievous kind of grin at times. The young reporter considered it an endearing quality.

"Do you want me to recite the history of December 7?" the young reporter asked. "I'm pretty good at history, you know—I got my degree in American Studies at UH."

The old man laughed. "No, I know you're qualified. You're a helluva lot smarter than I was when I was your age. Jesus Christ, when I was in my early twenties, I didn't know if I was supposed to crap in my pants or get crapped on. If it wasn't for everyone here, I don't know what I would have done."

The young reporter shook his head at the thought of this big old man some sixty-odd years earlier. Hard to imagine him scared and unsure of himself.

"You going to tell this story or not?" the young reporter teased his older counterpart.

"Yeah, I'll tell you, young man, but you need to know that there's much more than just the events of December 7, at least as far as I was concerned. I guess you could say it started in Hollywood and led to here."

A Hollywood mystery in Hawaii, the young reporter thought. This he had to hear.

"I consider John Gillespie like he was family," the old man said. "I know you're probably most concerned about history, but back then, I was more concerned about family than anything else."

"Why was that?"

"Because mine was gone. I had no one left, or so I thought."

"How does Hollywood and Hawaii, your family and the famous John Gillespie and World War II all tie together?"

"I guess that's the mystery. Tell me what you know first, and then I'll fill that little notebook of yours, plus a few more besides."

"Fair enough." The young reporter folded up his notebook and stuck it his back pocket. He paused himself to gather his thoughts.

"I want to hear what you think you know," the old man repeated.

The reporter looked at the old man and waited for more. But the old man wanted the tables turned. The reporter smiled.

"Okay," he said. "I know that Kailua has had its share of very important people over the years. Governor John Burns was a Kailuan—I think they called him Jack back then. He served as the state's governor during the 1960s and 1970s. He was the state's second governor after statehood and became one of the most powerful men in Hawai'i's political history. Then, there's John Gillespie, your friend, the diplomat."

"Yea, Burns was from Coconut Grove. John was from right here," the old man interrupted. "His parents' house was across the street and down the way toward the ridge." He pointed in the direction of a ridgeline that cast a large shadow on the surrounding neighborhood in Lanikai. The reporter waited for more information, but the old man stopped again. The reporter knew it was his turn once again.

"That's true. That was in all the newspaper reports. But Gillespie didn't spend much time here as near as we can figure. After graduating from Columbia, he was accepted into the diplomatic corps just before World War II. He served in the Navy Department and then directly for President Franklin D. Roosevelt; later he was appointed to a cabinet position under President Truman as still a very young man. He eventually served under all presidents from

Roosevelt to Reagan and was named ambassador to both the Philippines and to Japan."

"John was a very good man—one of my best friends," the old man said. He smiled again. "You had all that information you just recited in your newspaper report, but you missed maybe the biggest event in his life."

"That's what you keep saying, but I can't find anything in our files."

"No, I guess you wouldn't. Most of what you don't know is stored up here." The old man pointed to the side of his head. "Only a few people knew. She knew. And a few others. And John knew, but he made it a point to keep it a secret. He stayed away from controversy. He actually tried to resist controversy; he was that diplomatic in his approach."

"Until now," the young reporter interjected. "I guess I should tell you that we got a hold of his private papers after his death."

The old man smiled. "So I guess some of what is in those papers might cause quite a stir," he said.

"He mentions your name in there. I read his account and I'll admit I was startled. How did you manage to stay out of the spotlight all these years?"

"Just luck, I guess. If John mentioned my name in official papers, then I guess I should feel honored."

"Those papers tell a story that seems almost too fantastic to be true. He doesn't seem like the kind of person to make things up."

"Oh, he didn't make it up. I know; I was there."

The young reporter took the notebook out of his back pocket and began to scribble once again. He looked up from his notes to continue his story. "The papers suggest that a few people in Kailua, including you, may have played a significant role in the days before and after December 7."

The old man removed his hat and ran his fingers through his thinning white hair but said nothing. He listened intently.

"The papers claim that there may have been a spy ring in Kailua at the outbreak of the war," the young reporter said. "We're aware of one spy. A former German naval officer who had homes in Lanikai and Kailua. He was arrested within hours after the December 7 bombing."

"I don't know whether I would call it a spy ring," the old man said. "There might have been two spies—only two that I know of."

"We don't have any records on anybody except a guy named Otto Kuehn. He was sentenced to death, but ended up serving only a few years at Fort Leavenworth," the young reporter said. "His wife spent the rest of his life trying to clear his name, but to no avail."

"Yeah, some of the old-timers around here refer to him as 'the spy from Kailua,'" the old man said. "But there was another."

"That's the part I don't understand. Gillespie's papers are very detailed in spots, but sketchy in others. Until we saw your name and eventually located you, I would have dismissed what little he wrote about it in the papers."

"Why dismiss it?"

"No corroboration."

"What did he write?" the old man asked.

"Gillespie said he found a Japanese intelligence report that referred to an unnamed foreign mercenary being deployed from a Japanese submarine well off the Windward coast of O'ahu just before December 7. We checked the U.S. military records, but we have no report of such activity."

"What John says is true," the old man said. "We all suspected it was true."

"Who is we?" the reporter asked.

"Oh, she was there and so was her brother, and I was just a *haole* kid from Hollywood." The reporter wrote it all down. "We didn't know he was a spy for sure. But we did know that nobody would have believed us."

"Why?"

"Everyone was in a panic after the surprise attacks," the old man said. "People were conjuring up the wildest stories—everything from a Japanese invasion in Waimānalo to Nazi planes over Tantalus and paratroopers in St. Louis Heights."

The young reporter wrote down the quotations in his notebook.

"The military authorities were sick of the rumors, so they didn't want to have anything to do with us. They made a point of that. What else did John's papers say?" the old man queried.

The young reported looked up. "It's not a whole lot. He later wrote that he came back here to Kailua a few years later and went on a diving expedition with a friend. He said they buried something that 'needed burying'—to use his words—deep out in Kailua Bay under the reef. He and someone named Jorge Luis. You ever hear of this man?"

"Yes. He was my other best friend. A very good man. He was a war hero, you know. Passed away a few years ago, having served his nation well in both World War II and the Korean War. He was much decorated."

"I see," the reporter said, as he wrote down the information in his notebook. "I'll look it up. But what did they bury? What was it that they buried under the reef? Gillespie doesn't say."

"Something that needed to be buried away forever, or at least until you found me."

"I'm putting two and two together here, and I'm guessing you mean the spy, but that's not clear. Gillespie's papers say the mercenary's mission was to use a piece of crude signaling equipment and climb to near the top of the highest peak in the nearby Koʻolau Mountains—that would be 3,105-feet Mount Kōnāhuanui—in the days after the attack."

"So that's what he was doing."

"You saw him?" the reporter asked, his voice nearly raising an octave. "How come nobody ever knew about this?"

The old man said nothing. The young reporter waited.

"Go on," the old man said. "What else did his papers say?"

"They said it was the spy's job to signal a submarine far off the coast, to tell the Japanese forces how the island was reacting to their attack. Gillespie found this previously secret information when he was the ambassador to Japan. His papers said if the right signal was sent, then the Japanese would turn their ships around and follow up their first wave of attacks with a small invasion force, followed soon thereafter by others." The reporter stopped for a moment. "Do you realize what this means? If that had happened—if a signal had been sent and received—and an invasion of some kind occurred at that vulnerable moment in time for American forces, it would have changed the entire course of the war."

"That wasn't going to happen," the old man said, almost under his breath.

"What?"

"I said we weren't going to let that happen."

"And John Gillespie was in on this? How?"

"We were all in on it," the old man said.

"If what you say is true, then this was an early turning point in the war."

The old man closed his eyes momentarily and ruminated for a few moments. "No, young man, it was the turning point of my life."

"I'm not sure I understand, Mr. Sands," the reporter said. "That is your name, right—Paul Sands?"

The old man smiled and then nodded.

"From the moment we found out about you, Mr. Sands, we've wondered about the veracity of Gillespie's papers. You're going to have to let me in on what happened. You may be the only person who can corroborate these papers. If you think you know something that changed the course of history, then spill the beans. If you think you know better than all of us, then for God's sake, let us know."

Paul Sands removed the big straw hat from his lap and placed it over his thinning white hair. He paused for a moment and looked skyward. At first, he said little. Then, he smiled again, and brought his gaze down. He looked the young reporter squarely in the eye.

"I do know better," he said.

And so for the next couple of hours, he told the reporter of the secret that he was never supposed to reveal. But he felt secure in his revelation. After all, almost everyone was gone. Almost.

When he got to the end, the reporter sat in his place with a shocked look on his face. He had filled four full notebooks and most of a fifth one.

"And you say all of this is true?"

"Of course it's true," Sands said, as a car pulled up alongside the beach entrance.

"But what about the force you said you felt when you were in the mountains. Is that what you're saying killed this man—this mercenary, as Gillespie called him?"

"You don't believe that the island can have its own powers? Look around you! You have a lot to learn, son. You need to learn to believe." Sands waved toward the car and began walking in that direction. "Gotta go now," he said.

"But Mr. Sands, I need some kind of tangible evidence!" The reporter chased after him. "What about divers going into Kailua Bay to find where you say the body was ultimately disposed?"

"It's gone," Sands said, as he continued walking down the beach access.

"What do you mean it's gone?"

"I dove down there many years later because I was curious, but it's gone. The sharks come and go from the reef all the time. I can only make an assumption on what happened. All I know is that nothing's there."

The reporter stopped. "So, Mr. Sands, please, how do I know if what you've said is really true?"

"You'll have to trust me, son."

"But how can I know? None of this is in any book I've seen—or at least most of it anyway."

"Sometimes you just have to believe," Sands said, stopping at the car that had pulled up at the beach access, and then he opened the door. "Sometimes, you have to believe even when common sense tells you otherwise." He then spoke in the direction of the person sitting inside the car. "Isn't that right, dear?"

The reporter could vaguely make out an elderly woman sitting in the driver's seat. Her face was difficult to see because it was blocked by a large hat.

Paul Sands closed the passenger door and rolled down the window. He motioned toward the reporter. "Sweetheart, this man doesn't seem to believe our story." He chuckled.

The woman opened the car door and stood up. The reporter was amazed at her elegant appearance, dark-skinned with silvery hair that seemed to wrap her face just perfectly. The elderly woman smiled toward the young reporter and took off some of the flowers that adorned her hat.

"They're blossoms," she said. And she tossed them playfully in the reporter's direction. "They're *hau* blossoms. Does that help you?"

She smiled a most beautiful smile and then got back into the car. The reporter picked up the *hau* blossoms and stood with a stunned expression on his face as the car with the tall *haole* gentleman and the lovely Hawaiian lady drove off toward Kailua Town.

AUTHOR'S NOTE

I've never been a professional historian, but I love history. I always have. My journey to write this piece of historical fiction began several years ago when I sat quietly on the beach in Kailua and imagined how it might have looked many years ago. I was reading a World War II novel at the time, and that led me to speculate what might have happened had the Japanese military been successful in returning to the island after their December 7 surprise attack. Eventually, that speculation led to the story you've just read.

The research for the book was tremendously enjoyable. I spent a number of days in both the Kailua and downtown Honolulu libraries—reading old newspapers and other books on the period. Some of the best information came from first-person accounts, some from people I interviewed, and some from an old interview project that is kept in a file drawer in the Kailua Library. The staffers in the Kailua library were very helpful, as was W. Thomas Hall of the Waimānalo library, who wrote the book *The History of Kailua*. The stories from all these sources helped me get a real feel for life during that time, and many of those true stories were woven into my fictional account.

Several people helped me along the way—including my daughters, Becky, Jesica, and Amanda, who patiently listened to my first attempts at creativity. It's not always easy hearing or reading what dear old Dad has to write, so I am forever thankful for their love and support. My parents, Dale and Ale Hogue, who were married in Hawai'i, also offered comments. My mom had grown up in Honolulu during the time period of the book, and she was patient enough to read the very rough first draft and make personal observations. There were many new friends along the journey, including Dale Madden of the Madden Corporation, who first told me I might have a publishable novel. He and his wife, Lynne, gave me the push I needed to eventually get this into final form. Then, there were those who helped me with editing, Karen Valentine, Robinson Paulino, and Mikayla Butchart. I couldn't have finished without their awesome assistance. There are many others, too, who came along during this long journey. Thanks to all of you who gave me kind words and suggestions during this very exhilarating process.

People have asked me how much of the story is true and how much is fiction. Well, some of the Hawaiian characters who are weaved into the story are very real—Jack Burns; Harold K. L. Castle; Henry Wong; FBI Director Shivers; Governor Poindexter; Queen Lili'uokalani; even the jockey who won the horse race at the Kailua track, Tommy Kaneshiro; and, yes, the man known as "the spy from Kailua," Otto Kuehn. I tried to stay as true to their memory and to historical events as possible, while still moving my little piece of fiction along. In fact, I appreciate the good counsel from former judge Jim Burns, the son of the former governor, who gave me permission to put his famous father into fictional situations. You don't have to ask my permission, he told me; these are public figures.

The events, on a grand scale, are true. The Japanese attack planes did in fact strafe and bomb the Kāne'ohe Naval Air base minutes before their more famous attack on Pearl Harbor, and some of the planes flew directly over Lanikai on their way to shooting up the base at Bellows. The reaction by the locally stationed military and many of the Kailua townspeople was fairly close to how I wrote it, especially the rumors, chaos, and war preparation afterwards. I made my best effort to keep to the actual timetable of news and events of that period between Thanksgiving and Christmas 1941. And finally, the streets and businesses of Kailua, including the old race track and nine-hole golf course, are written as they were then. The lovely but very rustic small town looked fairly much how I described it, based on personal interviews and photographs from the Kailua Historical Society.

It's also interesting to note that many years later, after he was elected our nation's chief executive, President Barack Obama brought his own growing family back home to the island of Oʻahu, and they vacationed together in Kailua. In fact, the vacation home they chose was the old Castle beach house that was built along the Mokāpu Peninsula on the shores of beautiful Kailua Bay in the 1930s. President Obama knew what others who have lived in and visited Kailua have known for years—that it is truly one of the most gorgeous places anywhere on the globe.

The rest of the story is from my imagination. Any coincidence to persons living or dead is not intended, although I will admit that the characters of Nan and Mr. G. are based on my grandparents, Nan and Peter Gillespie McLachlan, who came to Hawaiʻi from Scotland in the 1920s, raised their family in Mānoa, and spent many wonderful weekends driving over the old Pali Road to visit friends' beach homes along the sands of Lanikai.

What better place?

ABOUT THE AUTHOR

Bob Hogue is the commissioner of the Pacific West Conference and a weekly columnist for *MidWeek* magazine. He also is a long-time broadcaster, writer, and coach, as well as the former sports director at KHON-TV. He served two terms in the Hawai'i state legislature as the state senator from Kāne'ohe and Kailua.

P.O. Box 23124
Honolulu, HI 96823-3124
senatorbobhogue@yahoo.com